LIMIT UP

Limit Up

Russ Crawford

Agrinomics Publishing

Limit Up
© Russ Crawford 2022
Published by Agrinomics Publishing.
For story background visit www.LimitUp.ca
Cover by Force Ten Design, Calgary

Paperback ISBN: 978-1-9992805-2-9
eBook ISBN: 978-1-9992805-3-6

This book is dedicated to grain traders of a day gone by. Some alive, some since passed, some are mentioned here, some are not. I salute commodity market veterans of the 1970's and 1980's. Traders who knew how to interpret government programs, exchange data and S&D's. And more importantly, they knew how to take action. They were risk takers on a very large scale. They were merchants of grain.

I'll pay tribute to two traders who don't appear in this book. The first, a Russian named Leonid Kalitenko, who is represented in the story if you know the characters. And second, my own mentor in Canada, Arthur Corbiere, who taught me many things, including things I probably shouldn't know.

Contents

Preface

Moscow, Russia   June 9, 1972

The ancient black cobblestone parade yard of Red Square, worn smooth by decades of marching troops and resplendent military vehicle processions, radiated shimmering heat waves under the blazing sun. City parks and boulevards were parched. Tree branches and leaves drooped sadly. It was one of Moscow's hottest and driest years on record. The area was enduring the effects of a month-long high-pressure system over much of the Soviet Union. New temperature records were being set daily as the dome of heat locked itself into place. Thermometers soared into the mid-30 degrees Celsius range during the long days of June, while the nights offered little respite. Hot, dry winds from the south parched the countryside and cities alike. There was no escape, and no relief in sight. Precipitation was one third of normal for the year, most of that coming as snowfall during the earlier winter months. It was one of the most pervasive and persistent weather patterns over Eastern Europe and Asia in recorded history.

Even in the early morning hours, the oppressive heat was unavoidable. As citizens headed to work, they were crushed by its intensity and the unbearable humidity. There would be no reprieve inside the sweltering office buildings either, as only elite Soviet workers or leaders were bestowed air conditioning. Some office workers were fortunate enough to have fans blowing in their workspaces, which for the most part just moved the hot air around. Inside or out, it really was quite insufferable, with nowhere to go to avoid the furnacelike conditions.

Russians owned closets full of heavy warm clothing for the winter, but lighter-weight clothes designed for hot summer days were scarce.

Men's jackets had been abandoned, sleeves rolled up while prudish women's traditions were tossed in favor of open necklines and shorter skirts. Russian winter would come soon enough, though, and complaining never helped.

Apparently oblivious to the heat, one man wearing a full suit and tie entered the Soviet Department of Agriculture building and rode the elevator to the top floor. He was thickset and blockish and moved with the directional certainty of an army tank. His shape and likeness could be easily re-created using LEGO blocks. It was 7:00 a.m. and, while he chose to ignore it, sweat was already trickling down his forehead from his shaggy, unkempt hair. His bushy eyebrows redirected the flow of sweat to the sides of his face. His shirt clung to his body.

Mikhail Fisenko was the vice president of Exportkhleb, the Soviet Union's grain export agency. Formality and reverence for the office were paramount to Fisenko. He took his job very seriously, religiously demonstrating loyalty and respect for the position and his country. He wore a suit and tie every day. He was also one of the fortunate few with air conditioning.

Today, he would escape the intensity of the heat wave, but he knew there were greater concerns awaiting him at his desk. Fisenko oversaw the grain export program for all the countries of the Soviet Union. As he made his way to his office, he wondered how he would complete his assignment this year. There would be no exportable grain surpluses due to the drought. Worse, he was beginning to suspect many of the various politically unified countries of the Union would need to import grain to be able to feed their people and their livestock. This most certainly meant the Russian agency would be assigned the task of importing critical foodstuffs for as many as one quarter of a billion people.

The Soviet Union had operated under the mandate of a perpetuating Five-Year Plan. It contained many facets, including agricultural targets designed to harness human and land resources and export surplus production of an important and renewable resource: food. The desired shift from being dependent on grain imports to being a prolific exporter was intended to boost the national treasury. The 1971 to 1975

Plan called for increased grain production and expanded livestock feeding to improve the standard of living for all Soviet citizens. The Union's leaders believed that providing more meat to citizens, in place of plant protein, would motivate the people. Fisenko's role as head of agriculture also included oversight of all the collective farms in Russia. Any failure on their part would reflect directly on him. The poor weather would not be a defensible excuse. He knew he would be singled out as the person responsible for any production shortfall and the inevitable catastrophe to follow.

* * *

Fisenko's office, double the size of the standard worker's space, was strategically located along the perimeter of the floor, giving him windows and a glorious view of the city. His desk and chair were standard issue, old but durable, nothing fancy. The floors were the ubiquitous yellow-gray linoleum common to all government buildings. His walls were spartan, featuring four pictures hung in an organized manner. One was a print of a painting of a proletariat grain harvest from the 1920s, and the other three were government-issue portraits of distinguished Soviet leaders Lenin, Stalin and Brezhnev. The photo of Brezhnev had mysteriously appeared one night in October 1964, replacing the previous image of Nikita Khrushchev. This was how change happened in the Soviet Union. One day Fisenko's mentor was here, the next he was gone. He wondered if his own future held a similar destiny.

Fisenko had earned his position as vice president on the basis of twenty-seven years of dedicated service and hard work. He was assigned to the agriculture department after doing his duty as a soldier during the Second World War. Throughout his working career, he had served under four leaders of the Soviet Union, including the current one, Leonid Brezhnev, but Nikita Khrushchev was his favorite. Khrushchev had secured grain during 1963 when the Soviet crops experienced widespread failure. Fisenko was aware of the déjà vu aspect in his own situation. He had learned a great deal during those days and had great respect for Khrushchev. He missed his counsel. He missed having his picture on his wall.

Later in the morning, Fisenko was scheduled to meet with his boss, Exportkhleb's president and Committee Chairman, Viktor Pershin. He would be updating Pershin on the status of production and provide his preliminary estimates for exports for the 1972–73 crop year, which ran from August of one year to July of the following year, in line with the harvest cycle. Soviet agriculture was now expected to provide important revenues for the national treasury and, like Fisenko's, Pershin's career depended on performance.

Summoning his courage and managing his emotions, Mikhail Fisenko entered Pershin's office precisely at 10:00 a.m. to break the news to him. Pershin's office was the same size as his, but the furniture was a decade newer. The same three leaders' portraits adorned one of the walls. In spite of the air conditioning, Fisenko was still sweating.

"Good morning, Comrade Pershin," he said.

There was no reason to slow play his news. It was bad, and he wanted to get it over with. "I have the information on this year's grain crop as you requested. I collected the reports from eight farm managers stationed across Russia as well as our agents in the Ukraine, Belarus, Kazakhstan and Turkey. The story is the same everywhere. Our crops are devastated by drought. If my estimates are correct, and the production is as poor as it has been reported to me, I fear we will need to import grain this year… a lot of grain."

"Have you seen this with your own eyes?" Pershin asked. "This is extremely concerning to me."

"No, sir, not recently. But I trust their reports. I last toured our country operations just after crops were seeded in April. I usually conduct a second trip prior to harvest to better understand the amount of grain we are likely to produce and what the quality will be like. I have been relying on regular reports from the farm bosses. Based on those reports, I decided not to sell anything for export this year."

"Well, that's a good thing, I guess, but it would appear we still have a very big problem this year, Fisenko. What are you going to do about it?" Pershin snapped. "I think you need to get out to the farms and see what's going on for yourself. We have struggled with these damn collective farming programs in the past. Our yields don't come close to those of North American farmers. I want to know why."

"I agree, President. Based on the situation, I have scheduled a trip for next Monday. I will fly to the Ufa airport in the Volga Plain and meet with our farm manager there. I will tour the fields myself."

"That sounds like a good idea. I'll come with you! Make the arrangements. I want to see and hear this for myself. If I am going to be responsible for telling our minister of agriculture the situation is dire and we may have to import grain, I want to be one hundred percent certain I am right, and I will need to tell him convincingly. This could go very badly for both of us, my friend."

1

The Volga Plain

Volga Plain, South Russia   June 12, 1972

The Volga Plain is home to the Volga River, the longest river in Europe. The river basin and surrounding region is one of the most lush and productive grain-growing regions in the entire Soviet Union. It is the Russian breadbasket. Year after year this area typically accounts for 50 percent of the Russian production of cereal grains such as wheat, rye, barley and oats. This year was not a typical year.

The once-shiny late-model black town car rumbled along a rugged country road in the agricultural plains of Russia. More of a trail than a road, it was meant for industrial vehicles, not a highway cruiser. Even the sophisticated engineered suspension of the Soviet-built ZiL limousine failed to smooth out the ride for its two occupants. Rutted country roads were clearly not the terrain the ZiL was designed to traverse. As the car rocked and swayed, the passengers were thrown from side to side, bouncing on the luxury leather seats like crash-test dummies. The driver, a Soviet soldier, had picked Fisenko and Pershin up at the Ufa airport over an hour ago. Their progress was slow and grueling.

As they crawled along the parched dirt and gravel road, the statically charged cloud belching from the rear of the vehicle clung to the car's exterior and left a long snake of dust floating in the car's wake. The finer particles permeated the inner cabin, triggering the passengers' coughing and sneezing. The men, in their dress shirts and suit pants, looked as misplaced as the car in the rural setting.

"Comrade Fisenko, we've been driving through a wasteland for over an hour. We came here to view the green fields and the bountiful crops being produced on our collective farms. All we have seen so far is bare land and shrunken or dead plants. I just have one question. Where is the wheat?" Pershin said sarcastically.

"As I've been telling you, Mr. President, the wheat has not grown for us this year; there's been a massive crop failure. We have no control over the weather." Fisenko's tone implied this should be obvious to anyone.

"All the wheat? I haven't seen a single field worth harvesting!"

"This year we are suffering one of the worst droughts in our country's history. I don't remember a year this bad. It has devastated the entire Russian grain belt. From these plains on the west all the way to southern Siberia it is like this. And our southern neighbors are not faring any better. Kazakhstan, Mongolia and the Ukraine are all experiencing similar catastrophes. It's very bad."

"This isn't *very bad*, Misha. This is a desert!" said Pershin as he shifted to the less formal use of Fisenko's first name. The two men had been business associates for the past decade and had come to like and trust each other. The performance of Exportkhleb had been stellar in those ten years, gaining Pershin his first Order of Lenin award last year. They enjoyed success and accolades together, but this situation had the potential to undo all the progress they had achieved. Their frowns and serious gazes revealed their inner feelings.

Over the past decade, they had traveled the globe, representing their country during important commercial trade negotiations. They were well known in international grain-trading circles and respected among their peers. Both were also known to be well-prepared and tough negotiators. Pershin oversaw Exportkhleb and Fisenko was responsible for grain-trading activities. They held similar values and maintained a high level of respect for each other. They were part of the same team. But the men couldn't present themselves more differently.

Pershin had developed a fondness for expertly tailored suits and hand-crafted footwear. His trips to Italy and France introduced him to a quality of garments unavailable in Russia. He had become a regular customer of fashion shops during his travels. His tall, thin frame was ideal for European cuts, which enhanced his aura of authority. His face indicated his roots were western Russian, with a finer bone structure and sharper features in comparison to the thicker features of most Russians. His air of authority was backed by a strong, deliberate voice. There was nothing wishy-washy about Viktor Pershin.

Fisenko, on the other hand, was a tractor to Pershin's Ferrari. His five-foot-nine-inch, 230-pound frame was physical evidence of his durability and strength. He dutifully wore clothes manufactured in the Soviet Union and could easily be taken as a Russian factory worker. Since the passing of his wife three years ago, his attention to personal grooming and presentation had suffered somewhat. He mostly remained quiet, deferring to Pershin when they were together, but when he did comment his speech was short and gruff. Nevertheless, inside this unwelcoming, crusty shell was the mind of a brilliant man. Fisenko was fluent in English and an expert in global agriculture. His language skills were vital to successful negotiations. And he maintained a deep knowledge of the workings of state trading agencies such as the Canadian and Australian Wheat Boards and knew US agricultural policy as well as any American. His expertise was invaluable to his department in understanding their competition when Exportkhleb was a grain seller and their options now, when Exportkhleb's usual role would be reversed, as a buyer.

* * *

The car persevered along the trail as the prairie winds swirled. Visibility diminished and a brown wall of dust and debris pounded the exterior. The sun was obscured by the thick dust stirred by the winds across the plain. This is a lot worse than I expected, Misha thought. We're in trouble.

As his mind raced through calculations of lower production numbers and their potential impact, Pershin was preoccupied with the dead bugs smeared across the windshield.

"If our goal was to raise grasshoppers, we would be getting an award from General Secretary Brezhnev himself! How do you expect us to meet our wheat export targets without crop production? The agriculture minister will have our heads, I fear." Pershin looked out past bug body parts, seeing only more barren fields. "What about the winter wheat? There should be crops getting close to harvest by now. We haven't seen any of them."

"The winter was exceptionally cold, Mr. President, as I am sure you remember. That's not unusual, but the problem was a lack of moisture. We've had very little snow cover on the crops planted last fall, so the winterkill was extreme. We estimate the crop loss to exceed 30 percent of our total anticipated production, although from what I am seeing today, it could be worse. The winter drought continued into the spring, delaying seeding and preventing germination of the crops we did manage to plant. It has been six terrible months for Russian farmers. I stand by our department's assessment; we will not have surplus grain to export this year. Let's see what the farm manager has to say, but I'm even more convinced now that we will have to import grain."

"Importing grain is not our long-term plan, now, is it, Misha?" Exportkhleb's president was half asking and half telling. He softened his tone. "We are both accountable for the success of our department. Our leaders demand this of us. I am not looking forward to updating the Minister with this news. And it is even more important we not let news of this grain production failure leak to the western world. Remember what happened in 1963? That's the main reason your comrade Khrushchev isn't around anymore. You remember what they said, don't you? *He planted wheat in Kazakhstan and harvested it in Canada!* I wouldn't want to be either of us if a similar disaster repeats itself. If the world outside the Soviet Union discovers this crop failure, they will force us to pay dearly for imports. I'm not exaggerating when I say it could bankrupt our nation's treasury."

Pershin's reminder of the economic problems endured by Russia during the early 1960s revived graphic images for Misha. He had been working for the government agricultural department for fifteen years at the time. In the subsequent decade, his responsibilities in the department had gradually increased to include oversight of the "sovkhozes and kolkhoz," the system of state-owned and collective farms. It was an honor for him to receive this assignment to serve his country. For as long as he could remember, he had been a faithful believer in the path of Communism as a way of life. In his mind it was an obvious fact that equal effort would result in a balanced and fair distribution of reward. It was his life work to realize the farm-production goals of the Communist Party. But even with productive land and suitable, arable conditions over the past four decades, the Soviet Union's Socialist Farming Program failed to match the successes of capitalist farming in other countries around the world. He took this failure personally.

The Soviet crop failure of 1963 was the first and only other time the grain-export agency Exportkhleb had reversed its role. The name of the government department described its function. *Khleb* means "bread" in Russian. They were the exporters of bread (in the form of wheat). Due to a lack of domestic production, Exportkhleb had pivoted to become an import agency. The agency as a whole, and Khrushchev and Fisenko specifically, became buyers of wheat for their country. At Khrushchev's directive, he and Pershin met with grain-marketing agencies in Canada and Australia and with senior executives of private grain companies in the United States and Europe. They managed to acquire enough grain to backfill their shortfalls, but the unexpected costs to the Russian economy were severe and long-lasting.

The experience was a dogged reminder of the ongoing failure of the thirty-year-old communist farming program. As Pershin reminded him, many believed this failure was the final straw for Nikita Khrushchev and the ultimate cause of his removal as Chairman of Ministers. In dismissing him, the government sent a strong message to everyone in the department of agriculture and even other branches of the government. Failure brings serious consequences. Anyone who does not perform is removed from their position and discredited by the nation. Khrushchev earned the ultimate disgrace when the government declared him a "nonperson" and removed his name from the *Soviet Encyclopedia.*

As Misha continued to fight the turbulence of the ride along the country road, he had an ominous premonition. His stomach twisted, and he hoped he would survive the events about to unfold in the coming months.

* * *

After another twenty minutes, which felt more like several hours, the two executives reached the meeting point. The soldier parked the car nose to nose with a vehicle more suited to the terrain—a rugged Russian-manufactured GAZ truck. Its two passengers climbed down from the elevated cab as the limousine approached. They were dressed in more fitting attire for the conditions, more working class and durable—the couture of farmers.

As the four men came together in the lee of the truck parked on the edge of the road, a miniature cyclone raced across the adjacent barren field heading directly for them. Both vehicles were already covered with dust, along with the grizzly, deformed remains of insect carcasses smattered on the grills and windshields. The "duster" tracked its inevitable path toward them, collecting loose, dry topsoil on its way. One by one each man turned his head away from the choking cloud. The searing 40-plus degree Celsius heat added to the discomfort of the moment.

Pershin braced himself for the impact of the twister by raising his arm to his face and turning to avoid the blast. As he cast his view to the ground, he noticed his once-shiny Italian shoes were covered with the same fine, light-colored dust that plastered their car and, now, their clothes.

Misha mirrored his boss's sheltering motion. His shoes were equally dusty, but their Russian manufacture leaned more toward function than fashion anyway, as did all his proletariat clothing. His rugged frame helped him fend off the torrent of wind, but as the small dust storm encompassed them, he felt caught up in the maelstrom, subject to its whim.

As the mini tornado proceeded on its journey, the men brushed off its gritty remnants and greeted each other with hearty handshakes, Misha providing introductions.

"President, this is the Volga Plain Collective farm boss, Director Anton Yelchin and his assistant director, Alexei Alexandrov. Gentlemen, meet Exportkhleb president Pershin." The collective's men remained silent, tentative.

"Greetings, comrades," said Pershin. "I am pleased to meet you; however, I must begin by saying I am very unhappy with what I am seeing. Your section is known to be one of the most bountiful areas in the Russian grain belt, and yet what I have seen for the past hour disappoints me and the government agency greatly."

"No one is more disappointed than we are, President Pershin," replied Yelchin. "We have done all we could, but what little rain we got came too late, and most of the seed we planted never had a chance to germinate in the hard, dry ground. There is no hope for a crop in our region this year. What does grow probably won't be worth harvesting in most areas. It is the worst year for grain production I have ever seen."

"Gentlemen, I don't say this lightly, the actions we take in the next two months could dictate the fate of the Soviet Union," predicted Pershin. "A great deal is riding on us. Misha, you must perform at the highest level of your career and somehow complete the impossible task of saving our countrymen from certain starvation. This is a pivotal point in Soviet history!"

2

The Lake Office

William Wallace Cargill, the son of a Scottish sea captain, founded a small grain storage business in Iowa shortly after the Civil War. The Cargill family went on to forge one of the largest commodity corporations in the world. As a privately owned company, it enjoyed privileged immunity from normal reporting requirements and the scrutiny imposed on publicly traded companies. Revered by its competitors, it was nevertheless viewed by most outsiders as a secretive, illusive entity operating in relative obscurity, exempt from regulations other than minor rules imposed by the Department of Agriculture. The global business center for this mega conglomerate was based in downtown Minneapolis, Minnesota. In total, Cargill employed over seventy-five thousand people in more than thirty different countries around the world. Its corporate goal was to double the size of the organization every seven years. This self-imposed challenge meant reaching well beyond the standard American crops of wheat, corn and soybeans to include new commodities such as meat, sugar, salt and coffee along with value-added processing industries such as soybean crushing, corn and wheat milling and barley malting. It meant further global expansion to untapped regions of the world such as South America, Australia and

Southeast Asia. In terms of international organizations, Cargill was already big, but its plan was to get bigger—much bigger.

Its nerve center, home to its intellectual brain trust, was located off-site from the main office building in a unique corporate head office covertly nestled away in the secluded woods of a nearby Minneapolis suburb known as Wayzata. Senior management and head commodity traders conducted their daily work from an opulent sixty-three room replica French-styled manor on the edge of Lake Minnetonka. Rufus Rand Jr., designer of the Art Deco Rand Tower in downtown Minneapolis, had built the chateau-style estate in the early 1930s. Cargill purchased the property during World War II and converted it into an office center in the 1950s for approximately forty senior Cargill managers. Cargill employees considered the "Lake Office" to be hallowed grounds, and an invitation to "the mansion" conferred status. To actually work there was akin to being knighted.

From this lavish, state-of-the-art telecommunications bunker, Cargill's senior executives and a cadre of elite, handpicked traders masterminded one of the most powerful private trading firms on the planet. The company's public face was a country network of grain elevator storage facilities, branded with their bold corporate logo, but their world of commerce was the highly leveraged shadowy world of commodity markets. An internal communications network, one of their unique advantages, reached across the globe with modern technology and instantaneous connectivity. Their traders utilized a sophisticated short form language to minimize "individual keyboard click" connectivity costs. The Cargill "wire" was an advanced communications tool, surpassing both the speed and reach of most government networks anywhere in the world. Cargill was in a league of their own with respect to technological sophistication and market intelligence. They were first to gather market intelligence on crop conditions, trades and general supply and demand factors. Often they were the source of market news. Their power and influence were disproportionate to the largest players in other industries.

Entering this mysterious and powerful center was a daunting experience for a promising young trader from Cargill's Tuscola, Illinois, grain elevator. On this momentous day, Jim McCrea reported to his new job at the epicenter of Cargill's global enterprise. He parked his car in the employee parking lot behind the out-of-place stately red-brick mansion. This building would be his base of operations for the foreseeable future.

He felt both excitement and trepidation as he made his way to the chateau's rear entrance. At twenty-six years of age, he knew he would be the youngest person in the building, perhaps by as many as ten years. He also knew his off-the-rack suit and tie, along with his shoes from Marshall Field's department store in Chicago, would be a fashion world away from the deep-pocketed, well-traveled executives with whom he was about to share workspace. He would be working beside some of the most experienced and skilled grain traders in the world, maybe in history. He knew he had a lot to learn, but he was confident; he was up to the challenge.

* * *

Unsure of where to go, Jim reported for duty to the main receptionist. The polished brass, thick carpets and luxurious wooden railings and wainscoting of the Lake Office were a world away from his previous workplace, the dusty driveway of a country grain elevator. He was startled by the sophistication of the receptionist's hair, makeup and clothing. She appeared to be ready for an evening at the theatre rather than a day at the office. As the first example of Cargill personnel, she set the bar remarkably high. He suspected his penny loafers and khaki pants probably needed an upgrade.

"Just one moment, please, Mr. McCrea. I'll tell Mr. Larson you are here."

The "Mr. McCrea" caught him off guard a little. The receptionist was old enough to be his mother, he thought. The formality was foreign to him, but he decided to go along with everything and take it as it comes without seeming to be too much of a country rube.

After a few brief minutes, the receptionist returned. Stella, as she requested Jim call her, led him to his new desk, where a familiar face awaited. Doug Larson had interviewed him at college, and he was also the person who had contacted him with an offer to transfer to the Lake Office. As it turned out, Larson was also in charge of intern orientation and introductions. He was the most at-ease person Jim had ever met. His speech was quiet and calm but always clear and confident. When he sat on a couch, he really knew how to stretch out and relax his long, lean body. It was almost like he was going to snuggle in for a quick nap and he might nod off. But he didn't; he just operated from a lower plane.

Jim's new desk was part of a four-desk configuration, flush and facing each other in a quadrant format. The massive room looked like it had once served as a large dining room or even a small ballroom. The workplace designers had remarkably blended the historic beauty of the mansion with the functional starkness of an office space. It now functioned as a central trading center.

Several conversations were taking place in other similar desk configurations in the room, creating a droning sound, not as loud as in a college auditorium but persistent and mostly undecipherable. In all, there were four sets of desk quadrants, which Jim later learned were the wheat, corn, soybean and freight trading desks. Every desk had one or two display screens and copious piles of paper. More than half of the traders were on their phones while simultaneously conducting conversations with other traders. This was the hub of commodity trading for Cargill Inc. He had expected they would talk in another room where they wouldn't disturb the traders, but he quickly realized everyone had an unwavering level of focus, concentrating on their desks and the live market quotes posted on the monitors. The energy was intoxicating.

"Good morning, Jim," Larson said, extending his hand in greeting. "Welcome to the 'wheat desk.' Our plan is to get you started here and introduce you to the way we do things but, more importantly, how we make money at this game. Make no mistake, Jim; that's the driving force here. We don't buy and sell grain for the fun of it. We do it to make a profit. Mel Middents is our senior wheat trader." Larson pointed to the man approaching them. "You'll be working closely with him every day."

"Hi, Jim, nice to meet you, and welcome to the Lake Office," Middents said. "I'm sure you'll find this a stimulating experience. You're in for some excitement right away. We're trying to figure out what's happening to the winter wheat crop in Asia—well, Russia, specifically. We've heard some great things about you, Jim. I'm glad you're here. I can use some help."

As Middents spoke with Jim, he multitasked with the quotation screen on Jim's desk, a half dozen slips of paper from the internal Cargill messaging teletype service he carried in his hand and randomly interjected side comments from other traders. He wasn't missing anything, Jim noticed. He looked more like a banker than a commodity trader. His gray hair was thinning, his glasses seemed permanently attached, and his thin dark tie and white shirt completed the appearance of a mild-mannered clerk. Jim would learn Middents was one of the most successful and highest-risk–taking traders at Cargill. Looks could be deceiving.

"Why don't you tell us a bit about your background and how you got here," said Larson.

"Sure, I'd be happy to." It was clear that this conversation was going to take place amid the din of the trading room. It was also clear he would need to develop the skills to absorb an abundance of information and still retain the necessary focus to do his job. The game had just moved into an exciting new phase for the young farm boy from Illinois.

"Well, you know I come from a farming background. I liked living on the farm, but I didn't love it as much as my brother did, so he's the farmer and I'm the one who went to university to study agriculture. Since I was hired by Cargill, I've been working at a great job at the Tuscola elevator. I particularly liked helping farmers develop grain marketing plans and providing them with advice. None of the other country elevator companies have insight that compares to Cargill's. The opportunity to come to Minnesota and work with this team is a dream come true for me. I can't wait to get started."

"Well, you already have," Middents said. "I'll let Doug get you organized with everything you'll need. Make sure he gets set up on the teletype with a username, Doug. You need to be on the network to send and receive messages, Jim. We have a cross-commodity team meeting at two this afternoon, so you'll be able to meet everyone then. You have a challenging year ahead of you with a pretty steep learning curve, but we think you're up to the task."

"Thanks, Mel. I wouldn't want to be anywhere else right now. I'm one hundred percent committed to this opportunity," Jim said, buoyed by Middents' confidence.

* * *

McCrea had graduated from Iowa State University two years prior with a degree in agricultural economics. During his studies he had demonstrated a dedicated work ethic and became known as a bit of a "research machine" who had acute skills in mathematics. He had been raised on a medium-sized corn and soybean farm near Champaign, Illinois, but he had always favored academics to farming. He greatly respected farmers like his father, but plowing the soil was not the career he sought. He attended postsecondary school to expand his mind and open new opportunities.

McCrea was a grounded, honest, straightforward kind of guy with a killer smile and a short haircut. He had no interest in the hippie drug culture of the sixties. He wore thick-rimmed glasses and possessed the handshake of a farmer. Jim McCrea was the embodiment of a typical mid-western American youth, evoking integrity and trustworthiness. As first impressions go, he made a great one wherever he went.

It was at Iowa State that he first learned about the intricacies of commodity markets. There he developed a fascination for the economic nuances of agriculture. He had a general understanding of grain market prices from his farm background, but he'd never given much thought to their origin or makeup day over day and week over week.

Commodity marketing was not a career path he'd contemplated when he enrolled in university. In fact, he didn't even know such a job existed. But the connection of mathematics and his knowledge of farming was just too enticing a combination to ignore. The concepts of commodity price risk management were a new and appealing world of economic complexity. He was a bit of a puzzle geek, and that drew him to grain trading.

His university studies also exposed him to the role of grain companies as commodity traders. He was familiar with Cargill, but only as the local elevator in Champaign, where his father delivered grain. His studies took him well beyond the Illinois countryside to the workings of US agriculture, international trade and the forces of the marketplace that drive the agricultural economy around the world. He studied transportation, processing and politics. He discovered there was so much more to learn on the business side of agriculture beyond growing grain on a farm in midwestern America.

McCrea interviewed with Cargill during a recruiting session at Iowa State and managed to attract their attention—and a job offer. After four years of study at college, he wanted nothing more in his life than to get a job in this business with this company. Their offer of employment as a grain buyer at a country elevator in Tuscola wasn't exactly the entry point he had imagined, but it was a start, and they assured him it was the type of job every college recruit started with at Cargill.

In July of 1970 McCrea went on the Cargill payroll. He worked hard. He listened and learned and never said no. Even as a university graduate with an economics degree, if a railcar needed loading or a pallet of fertilizer had to go onto a farm truck, he lent a hand. But his primary job was to interact with farmers. He helped them secure grain contracts and then managed the reporting of purchases into Cargill's business system. He followed grain markets and provided market insight for farm customers. Occasionally he fielded calls from the regional office in Chicago to discuss the trend in prices, farmers' expectations and the general condition and progress of local crops. He became part of the comprehensive information-gathering network at Cargill. These tasks gave him a feeling of importance and the sense he was participating in something much larger than himself. During his early years he learned the language of the business—futures, spreads, inverses, arbitrage, basis and grade discounts. This was a unique application of words and phrases exclusive to the grain industry, terms understood by farmers and traders, terms critical to commodity markets. He loved it.

McCrea was also fortunate to have access to Cargill's internal training programs. The art of grain trading isn't taught in schools. It is mastered by specialized knowledge transfer and experience. There was another level of learning Cargill's corporate recruits received from the "University of Cargill." He attended numerous regional meetings where new traders like him were given specific training on commodity markets and techniques to excel at their job. The Cargill philosophy was a simple one: train people for their next job so they're prepared to move higher in the organization—in the United States or internationally. It was necessary to support growth in the rapidly expanding organization, and the teaching mandate reinforced a motivational culture.

* * *

Earlier in the year, in January of 1972, after eighteen months in the trenches of country operations, McCrea had been invited to attend a special training seminar at Cargill's main office center in downtown Minneapolis. He didn't realize it then, but this session was limited to a select few candidates who had demonstrated exceptional potential in the organization. The two-week class was delivered by Cargill's senior training specialist and commodity mentor, Julius Hendel. At seventy years of age, Hendel remained a brilliant, unique individual. He had literally written the book, The Theory of Hedging on commodity trading at Cargill, and it was his job to convey this wisdom to new apprentices. There was no public academic parallel to this training. It was exclusive. The training session attendance was capped at eight: seven male and one female trader from various locations across the Cargill global network. Jim McCrea was in select company.

Cargill management had a specific growth plan hinging on maintaining their global advantage in trading knowledge and expertise. If they were to achieve their goal of doubling the size of the company every seven years, it would be accomplished through strategic planning and execution of innovation and managed risk. Having a pool of strong prospective leaders was a must. They used several external training programs to develop better managers, scientists and operational engineers, but they also had their own way of doing things based on the core business of grain marketing. This approach differentiated the company. It was their technique for bringing the best out in potential traders, or "merchants," as they became known—merchants of grain. McCrea was one of these potential elite traders, and Cargill management was counting on Julius Hendel to bring out the best in these young recruits. The global agricultural industry was expanding rapidly, introducing more opportunity along with more risk. As advanced as the company was, the leadership knew they needed to keep upping their game. Their future leaders had to be sharper than current management. It was critical for the company to continue to thrive.

Hendel had come to the United States from Russia and started with Cargill by developing the company's first grain-analysis lab. He demonstrated the potential to extract value from grain through a better understanding of different qualities of and handling techniques for grain and quickly became invaluable to the Cargill family. He broadened his knowledge over the years by focusing on commodity market pricing and the various influences that moved market prices higher or lower. He became a student of markets and futures exchanges, writing numerous papers on the subject—all exclusive to Cargill and its traders.

"My job today isn't to teach you about agricultural economics or even about grain markets around the world," Hendel began. "My special skill is gleaning information from the market and using that information to manage company risk and strategize grain positions. Should Cargill be buying or selling on any given day, and why? I'm a numbers guy, and I use numbers to understand markets."

Jim was in heaven. This guy spoke his language.

"Over the next two weeks, I will teach you how Cargill trading works, the tools we use and what we do with the information. No other company in the world is as well positioned as Cargill to gather global information instantly and interpret the effects the information may have on market price.

"You will learn the language of the markets, including a host of other grain terms you've heard and think you understand. I think you may be surprised and enlightened by the deeper meanings and 'cause and effect' circumstances corresponding to agricultural jargon you already know and use.

"Commodity trading is unlike any other business or career you can imagine," Hendel continued. "When I use the term 'commodities,' I'm referring to bulk, raw goods like oil, ore, lumber, grain and livestock as well as some others you might not think of, like precious metals, gems and food stuffs like sugar and coffee. If you aren't directly involved in one of these industries, it's unlikely you have a clue about the complexities of the business. No one person or company owns a commodity. They trade freely on global exchanges and physical markets.

"So, let's stop here and talk about that, about futures markets, or exchanges. What is an exchange and how does it function? I'll begin by saying commodity exchanges represent the most perfect form of trade ever invented. Anyone can participate. Prices are the result of a collection of all bids and offers entering the market during the course of the day. In the simplest of terms, an exchange is a facility where buyers and sellers negotiate terms on paper transactions for a specific commodity at a specific time and location. These are the variables of price—what, when and where. It's exciting because it all happens in real time and no one person or company has the power to control the process. Sometimes people think they are big enough or smart enough to 'corner the market,' but most of those cowboys get their hat handed to them!

"To create this perfect marketplace and simultaneously simplify price discovery for commodities and connect them internationally, commodity exchanges were developed. I use the term 'price discovery' because commodity prices aren't set by anyone; they are determined in an open outcry format based on supply and demand. The value of a commodity on any given day is what someone is willing to pay for it—no more, no less. Futures exchanges are the home for that discovery as well as the tool for buyers and sellers to manage the risk of fluctuating prices."

At that point Hendel paused. "How are we doing so far folks? Have you fallen asleep yet? Are there any questions?"

A junior trader from Kansas City raised his hand. "Does the stock market work the same way?" he asked

"In some ways it does," Hendel replied. "At least the open outcry part. Most people wrongly assume the commodity market is synonymous with the stock market. Of course, all of us here know this is obviously incorrect. Stock certificates are issued by a company and trade on a public stock market. Their prices move up and down based on profitability and prospects. Individual companies control the number of their shares outstanding at any one time and provide financial information on the progress of the business. But overall, aside from an open outcry trading format, there is little similarity between stock markets and commodity markets.

"Cargill participates in many commodity sectors, and yet how we manage risk is similar for all of them. Your job as traders for Cargill is to anticipate the direction of markets based on market signals. You will monitor the prices on the various futures exchanges to have a clear understanding of the prices and trends in the associated physical grain markets. After a while you'll begin to sense the rhythm of price movement and the factors causing a change in price over time. There are short-term rhythms or cycles covering weeks and months and longer-term ones spanning years.

"Ironically, you don't need any physical assets to be a commodity trader. By that I mean bricks and mortar, equipment, and so on. But Cargill, and many other large grain companies, own country and terminal elevators as well as trucks, rail cars, lakers and ocean vessels to stay connected to the full value chain and maintain control of the deals we make. We use those assets to drive revenue for our company. Many people assume we charge a fee for handling, cleaning and shipping, but we don't; we buy and sell grain. We profit on value-added activity like processing, shipping and storage. And we also utilize our expertise to profit on our market exposure through price fluctuation. We own grain through contracts and inventory. That is referred to as being 'long.' Or we can be 'short,' meaning our sales exceed our purchases. We can make money when the market goes up or down. It all depends on our position. We are indifferent to the actual price of the markets. For Cargill, it's all about the direction of price movement and our position being either long or short.

"But above all, I want you to have a crystal-clear understanding of the relationships we have with our suppliers, generally farmers, and our customers, generally end-use consumers. Without either of these relationships, we don't have a business. We succeed only when they succeed. Treat them well, and they will be our partners. Treat them badly, and they will move heaven and earth to make sure everyone knows about it.

"That's enough for an introduction. I've provided you with reading material in the form of a paper I wrote called 'The Theory of Hedging.' Please read it this evening, and I will see you at 8:00 a.m. tomorrow."

After a full day of listening to Hendel, Jim had more questions than answers. The material covered in Hendel's sessions was fascinating. His ability to cut through the complexities of commodity marketing, clarify the opacities and explain Cargill's role in the industry stuck with him. Some things were familiar to him, while other topics covered material he had never encountered. He liked Hendel's reference to respecting and valuing farmers and end users. This was a moral standard of Cargill's culture that he was particularly aligned with and willing to uphold.

* * *

The second day of Hendel's course began with the nomenclature and nuances of trading. "Let's start out with a widely used description of a trader's position in the market. If you have bought more than you have sold in the market you are said to be "long". Conversely if you sell more than you buy, you are "short". This includes all purchases of physical grain, inventory and futures contracts for the long side and all sales of physical grain and futures for the short side. This is true regardless of location, quality and delivery period. It all adds up to your position – either long or short. Or "even" if it balances. The daily long and short position report is the life blood of a trader. You can't operate without it. A good report further defines time and place but the most important number is the bottom right hand net tabulation.

If one was "bidding," they wanted to buy, and if they were "offering," they wanted to sell. An "offer to purchase" was an oxymoron in the grain business. The terms "cash grain or physical grain" represented the physical commodity, while a "futures contract" was a proxy for the commodity. It was a paper trade emulating the value of physical grain based on the commodity, location and delivery period. A futures contract could be converted to physical grain, but most of them were offset as part of a hedging or risk transfer strategy. The data known as the "Volume and Open Interest" of trading provided a wealth of information. It was exchange data tabulating the daily trades by commodity and month of delivery as well as how many contracts were open."

Hendel spent an hour explaining how open interest was created and offset and what it meant in conjunction with rising and falling markets. Jim was reeling after this session but determined to understand this more completely. It was clearly an important, yet lesser-known, feature of an exchange. He made a note to find more information on exchange data and how he could be a better trader by interpreting the meaning of the data.

Days 3 and 4 were devoted to Hendel's tutorial on supply and demand.

"The foundation of commodity trading is understanding the basic economic principle of supply and demand," stated Hendel. "This is what drives price. Each commodity has its own unique supply and demand, or S and D, picture. Similarly, different geographical regions have localized S and Ds. A local or regional S and D balance affects prices in that local market. Local S and Ds roll up into larger, national perspectives, which in turn add with other countries' S and Ds to represent the larger global picture. It's all connected."

"Supply" included a number of data sources representing the positive side of the ledger, such as inventory of grain held over from the previous crop year, production and imports. "Demand" was more complex, as it included both domestic usage and exports as well as subcategories like feed-seed-waste, resulting in an estimate of carryover stocks to the next crop year. Hendel introduced analytical measures like "stocks-to-use ratios" and "grain-consuming animal units." These weren't terms Jim had learned or used in his university courses, but it was clear to him they were fundamental to a deeper understanding of agricultural economics and trading.

In wrapping up the S and D section, Hendel laid out the methodology to translate this data into market signals and influence on price.

"I think you have gathered by now that the art of trading grain is not easy or simple," Hendel said to summarize. "There are many things to consider, not much time to react, and almost no one to call for advice. Above all, you will require discipline. It's not for everyone, but I hope when we are done here you will be prepared if the company comes calling."

Jim recognized this elite training as foundational in creating a clear advantage for all Cargill traders, especially the eight gathered in this room. This was where "the rubber hits the road," he realized. Of course, other successful grain companies practiced similar market analysis techniques. No one traded by the seat of their pants—at least not for long. But this was different than anything he had learned in school. It was next-level stuff, comparable to a condensed university course all on its own. It made him feel empowered to do a better job. But these skills were not especially useful in Tuscola, Jim realized. He hoped he was on a path to a trading position in the regional office. That was his immediate target, the next step in the corporate ladder.

Over the two-week session Jim learned about the history of commodity exchanges and why they became necessary as risk-transfer facilities. He learned how the trade in these futures contracts aligned with the underlying physical commodities they represented. He also learned about price variability over time and the relative values of the different calendar delivery months. The detail and depth of information used in these analyses opened a new level of understanding for him. Gradually the theory from college was starting to connect with the real-life world of the company.

As a part of the training session, the young traders took a tour of the Minneapolis Grain Exchange, or the MGEX as the locals called it. It was a short walk from Cargill's downtown office building. While at university Jim had visited the Chicago Board of Trade—the big exchange—and watched the action from the observation deck, but he had never been on an actual trading floor before and, while he knew the MGEX was a relatively small exchange, it was still an exciting opportunity to see commodity trading in action. He hoped one day to make it to the floor of the Chicago Board of Trade, referred to in short as "the CBOT," but even here in Minneapolis he was living out a dream.

The Minneapolis trading floor was a vast room with a thirty-foot-high ceiling, a large, centrally located eight-sided trading area, or "pit," elevated by three steps from floor level and back down five levels to the center inside the octagon shape. There were many grain-grading tables used by cash grain brokers and numerous private booths. Just prior to the opening of the market, over two hundred people milled about in numerous private conversations or scurried from booth to booth in anticipation of the start of trade. A loud bell clanged precisely at 9:30 a.m., signaling the opening of trade for the day. The gong was immediately followed by intense yells and aggressive arm waving by floor brokers physically jostling in the pit. How anyone could make sense of this cacophony seemed incredible to Jim. The excitement and robust activity were fueled by floor talk of speculation and rumors of potential Soviet crop problems due to a lack of snow cover on winter-seeded fields. The eight young Cargill traders soaked up the energy of the market in action.

"The Minneapolis Exchange provides a service to the local agricultural industry," Hendel told the group. "But it is a minor player in comparison to Chicago. I wish I could take you all there, but this will have to suffice. If you get a chance during your career with the company to spend some time on the trading floor of the CBOT, I promise you will never forget it."

The tour of the exchange wrapped up the two-week session with Julius Hendel. Jim got a great deal out of the training and, maybe as important, made excellent contacts with other potential future leaders of the company. He hoped his career path with Cargill included opportunities to work with some of the brightest people he had ever met. It was still a dream come true to be included in such an elite group.

As he watched the Lake Office traders and the memory of the training session flashed through his mind, he realized he must have impressed the right people at head office. Roughly four months after the training session he was offered a prestigious position as a junior merchant at the Lake Office. Somehow, he'd bypassed the regional office assignment, securing the "cherry" position in Wayzata. Jim couldn't contain his enthusiasm as he contemplated the thrill awaiting him in this exciting new assignment. Cargill gave him ten days to wrap up his affairs in Tuscola, train his replacement and 'get his ass' to Minnesota. That wouldn't be a problem.

3

The Politburo

Russian Politburo, Department of Agriculture, Moscow   June 14, 1972

Misha Fisenko circled the massive boardroom table, uncharacteristically fidgety, unable to sit and wait. Viktor Pershin remained seated, unaware of the incessant clicking of his pen. They awaited the arrival of their immediate superior, Deputy Chairman of the Soviet Council of Ministers Vladimir Matskevich. Two of Misha's analysts sat quietly at the table, opening files and preparing to take notes. Meeting rooms in the Politburo were massive; high ceilings, elaborate solid furniture and ornate accessories of red and gold were the usual decor. The ubiquitous images of Lenin, Stalin and Brezhnev adorned the walls. Conversations echoed in the cavernous chambers. Even this smaller room was no exception. The architecture and furnishings were meant to impress and intimidate at the same time. Mission accomplished, Misha thought.

Matskevich also held the position of Soviet agricultural minister, reporting directly to General Secretary Leonid Brezhnev. He was a powerful member of the Politburo. In his agricultural capacity, he was the central planning architect, ultimately responsible for the collective farming initiative, which had been developed in Russia at the very beginning of the Five-Year Plan system launched by Stalin in 1928. The primary goal of the initiative was, and remains, to transition the Soviet Union from a weak, poorly controlled agriculture state dependant on food imports into an industrial powerhouse.

Matskevich had already reviewed the brief supplied by Pershin and Fisenko. Both men had a desire to distance themselves from the information contained in the brief to the Minister given the foreboding news it contained; however, it was their duty to present their findings and own the responsibility, no matter how grim. Matskevich, short, stocky and bald, exploded into the room and quickly approached the Exportkhleb team. Two aids rushed to keep pace with the Minister as he charged forward. He welcomed Pershin, Fisenko and the two male analysts to the meeting then took his place at the head of the table in the ornate chair reserved for the highest-ranking individual.

"Thank you for coming this morning, gentlemen. Please proceed, as we have a lot to discuss," he said. "Let's get down to the urgent business at hand. Viktor, it is always a pleasure," he said formally with a nod. "Comrade Fisenko, it is good to see you again, and thank you for your report," he said slightly less formally. "Let me begin by stating I hope you are being overly cautious. Please tell me you are exaggerating the severity of the conditions and you are here today to advise me on how we will find a way to achieve adequate grain production in the Soviet Union this year."

Even though Pershin was the ranking official representing Exportkhleb, the Minister directed his questions and comments to the report's author, Mikhail Fisenko, as the long-time agent and best-known member of the department. Everyone knew Fisenko. He had been in the ministry longer than anyone could remember. He was regarded as the exemplar of how a good Soviet citizen went about his job. He displayed unquestionable loyalty and dedication in serving his country without any expectation of glory or compensation beyond his basic needs.

"Greetings, Minister Matskevich." Misha began with the necessary formalities. "It is our honor to meet with you today. We wish we had better news for you on the condition of crops across the Soviet Union. Unfortunately, the opposite is true. We face a dire situation. I can assure you we are not exaggerating. Winter kill, caused by extreme cold and a lack of snow cover, has caused irreparable damage to much of the winter crops. Additionally, planting delays and a lack of spring rainfall have combined to hamper progress in this year's crop. Now, drought and insects have taken over. We have some areas where crops are in average condition, but in many key production areas we are experiencing serious failures. It is no one's fault," he said in an attempt to lay groundwork that would cover the department's collective ass. "The problems are all related to uncontrollable effects of nature."

"It's true, Comrade Matskevich," added Pershin. "I concur with Vice President Fisenko's assessment. We traveled several hundred miles together in the past week, viewing field after field of withered crops and fields of dust."

They knew this was not the report the Minister wanted to hear, but it was truthful and had been corroborated by their own eyes. Better to be transparent about the situation than cover it up. Things weren't going to improve, and lying about it would result in more serious consequences in the future. As hard as everyone was working for the common goal, there were elements of farming out of their control, weather being at the top of the list.

"Gentlemen, I trust your assessment, even though at this point I have no desire to dwell on the serious problem this will create for our country. It has the potential to trigger devastating problems, including starvation, financial ruin and major setbacks in our long-term plan for global superiority. Misha, your report indicates we will not have a surplus for export in the coming year. You also state the countries of the Soviet Union must import grain. In your estimation, how many metric tonnes of grain will we need to buy and import to feed our citizens in the coming year?" Matskevich said.

Misha and his team had already given the question some thought and developed projections based on both "likely" and "worst case" scenarios. They were both just different degrees of disastrous, Misha knew.

"It is an estimate, Minister, but we believe we will need over 20 million and perhaps as many as 30 million tonnes—more than we have ever purchased before."

His answer hung in the air as Matskevich contemplated what he had just heard. His face began to contort at this unexpectedly large projection and the potential disaster it represented. He stared at the papers in front of him, digesting the news as his subordinates waited for his response. Then he looked both men in the eye to gauge their sincerity and back down at the brief in his hands, although it was obvious he wasn't reading it.

"All right. Assuming you are correct, how will you and your Exportkhleb associates accomplish this task without draining the country's treasury as we did a decade ago? Need I remind you, Comrade Fisenko, what happened then? You were here during that period, weren't you?" Matskevich pointed at him. "I would have thought we learned our lesson from that experience."

"I was here in 1963, Minister, and I remember the terrible situation very well. I remember our people endured empty cupboards, and I remember the depletion of our nation's cash reserves as we tried to purchase grain. I also remember international suppliers increased their prices, causing even greater damage to our economy. We were at the mercy of exporting countries. This was a lesson I have not forgotten. I believed our collective farming plan would prevent a recurrence of that disaster. But this year's crop failure will expose us again. I am quite certain of this."

"Well, what is your department's plan? Pershin, what are your thoughts on how to solve this situation? You're in charge of this now. What do you suggest?"

"Minister." Pershin paused. "Misha and I discussed this at length on our return from the crop tour. We realize we have very few options open to us and all of them require a lot of money. Most importantly, we can't let the citizens of the Soviet Union suffer. I should add to this, virtually all of our political allies in the Union are suffering the same agricultural setbacks. Not only will they be looking to Russia to help them through their difficulties but, ultimately, they will also be our competitors in securing adequate food supplies for the coming year once they realize we can't help them.

"Aside from Canada," Pershin continued, "our relations with international grain exporting nations are poor. The Cold War has been with us for more than thirty years and, until recently, a major barrier to trade. We know we have a great challenge ahead of us, Minister, but our team at Exportkhleb is up to the task, I can assure you."

He looked as unconvincing as he sounded, Misha thought as he watched Pershin scramble for answers. He knew Pershin's comments were wishes, not answers. There was no plan as requested by Matskevich. The best description of the situation that came to mind was a North America phrase he had learned from his associates. This was a shit show! Pershin was not helping. I'd better step in and try to save both of our necks, he thought.

"We'll heed the lessons we learned from a decade ago and handle this situation in the best way possible." Misha was aiming to be supportive without committing to anything specific. "There are a great many things we must address, but the most important at this moment is secrecy. In 1963, Chairman Khrushchev told the world about our poor crops, and they used the information against us by holding back sales and increasing prices. This time we must act secretly, strategically and quickly if we are to avoid a repeat of that error." This truly was his learning from their previous crop shortfall. At least that was something.

Matskevich responded with an icy and uncomfortable silence, resuming his blank stare at the report in his hands; he was letting his feelings be known in this frozen moment. His grim mood and intensity elevated the stress in the room, but everyone knew better than to say anything more. Time passed.

Finally, Matskevich ended his trance and spoke. Clenching his open hand and crumpling the brief in the other, he stared directly at the two men opposite him. Misha noted a vein in the chairman's bald, glistening head throbbing—on the verge of popping, he feared. Matskevich's fists landed hard on the massive table, startling everyone.

"President Pershin, Vice President Fisenko," Matskevich growled as he stood to face his audience. "Let there be no misunderstanding here."

He'd said this in a soft, deliberate voice. Misha recognized the significance of the Minister referring to them by their titles; he was emphasizing what was a stake. The volume of Matskevich's voice gradually rose in decibels, sentence by sentence, as he continued. "You two and your department are responsible for making sure our nation has enough food to feed millions of Soviets to the elevated standard set by our leaders. If we don't produce enough food across the Union, then we better get it—no… matter… what." Louder yet, he asked, "Do you understand me so far?" His voice bounced off the walls and echoed in the chamber.

Both men nodded. Now was still not the time to speak.

"Good! Now hear this," he bellowed. "If the government can't provide food for its people, the consequences would be ruinous. Let me lay this out for you." He began speaking in short bullet points. "This is more than just about starving people. Food shortages would lead to riots and angry citizens looking to overthrow the government. The future of our Union depends on the performance of its leadership. The Communist Party expects results. Bad weather is not an excuse. Your planning should account for unexpected disasters. Our gold reserves are limited. Our relationships with capitalist countries are aggravated, even hostile in some cases. We can't just buy our way out of this situation, and we sure as hell can't count on our enemies being there to *help us out.*"

More calmly, he went on. "So, you need to develop a plan and present it to me within the week. I look forward to it with great anticipation. We will meet here one week from today, and you'd better have more for me than you have right now. Understood?"

More nodding.

With nothing more to add, Matskevich gave each man one last burning glare. The men waited for the Minister to leave before they stood.

"Well, that was about what I suspected from him," said Pershin. "We already understand the dilemma. That's not news to us, but he certainly made himself clear. Obviously, we need to conceive a solid plan, Misha, or our days in this department are numbered, not to mention the possible starvation our failure could trigger. This state-owned farming plan has been a disaster for decades—long before I took over. And because we've exported our surpluses year after year, we don't have any reserves to help us through years of short production like this. It's a no-win situation.

"Misha, you've been here through all of it. I am counting on your years of experience and insight to develop a plan. I agree with the Minister; there should be contingencies for this kind of thing, but the truth is we don't have adequate grain reserves or an unlimited budget to prevent this exposure. Russia's plans to be an exporter of wheat will be set back this year, that's certain. You also feel, based on your estimates, that we will be forced to import more than ever before. More bad news. It's an embarrassment to communism and, potentially, a great financial catastrophe. We need to get creative here, Misha. What are your thoughts?"

Misha realized there was nothing to be gained by disagreeing or trying to defend himself or the Social Farming Program. Their position was clearly tenuous. Developing a credible and executable plan for the Minister would require Misha and his team to be more clever and innovative than ever. There were a lot of questions to be answered and ideas to be conceived in the one-week deadline imposed on them. How could he avoid the mistakes of previous administrations? How could he keep a thirty-million-tonne shortfall of grain secret from the world, at least long enough to cover their exposure? How could Russia pay for that amount of grain? How would it be physically possible to import such a massive quantity? And, perhaps most importantly, how could he overcome the political barrier imposed by the Cold War, which had become so entrenched between the Soviet Union and western countries? There was so much to consider, so much to get done. These were the thoughts and questions racing through his mind as Pershin unloaded the problem on him.

"Well?" Pershin said as Misha considered their problem.

"My thoughts are... we need a miracle, Viktor. We can't create grain out of thin air. Our member countries will not be able to supply us.

They will most certainly be looking to Russia to help them. I feel we will need someone from the Soviet leadership team to direct this critical task. Like Khrushchev's role in 1963, it is a matter of such importance it should be led by one of our top diplomats to be certain we maintain the confidentiality and assure the best result for the Union. We are just the leaders of a single government department, and our focus has been dedicated to sales of grain, not purchases. I fear we are at too great a disadvantage to be successful. It is too large a problem for us. This requires top-level negotiation between heads of state."

The truth was that Misha didn't want to be the bull's-eye if things went badly and the production shortfall caused harm to the Union. He didn't even want to share a spotlight with Pershin, as their futures would be similar and unpleasant. People disappeared in Russia all the time. Even people who had shown loyalty their whole life. It was clearly a no-win situation, as Pershin had suggested. How could his team change the will of Mother Nature and make a winning hand out of the cards dealt? At best this was damage control, and, in the end, someone would pay for the failure. He really wanted to hand this hot potato over to someone else—anyone else.

"Did you not hear Matskevich?" Pershin asked. "He told us to present a plan—not a suggestion to find someone else to take on the challenge! This one is on us, my friend. There's no way for us to walk away from the responsibility of our jobs."

"Yes, Viktor; of course I heard him. I just don't think we have the resources or authority to invoke the actions necessary to fix this. We don't control the treasury or the military. I think this problem exceeds the scope of the Department of Agriculture. In my view it is a problem of national security and international relations. This is way out of our league, Viktor."

"Do you really suggest escalating this to a national crisis, Misha? Have we exhausted all choices we might recommend? I think it is our responsibility to think it through, be creative and try to develop a plan. That's what the Minister has instructed us to do. I can't think of anyone more capable of rising to this challenge than you, Misha. Your experience and knowledge of global agriculture qualifies you to devise a mitigation strategy. Dig deep, my friend. Give this some more thought, and then we can discuss it further. But don't take too long. Time is not on our side now, is it?"

4

Global Trade Relations

Tension and distrust characterized the relationship between the USSR and the USA during the late 1960s and early 1970s. These two superpowers engaged in an ideological stalemate, pitting the philosophies of communism against capitalism, immediately following World War II. Hostility escalated over subsequent years with the advancements in nuclear power, culminating in the capability to wipe each other's nation off the face of the earth. While there were no direct military confrontations between these entities, the Soviet empire grew through military acquisition of neighboring Eastern European countries along with alliances with like-minded nations including North Korea and Cuba. The expanded American international presence and influence came about through provision of financial aid and military support. Both sides increased their nuclear military arsenals and strategic placement of troops, ships and armaments to a threshold of potential global annihilation if a conflict ever were to erupt. The Korean War lasted from mid-1950 to mid-1953. It resulted in each superpower supporting opposing sides of an international argument and waging a war through their respective allies. Political stress was high and the conflict was real. This was the Cold War.

Hostilities reached a peak in 1962 as the communists attempted to establish nuclear missile bases in Cuba, just eighty-five nautical miles from the southernmost tip of Florida. The United States government engaged in a naval blockade around Cuba in an effort to head off this threat. For thirteen days, American President John F. Kennedy and Russia's Nikita Khruschev engaged in a tense military standoff known as the Cuban Missile Crisis. Cooler heads prevailed, and an agreement was struck whereby the USSR would remove the missiles in exchange for a guarantee from the USA that it would not invade Cuba and would remove its missiles from Turkey. After two decades of escalation between these two nations, this event stood alone as a movement toward a pause in hostilities.

During the early 1970s, countries around the world underwent a period of powerful change born of the sixties. "Peace, love and happiness" was the mantra from an unsettled and vocal younger generation. The dominant nations experienced considerable pushback from their citizens, who publicly expressed their concerns and opposition to military conflict, escalating armaments and what many felt to be an accelerating trend toward global conflict.

Fresh from winning the race to land a man on the moon in 1969, the United States was flush with confidence and more than a hint of arrogance. During the early seventies President Richard Nixon emerged as a globe-trotting emissary of world peace, making high-profile visits to the previously unfriendly communist regimes of China and the Soviet Union. Conflict between these nations took on less lethal or confrontational tones thanks to the benign fields of chess, ice hockey and negotiating tables where arms-limitation pacts and trade deals were struck.

Russia's Boris Spassky and American Bobby Fischer dueled for twenty-one games to determine global chess supremacy. Canada and the Soviets met in a seven-game winner-take-all-bragging-rights series to determine the best hockey country in the world. The Americans and Soviets signed the Strategic Arms Limitation Talks Agreement that outlined a plan for ballistic missile arms control after a series of meetings at neutral sites, including Vienna and Helsinki. Nixon visited the Great Wall of China, and the two countries ended a twenty-five-year period without formal communications. In 1973, Nixon signed the Paris Peace Accord in an effort to bring an end to a conflict that set the United States and the Soviet Union against each other in a far-away war in Southeast Asia. In 1975, the United States withdrew their troops from that Southeast Asian country, Vietnam, ending a six-year war in the region.

This human desire for renewed global peace and security became known as "détente"—the easing of strained relations. During the first half of the seventies, the world experienced generally safer times and a shift to embrace the youth messaging of the sixties found in John Lennon's song "Give Peace a Chance."

This was the state of global relations the Soviet Union faced as Misha Fisenko pondered his fate and that of his countrymen. He suspected he would not be particularly welcome at trade tables around the world, and in the United States in particular. Memories of more adversarial times still lingered with the older generation of commodity traders, of which he was one. Unlike his Canadian and European contacts, there was no trust with American based companies. Would they even agree to meet with him, never mind actually provide offers of grain? Added to this challenge, the mere disclosure of a problem would greatly weaken his negotiating powers with the Americans.

Misha Fisenko's Apartment, Moscow June 14, 1972

Global peace wasn't uppermost in Misha's mind as he deliberated the challenge of finding enough food to feed his nation. He knew his adversaries all too well. His traditional suppliers of grain, Canada and South America, could not produce the miracle he was seeking. The solution was agonizingly obvious to him. There was only one country in the world with the supplies, production and shipping capacity capable of filling their unprecedented order book. He must find a way to negotiate with the Americans.

Ironically, thanks to a visit to Moscow by Nixon a month earlier, there was a new opening for trade with the United States for the first time in history. But could he trust the Americans? And could he negotiate with them? He knew he had the right contacts at international grain-trading companies. He had traded grain for decades, but rarely

United States–origin grain for shipment to communist countries. Now, he had no choice. Thanks to abundant grain production in recent years, the United States held surplus inventory. This serendipitous potential fix came with just one catch. Once the grain industry learned of the Soviet's predicament, grain markets were likely to explode. Prices would escalate rapidly, creating an economic problem for an already weakened Soviet government treasury. The very act of asking for an offer could trigger a spike in prices before he could get anything bought. Misha felt disadvantaged in any pending negotiation. He conjured an image of himself negotiating bare naked, a sight no one, including himself, would want to see.

Alone in his apartment later in the evening, he prepared a small meal and flipped through his collection of records looking for the right theme to stimulate his thinking. He and his wife, Liliya, now deceased, had enjoyed many evenings listening to their favorite songs. Misha favored more traditional Russian composers like Tchaikovsky and Sviridov while his wife had preferred more modern artists—even some American singers, she'd admitted. Tonight, he decided Sviridov's "Snow Storm" would be an appropriate inspiration.

Misha lived in a bland three-room apartment in a large suburban complex of Moscow. Even as a vice president of an important government department, he lived among the people. In truth, it was all he could afford and it was sufficient, no better and no worse than other citizens' homes in this huge city. His furnishings were modest, a little tattered and worn and, like him, aged. The rooms held a musty, blended aroma of cooking grease and stale air. He didn't open the windows often and paid little attention to cleaning. He hadn't changed a single thing since he'd become a widower. He was fine with things as they were. His apartment was his sanctuary, the place where he and Liliya had lived together. He couldn't imagine living anywhere else. It smelled like home: familiar, comforting.

Misha nibbled away at his sandwich and washed it down with large gulps of vodka. His food preparation was unimaginative and his appetite not what it had been when Liliya cooked for him. She had passed away from heart failure just over three years ago. She had worked in a clothing factory in Moscow. They'd had no children during their thirty-eight years of marriage, but they were a great team and a loving couple. She always brought a smile to his otherwise stern expression and called him her big bear. After she passed, he focused exclusively on his work, the one anchor remaining in his life. Misha's parents had died many years ago and he'd lost his younger brother during the Second World War. He was alone in the world, without any close friends or family connections. His work at Exportkhleb, his service to his country, was his life.

Misha delicately placed the album on the record turntable and clicked the start lever. As the familiar music filled the room, he began to contemplate his immediate predicament. He rummaged through his memory of previous years' events, looking for clues or ideas to help him puzzle through the crisis he and his nation now faced. The Soviet Union had experienced droughts and crop failures before. This wasn't new. In fact, it was more the norm, but two things had changed. The first obvious difference was the population of the combined nations of the Union had increased by over twenty million people in the past decade. The second change was a new policy the government had developed to provide more and better food for everyone. This meant more meat and animal products like beef, pork, eggs and dairy, all requiring ever increasing quantities of grain for animal feed. In addition to this increasing domestic demand, the government expected excess production to be exported and this new revenue adding to the country's treasury. This expectation dictated the need for significant increases in local grain production, not decreases. It was an excellent plan that included better farming practices and more acres seeded to crops that would lead to higher production. Unfortunately, the Farming Initiative failed to meet the plan year after year. The reality of lower fixed payments to farmers fostered revolt, which was met by higher government quota targets, creating a spiral of resistance. In summary, the collective farming initiative had been a failure.

Now, into his second full glass of vodka, Misha started to scribble down random thoughts and memories relevant to the current situation. He listed possible countries capable of supplying grain, companies or agencies working out of those countries, and other random factors like price, foreign currencies, shipping costs and schedules. All of these variables coalesced into an extremely complex puzzle. At the top of the page in large capital letters he wrote "TOP SECRET." Paramount to whatever plan he could hatch, the actions of his agency must remain confidential if they were to have any hope of success. And he didn't have much time to get this done. As good as the Soviet Union was in sequestering news, it wouldn't be long before the investigative skills of international traders zeroed in on the fact there was a grain-production problem in Asia. Rumors to that effect were already circulating.

After his third glass of vodka, Misha decided to try to get some sleep and start fresh in the morning. He had managed to create even more questions for himself and his team but he didn't have many answers. Buying up to thirty million tonnes of grain without creating a frenzy in the global marketplace was just not possible—was it? Even at current market values, the estimated quantity represented nearly four billion American dollars, a staggering sum of money and an amount the Soviet Union could most definitely not afford.

Misha Fisenko's Apartment, Moscow June 15, 1972

Misha was awake when his alarm rang at 6:00 a.m. Sleep had evaded him, even after drinking a "pail of vodka," a term his Canadian friends colorfully coined for a heavy-drinking session. After a quick splash of water on his face, a dozen swipes of a toothbrush and a mediocre scraping of whiskers, he was ready to go to work.

Outside, his chariot awaited. He proudly drove one of the very first Russian Ladas produced in Moscow by Fiat. The performance of the car challenged his loyalty at times, especially on the coldest days of winter. But in spite of its propensity to refuse to start, it was made in Russia, just like he was. How could that be bad? Today, it started. A good sign, he felt.

Misha always took the Leninskiy Prospekt to work, crossing the Third Ring Road and then taking the Garden Ring over the Moskva River around to the Agricultural Department on Academician Sakharov Avenue. He joined thousands of others on his daily commute, all in service to their country.

The heat wave created by the high-pressure system continued. Each day became a continuous reminder of the looming crisis created for him by the forces of nature—relentless heat, no rain. The problem was not going to solve itself, and it didn't appear Pershin was going to give him a pass on it either. He had some ideas, but his first task was to create a team. He employed good people in his department, and right now several good minds would be better than one.

Misha also knew he needed a strategically creative approach, something "out of the box," as the Americans said. Perhaps he needed to think more like an American, he considered, whatever that was. It may require a different perspective on the industry than the one held by him, Pershin and the Soviet Union's Department of Agriculture. The question was, who could he trust with the most sensitive and potentially damaging secret ever encountered by Exportkhleb? One man's name came to mind.

5

Project Kuznechik

Exportkhleb Offices, Department of Agriculture June 15, 1972

So much to do, so little time, Misha thought, arriving at his desk a little earlier than usual. The task before him was monumental, greater than anything he had faced in his long career at Exportkhleb. And the stakes were the highest possible: a starving nation and a depleted treasury. He could not afford to fail. He had formulated a plan for Day 1: build his team.

"Good morning, Comrade Fisenko." Misha was greeted by Gregor Yeremenko, a sector analyst who had attended yesterday's meeting with the minister. Yeremenko was one of the youngest department heads at the agency. His superior analytical abilities had proven extremely useful to the department and earned him additional responsibilities early in his career. Misha was pleased to see Gregor had anticipated an earlier-than-usual start to the day.

"Let me know what you need from the statistics and analysis group today. Responding to the Minister is our top priority."

"Thank you, Gregor. I need some time to rough out the complete plan. While I'm strategizing, I need you to gather information, contacts and costs. You can start by preparing a list of the grain company head offices and contacts in Australia, Canada, Argentina and the United States."

"The United States?" Gregor asked with surprise. "Of course you know we aren't on particularly good terms with the Americans, sir. Do we want to deal with them? Do they want to deal with us?"

"I don't know the answer to those questions, Gregor, but I fear we may have few other alternatives. I know it's early, but start to gather some production estimates for those countries as well. This information will tell us if we can pull this off without the USA or if we will have to deal with the devil. Above all, and I can't stress this enough, Gregor, keep everything you do and say confidential. I'm trusting you, but you must not share anything you hear or do."

"I understand. I'm on it, sir," replied Gregor.

Gregor was right, Misha thought as he prepared to get to work on his own to-do list. After all the haranguing between Brezhnev and Nixon over the years, trying to close a trade deal between their two countries would be difficult. But the leaders had met recently and talks were underway on a deal to limit strategic armaments. One thing Misha knew with certainty was that the United States had a surplus of commodities and they were actually paying farmers not to grow grain. What kind of an agricultural plan is that, he wondered.

Misha formalized team leads for a working group from his staff that would cover the basics: research and data collection, finance, and logistics. This team of department leads spent the rest of the day gathering information and compiling a database. Each person was tasked to be prepared to provide the most recent, accurate information available in response to the vice president's orders. Misha developed his own list of the necessary topics to cover and an order of events. He pondered all the uncertainties, strategized, eliminated bad ideas, considered risks and plotted out steps in the plan. Action plans would be developed tomorrow.

* * *

This was an undertaking unlike anything ever attempted at Exportkhleb, or within the whole Politburo, Misha suspected. How does one create a plan to purchase the largest quantity of grain in history and not simultaneously send market prices into the stratosphere? During his international travels, Misha had learned a great deal about markets in other countries. His travels to many European nations as well as western countries led to a deep understanding of the open market system. He had researched grain policy in countries around the world and become a student of the nuances of legislation and regulatory oversight. He had also developed strong relationships with government marketing agencies known as Wheat Boards in the Commonwealth countries of Canada and Australia. Most importantly, he understood people. After all, deals were made with people, not countries. He counted several people he had met on his trade missions as friends—especially those crazy Canadians. Through all the years, Canada and Russia had maintained strong trading bonds. He credited that to the management of the Canadian Wheat Board. He had already decided his first trade destination would be Canada. That is, if the Minister approved of the plan he and his team were developing.

Exportkhleb Offices, Department of Agriculture June 16, 1972

The following morning at 7:00 a.m. the newly formed team, now code-named "Kuznechik," convened in the Exportkhleb boardroom. The room had been converted into a dedicated war room for the duration of this mighty challenge. Misha shared the operation name with those gathered—in English, it meant "grasshopper"—and the team members shared a sympathetic laugh to get things started. The name was a personal but subtle nod to the president's sarcastic comment during their crop tour about receiving an award from Brezhnev for raising a record number of grasshoppers, he told them. "So, our goal is nothing less than an award from the Minister!"

Sitting around the table was the handpicked team of experts who would lead in those critical areas Misha had identified: production, logistics, and finance. Gregor Yeremenko was the statistician and manager of grain production, Boris Gryzlov oversaw ocean freight and port logistics, and Nadia Makarov was the senior financial manager for the agency. This was a highly qualified team of experts, capable of providing leadership, innovation and, most importantly, results. They would lead their own teams, but the four people assembled in this room would be the only ones privy to the big picture of their mission. No leaks.

"Good morning, everyone," Misha began. "Thank you all for arriving early. This will be our starting time for the next five days as we prepare our vital strategic plan for Minister Matskevich. Here's our schedule." He passed out the information to the three seated at the table. "We will work on Saturday, take a break on Sunday and then finalize the report for President Pershin's review on Monday. The final recommendations will be ready for our meeting with the Minister on Wednesday.

"For most of your careers in this department you have been responsible for the management of our country's grain-export operations. But this year, everything changes. You all know by now you must reverse your roles and become agents of grain imports. Our plan will be based on production shortfalls rather than surpluses; it will be a plan to manage the task of importing and storing grain and a plan requiring payment rather than collection of money. You are all department leaders, and this is what you will have to do—lead. It will be unlike anything you have done before, but I know each of you will do whatever you have to do in service to our country. It is critical your staff work in compliance and confidentiality. We must not discuss the extent of our production shortfall beyond this group unless it is necessary to guide your staff. You will have to figure out how to do that. Most importantly, no leaks!

"It will be my job to, along with President Pershin, negotiate international deals. Critical to our success is making sure we can make it all happen; the 'what, where and when' details of those transactions will be based on the work we do here as a team. I'm going to try to purchase between twenty and thirty million tonnes of grain from exporters in the next two months."

Misha's remarks shocked Nadia and Boris. Unlike Gregor, this was the first time they'd heard of the problem. Their silence indicated they were processing the declaration and assessing the impact of such a monumental shift in direction. Nadia was already tabulating figures on her calculator.

"Let's start by reviewing my list of assignments," said Misha. "Gregor, I need you to speak with all the bosses of the state-owned and collective farms and get their best estimates of grain production in their areas. I know it's early but I fear the worst, which is likely already quite evident. As a starting point, we need to know how much grain we must purchase. We can't underestimate, but I don't want to buy a kilogram more than we absolutely must secure. Do you have the list of grain-company contacts I asked you to compile?"

"Yes, Misha. Here it is." Gregor passed him a sheet of paper with names and numbers.

"Thank you, comrade."

"Boris, your job may be the most challenging. Buying the grain is only part of our task. Getting it where we want it in a scheduled manner will be especially difficult. If we are successful in securing as much as thirty million tonnes of grain, it will mean over six hundred ocean vessels need to be unloaded in Soviet ports in the coming year. We control a large number of suitable vessels, but we will need more—many more. Very quietly and under confidentiality you will need to contact ocean freight companies to book shipping capacity and notify our terminals to prepare themselves to become import facilities rather than export—and they will only have two months to incorporate all necessary modifications. Don't do anything publicly until we get approval from the Minister, but start planning right now so we can show him the steps we will need to take. I don't want this to leak out through the shipper networks, either, Boris. Be certain this is crystal clear!"

"Nadia, I'm guessing you have already done the math on this particular problem."

Nadia smiled and nodded, tapping her trusty calculator.

"All right then. For you two gentlemen, thirty million tonnes landed in Russia over a one-year period will cost our country just over four billion US dollars. This amount is what it will cost to cover our shortfall and feed our people over the next year. And we won't even come close to satisfying the increased targets of meat protein set by our government. It's back to basics for everyone for a year or more. It means more bread and less meat in our diets.

"Nadia, I need you to work with Treasury. Find out what money is available and put together some ideas on where we can get credit. Get firm commitments wherever you can. This is no time to be tentative."

"I'll do my best, Misha, but it will be a problem, I can tell you already."

Misha nodded knowingly. As his team dispersed, he felt confident in their start. They would come back with strategic details on the "what, where and when" as requested. The "how" was all on his shoulders. He still needed to develop a course of action that would lead to the transfer of huge American grain surpluses in storage bins all over the United States into import terminals, flour mills and oilseed processing plants in the Soviet Union. And he had to arrange this transfer between nations that didn't like each other very much. Even with the key players he'd assembled, he knew his team wasn't complete yet. He needed more help with these unprecedented actions. He needed someone to help him on the "how."

* * *

The team met daily to update and strategize, breaking only on Sunday to be with family, as Fisenko had promised. While the plan was taking shape, there remained weak spots; financing the endeavor was currently the single greatest hurdle. And the more he might be forced to pay for purchase contracts for grain, the worse the financing problem would become. A higher-priced market was a potential outcome the Soviets did not control, so they needed to prepare for a worst-case scenario. The plan had to include a range of possibilities, the worst of which were almost unthinkable.

The areas of focus Misha assigned to his team were hard-asset types of questions about port terminal capacity constraints, quantities of grain and availability of cash. His own challenges were of a more strategic nature. He needed to develop a plan to approach agencies like the Canadian Wheat Board. He decided to leave the Australian Wheat Board out of his plans since it was the middle of winter on their continent and they wouldn't be as open to trade as North American suppliers. Plus, Canada was the easier supplier, as there were open lines of communication for him to access. The greater, more difficult challenge was the need to approach private grain companies, because this was how the American system worked. There were no government agencies negotiating in secret and capable of trading large quantities. He would have to purchase massive quantities of grain from multiple suppliers, all the while keeping it quiet and preventing a run on the grain markets, which would be inevitable once this news became public. These companies controlled the trade in international commodities. Normally he sold grain to these trading companies, so he knew how they worked, but being a buyer seemed a much more vulnerable role. Strategically, Misha's thoughts kept returning to the one unbelievable coincidence: America was storing large inventories of grain—more than thirty million tonnes, in fact. *How do I turn this to my advantage?*

Back in his apartment, he worked through the evening. In this case, "work" was thinking, planning, and considering options and tactics. No vodka until the report was done, he decided. This had to be his best work.

"Where are you, Lily, when I need someone to talk to? Someone who will listen and tell me whether I am on the right track or just plain crazy."

6

The Board of Trade

Chicago Board of Trade Building, Chicago, Illinois   June 19, 1972

The oppressive Chicago heat and humidity, already settling in at nine o'clock in the morning, forecast another 'hot one' for the Windy City. Inside workers were thankful to enjoy the miracle of air conditioning. It was early in the year to be experiencing this excessive heat, but no one complained. Summer was officially only two days away, and the warm weather was so much nicer than the icy chill and frigid winds blowing in over the city from Lake Michigan during the harsh winter months.

Doug Larson and Jim McCrea walked east along West Jackson Boulevard heading toward the Chicago Board of Trade tower. They had flown in the previous evening expressly to meet the Cargill team on the floor and take in the action of the largest and busiest commodity exchange in the world.

The impressive and iconic CBOT Tower was a symbolic, stylized structure dedicated to agriculture and industry. The forty-four-story building was clad with gray Indiana limestone, decorative carvings emblazoned on corners, while the feature ledges paid tribute to the commodity industry. The centrally located Roman-numeral clock at the foot of South LaSalle Street, guarded by a Mesopotamian farmer holding grain and a Native American holding corn, performed the reliable task of measuring the minutes for all who passed. The glistening silver female figure capping the building was Ceres, the Roman goddess of agriculture, in honor of the commodities exchanged on the trading floor in the building below. Inside, the art deco motif rendered in glass, brass, marble and steel offered a visual treat to all who entered. The geometry of the decor featured pleasing symmetric patterns, stylized ornamentation and accented vertical lines. The building was an architectural and artistic wonder.

At just after 9:00 a.m., the two men entered the elaborate lobby of the Exchange Tower, happy to escape the stifling heat.

"Have you been on the trading floor before today, Jim?" Larson asked as they took the elevator to the trading floor, one level below the observation-deck floor commonly used by visitors to access the exchange.

"We went to the floor of the Minneapolis Exchange with Julius Hendel, and I came here as part of a class road trip with my ag economics class a few years ago. But we were only allowed on the observation deck, not right down here where the action is."

"Well, it's very different from up there, I can assure you." Larson pointed to the observation level. "Down here you can see and hear what is happening; you can feel the life of the market! You feel the pulse of trade, the joys and the anguish, the surge of the market. From here you won't just watch and listen—you'll experience the vibrancy of the business."

The overwhelming beauty of the tower and Larson's enthusiasm peaked Jim's excitement. The very act of entering the building created an emotional pull as he considered the significance and history of the Exchange. The trading floor had seen great wealth procured for some and terrible loss and ruin brought to others. While this rags or riches comparison was not the purpose of the Exchange—quite the opposite, in fact—this was part of the legacy of this institution. The magnitude of the moment made him feel small, like a speck in time of decades of commercial might. Would he ever feel comfortable, like he belonged on these hallowed grounds? It seemed unlikely at the moment.

Proceeding along a lengthy hall, they stopped at a regular-looking rather inconspicuous door with simple hand-painted lettering on it: CHICAGO BOARD OF TRADE – Members Only. As he read these words, Jim felt a rush of adrenaline surge through him. This was entirely different from his university class tour. He was now part of an inner group of people who played a role in agricultural marketing. The Exchange was host to traders from all over the world, both physically and electronically. They bartered on the exchange for a whole host of reasons. He was about to step onto "the floor," as it was referred to by locals.

Larson led Jim through the CBOT door as he showed his floor-access badge and Jim's visitor pass to the security guard. From this small ante room, they entered the inner sanctum, a cavernous space towering three stories above them. From outside the building, or even in the entry hall, you would never know this massive room existed. As Jim's eyes turned skyward, he stood in awe of the room. It felt like he had just entered the belly of the beast.

"This Exchange has been in operation since 1848 and at this exact location since 1930. Futures contracts have traded in the distinctive 'open outcry' manner since 1864," Larson explained, acting like a tour guide. That's over one hundred years, Jim quickly realized. "The CBOT was a cornerstone of Chicago business, an icon of world commodities. The trading pit was symbolic of the sophistication and uniqueness of this business marketplace. Stock exchanges have a similar look and feel, but there is something unique and fundamental about an enterprise dealing in the business of food and other bulk commodities."

Jim slowly scanned the great expanse of the room from left to right, trying to take in the panorama of information content and displays. From the elevated ceiling and the observation deck to the trading pits and member booths, his awe at the magnitude of the place remained. It was so different to view the trading floor from this vantage point compared to the deck above. It was so much bigger, for one thing, and there were so many people! The walls were covered with different commodity boards displaying prices and dates in abbreviated codes only the traders really understood. It was the language of the market. Board makers, armed with their sticks of chalk, waited patiently to transcribe prices to the blackboards. Everything here worked toward a single purpose: to facilitate trade in numerous commodities. The activity reminded him of a kicked anthill. Ants always looked busy, but when you kicked their hill a few times all hell broke loose. This place gave off the same impression. He wondered if this moment was before or after the anthill was kicked.

And the noise. The din arising from this many people, from telephones and the clackity-clack of teletype machines, forced everyone to raise their voice to be heard. The trading room had not been built with sound absorbency in mind, resulting in a layered cacophony of perpetual echo and reverberation.

Jim felt a tingling excitement and anticipation for the imminent opening of the market. Shifting his attention to more detailed activities, he focused on the spectacle of several hundred people traversing the floor from their booths to the trading pits, market monitors positioning themselves for the day in the pit booths and brokers and traders exchanging their thoughts and expectations for the market, which hadn't even started yet. Everyone was moving with purpose in preparation for the opening bell, now just a few moments away. From things he could see, he shifted his attention to things he could hear, picking up the low drone of dozens of conversations, either face-to-face ones or one-sided ones from people on phones. It was impossible to make out any single conversation as each blended into the chorus of noise. Phones were ringing from every corner of the room and teletype machines spewed out buying and selling orders in booths around the pits. It was an exciting, vibrant milieu, a flurry of activity where, in a few short minutes, the sum of every individual action would collide in the vocal discovery of prices, resulting in the ensuing commercial activity known as futures trade.

"Today, Jim, my plan is for us to spend the day on the trading floor." Larson's words broke through Jim's moment of wonderment. "With your farming background and economics degree, I know you have a basic understanding of the role of the exchange, and I know you got the 'magic of numbers' spiel from Hendel. But I'll take a couple of minutes to walk you through the history and features of the exchange as if you had no knowledge or preconceptions. I want you to see it from a grain trader's point of view. Okay with you?"

"Most definitely, Doug. Your enthusiasm has already given me new perspectives and a better understanding of grain markets. I'm a sponge today."

Jim noted Larson's demeanor had changed from his casual, uber calm persona to one more focused and alert as he took in the activity on the floor. Even his posture changed as he readied himself for the bell to ring. But Larson wasn't wowed or intimidated by the experience. He was reading signs and signals of the nuances of the market. This was clearly his domain.

"The vast majority of people in the world have little to no under-standing of the features and operations of a commodity exchange," he began, raising his voice to be heard. "The terms 'stock market' and 'commodity market' are often used interchangeably, but we both know they are two vastly different markets."

"Tell me about it! All of my family thinks I do 'something' in the stock market—and they are farmers!"

"Get used to it. My wife still has no idea what I do, and we've been married over thirty years.

"A common misconception is that prices are set for different com-modities by some mysterious and dishonest group of individuals con-cocting devilish plots to separate people from their hard-earned money. While there are some, shall we say, seedy characters trading here on the floor, I can tell you the exchange operates with rock-solid checks and balances to ensure fairness and value," Larson continued. "It's prob-ably the most transparent and honest price-discovery process ever in-vented." The lesson had begun.

"Trading floors are the most sophisticated and accurate tools for markets and risk management in the world," Larson boasted. "They're superior to any other price-discovery mechanism. It is the simplest and simultaneously the most refined technique available to determine a consensus value in a timely manner. The ability to share this information on a nearly immediate basis around the world ensures the information is accurate and timely. But the Exchange doesn't set prices, Jim; it discovers them. There's a world of difference. Let me give you an example.

"In a monopoly situation, where there is only one buyer or one seller—" Larson raised first one forefinger and then the other—"that one person normally determines the price. But if you have two buyers and two sellers, well, now you have a market. Expand the model to thousands of buyers and sellers and you have a robust and accurate representation of supply and demand. Those people or organizations who malign the CBOT do not understand its function or value. They are most often looking for someone to blame when the market has gone against them."

"That's a good way to describe it, Doug, but how can you be sure the seller will deliver what he promised or the buyer will be able to pay?"

"That's where the magic is, Jim. It's called the clearinghouse. I know Julius spoke with you about this too. When you trade on the Exchange you deal directly with another party to conclude a trade. But at the end of the day, all trades are converted to transactions with the clearinghouse. In essence, the clearinghouse becomes the intermediary, the buyer to all sellers and the seller to all buyers. We call it novating trade. This way, you can offset your position at any time and get out of the deal by creating an equal, offsetting position and then paying or collecting the difference in your trades. It's clean and simple.

"It's also why the Exchange requires membership. It pre-qualifies buyers and sellers and ensures performance. In other words, the grain gets delivered by the seller and payment is made by the buyer. It all fits nicely into scheduling, banking, storage and grain marketing—a complex system for sure. But I can tell you that extraordinarily little grain is actually delivered on CBOT trades. This place is a hedging facility designed to transfer price risk for a period of time. Most trades are offset."

"Who can be members of the Exchange?"

"Well, first and foremost, the Exchange doesn't care who you are," Larson replied. "You could be an insanely wealth sheik from Saudi Arabia or a small farmer from Kansas. It doesn't matter. As long as you have qualified to trade on the exchange, you are treated equally. Everyone trades through brokers, and the buyers' and sellers' names are never revealed to each other. This is the beauty and genius of these guaranteed transactions. And every day the market is 'brought to market,' meaning if you owe money against your position based on today's close then you pay a margin call. If your account is positive to the market, you have a cash credit. This way, if any one party fails to perform, everyone is protected financially. This allows market values to seek their own levels without creating risk for anyone with an open position. That's what I meant when I called the exchange a risk-transfer mechanism.

"The market is always right, Jim. You may not like it, but you can't argue with the price. It finds its own level every day based on the sum total of bids and offers. It's as close to a perfect price system as there can be.

"The Exchange discovers price through an open outcry of bids and offers," Larson added. "Many years ago I asked a mentor of mine why the market was higher. His exact quote, and I'll never forget it: 'more buyers than sellers.' His response to this same question rarely changed, although it alternated depending on whether prices had gone up or down. If market prices were down, he would say 'more sellers than buyers.' Of course, we know that statement isn't true. The volume of buyers always equals the volume of sellers. It's a constant of commodity markets. But for years this response frustrated me. In fact, it pissed me off on some occasions, until I finally came to realize this simple statement was the basic underlying reality of a commodity exchange. Price finds its own level based on the actions of all participants. What could be fairer?

"The Exchange is like a living, breathing beast. I say 'beast' because it can gobble you up one day and provide life-saving nurturing another.

It's like it has a pulse from the moment the opening bell rings at nine thirty until it goes back to sleep at the closing bell at twelve fifteen.

"So, tell me, Jim. What are your initial reactions here on the floor? What do you see, or hear or smell?"

"Smell was the first sense it triggered," Jim admitted, wrinkling his nose. "If 'old' had a smell, I think this would be it." He smirked and pushed on to get a rise out of Larson. "It's a bit funky with a musty tinge and a squeeze of human sweat thrown in."

"Yeah, several decades of smoking and perspiration can leave a trail, I agree. But that's all part of the experience of being here, as I see it. I smell the rush of energy from a market going your way and the angst of loss when it's not."

"You have a very insightful sense of smell, Doug," Jim teased. But he realized Larson was genuine in his feeling. To him, the sights and sounds of the Exchange were comforting.

"One can't appreciate the noise of the floor from the observation deck, either," Jim observed. "And I was just thinking earlier that the activity reminded me of an anthill."

"Wait until the market opens. That's when it gets really loud, and if somebody goes a little crazy and starts bidding or offering aggressively, it will be like kicking that anthill. It goes nuts in here!"

* * *

As the two men wandered around the commodity trading pits, chatted with various brokers and viewed information posted on walls and tables, the clock clicked down closer to the opening. Unbelievably, more people continued to arrive on the floor to participate in the ritual of the start of the day's trade. Many of them wore the same sky-blue jacket with their name badge pinned to their chest. These were floor traders. They would be the ones entering the pits with specific orders to execute.

Larson continued the lesson. "The Exchange is one hundred and twenty-four years old this year. While it's alive during the day, sticking with the metaphor, it has a mood and a pace. It can be a calm trading day or a frenetic, hell-raising day. Prices can move gradually higher or lower during the course of the trading session or they can move rapidly and aggressively to pre-established daily trading limits. The pace is set by the number of orders in the hands of traders and the urgency with which those orders need to be filled. When those daily trading limits are reached for a commodity, we call the market 'limit up' or 'limit down' and trading is halted. That doesn't happen too often, though. There has to be a set of extreme conditions for a market to reach a daily trading limit.

"As I said, people who don't understand commodity exchanges sometimes vilify them, suggesting the Board of Trade is a collection of thieves specifically gathered to cheat hardworking farmers and processors. The truth is, the exchange offers buyers and sellers an effective way to transfer the risk of price movement. Farmers can lock in prices for future delivery from a crop they haven't even planted yet, or a flour miller or soybean processor can establish a base price for a future sale of their products even though they can't actually buy the grain they need to fill their current product order.

"Come on over here by the corn pit and I'll show you how this whole place works." Larson waved his hand invitingly. The closer they got to the pit, the noisier it became, even though it wasn't yet nine thirty.

"In the early years of exchanges, there was more of a gentlemanly manner about them," Larson admitted. "Traders stood in different segments of this octagon pit, depending on which commodity they wanted to trade. The different steps leading down into the pit represented different delivery months. The top one would have been for May delivery, the next one down July, then October and finally December. Those are the delivery months used to trade corn. Traders would wave their hands toward or away from themselves to demonstrate an interest to buy or sell. They would use their fingers to represent price in quarter-cent increments. Each contract of trade, or board lot, was five thousand bushels. It was all very civilized back then, but it's a little more robust now, as you will soon see and hear."

"I've studied the history of exchanges, Doug. It's interesting, but there are still gaps for me. How do all of these people reach a consensus on a deal?"

"A good question, Jim. Three main components make up the price of any commodity. They are the what, where and when. If you know those three things, you can discover a price and create a market based on a mutually agreed value through this open, transparent process. Let me explain.

"The 'what' simply means what you want to buy or sell. Is it wheat, corn, soybeans, etcetera? 'Where' is pretty obvious, too. Is it in a farm bin in Iowa, loaded in a rail car by a country elevator in Illinois, sitting in a warehouse in Chicago or delivered to a port like Rotterdam? The 'when' is where forward pricing, or 'futures,' comes into play. Is the grain already harvested and sitting in a bin somewhere or is it a commitment to deliver or receive it at an agreed location at some point in the future? This is the origin of the term 'futures market.' Like I said, it's important to understand that these contracts are rarely fulfilled. They are most often offset or 'novated' when they are no longer needed to manage the risk of price volatility. They allow for a smooth functioning of the underlying physical or cash grain markets to trade.

"In the case of futures contracts traded on the exchange, the what, where and when are predetermined for each commodity so traders are merely negotiating price. When they ultimately trade out of that position, the same terms apply, and only the price has changed from their original deal.

"I'll give you an example of a typical transaction. In May a farmer wants to lock in a price for his crop, but it won't be delivered until October and the local elevator doesn't have a bid price yet. He likes the price today and he is afraid the market might be lower by the time he is ready to harvest. So, he sells a futures contract today for delivery in the fall. It means he is 'short.' When he harvests his crop in October, he goes into his local grain elevator and sells his crop. At the same time, he calls his broker and buys back his futures contract. If he was right, and the market at his local elevator is lower than the price was five or six months ago, he can live with a lower price because he will have profit in the short position he made in the futures market in May. It would have gone down by a similar amount. If the market is higher at harvest, he gets more for his grain to cover what would be a loss in his futures account. In either case, he has protected his return from changing market prices. Buyers can do the same risk transfer by applying the same technique in reverse. As I'm sure you know, the term for this activity is 'hedging.' The risk of price movement is transferred to someone else.

"Enough examples for now," Larson said. "Let's go over to the soybean pit. I know Cargill will be active there today."

They stopped at Cargill's trading floor booth on the way. "Jim, I'd like to introduce you to Oscar Muller, the busiest man in the whole company." Larson grinned as Jim and Muller shook hands. "Oscar manages Cargill's hedge desk. He collects orders from Cargill offices and country elevators all over the world and nets things out before sending them to the pit. We want to be careful we aren't buying and selling the same thing at the same time.

"This other cowboy here is our pit trader, Sam Southern." Southern sported the light-blue jacket common to many other individuals in the room. He was Cargill's bona fide trader. Pinned to his jacket was his official-looking name badge labeled "SOU," which Jim quickly realized was his trading ID in the pit. Southern carried a handful of teletype orders from Cargill traders along with a jacket pocket full of trading cards, to record transactions on the fly, and numerous pencils in his pocket and in his hand. His glasses defied gravity as they perched on his forehead, at the ready when needed.

"Nice to meet you, Jim," said Southern. "I gotta go. The market is about to open."

Larson led Jim to the outside edge of the soybean pit to experience the opening bell.

"The trade is likely to be pretty active this morning, Jim, since it's Monday. Lots happens over a weekend, triggering even more activity in the pit than midweek days. Get ready, we're about to get going."

Jim glanced high up to the three-foot diameter Bulova clock on the wall. The second hand ticked around to the top of the hour. At precisely 9:30 a.m. a bell clanged across the room, signaling the market opening. Traders in every pit were yelling and gesturing with their arms and hands. Jim jumped in reaction to the unexpected chaos and didn't know where to look first in this scene of what appeared to be uncontrolled mayhem.

"What in the name of….?" Jim started to speak, but he couldn't be heard above the deafening roar. Once again, he realized, the experience on the floor was not at all the same as watching the action from the observation deck.

"Pretty cool, right?" yelled Larson as he gave Jim a nod and a huge smile.

"How can anyone understand what is going on?" Jim asked.

"You would be surprised how effective this is, even if it seems messy. These guys are pros. They know exactly what they're doing."

Jim took in the action, watching as the trading in the pit was transferred by intercoms and displayed high on the boards above them. He watched the floor traders making deals with eye contact and nods of agreement. Deals happened quickly, and then traders moved on to other orders. One particular broker selling soybeans was surrounded by three other brokers vying for his attention and confirmation of deals. Grain prices were moving higher this morning. More buyers than sellers, Jim thought to himself. A little bit of heat on the crops early in June made some traders nervous, and the market reaction pushed grain prices higher.

"You really do like this place, don't you, Doug?"

"It's like church to me, Jim. I have such respect for the value this institution provides everyone in the grain market. Whether you like the prices or not, you can't argue with the process. The stakes are extremely high, but this place offers a way to manage risk and transfer it to someone else. Regardless of whether you're a hedger or a speculator in the market, there's a place for everyone. The market feeds on input from all participants in order to function properly."

The pace and volume of the trading session calmed after the initial rush of orders were filled. Jim was curious about Muller's role and how he managed what seemed like an impossible task, so they headed back to Cargill's booth.

"Oscar, can you tell me how you collect all the orders and make sense of it?"

"I'll try," Muller replied. "You know we have offices all over the world, but the biggest and best exchange is right here in Chicago. Most companies use this market to trade and hedge. For instance, we have our US soybean-crushing plant sending us orders to buy beans for October delivery. They would normally be sellers of bean futures, as they hedge sales from producers, so it's a bit unusual. They probably sold some product—soy oil or soybean meal—and can't buy grain from farmers to cover. So, they buy futures. Meanwhile, the bean harvest in South America is just finishing up and farmers there are selling. We had an order from our office in Brazil to sell beans. I crossed the two orders and ended by selling a small amount to tidy everything up. Not all companies can net orders, but we are very big and diverse, with our finger on the pulse of all markets. It's a huge advantage for Cargill."

"Gotcha!" Jim was gaining a slightly better sense with this example of the power of Cargill's communication network and global business power.

"It only makes sense for everyone in our company to share information as well as combine our trades so we can anticipate market moves rather than respond to them. This is one element of the secret of our success, Jim. I don't mean knowing why markets did what they did. I mean having the insight to know what markets are going to do. That's the key."

Jim looked back to Larson. He had another question to ask. "What makes someone a good trader?"

"Yeah, that's a really good question. I think if you asked five traders you would probably get as many different answers. There's no 'one thing,' Jim. But, at the outset, a good trader needs to have an organized, analytical mind with an affinity for numbers. That's a bare minimum, and it's why I recommended we hire you," Larson said. "You check off those boxes very well. But you need more than those basics. First of all, you need to know how to interpret the data you and the analysts collect. What does it all mean and how does it translate into useful information so market moves can be anticipated? Some of that is instinct, but I believe it's more about having more information than the next guy and acting on it faster than anyone else."

As the market quieted down, Southern joined them in the booth along with Oscar, the teletype operator and the floor runner, making for a congested cubicle. There was still a dull roar from private conversations, ringing phones, light trade in the pit and the undefinable continuing pulse of the beast.

"Jim just asked me what makes someone a good trader, Sam. What are your thoughts?"

"Nerves of steel, a cold heart and nice shoes," Southern replied instantly with his trademark big grin, pointing at his loafers.

"Very funny, you old codger," Larson said with a laugh. "Like I said, Jim, there are differing views. Some companies have different people responsible for trading futures in addition to the ones who trade the physical grain. They have a corn futures trader and a cash grain corn trader. We don't do it that way. Our corn trader handles both futures and physical grain for the simple reason they are tightly aligned, and movement in one generally dictates movement in the other. The physical grain is the underlying commodity for the futures contract."

"That's why our commodity position reports contain both grain and futures," Jim said.

"Exactly! But back to the analytical skills. A trader needs to understand the supply and demand Julius covered in his course. I'm sure he told you it's a perpetual document spanning many years. We use it to check back on the past and predict the future. We estimate numbers for the current year and, as they become known, we fine-tune the accuracy of the estimate. I'm talking about production numbers, exports, carryovers, etcetera. My best advice is for you to spend a lot of time getting to know the numbers. The last thing the trader does is buy or sell grain based on predictions, so you have to get the facts right. Good traders understand this."

"SOLD!" Southern bellowed as he crashed out of the booth, chair flying, heading to the wheat pit. "Dec wheat at forty-two," Jim heard him yell as he reached the edge of the pit, waving his arms. "Five, ten."

"What just happened?" Jim asked as he and Larson sorted the debris field of Southern's departure.

"While he was sitting here talking with us, he was also listening to the trade in the wheat pit," answered Larson. "He has orders to buy one hundred thousand bushels at a dollar forty-two or better. He said 'sold,' but he was actually buying wheat."

"How does anyone know that?" Jim asked.

"Somebody in the pit offered Dec wheat at a dollar forty-two. I didn't hear it, but Sam did. Specifically, they said 'Dec at forty-two.' Sam booked the offer by yelling 'Sold' before anyone else. If the guy in the pit wanted to buy wheat, he would have said 'forty-two for Dec. See the difference?"

"Yes, I do. But how did Sam hear that all the way over here?"

"He's amazing, is the only answer," Muller said. "He does it all day, every day. He's supposed to be in the pit to trade, but he takes some liberty in that rule. No one challenges him on it."

"Okay, I get the data analysis part, but there's more to it than that, right?" Jim asked Larson, eager to continue this important conversation.

"You're very right. It's not enough to know what is happening in our local market; you have to understand what's happening elsewhere in the world. Traders from many other countries use the Chicago futures market to hedge their positions. A soybean processor in Europe or a corn handler in South America might have orders in the pit. You can get rear ended and sideswiped at the same time."

"That's such a big playing field," Jim said.

"Damn right, and there's more. Take soybeans, for instance. Beans get processed into soybean oil and soybean meal. One day the market wants the oil as a food energy source and that's what's driving the price.

Six months later, soybeans could be driven by demand for protein in the meal. You have to understand the components of the crop, not just the seed itself."

"And that's true for all crops?"

"Yes, most of them. So, along with that analytical mind comes the 'nerves of steel' Sam mentioned. He's right—this is not a job for the faint of heart. A cold heart may be the right characteristic. I won't comment on the 'nice shoes' requirement." Larson grinned.

"A final characteristic I would add is judgment," he continued. "A good trader needs to be able to admit when he is wrong and get out of bad positions. I've seen too many young traders get married to their position and lose their objectivity. I'm sure you've heard it said, your first loss is your best loss. It's true. If a position isn't working for you, double-check your assumptions. If they aren't rock solid—get out."

* * *

They spent the rest of the morning on the floor chatting up brokers, reading posted reports and following the movement of price as orders trickled in through the day. Most of the price change occurred at the outset of trading, but sometimes an outlier order would come in and, without anyone willing to fill it, the market would move one way or another. Larson introduced Jim to a dozen different traders and brokers. There was no way he could remember them all, so for today he would be happy remembering his new Cargill contacts, Oscar Muller and Sam Southern.

As the market approached the close at 12:15, the activity started to escalate.

"What's happening all of a sudden, Doug?"

"Quite a lot really, Jim. Some companies who expect to buy grain overnight based on the close today are pre-hedging or selling futures before they buy grain. Exporters may be doing the opposite: buying grain in anticipation of sales. Speculators may be evening up their trading book for the day and brokers are filling market orders to lock in a purchase or sale at the closing price—whatever it is. You never know how this will end, but you can be sure it will generally be with a bang rather than a whimper."

The market didn't disappoint. The excitement at the close was as loud as the opening had been, and almost as robust. Then, sharply at quarter past the hour, the bell rang, the noise level lowered and the market went to sleep until tomorrow morning.

After thanking Muller and Southern for an educational morning, the two men headed for the door.

"Man, that was fun!" Larson exclaimed. "Now, let's go get us a Red Hot and a beer!"

7

Russian Roulette

Exportkhleb Offices, Department of Agriculture   June 19, 1972

Misha Fisenko wasn't a gambler. He avoided risk as part of his job as well as in the way he lived his life. Ironically, his job entailed a lot of risk. That was the nature of commodity trading, but he went to great lengths to remove the aspect of chance from decisions he made and outcomes he delivered. But not all scenarios can be managed with care and precision. There are times you must make a decision or take an action that offers no guarantee of success, where the alternatives either may not differ much or may mean life or death. On these occasions, people often find themselves immobilized by fear of the prospect of failing or making the wrong choice. This was the weight squarely on Misha's shoulders as he accepted the inevitability of the responsibility and the challenge of his job. He understood the urgency and the task at hand but had no inkling of how much time he had to succeed or what action he could take. He assembled his team Monday morning to take stock of the situation.

His trio of specialists had dedicated themselves to their duty over the weekend. All three members had passed on his promise of Sunday as an off-day. They understood the critical need for success, and there was too much work to do and not nearly enough time. But all their preparation relied on one key element: Misha's ability to acquire the grain. If he couldn't find twenty-five to thirty million tonnes, it wouldn't matter what the rest of them accomplished. No one knew that better than Misha himself. The clock ticked in his imagination as every critical second slipped away.

By end of day on Monday, Operation Kuznechik had the makings of a plan—at least the physical components required to handle imports and then distribute the vital grains to domestic food processors. Boris's review confirmed that the Soviet infrastructure could handle the volume of imports estimated by Misha. And Gregor's estimates confirmed Misha's earliest predictions: the Soviets would indeed require a minimum of twenty-five million tonnes of grain to meet the demands for the most basic food-consumption requirements. Even at this level it would mean, as Misha had predicted, more bread and less beef. It forecast food lines and empty shelves. Even if they were successful, the nation's prospects remained grim. They were afraid to imagine the circumstances if they were to fail. And what about next year? Would this problem repeat itself into the future?

Boris outlined a distribution plan outlining terminal capacities and processing facilities within reasonable distance to the various ports of entry. He broke it out by region, by grain type and by delivery schedule. Misha was impressed with the detail Boris had accomplished in such a short time. Much of this information came from Boris's knowledge of the Soviet infrastructure. He provided the analysis and advice of a seasoned department veteran and long-time confidante of Misha's. Based on Boris's overview, Misha quickly realized it would be challenging, but achievable. Ocean vessel freight was not within their control to the same extent as the facilities inside the Soviet Union were, so Boris's confidence level in shipping capacity was not as high as his terminal capacity projections. But whether boats were loading grain out of Soviet ports or bringing grain into them, there should be adequate capacity. The cost? Boris didn't know, at least not yet. And he was reluctant to ask vessel agents too many questions at this point and trigger speculation and a possible run on freight costs.

Somehow, Nadia had managed to secure a commitment from Soviet Treasury for the equivalent of three billion US dollars starting in October and spread out over the following twelve months. Nadia confirmed she had reached out to Minister Matskevich's office and the minister himself had directed the Treasury to approve the financing. At least that number won't be a surprise at our meeting with him, Misha thought. It was still less than the full amount they would need, meaning they would have to secure long-term credit financing along with the actual grain purchases. Nevertheless, it was significantly more than he had expected.

"Let me start by acknowledging the excellent work you all have accomplished in such a short period," Misha began. "Nadia, well done. Securing this commitment is a significant achievement during difficult financial conditions. Boris and Gregor, your work on this project has been equally excellent. I'm proud of each of you for a brilliant effort under unprecedented and difficult conditions."

Misha was diligent in recognizing the work of his team. This behavior was uncharacteristic of Russian managers, but it's what made Misha different and why he was well-liked in the department. He could thank his dear departed Liliya for teaching him kindness.

"Unfortunately, the hardest part is ahead of us." His team nodded in understanding. "We actually have to find the grain we now know we will need, assuming we get approval from our leaders to proceed."

At 4:00 p.m. on Monday, the team met with Exportkhleb president Pershin to present the plan to be submitted to Minister Matskevich.

"President Pershin, I can now provide more detail on each of the elements of the plan we propose for the Minister," Misha began. He spoke assertively, confident in their knowledge and analysis. It wasn't easy, but he had to appear capable—in control of a situation that many might view as catastrophic.

He walked through all the elements of the team's plan with Pershin. He left the final strategic component of acquiring grain until the end. Eagerly, Pershin pushed him to explain how he planned to execute this monumental endeavor and protect Soviet interests.

"I see your outline, Misha. You have identified what we need to do to manage the undertaking and even how to pay for 75 percent of it, assuming the prices don't go higher as you buy grain, which seems very unlikely. But still, I don't see 'how' you propose we get this done."

"Yes, President, I do have a proposal that I think will work. Let me play it out for you, and I look forward to your review."

Over the next hour Misha laid out an elaborate plan to secure both grain and credit. It focused mostly on unprecedented grain-supply agreements with the United States. He outlined a plan to deal with both American and international grain companies trading in the USA, which included some grain coming from traditional sources with whom they had enjoyed a history of long-term trade agreements. Misha would secure the grain deals while Pershin secured credit. He knew this would appeal to the president, as it played to his strengths and meant he would take on a key role dealing with high-powered government officials.

"Your plan is bold and simultaneously delicate. Timing will be critical. However, this carries a high level of risk and a great potential for failure," Pershin said. "We have no history trading with the Americans, and, let's be honest, I don't like our position as we try to open this trade relationship. But I admit I don't have a better idea. Misha, you have a lot more experience in agriculture than I do, so you are a better judge of whether this idea will work or not. It makes me nervous; I can see the whole thing blowing up in our faces. You aren't dealing with uneducated people at these giant corporations. They are sophisticated, experienced traders who do this for a living. I feel like we will still be exposed by revealing more information than we should, but I don't know how else to proceed.

"I would suggest you prepare a more detailed description of the American support programs and the workings of the open market trade for the Minister," he continued. "His knowledge of those mechanics is less than ours, and it will help him understand the economic infrastructure we hope to use to improve the potential for success of this plan. With respect to my concerns, do you have another option, Misha? A plan B, as the Americans say?"

"I don't, Mister President," Misha admitted. "We have analyzed production in other countries, and the only chance we have is to try to secure the large inventories of grain being held in the United States. No other country can come close to filling the void we are projecting."

"But if we do declare our production shortfalls, how can you be sure it won't trigger a market frenzy, exposing us to significantly higher cost? They appear to hold all the cards," Pershin said.

"I can't make such a promise," Misha conceded. "Commodity markets move on their own accord and no one has control over them—not the large, private grain companies, and not the American government. Here in Russia we would just set the price and that would be the end of it. But in the capitalist world, markets work differently, as you know. We must act quickly by arranging closely scheduled meetings with companies to prevent the spread of information. To my mind, it will require precision and action. We need to make sure we lock in business before the market learns of our predicament and reacts to our actions. What happens in the market after we make our deals will then be their problem, not ours. We are exposed right now, though; there is no question."

"You're right, Fisenko," Pershin said. "As far as securing credit, I will take on the task, as you suggest. We will have to work quickly and in unison so we don't tip anyone off. I expect you can lock in financing with the Canadian Wheat Board when you buy their grain, but I will have to meet with the American politicians." Pershin was already showing more enthusiasm for a plan that would enable him to play a role. "Very well, let's take it to the Minister. Send me the final version by tomorrow and we will meet with Matskevich on Wednesday morning."

Cargill's Lake Office, Wayzata, Minnesota   *June 20, 1972*

One week after arriving at Cargill's Lake Office, Jim had oriented himself logistically and even a little culturally. He could find his way from his desk to the boardroom, cafeteria and washroom. The rest of the interior of the Lake Office was uncharted territory. Beyond the walls of the Cargill castle, he had experienced a day on the trading floor and had his first Chicago Red Hot hotdog. There was a lot to take in, and he knew there was a great deal more ahead. But the new assignment energized him more than he would have imagined. The pace of the action, the stakes in play and the tension of the situation combined in a way he couldn't describe.

The luxury of having his own personal screen displaying futures market price information was a new treat, but his biggest surprise was the rapid pace of an enormous amount of information moving on and off his desk. The intellectual responsibilities of his assignment were becoming more evident to him each day. He had to get up to speed on a communications system, the language of the commodity world and a global directory of people who relied on the Lake Office for market insight, opinion and leadership. And the reports—my God, the reports! Cash grain position reports, futures position reports, consolidated reports, weather forecasts, regional production estimates, international summaries; the list went on and on. He could read all day and get through only half of it. He had to make prioritizing and selective reading a key strategy.

The daily merchant update meeting occurred at 9:00 a.m. For the first week, Jim got a pass as a listener, but starting today he would be providing a portion of the update from the wheat desk. Intimidating, for sure. At least his contribution would play from his strength: US wheat production.

Trading manager Barney Saunders hosted the meeting. He was a tall, lean man with thinning, brushed back gray hair that exaggerated his receding hairline. His height and large hands would lead one to suspect he had played his share of basketball—which would be correct. He had completed his college degree on a basketball scholarship, but his court skills hadn't matched his intellectual potential, so it was no surprise he ended up in a white-collar job. Cargill was fortunate to snag him. He had been on this team for over twenty-five years, leading it for the past five, and was widely respected inside and outside the company.

The setting of today's sanctum and yesterday's free-for-all struck Jim as comically opposite. From the raucous and chaotic frenzy of the trading floor to the serenity of the Lake Office boardroom, he had been immersed in the rich diversity of the commodity industry, well distanced from the grassroots production of his recent past.

"We'll start with the wheat desk and move around the table to corn and beans," Saunders suggested, interrupting Jim's musings. "Let's focus on global production today, gents. Tomorrow we will look at the export picture, and on Wednesday we will drill down to look at domestic processing. By Thursday I want a complete revision to the supply and demand outlooks for all three crops.

"Jim, you've had your week of grace to see how we do things here, so now's your chance to add your voice. Let's get your maiden presentation out of the way and put you out of your misery," he said with a smile.

"Thanks, Barney. I've actually been looking forward to this," Jim said. "I'm grateful for this opportunity and anxious to take on the challenge." He launched into his update for the merchants like a typical enthusiastic rookie.

"It's still very early to make a firm prediction for 1972 American wheat production, but, using last year's average yield per acre and the amount of land seeded to wheat this spring, the USA is on track to replicate last year's record production," Jim said confidently. "In some areas, farmers are still planting wheat, and the weather has been accommodating," he added for color. "I've prepared a state-by-state production estimate along with estimates of available grain tributary to each export port on US coasts." He began passing out copies of a chart. "My next step would be to reduce the available supply by domestic use estimates, which are pretty static year over year, and finish with an estimate of export supply by port. This will give us some idea of potential grain supply for Cargill's export terminals. These steps will help us monitor movement and predict areas of tight supply or overage. I have to factor in the location of US-government-held inventory as well, but that's easy to find."

"Well, that's a helluva a way to start, Jim. Great initiative. Nice work," Saunders said. "Mel, can you give us your global outlook?"

"As you know, we've been monitoring the wheat crops across Asia, specifically the Soviet Union countries," Middents began. "Mostly this includes the grain belt in southern Russia, but it takes in the western member countries like Czechoslovakia and Ukraine as well. As usual, information is scarce from these places, but a couple of the bordering countries give us some insight. Joe the Blinker is always good for some early intel on situations, and he's sending us strong signals that Poland wants to buy a lot more than usual."

"Joe the Blinker?" Jim asked.

"Yeah, Joe Jankowski, the grain buyer for Poland. His nickname is 'the Blinker' because he has some kind of nervous condition that makes him blink quite noticeably. I know, I know—it's not nice to point out someone's affliction, but we know him well and he's a good sport. He's well aware of the nickname, and I think other companies use it too. When he gets really excited the blinking gets faster. He can't play poker anymore because his nervous twitch gives him away," Middents said with a laugh. "He's a great guy and wants to be everyone's friend, but he really can't keep secrets. He's an open book!

"Joe is often the first indication things aren't just right in Ruskie land," Middents continued. "Our merchants in Geneva confirm that their sources across Eastern Europe indicate the signals we got from Joe are consistent with their findings. The winter wheat crop is a write-off, and the early indications show low rainfall and poor germination for much of the spring-seeded production. The clincher for me, though, is intel coming from Dick Dawson in Winnipeg. We all know how close he is with the Russians. He's been dealing with them for a decade now and stays in regular communication. We spoke last week, and he told me he sees signs of their concern. Nothing specific yet, but I trust Dick's instincts. The whole collective farming initiative in the Soviet Union is still a clusterfuck, so when you put it all together it looks like we should be expecting a call from Exportkhleb any day now."

"What makes you think they will call us, Mel?" Saunders asked. "We haven't sold US grain to the Soviets in decades."

"A couple of things. I don't think they'll find everything they need from traditional suppliers, for one, and Nixon's road show to Moscow last month may open some trade talks. If the government qualifies the Soviet Union for the Wheat Export Subsidy Program, it could be a new ballgame.

"Jim, I'd like you to take the same approach you did on US production and see if you can apply it to what we know out of Russia. See what you can discover at a more detailed level using yields at, above and below average. I'd like to get a range of severity so we can position ourselves for a future opportunity. Even though we're looking at record wheat production here in North America, we're starting to build a long position in wheat futures in anticipation of this potential export demand. On the surface, it sounds crazy and getting long wheat is in opposition to just about everyone else's view of the wheat market, but that's not new for us. We'll start small for now, but this situation bears watching."

"Doesn't the US government export subsidy program put a ceiling on wheat prices, Mel?" asked Jim. "The government subsidies put a port price limit of a dollar sixty-three per bushel on wheat. How much money can we actually make going long if there's a price ceiling?"

"It does create a price ceiling," said Middents. "And with large local production, the domestic market isn't likely to drive cash grain or futures prices higher, so going long does seem like a bad idea. But if this Russian production problem turns out to be as large as I fear, then all bets are off. It could potentially even mean an end to export subsidies. This could be nothing, or it could be a turning point in global agriculture trade. I think we need to move carefully right now, but there is a possible opportunity here for us and American wheat farmers. There's also a ton of risk if we're wrong."

Jim had nothing more to add. His mind was already racing through scenarios. Middents had just raised the stakes in the game. The scope of this conversation spread well beyond his humble role in Tuscola and even beyond the borders of the United States. What Middents had laid out was a possible tectonic shift in ag economics and international trade. Markets weren't reacting to this signal—not yet, at least. This insight was a solid example of Cargill's reach and intelligence network in action. It wasn't just gathering information. What he was witnessing was gut instinct and an ability to read a developing situation. Cargill was ready to risk money on the consensus of this team. It was a serious responsibility.

Russian Politburo, Department of Agriculture   June 21, 1972

On Wednesday Pershin sat with Misha, Gregor, Boris and Nadia at the same table in the same massive room where they had met with Minister Matskevich one week earlier. The Minister entered along with his aide and resumed his position at the head of the table. He looked a bit frazzled, frowning with a no-nonsense expression, no doubt dealing with the pressures of the agricultural situation. This was a serious, troubling situation. The meeting wasn't going to be fun, Misha realized.

"Good morning, comrades. I'm anxious to hear what you have to share with me today. Thank you for sending the basics of the report in advance. Your information was helpful, but there are still some gaps you must address."

"Minister," Misha began, taking the lead as he and Pershin had decided. "After additional research and study, I can confirm the situation is as desperate as I had imagined." There was no sense in hiding from the bad news, he knew. Delaying the admission would only make things worse. "The entire crop is not a failure, but we will suffer large production shortfalls. We will need to import wheat and rye for flour, soybeans for protein, and oil and corn for food and animal feeds. We believe we have the physical capabilities to import what we need. I'm speaking of port capacity, transportation and labor. I'm not sure how we will pay for everything yet, but your help in securing the finances allocated so far has been essential.

"My proposal is a like three-legged stool, the legs being quantity, price and credit," Misha continued nervously. "Most importantly, we know where we must go to get what we need. Unfortunately, we have no choice but to deal with the Americans." He was close enough to Matskevich to see his jaw tighten and teeth grind.

"In the past decade, their grain crops have been bountifully productive, resulting in huge grain inventory surpluses. The government set-aside programs are mechanisms developed to actually pay farmers not to grow crops in order to manage this surplus. Their government has financed huge quantities of inventory through their Commodity Credit Corporation agency to support grain prices and put cash in farmers' hands. The United States has twenty-four million tonnes of wheat in storage, and another large crop expected this year. They have positioned themselves as a major global exporting nation, producing well beyond their own domestic demand. They have managed to accomplish what we in the Soviet Union are trying to achieve.

"The next leg in the stool, which the Americans are kindly providing, is an export subsidy payment. This program is designed to preserve American competitiveness in international markets while maintaining stable, higher prices in their own country. It is essentially a ceiling on world prices and a bane to other exporting countries like Canada and Australia. If we can qualify and continue to capture the export subsidy until we have covered our business, we will be the main benefactor of this program. US grain exporters will work with us to secure this support, because it is to their greedy financial interest. Our plan requires us to strike quickly and aggressively. If the American government decides to remove the subsidy, world grain prices are likely to move much higher, very quickly.

"Lastly, the US government is prepared to provide credit for export sales. This negotiation is separate to the actual purchasing of grain, so our plan is to meet simultaneously with US government officials and grain exporters. We hope to secure as much as one billion dollars in commercial credit, which will address the shortfall of funds according to our estimates and allow us to purchase twenty-five million tonnes of their grain all at the same time—a coordinated, tactical maneuver. US President Nixon's recent visit to Moscow in May included an offer to secure trade credit through direct dealings or by way of their Money for Peace program, known as PL 480.

"I propose we accept his kind offer," Misha concluded with a wry smile. "The grain companies will work in their own best interests, not in the interests of their country. Hopefully, this plan will allow us to secure the grain we need and the credit to pay for it."

Looking up from his notes, he was discouraged to see that the dour look on the Minister's face had not been lifted by the description of the plan thus far. If anything, he appeared even more stressed by the frank details. That was unfortunate; this was the best news Misha had to present. Clearly, dealing with the Americans was not the tactic the Minister wanted to hear.

"Okay, I see the numbers in your report and your strategy, Misha. This is all helpful," Matskevich said, holding the report in the air. "But I don't expect the Americans to just roll over and agree to supply us with twenty-five million tonnes of grain at the current price and lend us the money to buy it. They will hold us ransom somehow, I'm sure. I could believe in your plan more if you were talking about dealing with another state agency we could trust to keep quiet, but not with international, private companies. This is a weak negotiating position for our country. Should we bring in some of our top diplomats to hammer out a trade deal?"

"Initially, I thought that would be necessary, Minister, but after some consideration I believe that would be a mistake," Misha said. "I feel such a move would draw unwanted attention to our situation. After all, we have been saying how much we plan to export under our current agricultural plan. If we walk into Washington or New York with a contingent of Soviet officials, we'll be waving a big red flag in the Americans' faces. The market will react to this move, and any advantage we have would be lost before we even sit down at a negotiating table. I suggest we base our plan on a quick, precise, sequenced strategy dependent on rapid execution and confidentiality."

As he had with Pershin, Misha outlined his 'art of the deal' strategic plan to Matskevich. He explained how he would approach the delicate task of buying so much grain without triggering a price surge. Timing would be everything.

"Oh, this is risky, Misha," Matskevich sighed. "So many things could go wrong. There is one right, positive outcome and a host of potential catastrophes." He paused. "But the prospect of food shortages and starving Soviet citizens is not an option. I know you both understand this." He looked at both Pershin and Misha. "However, I need to emphasize the very future of the Union depends on a strong workforce. Nutrition is the basis of our strength. You cannot fail. Can you make it work? Do you really believe this approach to be possible?"

"I think it plays into our strengths and targets the weaknesses of the open market, Minister," Pershin said. "Actually, I believe we could never do this secretively with central agencies like the Wheat Boards. We would have to put all our cards on the table with them. But the open market leaves itself vulnerable. Misha has developed a clever and tactical plan. Knowing how these large grain companies operate and knowing their penchant for secrecy is as critical as ours puts us in a stronger position. I support the plan developed by Misha and his team."

Well, there it was, thought Misha. Pershin had tied himself to his plan. They would succeed or fail together.

"We could all be heroes or goats, my friends, yes? What other options do we have?" asked Matskevich. Pausing for effect between each word, he asked, "What…else…can…we…do?"

"This is it, sir," replied Pershin. "This is the only way for us to act quickly and quietly. No other country can come close to supplying the large volume we seek. No one else can give us credit to pay. We have little choice but to present ourselves as non-threatening and cordial."

The Minister pondered the proposal. "I know the stakes all too well, and I hate to be forced into dealing with the Americans at all. Maintaining our independence from international supplies is a priority for the Soviet agriculture department. But I fear you are right, gentlemen. There is no other real alternative that wouldn't be very expensive.

"All right, President Pershin and Vice President Fisenko. You have my authorization to proceed with your plan. We don't have much time; every day exposes us to greater disaster if our situation is revealed. Tell my staff what you need and I will support you. I want a weekly update on your progress."

"Thank you, Minister," Misha quickly responded. He didn't want to leave the Minister time for second thoughts or regrets. "We will do our best. I will need some external help if I am to be successful. With your permission, I would like to recruit a man who can develop tactics with me and open some doors with the Americans. You know who I am referring to: Doctor Michal Slaski."

"Ah, Slaski." Matskevich nodded. "The ex-Cargill trader from Geneva. He has been helpful to us before, hasn't he?"

"Yes, Minister. He has been extremely valuable in negotiations and trade arrangements, although I'm never completely sure whose side he is on most days. His own, I believe. But he is smart and well connected and he has always delivered. He is also quite popular with our staff at the office for some reason. Maybe it's his good looks and fancy European suits, but regardless of his background or loyalties, I need his help."

"Okay, Misha, bring him in on this, but be very clear—no leaks!"

* * *

Back in his office, Misha mentally reviewed and summarized the directions of the Minister . He had been given the permission and empowered to take on the single biggest responsibility of his career, possibly the largest single commercial trade transaction in Soviet history. He had the tools to succeed, but he also knew this assignment had the potential to end his career. At this point in his life, it probably didn't matter that much. He was close to retiring, so his future would be predominantly dreary, alone in his little apartment whether he was a hero or a failure. But it would be nice to say his goodbyes as the former. This was a once-in-a-lifetime chance to serve his country.

He opened his file and searched for the list Gregor had created. Slaski's name and number were there. He dialed the Switzerland number.

"Mike? Misha Fisenko here."

"Misha, it's been a long time since we spoke. How are you?"

"Well, thank you. I have a proposition I would like to discuss with you."

"By all means. What can I do for you?"

"I would rather speak to you in person, confidentially. Can I meet you in Geneva tomorrow?"

"Certainly. I'll pick you up at the airport and we can meet at my place. How's that?"

"There's an Aeroflot flight arriving at eleven fifteen. I'll see you then."

"I look forward to seeing you, Misha."

8

The Doctor's Appointment

Cointrin Aéroport, Geneva, Switzerland   June 22, 1972

In 1968, the fifty-year-old Cointrin airport in Geneva upgraded its main terminal to handle rapidly expanding international travel. Geneva was home to some of Europe's wealthiest people thanks to the country's stunning beauty as well as its attractive tax regime, a one-two punch making Switzerland an attractive haven, difficult for most other European countries to copy.

Geneva was also home to Cargill's European trading arm. "Tradax" was the base of operations for a contingent of Cargill's best traders. Mike Slaski had been the senior manager of the division until two years ago. He left the company to pursue a career as an independent consultant, a choice already resulting in a more lucrative income than he had earned with his Cargill salary. In addition, the change in career created an independence exceeding his expectations and matching his personal style very well.

Michal Slaski was born in Czechoslovakia in 1926. His family roots traced back to nearby Poland. Like all Czechs at the time, he and his family endured a difficult life under Soviet rule. As a very smart and ambitious young man, he managed to leave the country to attend school in Switzerland. In 1951 he graduated with a doctorate in philosophy. He joined Cargill in 1954 as a commodity trader, which may have seemed an odd choice for a doctor of philosophy, but he was lured by the challenge and earning potential of the job and gravitated to it naturally thanks to his intelligence and personality. His degree earned him the nickname of "The Doctor," a respectful salute that spread from the inner Cargill circle to the industry at large. Along with being extremely intelligent, Slaski was a schmoozer and a very likeable individual. He appreciated the knowledge and contacts he gained at Tradax; however, he saw a greater opportunity to leverage his knowledge and reputation as a freelance consultant, so he ventured out on his own. His contacts in Russia became his bread and butter. He needed the work, and they needed someone with his experience and insight beyond the borders of the Soviet Union. Initially he acted in the capacity of an export sales consultant for the agricultural ministry, but right now Fisenko needed him to be an import consultant.

* * *

Was this a mistake?

On the flight to Geneva, Misha asked himself that question multiple times. He had permission to discuss the current crop problems with an outsider, but Slaski was no ordinary consultant. He made no secret of his capitalistic outlook, and, while he never spoke openly or negatively about communism, his history was well known and his bias obvious. Revealing the current Soviet weakness to anyone outside the inner circle of Exportkhleb and the Kremlin was a dangerous undertaking. Misha balanced the pros and cons for the entire flight. As the wheels touched down, he decided he had no choice; he would have to trust this man with their secret and hope he didn't live to regret it.

Exiting the luggage claim area with one small suitcase, Misha spotted Slaski immediately. His engaging smile and welcoming wave were unmistakable. Slaski also maintained an immaculately manicured moustache and carried his trademark walking stick. "Not a cane," he would frequently clarify—a walking stick. And the tailored suit— my goodness, Misha thought. Even for a casual meeting, Slaski looked like a million dollars. He quickly glanced at his own suit and couldn't help but feel like it had been sewn by a Russian tentmaker, and a bad one at that. Slaski's whole look was one of sophistication and success, but not in a garish or boasting way. It was just Mike Slaski, one of a kind.

"Greetings, Doctor Slaski," Misha said in a friendly teasing tone.

"Misha, my friend, it's good to see you. Drop the 'doctor' stuff, okay? You really have my curiosity piqued with this secrecy and face-to-face meeting. I'm glad you called, and I hope I can be helpful."

"So do I, Mike. So do I."

"I have lunch waiting for us at home. I hope you like the local cuisine."

"If it isn't borscht, I know I will love it," he replied with a broad grin.

* * *

Misha adored the city of Geneva. The architecture retained the beautiful character of old Europe, but by all measures this was a modern city. Language flowed easily between French, German, Italian and English, so he was able to communicate, although not in his native tongue. As they drove to Slaski's home, he was awed by the prosperity of the city, indicated by the houses, cars and the people. Everything was just so beautiful, so perfect. Wherever he looked there were lavish chalets, restaurants and shops. The older streets had a quaint elegance, an inviting ambiance enticing one to walk along the cobblestone sidewalks and into the shops for pastries, clothing and tobacco. The more modern areas of the downtown core reflected the affluence of the country's economy. There was a lot of money in this small city.

Slaski's home was no exception. He owned a country house in Villars-Sainte-Croix on the northern end of Lake Geneva, about forty minutes from the airport. They drove off the main road onto a long driveway through a wooded area. Hidden about a half kilometer into the property was a magnificent chalet-style home built on solid rock. A three-car garage stood adjacent to the main building. The BMW sedan they were riding in no doubt belonged in one of those three doorways.

The front of the Slaski home was highlighted by a thick wooden double door that when opened revealed a two-story-high ceiling and a tastefully decorated main living area to the left. In that room, a massive stone fireplace covered most of one wall. A stairway to an upper area and a hallway to deeper recesses of the first floor stood before them, and to the right was obviously what was Slaski's office, library and refuge. Another fireplace covered most of another wall. The two men headed for the office, where Misha removed his jacket and rolled up his sleeves. Slaski invited him to join him by the fireplace as they settled into comfortable leather chairs.

"All right, Misha, you've kept me in suspense long enough. Out with it my friend. What brings you here?"

"What I am about to share with you is of the utmost confidence. I know we always say that to you, but this time I must emphasize it. I really mean it. If what I am about to tell you becomes public knowledge, it will create great hardship for the Soviet Union and, if the leak of this information is traced back to me, will mean my certain disappearance. I'm not joking, Mike." Misha spoke with a serious clarity.

"Misha, I hope you know you can trust me. I don't think you would be here if you didn't feel that way. But I hear you—super secret. I get it. So, lay it on me. What's going on?"

For the next hour Misha shared the revelation of the Soviet Union's crop-production problems, their need to import an unfathomable amount of grain and their limited cash reserves. He replayed meetings with Pershin and Matskevich and outlined the tension this problem was creating. He didn't hold anything back from Slaski, knowing full disclosure was essential in outlining the complexity and magnitude of the situation.

"Before I continue with our proposed plan of attack, I want to stop now and get your thoughts and ask for your assessment."

"Jesus Christ, Misha, that's a helluva story. I believe you and I know there are problems with crops in Europe, but it's overwhelming at the same time. Twenty-five million tonnes? Are you sure? That's nearly a billion bushels."

Misha nodded.

"Jesus Christ!" Slaski repeated. "Okay, what do I think? I think you have a really big problem. If your bosses feel they need to buy so much, they're going to have to pay for it... for sure. You have to find the money somewhere. I have a few thoughts off the top of my head, but there is no single solution to generate money to pay for the grain. It will have to come from a number of sources and different strategies. I'm going to leave all the finances to you and your team. You called it 'Operation' what?"

"Kuznechik. It means grasshopper. It was all we could see on the Volga Plain last week—grasshoppers."

"Jesus Christ! Okay, Misha, let's break this down. Twenty-five million tonnes," Slaski repeated, trying to come to grips with the seriousness of the problem and develop some options to consider. "You might get as much as five million from Canada. That leaves twenty million, or maybe more still, to cover. You might be able to pick away at it with grain from Australia and South America, but, let's face it, the obvious source is the United States. Now, I don't think Brezhnev and Nixon like each other very much. This isn't going to be easy. What's your plan, Misha?"

"I concur with your view we must buy the bulk of our needs from America," Misha said. "As distasteful as this is for me, we have no choice. As you know, there's been a great deal of tension between the two geopolitical powers since the end of the Second World War. Both nations have experienced strained internal circumstances as well. The Soviets with the invasion and backlash to the incorporation of Czecho-slovakia as part of the Soviet Union, and the Americans with civil rights unrest and repercussions from the war in Vietnam. These have been turbulent times for both nations.

"Also remember that we came dangerously close to conflict with America during the nasty affair where we were accused of shooting down their U2 spy plane in 1960. Then there was the Cuban Missile Crisis in 1962. We weren't getting along very well back then. Confidentially, the dismissal of Khrushchev has been a turning point in negotiations and peace talks. President Nixon signing the Strategic Arms

Limitation Treaty last month in Moscow may represent a huge leap toward peace between our countries. Based on this outreach of peace and cooperation from the Americans, I believe Exportkhleb can leverage the symbolic nature of this agreement by accepting their invitation to trade and initiating trade discussions with our newest ally. Of course, I am just an opportunist, between you and me, but I believe this is a key tactic and a brilliant opening move in this game of chess we are about to play with the Americans." Misha paused to let this sink in.

"Relations are improving, according to our diplomats," he continued. "No one wants a war. The stakes are too high and the weapons too dangerous. Let's be realistic; millions of people on both sides would perish in a nuclear holocaust. Only a crazy person would go down such a road.

"I believe we have commercial tools at our disposal, Mike," Misha said as he moved into describing his tactical plan. "The USA has a large inventory of grain, and they are subsidizing farmers not to grow along with importers to buy. It's an expensive exercise I think the government would be happy to halt. It isn't sustainable.

"The final amount may not be twenty-five million tonnes, but that's our worst-case scenario right now. I propose we position ourselves as helping the United States reduce the huge surplus of grain stored in their grain elevators and farm bins. Number two, we request assurances for the continuation of the US Wheat Export Subsidy Program. I'm not so naive to think the government won't eliminate or reduce this subsidy, but my strategy is to get all or as much as possible of the grain we need bought while export companies believe they can still get the subsidy from the government based on current program parameters. It is my belief that timing will be critical. We will notify the American exporters that we are shopping for twenty million tonnes from them the day before we meet with them. This will limit the time that word can spread and the futures markets react."

"Okay, I get that part," Slaski said. "You feel the Americans will buy into your 'We want to be trading partners' gambit. Tell me more: what leverage do you have? How can you get them to agree to acceptable financing terms?"

"The third leg of my strategy is convincing the US government that a long-term trade deal is a building block to peace between our nations. This fits nicely into President Nixon's messaging."

"I can see I haven't given you enough credit for your knowledge of US farm policy, Misha. You have thought this out well. The timing and coordination required to pull this off is astronomical, though."

"I know, but the Americans are basking in the glow of world dominance right now. They don't have much respect for Russia. I plan to play on their ego and slide in under their hubris."

The conversation carried on through the afternoon as the two men had lunch and talked about meeting various companies and people within those companies. This was the value Slaski brought to the project. They discussed American agriculture policy and the comparisons of US and Soviet production success and failure. This was a sensitive subject for Misha, but Slaski spoke the truths he had been feeling.

"You've given me a lot to consider, Misha. I will need to ponder this further, develop some suggestions and figure out how much it will cost you for my brilliance." Slaski grinned. "Do you have a flight home this evening? I can take you back to the airport."

"Actually, I have a couple of things to look after tomorrow morning before returning home, so my flight isn't until tomorrow afternoon. I plan to stay downtown in a hotel tonight if you have a good recommendation."

"You will not! I want you to stay here as my guest. We have lots of room, and it will give us time to think this through some more. There is a lot to think about, wouldn't you agree?"

"Yes, this is true. Very well, I accept your kind offer."

Later that evening, he enjoyed a fabulous gourmet meal prepared by Slaski and his wife, Ginnie. Misha was enamored with the tastes and selection of foods. They enjoyed some wine and then more wine before switching to vodka at Misha's request. He was feeling a little less stressed now that he'd been able to share the challenge with someone he felt could help him succeed. And maybe the liquor was helping a bit, he admitted to himself. He had reduced his alcohol consumption considerably since returning from the crop tour.

After dinner the men moved outside to enjoy the mild evening, some brandy and fat Cuban cigars. As they settled in to enjoy the peace and tranquility of the Swiss evening, both men knew the next thirty days would require a serious, intense effort. If they didn't have the bulk of this challenge resolved by then, it probably wouldn't happen—but bad things most certainly would.

"Let's go back over everything you need to do, step by step," Slaski suggested. "The first thing is to appear as though everything is normal. You always buy grain from the Canadian Wheat Board to secure a supply of their high-protein wheat, right? So, Canada is where you start. Go to Winnipeg, meet with Frank Rowan at the CWB, buy as much wheat as you can from them without triggering their suspicion and then mingle with some of the locals. Just as you would normally. You and Dick Dawson at Cargill are good friends, aren't you?"

"Yes, Dick and I have been close friends since 1963. He's a good man, a good friend."

"Okay, make sure you connect with both of them. Just be normal. Then go back to Moscow, and you and I will move on to Phase 2, where we put out a tender to international traders to buy more wheat. Then we spring the trap. Right?"

"*Will you walk into my parlor, said the spider to the fly.*" Misha grinned and raised his glass of vodka in an inviting, scheming manner.

* * *

The next morning, the men enjoyed breakfast on the outdoor patio under the bright summer sunshine. Misha was feeling a modest amount of relief thanks to his discussions with Slaski. Having him validate the tactical plan was encouraging.

"Good morning," Slaski said as Misha entered the kitchen, where he saw a massive spread on the counter.

"I didn't know if you leaned more toward the French cuisine," Slaski said, gesturing to the jam and breads, "or the German fare of cheese and meat. Suit yourself. I recommend a bowl of this—we call it bircher muesli, a classic Swiss breakfast treat."

"Even for breakfast you outdo yourself, my friend." Misha didn't know where to start. He thought he would very likely try a little bit of everything.

* * *

After they had finished eating, Slaski suggested they go for a walk in the woods behind the Slaski chalet. This was music to Misha's ears, as he felt he had overindulged and would enjoy some fresh air and a stroll around the magnificent grounds.

"Misha, I've been thinking about this, and I have an idea I would like you to consider," Slaski said as they sauntered along a path in the beautiful mountain forest. "You told me your plan was to release the tender for purchase just before you meet with the grain companies to try to manage the risk of the price taking off. I don't think your plan will work. Once you alert even one company to the fact you're looking for twenty million tonnes, the cat is out of the bag. No one will fill that whole amount, and it's possible they could alert the whole trade—after they get long a shwack of grain. You can't keep news like that quiet for long. Somebody will spill the beans."

"I realize the risk, Mike, but I don't know how else to notify the sellers so they come prepared to deal and enable us to secure grain on the spot. If I don't tell them how much we need until we sit down with them, we aren't likely to make a deal that day. Then the information is out and we have lost our leverage without buying anything. It's critical that we make deals immediately. What do you suggest?"

"I think you should tender for less."

"But we need to buy all twenty million tonnes from the Americans. If I buy less, I fail."

"I didn't say to buy less; I said 'tender for less.' There's a difference."

"I don't follow."

"Here's what I'm thinking. If you tell the sellers you want to buy four million tonnes, they will come prepared to deal most or all of the amount. If you meet with all six companies and buy three to four million from each of them, they will each think they got the lion's share of the business. They will be quiet until they cover their sale, and you'll be out of town with 20 million tonnes or more before they know what's happened. Even if you don't get it all bought in the first round of trading, you will likely have another shot at it in a week or so. The traders who don't deal will be pissed they got shut out, and the ones you buy from won't be talking. It will buy you more time to deal. See what I mean?"

"I do, Mike. It's brilliant. Devious and brilliant."

"I know. I'm not just good-looking, you know. I've got some smarts going on up here." Slaski tapped his head.

"Okay, let me recap to make sure I've got it. We say we want only four million tonnes even though we want twenty million. Then we make each company think we're dealing exclusively with them. When we're done, we will have bought five or six times more than we said we wanted but exactly what we do want."

"Right! Simple but effective. You told me your team is working hard on getting the other pieces to fall into place: logistics, cash or credit and price controls from US programs. The only wild card is finding willing sellers. I think this will help, without scaring them off. Maybe some of them will even give you credit on their tonnage in an effort to seal the deal."

"And there's one last consideration," Slaski continued. "If the US government is dumb enough to keep paying the wheat-export subsidy, regardless of how much you buy, the grain companies aren't really at risk. If the market goes up, so does the subsidy, and they are covered."

"I understand how this might work, but what about the longer-term impact on trade relationships? Won't they see this as manipulative and even dishonest? What about our reputation? I feel like it is a questionable way to deal with companies who have worked with us over the years."

"Don't worry about that, Misha. You're dealing with seasoned international traders. They have thick skins and short memories. You have relationships with many of them already, don't you? Have you heard the familiar Latin phrase *caveat emptor*—let the buyer beware?"

"Of course."

"There is a slightly lesser-known phrase: *caveat venditor,* or let the seller beware. Well, this is what we have here." Slaski broke into a huge smile and pointed to the sky as if presenting a defense in court.

This was the missing piece, Misha thought. He knew he had a good plan but, as Minister Matskevich had pointed out, there were gaps. The mistake Khrushchev made a decade ago was being too honest and open, and the Soviet Union had paid dearly for it. Learn from the past, he told himself. Don't make the same mistake twice, or one will surely pay a large price—personally. There would be a price to pay down the road for this misdirection and deceit; he knew it. But he would deal with the fallout as necessary. Right now, his focus was more on his survival and completing his mission. Besides, achieving either success or failure, this challenge likely represented one of the final trade deals of his career.

* * *

Misha had asked Slaski to drop him off in the downtown financial district of Geneva after their discussion. After Slaski was out of sight, he headed for the headquarters of the Julius Baer Bank, an eighty-year-old financial enterprise specializing in the services he required on this day. Two hours later he took a taxi back to the Cointrin Aéroport and boarded his return flight to Moscow.

After a three-and-a-half-hour flight, Misha arrived in Moscow late in the day. Nevertheless, he headed straight to his office. The eight-hour time difference between Moscow and Winnipeg meant the people he wanted to talk to were just arriving at work. He contacted his old Canadian friends, Frank Rowan, sales manager of the Canadian Wheat Board, and Dick Dawson, wheat merchant at Cargill in Winnipeg. Both were eager to meet with him and committed to clearing their calendars to suit his schedule. Since Exportkhleb had been more of an exporter than an importer in the past decade, they didn't buy much grain from Canada. But, historically, Misha's trips to Winnipeg generally resulted in important sales of Canadian grain. He hoped this one would be no different. On a personal note, he looked forward to reconnecting with the Canadians. They were honest, trustworthy people, and they always treated him well. He also knew some consumption of vodka would be involved.

9

Executing the Plan – Round 1

Canadian Wheat Board Offices, Winnipeg, Manitoba June 27, 1972

Winnipeg, Manitoba, had been the base of operations for the Canadian Wheat Board, aka the CWB, since its inception in 1935. The original mandate of the single-desk monopoly agency was to bring price stability to grain markets during the Great Depression. Commodity markets collapsed during a time when food supplies were critical. The Canadian government stepped in to control prices and assure production with the establishment of this new agency. The Board took on greater meaning and an enhanced role to guarantee food supplies to Allied nations during the Second World War. Once again, global conditions dictated the need for legislative intervention to assure grain supplies for the war effort by stabilizing production, sales and distribution.

The Board was a federal government creation that reported to Canada's agricultural minister. It was overseen by a farmer commission and managed by a senior staff. Their responsibility was to oversee the aggregation and commercialization of all wheat, oats and barley produced in Western Canada. The returns were shared equally with farmers in a cooperative manner based proportionately on the quantities they delivered individually. A delivery-quota mechanism and initial and final payment structure assured equality and fairness for all farmers. Farmers weren't guaranteed the best price, but they were all guaranteed the same price.

Ironically for Canadian industry, the principals and operations of the Board more closely paralleled a communist system than a capitalist one. This was a challenge for independent grain companies, and many farmers opposed the single-desk format of the CWB. Arguments were made that the original motives for the development of the Board no longer existed nearly four decades after its inception; it was time to move to a system like the American open market. However, the political/philosophical debate persisted, and any change would need government assent. Change seemed unlikely.

Misha liked dealing with the CWB—a lot. Russia could purchase large quantities of grain from them in a single transaction, the dealings always remained confidential and he was always able to negotiate extremely attractive pricing and terms. Other Eastern European countries like Poland and Czechoslovakia also liked dealing with the Board for similar reasons. Year after year the CWB maintained a loyal relationship with its international clients, guaranteeing minimum quantities as a reliable supplier. The prices were always negotiated, but the CWB had a global reputation for competitive pricing. Competitors viewed CWB pricing as a discount to world values for this high-quality grain, but the Canadian organization valued long-term relationships over squeezing the last nickel out of its customers.

Even though his meeting with the CWB was scheduled for Tuesday morning, Misha had arrived early the day before in order to adjust to the significant time difference. He had had no trouble shaking it off as a younger man, but in the past few years it took longer to adjust his internal clock to the local time. Being sharp and alert would be critical for the important negotiations ahead.

As a means to protecting Soviet interests, Misha had lied during trade talks before. It wasn't his preference, but in every case the needs of the nation outweighed his own moral standards. This time he had to be completely convincing. Everything depended on him leaving

Canada with a large grain purchase in hand along with intelligence on North American crops and everyone's belief that Soviet Union crop production was close to normal. He didn't fancy himself to be an actor, but he had a well-developed "stone face," which had served him well during past negotiations.

* * *

Just before 10:00 a.m. Central Time on Tuesday, June 27, Misha walked two blocks from the famous intersection of Portage and Main and entered the lobby at 423 Main Street, a familiar venue for him. The CWB building was a solid gray sandstone edifice, unmistakably the home to government services thanks in part to the architecture and carvings of the four prairie province emblems over the front entryway. It evoked a sense of strength and stability, an image the CWB vigorously portrayed to Canadian farmers and international customers.

Once inside, he proceeded to the seventh-floor reception, the trader's floor. "I am vice president of Exportkhleb, Mikhail Fisenko, here to see Mr. Rowan," he said formally to the receptionist. The mask was on. His performance had begun.

"One moment, please, while I call Mr. Rowan. He is expecting you, Mr. Fisenko," replied the young lady with a warm smile and reciprocal formality. "Can I get you a cup of coffee?"

"Thank you, no."

"Misha, welcome to Winnipeg," Frank Rowan said as he approached with an extended hand. The men exchanged a firm handshake; it was a genuine greeting of two old friends happy to see each other. Rowan was tall and lean, the result of an active lifestyle and a focus on his health. He was one of only a few people in Canada who referred to him as "Misha." They had developed a strong friendship during the early 1960s based on annual meetings in Canada and Europe. Misha, along with his predecessors, valued the personal relationship he had developed with senior grain traders around the world, but none of them were more important than the one he shared with Rowan and his associates at the CWB.

"Frank, it is very good to see you looking so well. I hope you and your family are well."

"Yes, yes, we're all fine. Please come with me and I'll introduce you to our marketing team. How's everything in Matushka Rosa?" he asked as they proceeded down the hall.

"Ah, you remember the Russian I taught you, my friend. All is good in the motherland," he replied. He hoped he wouldn't have to mislead his friend too much in the coming negotiation. His conscious burned a little bit with the thought. Lying didn't sit well with him, especially to friends, but he had a job to do.

The main boardroom at the CWB was a massive wood-paneled chamber equipped to handle large audiences of farmer representatives and CWB management. The central table was an uninterrupted piece of pine that made one wonder how it had been possible to bring this massive slab into the room. The truth was the table had been assembled in the room.

The end wall was dedicated to portraits of the Queen and the current prime minister, Pierre Elliott Trudeau, along with group shots of the current CWB executive and board of directors. Hanging along the longer walls of the room were numerous framed images telling the tale of the Canadian agricultural industry. They included historical sketches of early settlers harvesting grain by hand and loading it into horse-drawn wagons. Images of the original grain elevators along truck and rail routes depicted early export-handling facilities. The opposite side of the room was dedicated to more recent photos, including large tractor and combine activity on the prairies and export terminals with huge downspouts and massive flows of grain cascading deep into vessel holds. These ocean vessels were loading large, aggregated quantities of wheat and barley destined for international markets. It was a bragging wall used by the Board to impress guests with images of the country's agricultural industrial progress in just a few decades.

Trade negotiations between state agencies always had a formality and pace to them. No one wanted to rush the process. Both sides were confident they would make a deal. What was in question were the terms. How many tonnes, what shipping period and, most important of all factors, what price. The price had its own level of complexity. There would be different price ranges for different qualities, different prices for different shipment periods and variations based on who provided transportation. It was a complex, time-consuming exercise made all the more difficult when the negotiators were stubborn. Rowan and Fisenko were both stubborn. It was expected but annoying at the same time. For some of the newer, younger members of Rowan's team around the table, this was the first time dealing with Exportkhleb and Misha Fisenko. The Russians were in a league of their own when it came to international trade. To them, the guy across the table was almost royalty.

But this was familiar territory for Rowan. It was, in fact, Rowan who had worked with the Russians to help them understand the nuances of grain contracts in the early 1960s. They were new to international trade at a time when they needed to buy massive quantities of grain to offset a 1963 drought in the Soviet Union. Rowan built a bridge of trust with his Soviet counterparts, working to help them comprehend contract terms for quality and price. He explained that by purchasing lower-quality grain they could secure larger quantities at those lower prices. He even traveled to Russia with Exportkhleb on numerous occasions to advise them on grain handling and storage, ensuring their imports would be handled efficiently and safely to protect the quality grain they were buying from Canada. Rowan was held in high regard by the Russian Department of Agriculture as a result of his efforts. Misha knew this trusted ally would treat him as fairly now as he had a decade ago.

"Misha, it is always a pleasure to welcome you to Winnipeg. The Wheat Board values the long-term trading relationship we have with Exportkhleb and the personal relationships we enjoy with you and Viktor," Rowan said as he went through his formal welcome and acknowledged his respect for Misha's boss.

There was an unwritten, sequential process to every international trade session. There were the formalities of introductions, updates on the two respective agencies, tributes to those who were not in attendance and a modest, symbolic gift exchange. These items ultimately hung on walls in boardrooms and private offices as symbols of historic trade deals. Misha had brought several exquisite black lacquer boxes of various sizes, while the CWB presented miniature cattle branding irons with the Board's logo on them. They had a very western Canadian flair to them. At first Misha was puzzled, having never seen a North American branding iron, but one of the traders described the purpose rather graphically and he got the idea quickly enough. The room filled with laughter at his sudden understanding and feigned revulsion for the branding process.

The morning session was dedicated to exchanges related to crop conditions around the world, political actions in other countries and updates on the Canadian and Russian crops—both being questionable variations of the truth. At noon, the group broke for lunch. Nothing had been agreed to at this point. Misha did not want to appear anxious in any way. He knew he would close a deal by the end of the day, and he had dinner plans with an old friend.

After lunch he took the floor and laid out his version of Russia's grain requirements from Canada. The CWB would deal with other Soviet countries independently, but trade with Russia set the groundwork and price for all further discussions.

"Thank you, Frank, for meeting with me on such short notice. This is a sign of the strong relationship between our governments as well as our respective agencies, the CWB and Exportkhleb. It also speaks to the personal relationships between each of us." He extended both hands out, palms up, to the group and then drew them back to himself in a gesture of friendship. "There is a long history of trade between our countries, and I am proud to say that agriculture in general, and wheat specifically, forms the cornerstone of our bond. For many years the Soviet Union has relied on Canada to supply us with your high-quality protein wheat, and it has fed our nation well."

The CWB traders really had no idea where this was heading in terms of how much buying interest Exportkhleb would present. Some years Russia was a buyer and other years they were sellers. They had heard some preliminary reports indicating crop production in Russia wasn't meeting early expectations, but gathering this information from the Soviet Union wasn't easy for the board either. They also dealt directly with the Soviet states of Czechoslovakia, Poland and the Ukraine. The big unknown was always Russia.

"During 1970 and 1971, the Soviet Union's plan for grain self-sufficiency and improved nutrition for our citizens was successful. The low volume of trade from Canada is proof of our internal development. As you know, we faltered a bit last year due to production problems. Once again, in 1972, we find ourselves a bit short in achieving our goals of increased grain production to meet the increasing demands for more and better-quality food for our people. I am at liberty to share with you, confidentially, that we have a disappointing winter wheat crop. Please do not share this with the international grain companies. This is confidential between our agencies. I can also tell you the problem is due to poor weather conditions, not to our collective farm process." He spoke the last sentence a little defensively.

Misha had chosen to blame the grain production shortfall on the winter wheat crop and not reveal their spring wheat crop was also in trouble. A higher level of transparency would not help him negotiate the best price for this deal. He needed to sequester negative information as long as possible. Traders have a way of sharing news, and he could not afford to have the Americans alerted in any way.

"What about your spring wheat crop, Misha?" asked Rowan. "Our international reports tell us it's very dry right across the Ukraine."

So much for avoiding that topic. Rowan was a clever and experienced trader. He knew the right questions to ask and got right to the point.

"We are pleased with the current development of the crop," Misha lied. "We expect production to exceed last year's total." Another lie. "Our dealings today will cover our current estimated shortfall." Not even close, he thought to himself.

Fisenko's only hope was that this declaration, and his continuing assurances their crop was close to normal, would lead the CWB traders to believe they would be securing a coup in locking up the only business the Soviets expected to conduct. The CWB's relationship with Exportkhleb had fostered massive deals in the past, providing proof of the value of the single-desk agency marketing board for Canadian farmers. Proof, at least, in the minds of the government agency. The secrecy of the deals always obscured the dollar value of the trades and, additionally, the terms regarding schedules, pricing and transportation costs. Having set the stage from Russia's perspective, he continued with the specifics of their buying interest this year.

"The quantity of Number 2, 12.5-percent-protein Canadian Western Red Spring wheat we would like to contract with the CWB this year is 120 million bushels with an option of another 30 million bushels to be confirmed before September 1, 1972." This was about four million metric tonnes. "In addition, we would like to contract fifteen million bushels of Number 2 durum wheat and fifteen million bushels of feed barley."

This was truthfully the full amount he expected to buy from the CWB, and he wanted to maximize his purchases from the government agency. He hoped to buy additional Canadian wheat and barley from private companies so he could keep those lines of trade open. He still had a long way to go to cover his government's target, but his Canadian purchases would be a start. He was certain the trade would remain confidential, as the CWB didn't use futures markets and they never, ever announced transactions. If they used futures markets to hedge their trades, their buying in the market would set off signals for other traders. But they didn't, and he knew it. It's why he started here in Canada. The Soviet problem would remain a secret—for now, at least, and for as long as he needed it to remain confidential.

"The price we are prepared to pay is a dollar sixty-three per bushel in US dollars for the 150 million bushels of wheat loaded on vessels at St. Lawrence points for shipment between September 1972 through August 1973. We would ask you to cover the cost of shipping and storing the grain to move it into export position on the Saint Lawrence Seaway as usual.

"As you know, gentlemen, a dollar sixty-three per bushel is equal to the export value offered out of the United States, net of their export subsidy program. I don't need to tell you they have a huge surplus of grain in-store and are very willing sellers."

Misha knew the CWB had little negotiating power as long as the US government kept a ceiling on world prices. The Canadian and Australian wheat boards had tried, in vain, to encourage the US government to remove their trade-incentive subsidies and let markets find their own levels, but so far their pleas had been ignored. Misha knew this too.

"Next, let's talk about credit," he said. "We require financing for a term of three years at two-percent interest per year with settlement in twelve equal quarterly tranches. My government chooses to be fair with Canada, but we don't want to pay a premium. We think this is a competitive proposal respecting the most-favored-nation status between our countries. So, Frank, if you just nod your head in agreement, we are all done here." He said this last sentence as a joke. He knew Frank would counteroffer. That's how it worked.

Rowan rose from his chair and started to walk around the table in a slow, confident, authoritative manner. He was most definitely accustomed to these types of negotiations, and at that moment he owned the room. As he circled the table, he began his response. His tall stature, coupled with him being out of his chair, forced everyone to look up to him from their small boardroom chairs. It was a negotiating tactic designed to create an air of dominance and authority for the speaker. It worked.

"As usual, Misha, you lay out a clear picture of your needs, making our options clearer to us. We appreciate your open and honest approach. You know we have several traditional buyers who depend on supplies of Canadian wheat annually. Countries like Great Britain, Japan and China. These buyers' demands are predictable, and we endeavor to ensure we have enough grain to meet their needs, as we try to do with your country. The Soviet Union's demand has fluctuated greatly over the past decade, but nevertheless you remain a valued customer."

By the time he returned to his starting point at the table, he had created a calm in the room. Rowan assured his guest that the CWB would continue to be a good supplier for the Soviets.

"Lower wheat prices in the global market have discouraged wheat planting in Canada this year. Based on our early estimates of our wheat production, we are forecasting a tighter supply. We would very much like to meet your terms, but, unfortunately, we are not able to commit to such a large quantity this early." Rowan paused to let this sink in and take Fisenko down a notch in a diplomatically gentle manner. "The most we can offer you today is ninety million bushels plus your option to buy thirty million more. The price, as you state, is what it is. The Americans have put a ceiling on the market with their export subsidy program. There isn't much we can do about that."

Misha nodded in agreement. He started making notes on the terms of the deal.

"We will also agree to the smaller amounts of durum wheat and barley you have requested at the normal Soviet discount of ten percent off our export price list. I hope these terms are agreeable to you.

"As far as location, we have grain much closer to Canada's west coast shipping ports. Of the ninety million bushels of spring wheat, we would propose seventy million out of the Saint Lawrence and twenty million out of Pacific ports. Both locations have the necessary water depth and loading capacity to accommodate your larger ocean vessels. We can decide on the export position on the optional portion if you exercise it."

Once again Misha nodded positively to the offers of durum and barley and the proposed ports for wheat exports. Shipment across the Pacific to Eastern Soviet ports would actually work very well for them. He made more notes.

"Finally, Misha, I can't speak to credit terms today. Financing will be determined by our Federal Treasury Board, but I know we will come to agreement on this as we have in the past, and I don't see it being a barrier to this deal."

"As usual, Frank, you are a gracious host and a fair dealmaker. I believe we can work within the revised terms as you have proposed."

After some dickering on export port differentials and grade price spreads, the two principal speakers closed their note pads. It was 5:00 p.m. when Rowan stated, "I think we have a deal, then. Do you agree?"

"Yes, we do." Misha stood to shake Rowan's hand and then walked around the room shaking hands with everyone, talking as he circled the large table. "My good friends in Canada are worthy negotiators and, in the end, I believe we have a deal favorable for both our countries."

He knew this was not likely to be the case. This deal would likely be the cheapest grain he would buy in 1972, and next year he would have a challenge dealing with the CWB. But he had to deal with the most urgent problem right now: securing food for Russia this year.

"Now, my friend, before I leave, I must ask you a favor," Misha said. "In years gone by, I have always been able to secure some Canadian wheat and barley from private grain dealers. I know these traders buy grain from the CWB on speculation. Since you cannot fill my full order, could you tell me which companies I might contact that might have Canadian grain for sale?"

"I'm sorry, Misha. As much as we tend to avoid dealing with the private companies, they do reach markets the CWB can't or won't penetrate. I see these trading houses as necessary evils," Rowan said with a wink and grin. "It really wouldn't be appropriate for me to reveal any grain positions they might be holding with us."

"Very well. I understand. Let me try another approach. I am having dinner tonight with Cargill's Dick Dawson. Do you think he would be interested in speaking with me about supplying wheat to the Soviet Union this year?"

Rowan laughed, clearly entertained by Misha's persistence and investigative creativity.

"I believe Mr. Dawson would be very interested in speaking with you, Misha," he replied formally and a little conspiratorially. "Ha! Enjoy your evening. I will send the contracts in the mail and speak with you regarding the credit terms when you return to Russia."

"Excellent, my friends. Thank you for your continued collaboration with Exportkhleb. Frank, we anticipate the need for you to return to Russia once again in the fall in an advisory capacity to reassess our handling systems. If you can come, we extend the invitation to you and your wife as guests of Russia to attend tours of some of our best museums as well as a night at the Bolshoi ballet. Goodbye for now, and we hope to see you soon."

Misha headed for the elevator and a quick wash-up before his next negotiation session with his dear friend, Dick Dawson. Misha had fallen short of his target with the CWB, but he felt he had purchased as much as he could, at least on this trip. He would most certainly exercise the thirty-million-bushel option. His strategy had merely been to slow-play the original amount and imply they might not need the extra tonnage. Of course they would need it, and much more.

10

Moscow Nights in Manitoba

The Velvet Glove Lounge, Winnipeg Inn, Winnipeg   June 27, 1972

Richard Dawson had been Mikhail Fisenko's closest Canadian friend for nearly ten years. The year they first met, the Soviets bought five million tonnes of Canadian wheat to backfill their disastrous crop. Since then, they got together at least once a year and spoke on the phone regularly, and now referred to each other as "Dick" and "Misha." Dawson had flown for the British Royal Air Force during the 1950s and Fisenko had served in the Russian Army for a period during the Second World War. The two men had a lot in common and were close to the same age. A strong trust and mutual respect had developed and flourished over the years.

Fisenko negotiated deals with senior grain company officials all over the world, including federal agency guys like Frank Rowan and owners of the largest privately owned companies in the world. He maintained professional relationships with many people, but his relationship with Dawson extended beyond the formalities of a professional relationship. He trusted him and valued his friendship. As a British immigrant to Canada, Dawson related to European culture. Not communism, to be clear, but he still had an 'old world' outlook. He was a Brit through and through. His distinctive English accent was well known in Canada and abroad. He was highly regarded in the agricultural industry as a man of honor and a trustworthy trader for Cargill. Dawson could always be relied on for a good dose of British humor and a contagious laugh following every punch line he delivered.

In their many encounters, Dawson and Fisenko would notoriously get exceedingly drunk together. Long evenings, no food and way too much vodka—"pails of vodka," in fact, according to Dawson—resulted in some entertaining and often regrettable performances.

Misha thought this night had all the makings of just such an evening. Once again he wrestled with the morality of trying to buy grain from Dawson's company, Cargill Grain Canada Ltd., when he was covertly trying to manipulate the market in his country's favor. Dawson was his comrade and had been particularly good to him over the years. He decided to make sure any transaction would not leave Dawson in a position where he would have to cover a sale later. He suspected "later" would mean the likelihood of higher prices.

Dawson called Misha's room on the house phone when he reached the lobby of the Winnipeg Inn and then waited for him in the bar, the Velvet Glove Lounge, where many grain deals were struck and many late-night drinks were consumed. Misha took the elevator to the main floor and headed for the lounge. Waiting for his eyes to adjust to the darkness, he stood in the doorway of the dimly lit, smoky room, looking from table to table for Dawson's familiar face.

"Misha... here," Dawson called from a booth on his right. His unique and out-of-place English accent was unmistakable. Its recognizable timbre immediately brought a smile to Misha's face. Dawson had chosen a booth against the wall. Excellent, he thought. Much more privacy, as the room was known to have eyes and ears when it came to grain-trade eavesdropping.

"Dick, Dick, Dick, my good friend, how are you?" said Misha in his equally out-of-place Russian accent as he extended his hand in greeting.

"I am well, Misha. I'm so happy to see you."

The two men reconnected on both a personal and professional level for the next two hours, enjoyed some of Canada's finest steaks and updated each other on current conditions. Both maintained moderate alcohol consumption until their business was finished. So many deals had been struck in this very bar. There would be plenty of time later to drink to excess.

"How much grain do you need to buy this year?" Dawson began, getting right to the heart of it. "Were you able to get covered by the CWB today, or do you have a little more to buy from your old friend?"

"Ha, you don't waste time, do you?" Misha grinned. "I can't tell you what we have done and I can't tell you our plans, you know that. But I can say I am here to buy our usual amount and maybe a little more as we try to improve food quality for the people across the Soviet Union. Here's what I would like from you and your company, Dick. Tell me if you can make this work. Sell me one half million tonnes of Number 2 Canadian Western Red Spring Wheat loaded on a boat at your nice new elevator in Baie Comeau, Quebec, for a dollar sixty-three a bushel in US dollars. We will take it out over the next twelve months and pay you over the next thirty-six months. Can you do that?"

"That's a tempting quantity, Misha." Dawson was clearly taken aback by the magnitude of Misha's proposed order. "But your terms leave a lot to be desired. Our people in Europe report crop conditions across the Union to be dismal, and they expect the drought will cause huge shortages this year. It shouldn't be surprising to hear we think prices are going higher."

Misha knew Cargill had, arguably, the most sophisticated and comprehensive communications network in the global grain industry. Their far-reaching presence connected every one of their offices around the world. They knew more about crop conditions than either the Soviet or the US government, no question. He couldn't fool Dawson, but he could cloud the issue or avoid the question at least.

"Dick, you will never get a chance to sell this much grain at one time—ever. This is an opportunity of a lifetime for you," Misha countered as they dug into negotiations. "Prices won't rise as long as the Americans maintain their export subsidy program; you know that."

"That's true for US-origin grain, Misha, but we both know Canadian grain is better. It deserves a premium."

This was also true, Misha knew. *Damn this guy. He is well prepared. But so am I.*

"I will agree, Dick, a little bit. High-protein Canadian wheat is the best in the world. That's why I am here at all. What do you think about a two-cent-per-bushel premium?"

"Four."

"Ah… Okay, four," Misha said after a suitable pause, some muttering and face contorting. Given the CWB's reluctance to fill his initial request, he would have paid a five-cent premium.

"Now, as far as payment goes, Misha, we are Cargill Grain company, not Cargill Bank. I know the CWB can finance you with help from the Canadian federal government, but we aren't in the business of lending money. It's a nonstarter for us, I'm afraid. But let's see what we can do with the Export Development Corporation. This is the same way we financed your purchases in 1963. If you pass their screening, they will likely cover you for the thirty million American dollars you will owe us."

"Okay, I understand you, Dick. Please make the inquiry on our behalf. Otherwise, are we good? If you think markets are going higher, I suspect you own enough grain to make this sale, my friend. I wouldn't want to see you lose money if the prices do move higher somehow."

His affection for his friend motivated him to try to protect Dawson and his company from a negative outcome. Markets don't have to move very much to generate a huge loss. A ten-cent-per-bushel bump would mean a loss of 1.8 million dollars, a tidy sum in anyone's world. He had already paid Cargill a higher price for a smaller quantity than he had in his CWB deal earlier in the day. But securing bargains was generally how it happened when dealing with the CWB.

"Thanks for your concern, Misha. I will take your comments to heart. All right, we're done dealing for the night. Correct?"

"Yes, it is agreed. Send me your contracts tomorrow. Are we dealing with Cargill Canada or Tradax Geneva? We are fine either way, but if it is Tradax, I get to make another trip to Geneva." Misha nudged Dawson with his elbow.

"It will be Tradax," Dawson said. "Say hi to Huub Spierings for me when you're there. He's been our man in Geneva since Slaski left us."

"Yes, I met Mr. Spierings last year when he came to Moscow. Thank you for this, Dick." He did not acknowledge the mention of Slaski.

"Thank you for the business, my friend. Now, let's get our server back here and have a drink to celebrate."

"Let's get her back here and have a lot of drinks to celebrate!"

* * *

Finalizing a deal with Cargill concluded Misha's goals for this trip to Canada. Round 1 was complete. He had acquired 3.75 million tonnes of grain and also secured an option on another three-quarter million tonnes, which he knew he would exercise. This equated to roughly 4.5 million tonnes, 15 percent of his goal of 25 million tonnes. He was confident he could secure three-year credit on the bulk of the grain, and he had paid slightly less than the current market for most of it. This was probably the easiest part of his multi-stage plan; nevertheless, it was a success. He felt some relief because of this progress and allowed himself to take a break from his job, for one evening at least.

The two men enjoyed each other's company while consuming seemingly impossible quantities of rum and vodka. They genuinely liked each other and shared a level of trust and candor more commonly associated with lifelong friends. As the night wore on, their decibel level and energy increased, culminating in the decision to look for a venue a bit more lively than the sedate hotel lobby lounge. Answer: the hotel's night club, the Stage Door. It was adjacent to the lounge and offered more action thanks to live music and the energy of a younger crowd. And, of course, more booze.

"We do not have these 'night clubs' in Russia," said Misha. "We drink at home, quietly. But I have to say there are some interesting things to see here." He smiled and nodded at the younger women dancing near the stage. "My music tastes lean more toward the symphony," he added.

"You're such an old fogey," Dawson yelled above the music.

"Fogey? What is this you call me?" he asked, feigning hurt feelings.

"A fogey is someone with old-fashioned, outdated ideas."

"Ha, you are probably right, Dick," Misha grinned. "Guilty as charged."

They found a table, ordered more drinks and carried on their conversation, which predictably turned to politics and whose country and agriculture system was better. Both men enjoyed bantering like this and knew each other well enough to be challenging and even a little argumentative. The alcohol made them both a bit more animated and vocal.

"Look at your agriculture system, Misha. After forty years and so many Five-Year Plans, you still can't produce enough to feed your people. It's a disgrace."

"What about Canada?" Misha said. "You have a perfectly good marketing agency selling your production, but many farmers and companies fight to have it removed. That is crazy!"

"Don't get me started on the CWB, Misha. You like it because they sell you grain below the market. Admit it!"

This brought a smile to his face. He regretted revealing this to Dawson, but it was true, and Dawson already knew it anyway. The debate raged on about a wide variety of their countries' offerings, declared by one or the other as superior, from transportation to sport to food. Dawson decided to turn the conversation around to find something they could agree on.

"Misha, let's have a toast. I drink to your leader, Brezhnev. He is a worthy leader of the Soviet Union."

"To General Secretary Leonid Brezhnev," Misha slurred, raising his glass. Feeling the need to reciprocate, he said, "To your prime minister, Pierre Elliott Trudeau, a fine man and friend to the Soviet Union!"

"Ah! Don't make me drink to him, Misha. He doesn't support Canadians in the west."

"Come on! Be a good Canadian and drink." He laughed and downed his drink. Dawson relented and downed his as well, but only because he needed to keep pace with the Russian.

An hour of loud music and many more drinks was enough in this place. Dawson paid the bill and they headed out the front door of the hotel onto the streets of Winnipeg.

"Let's find a new watering hole where we can get in trouble," Dawson suggested.

"Watering hole?" asked Misha, unfamiliar with the term. "I want more vodka, not water!"

"It's an old 'wild west' cowboy term, Misha," Dawson said with a laugh. "Like an oasis in the desert or, for us now, another bar along the streets of Winnipeg."

"That is good, then. On to the watering hole! We will be Russian and English cowboys. Giddyup! Perhaps I can use my new branding iron," Misha joked.

"You brought a branding iron?" Dawson asked, confused. But Misha just carried on and Dawson had to catch up.

In the basement of the Lock, Stock and Barrel, the mission to get extremely drunk shifted into a higher gear. The atmosphere better suited their current condition; it was rustic, grittier and a little less tidy. It was only a block away from the Grain Exchange Building and occupied mainly by grain-industry people, so their conversation had to be subdued.

"Dick, I have something to share with you because you are my friend and I trust you." Misha leaned closer to his friend. The booze consumption had lowered his guard. "All those things you say about the failure of our system have some truth in them, I must admit," he whispered. "There are many days I wonder if my efforts have been worth it. Since Lily died, I am alone with my thoughts, and I look at where I am, what sort of future there is for me and my fellow Russians. When I see the prosperity in other parts of Europe and North America and I look at Russia, I am secretly disappointed."

"You have choices in life, Misha. Nothing is forcing you to stay in Russia."

"It is not so easy to just leave. The government pays close attention to the comings and goings of its citizens. Besides, I am loyal to my country," Misha said defensively. "My whole life is there. My work, my few friends. And I honestly believe in our leaders and our way of life. It is my country! But you are right. It isn't improving, no matter what we do. But I will soon be too old to work and unable to help build the Soviet dream. I honestly don't know what lies ahead for me. It is not a bright future as far as I can tell."

The men fell silent as Dawson sympathetically considered Misha's revelations and Misha considered his own prospects and options.

* * *

Two bars and many, many drinks later, it was time to call it a night. Misha had a plane to Moscow to catch at 10:00 a.m. Heading back to the hotel along Portage Avenue, Misha's arm over Dawson's shoulder, the men stumbled and slurred their way back to where the evening had begun.

"Look at the amazing sky we have in Manitoba, Misha. So many stars, and look at that full moon. Spectacular, isn't it?"

"It is impressive." Misha looked skyward and lost his balance, staggering backward. "But it cannot match the night sky in Moscow. There is a famous song, 'Midnight in Moscow,' sung by a most beloved Russian woman named Yulya. You know the words, no? I will sing them for you." Without waiting for Dawson's endorsement, he launched into a loud, alcohol-infused tenor rendition for Dawson and anyone else nearby.

Promise me my love, as the dawn appears

And the darkness turns into light

That you'll cherish, dear, through the passing years

This most beautiful Moscow night.

Misha bellowed the words with great commitment and emotion, his voice rising to a crescendo at the end. His deep connection to his homeland was obvious, but it conflicted with the doubts he had shared with Dawson.

The two men parted ways with a genuine, hearty hug as Dawson delivered Misha safely back to the Winnipeg Inn and then boarded a cab for home. He knew he would have to be at his desk first thing in the morning and recap the night's events to traders in Minneapolis, Vancouver and Geneva. It would certainly be easier to stay in bed and sleep through the inevitable pain about to crash down in his brain, but Dawson, like all other Cargill traders, lived by the decree "If you are sick, stay home; if you have 'self-inflicted' wounds, get your ass into work!" He would be at work on time.

Cargill Canada Office, Winnipeg   June 28, 1972

At 8:00 a.m. Central Standard time, Dick Dawson sent the following telex message to Cargill and Tradax offices, using their abbreviated language to save cost:

Cgl Cda sld Viktor 0.5 mil MT 2CWRS 13.5 pro @ US$60/MT FOB St Law for Oct/Sept delvy Z CWB also sld/optnd 4.0 mil MT – same px Z Tndrg 4 mil MT in USA nxt wk Z Thnk he wnts more Z Lts hv conf call in 1 hr Z
RLMD

At 9:00 a.m., Dawson was speaking with Mel Middents, Barney Saunders and Jim McCrea at the Lake Office along with the senior wheat trader, Huub Spierings in Geneva.

"Half a million tonnes, Dick! Is that the biggest deal you've ever closed?" asked Middents.

"No, we sold them more in 1963, but this is a sweet one, and I'm certain that besides the CWB we are the only company he dealt with in Winnipeg."

"That says a lot for your relationship, Dick. Well done! Huub, what are you hearing from your side of the pond?"

"I'm not surprised, really, guys," Spierings said. "It's a bad year for crops in Europe and Asia, particularly the normally productive Volga basin. Did you get a sense of how much they plan to buy, Dick?"

"Fisenko told me his agency would be tendering for four million tonnes of US wheat in the next few days, but that's all I could get out of him. He's too difficult to read, and even after hours and hours of drinking he won't reveal anything he doesn't want to share. Believe me, I tried!"

"Ha! I'll bet you did, mate," said Spierings. "Tough job, but you're the right man for the task."

"And that Russian son of a bitch is getting on a plane right now, heading home," added Dawson. "He gets to sleep for the next six hours!"

"Your dedication is appreciated, Dick," Middents said. "I have to say, this confirms my feelings as well. My intuition has been ringing on Russian buying for a while now. A conversation with the Blinker got my attention. Even though we have lots of wheat in the United States, I just don't feel like being short is where we want to be right now. Even or long is where I'm at."

"Great, we just sold half a million tonnes," Dawson exclaimed.

"We'll take half the book on, as usual, Dick," Spierings said. "We won't leave you hanging."

"Agreed," Dawson said. "Let's stay close to this over the next couple of weeks, guys. Something is going on here."

Jim was impressed with Middents' prescient prediction of Russian buying interest. Based on a single call with the Polish buyer, he had sensed a potential turn in the trend of the wheat market. On its own it wasn't enough to risk serious corporate funds, but, in conjunction with corroborating evidence from a reliable source, he was building a strategy. Here was Cargill's global reach and world class brain trust at work, Jim realized. He would never undervalue that tool.

"Jim, I want you to get to work discovering everything you can about the condition of crops across Asia," said Middents. "I'll introduce you to our crop economist and weather guy, Maury Brannan. I think you and he will hit it off right away. He's a very humble, intelligent man who isn't afraid to tell it like it is. We love him! But I also want you to reach out to our global network. I'll introduce you to some people to get you started. Weather forecasts will be key, Jim. Are things going to get worse or better than they are right now? We need to know that. The information is out there; we just have to be the first to find it."

11

Setting the Trap

Exportkhleb Offices, Department of Agriculture   June 29, 1972

"That's all you bought? Four million tonnes?" gasped Pershin. He looked concerned and confused. "It's a disappointing number when we have so much more to accomplish, Misha! What were you thinking?"

"I understand your concern, President, but this was Phase 1 of the plan we agreed to execute, was it not?" Misha said calmly. "Getting our Canadian supply covered first doesn't jeopardize what we need to get done in the United States. The next phase of the contracting will take place next week in New York."

Pershin did not respond, and Misha carried on. "Continuing with our report, we would like to update you on the ocean freight bookings we have accomplished while I was in Canada. Mr. Chairman, you remember Boris Gryzlov, our logistics expert. He has already managed to secure fourteen million tonnes of shipping capacity for the coming year, more than half of our projected requirements. Most of this cargo capacity is on Russian vessels. Some booking information is leaking out to the market, as we had expected it might, but the news doesn't seem to be setting off any alarms so far. The non-Soviet quantities are small, and no one knows where the ports of origin or destination are relative to the shipments, so the news Russia might be buying grain has not been linked to these bookings. On the Chicago futures exchange, wheat prices are not increasing. We have the US export subsidy program to thank for that, I believe. It is keeping prices from rising, at least for now. So far everything is working as per our plan; however, the most challenging phase, actually buying grain from the private companies in America, is yet to be executed. I would like to review the next phase with you, Mr. Chairman, as your role is vital to the overall success of our plan."

"Of course," Pershin said. "I will schedule an appointment with Agriculture Secretary Earl Butz in Washington for Monday morning, July third. Our intention is to request one billion dollars in trade credit over three years for the purchase of grain and grain products from the United States. The US government seemed very receptive to our preliminary contact and has already established diplomatic channels between our governments to facilitate these discussions and a potential agreement. We won't inform them that we expect to use the whole amount in the first year, but we will make sure we include that option.

"Comrade Makarov will join me and two staff on the trip to Washington, as she is closely involved in this process on behalf of Exportkhleb." Pershin nodded to Nadia, and she smiled to acknowledge her understanding. Misha was glad to hear Pershin was including her in the international meetings. It would be good experience for her, and, above all, Misha trusted her to report back to him on any potential problems.

"Excellent," Misha said. "That will help cover the credit shortfall we anticipate. Combining this one billion dollars with the three-billion commitment from our own treasury, secured by Nadia, gives us confidence we will be able to pay for everything we purchase. Let's not forget, if grain prices start to rise before we lock in prices, we will not be able to buy the quantities we have identified without more money.

"Next week," Misha continued, "Exportkhleb will officially announce the tender for US-origin wheat, and we will meet with the grain companies one by one to lock in deals. After meeting with the Canadian Wheat Board and Cargill in Winnipeg, I believe there is a general belief across the industry that we have problems with our winter wheat crop; they just don't know how bad it is. This will confirm their suspicions, but the quantity is still unknown, and we will not expose anything regarding our concerns for the larger acreage spring-seeded crops. We still maintain secrecy around this information. My plan is to reject anything Cargill offers us at the outset, as they are the one company that knows we are buying. If we reject them, it will help convince the trade we are not desperate. My meetings with the grain companies will coincide with your meeting, Chairman, and, hopefully, by the end of next week we will have covered most of our grain shortfall."

"Which companies have you arranged to meet with, Misha?" Pershin asked.

"Later today, as the Americans start their day, I will reach out to Cargill, Continental, Dreyfus, Cook, Garnac, and Bunge Corporation—all six majors. I hope to arrange negotiation sessions with each of them over the span of a week. I can only succeed if I stay in one place and request they come to me. I hope they agree to those arrangements. I will send them the grain tender sheet outlining our requirements after the calls and request confidentiality until we have met to negotiate."

"Very well, Misha. Let's meet again tomorrow afternoon one final time before we travel to the United States."

Exportkhleb Offices, Department of Agriculture   June 30, 1972

The following day, Misha decided not to mention to Pershin that he had altered the tonnage amount in the tender from twenty million tonnes to four million. He knew Pershin might get stressed if he changed the plan on him. The responsibility for the grain negotiations was his domain, not Pershin's. How he got the job done mattered less than actually getting it done. Besides, he already had Minister Matskevich's approval to execute the strategy. Mike Slaski's innovative plan was sound, and the more Misha considered it, the better it felt.

"Misha, let me start by telling you I was able to arrange a meeting with United States Secretary of Commerce Peter Peterson and Agriculture Secretary Butz for Monday at the same time you are scheduling your meetings to purchase grain from the export companies," Pershin said. "As you know, the Americans have been open to secure a trade deal with the Soviet Union for the past year, and we have been dragging it out. Even when their president Nixon was here in Moscow in May promoting his 'wheat for peace' proposal, they tried to get us to agree to a credit package, but we held out. I now have Politburo permission to attempt to close a deal with them for up to one billion dollars over the next three years at our option. This will be critical to locking up grain contracts. Minister Matskevich lobbied well on our behalf with the Politburo to gain this approval."

"This is excellent news, Mr. President," Misha exclaimed, pleased and relieved to hear another potential roadblock had been removed. "I hope you can close a deal early next week, as I too have scheduled numerous meetings starting tomorrow. Securing this credit will enable our grain transactions to proceed. It's perfect for us!

"Cargill is first on our list to meet with on Saturday afternoon, followed by Continental Grain on Monday. Gregor and I are actually joining Clarence Palmby, who is now working with Continental, in Washington on Sunday to tour their nation's capital," Misha continued. "You remember him from his position in the US government. Continental's president, Michel Fribourg, is returning from Europe specifically to meet with us on Monday morning. They seem to be the most eager to make a deal. We have put the wheels in motion. Now we must execute the plan."

12

Dealmakers

Commodity trading is, without doubt, one of the most mysterious and least understood industries in the world. It doesn't have a store front. On the whole, the general population is oblivious to the breadth and depth of trading activity that precedes the arrival of food on grocery store shelves, at restaurants, in bakeries and specialty food vendors. Those who may be aware of commodity markets are unlikely privy to the high-stakes, mega-million-dollar industry or the use of commodity exchanges in the process. Aggregators and processing industries utilize exchanges to manage and transfer the risk of fluctuating commodity prices. Some people may be suspicious of shadowy, confidential activities of goliath, privately owned food companies, but few are able to follow the day-to-day market intelligence and transactions taking place. It's an industry obscured by secrecy, covertly exclusive.

Commodity buyers and sellers prefer quiet, confidential negotiations. At the highest level, there are very few players. The global grain industry is comprised of numerous state trading agencies, or boards, for both selling and buying commodities as their needs dictate. Parallel with those government boards are many private entities acting as agents, brokers and principals. But the lion's share of trade is dominated by six major private firms. In the early seventies they were family-owned businesses, dating back more than 100 years in some cases. Most of these companies carry the family name of the ancestor who started the business as a small vendor or warehouseman. They bear names like "Cargill," "Cook," "Bunge" or "Louis Dreyfus," while others have gone for names with more international flair, like "Continental" and "Garnac." These corporate giants are mysterious and invisible to the general public due to their private ownership. They don't have public listings and they don't report to anyone but their internal boards of directors, usually composed of family members. The commodity industry where they operate is low-profile and exclusive. Commodity trading is steeped in contradiction. Price information is fully transparent through the exchanges, but actual deals are never known beyond the principals. The results of transactions ultimately become known, but normally well after the fact and too late for anyone to act on the information. After all, that is the basis of their success.

The irony of this is the impact of commodity markets on the food we eat. We are all customers of a market we know little about—hence the mistrust and suspicion of the market in general and of the specific participants. These companies control major links in the global food chain, from the farm gate through handling and processing, right through to commercial shelves. They deal in bulk agricultural production like grains and oilseeds but also in food commodities such as salt, sugar, poultry, livestock and dairy.

The overlords of the industry deal in billions of dollars in global trade. They often link government trading agencies together in transactions and enjoy communications networks and market intelligence vastly superior to any single national government agency. They frequently trade among themselves, although they prefer the advantages of vertical integration wherever possible to enhance margins and extend their privacy. Reporting to small closely knit boards assures their secrecy and corporate performance. No one really knows the value of these mega corporations as their names are not well-known commercial brands. This adds to the mystique and opaqueness of the commodity industry.

At one end of the commodity supply chain, grain companies buy small quantities from farmers—a ten-tonne truckload or roughly 350 bushels, for instance. At the other end they sell cargo-size quantities like 1.5 million bushels.

They are aggregators. They are risk managers. They are traders.

In truth, the marketplace would not function without them. These businesses have evolved over the years from small local enterprises dealing with individual farmers and village markets to their current status as international powerhouses. They carry enormous clout and the responsibility for large measures of employment, commerce and government revenue. They possess disproportionate influence with regard to agriculture policy and the food-supply system.

They are also smart enough to maintain a low profile and not behave too greedily, at least where they are unable to hide their activity. They know their place in the structure of their respective countries and, while they trade internationally, they abide by local laws and convention to maintain an acceptable status quo. This doesn't preclude them from setting up offices in tax haven countries to improve their profitability. Strategically, they are well positioned in the market to anticipate global grain activity before the general public and often before government intelligence services. In short, not much gets by them.

Nevertheless, it is the very secrecy and apparent oligopoly of the commodity industry that attracts the attention and earns the suspicion of a mistrusting public. Academics and citizen coalitions are known to be vocal in their opposition to the market power and lack of transparency afforded these corporate titans of the food industry. Are prices covertly set during the course of secret meetings? Is the doctrine of supply and demand a myth, perpetuated by those who stand to gain from market control? Does the powerless consumer pay excessive prices for food, thereby lining the pockets of the superrich?

These were the questions on the minds of market watchdogs as the events of a crop failure in Eastern Europe unfolded in global commodity markets during the summer of 1972.

* * *

Cargill and Continental traders were not particularly surprised to receive a call from Exportkhleb's deputy director, Mikhail Fisenko, in late June requesting a meeting in New York City to discuss grain purchases. The subsequently released Soviet buying interest or grain tender amount they received for four million tonnes was also not a surprise. They already knew the Soviet winter wheat crop was under stress and would not meet production targets. And some knew Fisenko had participated in meetings with the Canadian Wheat Board, where a four-million-tonne deal was ratified the previous week in Winnipeg. There were few secrets for these market leaders.

The fact that representatives from Moscow were traveling to the United States to enter trade talks was unprecedented. Food trade between these global superpowers had been virtually nonexistent for the three decades of the Cold War. Any trade taking place had been in the Soviet Union or on neutral ground. Unlike many other exporting-grain countries, the United States didn't have a national trading agency, so the door was wide open for dealmakers like these private companies and other commodity trading entrepreneurs to negotiate freely—and secretly. Traders were anxiously awaiting the opportunity to participate in what would potentially be the largest deals of their careers at a time when markets seemed predictable and safe.

Madison Hotel, Washington DC   July 1, 1972

Misha Fisenko and Gregor Yeremenko checked into the luxurious Madison Hotel in Washington DC on Saturday afternoon. Their grain dealings with Continental Grain, often referred to as "Conti" by those in the industry, and others would be in New York starting on Monday, but they had been invited to spend a day touring the US national capital with Conti's corporate representatives. The lead representative was the company's newest vice president, Clarence Palmby, an acquaintance of the Exportkhleb team when he was the assistant secretary at the US Department of Agriculture.

The trading relationship between Exportkhleb and the French-based firm had flourished over the years as they struck deals on grain from countries all over the world—excluding the USA. The head of the company, Michel Fribourg, was well acquainted with the staff at Exportkhleb, having dealt with them regularly over the years, most extensively during the 1963 grain-production shortfall in the Soviet Union. As bad as it had been for the Soviets, they were grateful to Fribourg and his company for providing the bulk of the grain they required that year.

Misha hoped this year would generate a similar result. He was delighted to accept the invitation to spend some social time with Palmby and his wife. Misha was a history buff with extensive knowledge of his own country's past, but he relished the opportunity to learn more about America's history from the great Smithsonian museums in Washington. This special treatment was one of the perks of traveling internationally in his role, and, while he did not display his sheer delight outwardly, inwardly he reveled in the attention and luxuries he was afforded. However, he was adamant the attention would not affect the execution of his duties in the best interest of his country. He was determined to maintain a distanced, professional image for the weeks ahead.

The Soviets had, however, decided to take advantage of their early arrival and secretly arranged to meet with senior Cargill representatives in the late afternoon and evening of July 1 at their hotel in Washington. This was a little awkward, as Continental was paying for the hotel rooms. Misha just hoped no one learned of this meeting. He had no intention of buying any grain from Cargill at this meeting. His plan was to create confusion and downplay any suspicions they might have pertaining to Exportkhleb's urgent demand. Cargill's senior management knew about the deals in Canada, so Misha wanted to start his plan to slow-play his deal making, hopefully negating any sense of urgency.

* * *

The invitation from Misha Fisenko to meet privately in Washington two days before formal trade discussions encouraged the Cargill brass. After Dick Dawson's huge trade in Winnipeg four days ago, they were bolstered by the prospect of additional business—American wheat business. Cargill obviously had the inside track thanks to Dick's relationship with Misha. Their optimism overflowed.

Cargill's corporate jet landed senior traders Barney Saunders and Mel Middents in Washington at approximately 3:00 p.m. They'd flown three hours from Minneapolis for a single meeting and would be flying home later that evening. The cost of their trip was not a consideration. Neither was the time. They disembarked their taxi at the lobby of the Madison Hotel at 4:00 p.m. Saunders and Middents made for an amusing pair, one tall and lean and the other short and stocky, but they shared a serious intensity.

Jim McCrea had led an outstanding effort to research the crop outlook in Eastern Europe and, from those discoveries, provided Saunders and Middents with the most current information on the actual condition of the Soviet crops. The Cargill team was convinced the Soviets were in a real bind and they held the advantage in any potential trades. The urgency of the meeting, on a weekend no less, convinced them they held all the cards. It didn't matter to Saunders and Middents that they were working on a Saturday, as this meeting had all the potential to be an extraordinary and even historic one. Using the lobby phone, they connected to Fisenko's room.

"Good afternoon, Misha. Mel Middents here. We are downstairs in the lobby. Are you ready to meet with us?"

"By all means, Mel. Please come to the twelfth floor and I'll meet you at the elevator. Come on up."

* * *

While waiting for Cargill and pondering the potential outcomes of the days and weeks ahead, Misha thought back to his strategic discussion with Mike Slaski before he'd left for North America.

"Okay," Slaski had said. "Let's talk about Cargill. They already know you're set to buy more grain since you dealt with the CWB and Cargill Canada. This may sound crazy, but my suggestion is to blow them off the first day—don't agree to anything."

"Really? That sounds risky to me, Mike. What are you thinking?"

"Appearing too eager would be a mistake. Cargill already knows you're a buyer and not a seller this year. But they don't know how much you really need. They may suspect you're desperate, so you need to remove any of those suspicions if you can. I know you tendered for wheat, but if you avoid talking about it altogether and play them along with a false line about corn and barley, they will come away from your first session very confused. You will get another chance to buy from them later, but initially they leave without a deal."

"I understand your thinking, Mike, but it still feels risky. I feel like we should strike quick and get it done."

"It's your call, Misha. I just think you will create more confusion by blanking them out, at least for the first meeting. Make them wait and then schedule another meeting the next day or two. The same for Continental. Drag it out a bit. Give them time to think about it. They will be hungry to deal, especially once they realize you're meeting with a number of companies and they might be left out. Make sure you let it slip you have other meetings, right?" Slaski smiled conspiratorially. "Remember you want to come across like all you need is four million tonnes, and you will be speaking with a number of sellers before making a deal. This will take some acting out your part, Misha. But you're such a hard read in negotiations that I know you can pull this off too."

"I like your thinking, Mike, and it makes sense. But I'll decide during the meeting if it's too risky to try."

"Like I said, it's up to you. But remember, Dawson got one on you for the four-cent protein premium for Canadian wheat. This is your chance to get it back. Right?"

"That is true," Misha smirked. "They owe me one, right?"

"Exactly!"

* * *

Misha hurried down the long hallway to the bank of elevators to greet his visitors. The elevator bell's "ding" sent a rush of adrenalin through his stomach, but his facial expression never altered. He expected Cargill to be determined in their dealings, which would make it more difficult to reach the desired stalemate Slaski had proposed. Misha greeted the two men and led them to his room, where he introduced Gregor and told them a bit about his assistant's role at Exportkhleb.

Misha knew Saunders and Middents fairly well. They had been to the Exportkhleb offices in Moscow several times. Cargill actually owned a suite in Moscow for traders or senior management who traveled there for meetings. Normally the Soviets met with Cargill's Geneva-based Tradax team, but at least once a year senior company officials from the United States came to Moscow. But those meetings were more often about buying grain, and they never involved discussions about American grain. Today's meeting was breaking new ground.

Saunders began with small talk, building rapport, calming nerves, but Misha didn't lose his focus; it was all business. Both Cargill men had a lot of questions. They wanted information on the condition of crops on a Soviet state-by-state basis. They wanted to know about the amount of rainfall. And they pushed Misha hard for his estimates of production this year. This data was not readily available outside the Soviet member states, so this was an excellent chance for them to gather intel. Whether they trusted Misha to be honest in his replies was anyone's guess. Maybe they were trained in eye movement and body language, Misha thought. No matter; he would present an unreadable front, be vague where he had to be and lie when necessary.

Misha was happy to wax on about the great success of the Soviet collective farms and of the Five-Year Plan. He dodged the critical questions masterfully. Everyone in the room knew he was full of crap, and both sides also knew he had confided truths to Dawson in Winnipeg already. There were production problems in the Soviet Union—full stop. The Americans just didn't know how severe the problem was.

As the discussion on crop conditions wore out, Saunders moved on. "Well, let's talk about your wheat tender, Misha. That's why we're here. You're looking for four million tonnes of hard red winter wheat from the United States. Correct?"

"Yes, that is the amount we tendered," Misha said.

"Excellent. Can we move on to that? We might as well get our immediate concern out of the way first. How are you planning to pay for it?"

Saunder's forthright question caught Misha by surprise. They wanted to know about payment terms before they even had a deal in place. Rather bold, he thought.

"Exportkhleb is open to financing a deal with you if you would like to include terms in your offer," he replied. He already knew the answer based on the response he'd got from Dawson—Cargill didn't like being a bank. Saunders didn't disappoint him, as he responded with the same storyline.

"No matter," Misha said. "We are prepared to sell gold from our treasury to generate cash. I will also share with you confidentially that we are meeting with your country's commerce department to secure trade financing proposed by President Nixon in Moscow in May. With financing of one billion dollars in place, we could purchase the same four million tonnes every year for each of the next three years, although I doubt that would be necessary. We feel this will meet our needs for this year nicely. It also supports a longer-term relationship, which we are also seeking." Misha felt that sharing this information, even though it wasn't yet confirmed, would impress Saunders and Middents and help build trust.

"That's exactly what we want to hear, Misha. Now we can get down to dealing," said Saunders. "Mel, I'll turn it over to you for the details."

"Thanks, Barney," said Middents. "Misha, Gregor, as an introduction, I'm the senior wheat trader for Cargill globally. I'm responsible for all wheat sales out of the US and for our global position in the wheat market. We are empowered to make a deal with you today if we can agree on terms. I'll start by giving you a quick snapshot view of the wheat market here in the United States.

"Misha, I'm sure you're not surprised to hear we have a large inventory and a promising crop coming at us from our wheat belt this year. Supplying you with four million tonnes is not a problem. It's a huge trade, make no mistake, but it's very possible in our view. My biggest concern is price. If the government cancels the export subsidy program, we could see wheat market prices start to move up. That is a very real possibility."

"We understand. And we are hopeful the US grain companies can express to their government contacts the extreme importance of maintaining competitive prices with other global suppliers. This is a politically charged topic of utmost importance to ongoing, good-faith trade negotiations between our countries." Misha was delivering a practiced response. "The offers we are getting from other countries are in line with the price levels available through the US subsidy program."

"Fair enough, Misha," said Middents. "Assuming the subsidy remains in place, establishing that upper limit on sales prices, we can talk about price and the quantity of hard wheat we can offer Exportkhleb."

"That sounds reasonable, Mel, but before we discuss wheat, I would prefer to receive an offer from Cargill for feed grains, corn specifically. This was not part of our tender, but I hope to secure two million tonnes of corn while we are here in Washington. We can talk about wheat another time. I don't plan to ask for an offer from corn from any other companies, which is why it wasn't part of the tender."

Middents and Saunders looked at each other quickly, their expressions confused. That was encouraging, Misha thought.

"Corn. But we thought…"

"I know." Misha filled Middents' pause. "I didn't mean to bring you here under false pretenses. We will get to wheat eventually, once my more pressing need to secure corn has been addressed with you gentlemen."

"Can we reschedule a meeting to discuss this, Misha? We didn't come prepared to make you an offer on corn."

"Yes, that is fine with me." Misha liked the concern his comments had instilled in the two men. Delaying them, as Slaski had suggested, appeared to be easier than he imagined. He decided to follow through with the strategy. "I will contact you later this week to reschedule a time for us to meet."

During the conversation with Cargill's traders, Misha's confidence had grown. He felt the anxiousness in their speech and their pressing style bordering on urgency—maybe "desperation" was a better word. Once again Slaski had called it. There was no need for Misha to act too quickly. Besides, the sooner he finished his dealings here in the United States, the sooner he and Gregor would have to return to Moscow. Living in fancy North American hotels was a nice break from his normal routine, not to mention the unbearable heat at home. Slaski was right about another thing: this was fun.

"Can we get back to your wheat tender, Misha? We would like to put some numbers in front of you and conclude some business today. You've come all the way from Moscow. We wouldn't want you to go home empty-handed," Saunders said with a smile.

"Don't worry about that, Barney. I'm sure we will find everything we came here to buy in due time," Misha replied coyly. "Hang on to your offer until we meet again. That will give you time to confer with the USDA on the export subsidy program as well. I think we are done for today's meeting."

Both Cargill traders looked at Misha in confusion. "Before we finish, Misha, we have one quick question. Besides the corn, if we could agree on a wheat trade today, what amount are you thinking?"

"One million, maybe two million tonnes," he replied.

Immediate smiles from the traders revealed their satisfaction with the prospect. These guys have trouble keeping their emotions in check, Misha noted. Even the Canadian Wheat Board presented a better front, but there was little they could do when the US oversupply of grain was so obvious. There was nowhere to hide.

"All right," Saunders replied. "We'll get to work on it and come back to you with offers on two million tonnes each of corn and wheat. Can we schedule our next meeting now?"

"Go back to Minneapolis, Barney. I'll call you."

Misha's aloof tone was obvious. Saunders and Middents both looked perplexed and frustrated. He guessed the Cargill guys felt they had really dropped the ball on this potential deal. And they had no idea why. The meeting had gone perfectly.

Madison Hotel, Washington DC   July 2, 1972

On Sunday, Michel Fribourg was still in France, quickly altering his plans to meet with the Russians in New York the following day. He would arrive in time for the meeting on Monday, but the short notice from Exportkhleb caught him by surprise. He could have traveled to Moscow easily from the French Riviera, but returning to North America added another day. For the opportunity to meet with the Soviets, the extra day would be worth it.

The Russian government never made these trade excursions easy for their traveling emissaries like Misha and Gregor. Soviet trade diplomats traveling abroad had an extremely limited daily expense allocation to cover their food and accommodations. The amount of money approved never covered the full costs, so they were always appreciative of the occasions when locals would pay for any of their expenses.

Misha and Gregor were thankful Continental Grain had committed to covering all their expenses in Washington, including their meals and accommodation at an exquisite hotel. In addition, Clarence Palmby and his wife had hosted their guests on a fantastic day touring Washington's landmarks: the Capitol Building, the Washington Mall, the Lincoln Memorial and the White House—the outside of it, at least. The impressive stretch of land from the US Capital building all the way to the Lincoln Memorial was reminiscent of Red Square to Misha and Gregor, although not as well designed for military parades.

The small group had managed to spend most of the afternoon in one minor but historic section of the Smithsonian Museum Complex, the National Museum of American History, immediately adjacent to the Washington Monument. The rooms were full of artifacts from America's history, but Misha had been drawn to the strong political images and history evoked by the third-floor dedication to American presidents and their wives.

Misha and Gregor had soaked up the relatively modern history of this young country, still less than two hundred years old, compared to more than the one thousand years of documented Russian history. The independence and spirit of the early pioneers and legislators intrigued Misha. The American evolution into a capitalist nation as opposed to their own familiar state control had always felt unruly to him, but they had managed to accomplish a great deal in those short two hundred years; he could not deny the facts.

Thinking ahead to the coming week, Misha expected tough negotiating from these traders. He was playing from a disadvantage, but only he and Gregor knew the real truth. The point of Continental's hospitality was to soften him and gain an advantage for their company based on building strong personal relationships. That was obvious. Misha had decided to play on the theme and let the Continental people feel like he was warming up and becoming more "friendly," but he wouldn't lose sight of his mission. He planned to be a tough negotiator. Letting one's guard down was never a good strategy. When this was over, Continental might not be happy with their position. That wasn't Misha's problem, though.

13

Continental Grain Flips the Plan – Round 2

Hilton Hotel, New York City   July 2, 1972

The Russians checked into the snazzy New York Hilton on Sunday night after a short flight from Washington. The glitz and glamor of a high-end New York hotel did not exist in Russia, or any Soviet country for that matter. This was unfamiliar ground for a Soviet trade mission. Soviet citizens being in the heart of New York was an extremely unusual event. Many Americans harbored hatred toward Russia based on little fact and a lot of public vitriol. The hostilities created by the Cuban Missile Crisis were ten years old now, but the persistent loathing of communism ran deep in America, and nowhere more so than in this metropolis.

The cool reception from most of the people they encountered was obvious. There were several languages spoken on the streets of New York, but their Russian accents were unmistakable. Misha's English was much better than Gregor's, but he couldn't hide the accent. They spoke softly and infrequently so as not to draw attention to themselves.

They had mostly acclimatized to the time difference after being in North America for two days. They would be living in this time zone for the next two to three weeks, or at least until they completed their mission. Adjusting their internal clocks was important.

Misha's initial plan to manage the pace of the meetings, dispel any sense of urgency and leverage one company against another in order to get the best offers was on track after their initial meeting with Cargill. In future meetings they intended to pounce on all the offers in rapid succession. With regard to the larger overall plan, so far everything was going as scripted, but the first stage in Canada had been the easiest part. The next few days would determine success or failure for Mikhail Fisenko and Exportkhleb. On this trip, Phase 2 as he referred to it, he was about to trigger the trap.

Misha called Slaski first thing Monday morning, late in the afternoon in Geneva, to get any last-minute market intelligence and try to absorb some of Slaski's confidence and build his own bravado for the coming days.

"No, Misha. There are no serious rumors of Russia's crop problems circulating in the market yet. Ocean freight bookings out of New York shipping agents caught a few eyes, but the reaction is as we suspected: Exportkhleb could be booking freight for wheat export, not import. It's not a concern yet," Slaski assured him.

"That's true, Mike. We do book a lot of freight every year. But we will need more than ever this year. The ocean freight industry is a notorious source of market intelligence and, more concerning, leaked information."

The freight booking, or "relet" industry, as it was known, had long been a bellwether for international market activity. Most international trade required ocean transport. The shipment of the cargo was part of the deal regardless of whether the transportation was booked by the buyer or seller. Smart traders kept a close watch on freight bookings, and vessel operators were quick to release the booking information in hopes of attracting more business and increasing their charter rates. They always loved a price run based on perceived shortages.

Misha proceeded to give Slaski a recap of their meetings thus far.

"We met with Cargill briefly yesterday. I laid out the opportunity but cut them off when they wanted to close a wheat deal. I sidelined them by asking for an offer of corn instead, making it sound like it was exclusive to them. They were clearly confused and unprepared for a change in plan. The strategy still makes me nervous, I have to admit. We're going to meet with Continental later today, Cargill again on Wednesday and then both Dreyfus and Bunge on Thursday. They all have the tender details for the four million tonnes of Number 1 or Number 2 hard red winter wheat FOB both east and west coast ports. I'm quite certain no one suspects what we have planned. How do you think they will react once they figure it out?"

"I think you don't want to be anywhere in the United States when the deals start to become public. It will take a few days or even weeks for them to leak out, but they always do," Slaski said. "But you are just doing your job, Misha. Don't worry about how they react. You're the buyer. You have the power right now. Let's go over the plan one last time."

"Yes. Yes, let's do that," he said thankfully. "I met with the CWB in Winnipeg and secured three million tonnes of spring wheat, durum and barley with an option on another one million tonnes of wheat. I also bought 500 thousand tonnes of wheat from Cargill Canada. We secured three-year credit on the CWB portion. We might be eligible for some trade credit in Canada through their Export Credit Insurance Corporation. We have worked with them before. Dick said they call it the Export Development Corporation now, but it's the same thing. Credit is credit as long as the terms are right.

"The Soviet Union has enough gold reserves committed for three billion in cash in US dollars based on today's gold price. It's the bulk of cash we estimate we will need for payment to the Americans, and we will be negotiating a trade loan with their government this week, hopefully for another one billion dollars. We feel the financing position is in fairly good shape. The actual cost of the grain will ultimately determine how much money we need and how much gold the Russian treasury will have to sell.

"We also have booked fourteen million tonnes of ocean freight. Just under half of what we need, but we hope the remaining deals can be finalized this week."

"All right," Slaski replied. "Just how we laid it out, right?"

"It is, but I'm very nervous about this phase," Misha admitted. "This part could explode in our faces. The sellers might not make offers. They could collaborate and move prices higher. A lot can go wrong."

"No, no, no! Don't think like that, Misha. You own this deal. You have all the cards. We've analyzed this. The Americans are sitting on huge inventories of grain. The only other country capable of helping the USA out of this mess is China, and the chances of a deal between them is really slim. Before Nixon went there this year, the Americans hadn't even talked to Chinese diplomats in forty-nine years! I know, I know—the Americans don't like the Soviet Union either, but they hate you less." Slaski chuckled. "And Nixon came to Russia, too, so they are open to trade. You will make the politicians look good, and they really like to look good!

"Misha, I wish I was you right now. You are going to make the deal of a lifetime, one of the biggest grain deals in history, and have so much fun doing it. I'm jealous, my friend. Really jealous."

God, how I wish I had this guy's silver tongue, thought Misha. He's just what I need right now to fortify me. Slaski had such a gift for planting all the positives in one's mind and excluding all the things that could go horribly wrong, things leading to a life in some kind of exiled Soviet purgatory for Misha and his team. Slaski wasn't in danger—but Misha was.

"Thanks, Mike. I'm glad we spoke. I'll let you know how the days go."

"Fantastic. You'll be great, Misha. Talk later."

* * *

Misha had arranged for a two-room suite at the Hilton to host his meetings. He had booked the suite for three weeks in anticipation of lengthy and difficult negotiations with numerous companies. He had informed the grain companies of the hotel and room number so they could come directly to the suite, avoiding unnecessary contact in the lobby or front desk. Anything he could do to maintain secrecy during the pending meetings would be worthwhile. He had no idea the grain companies had placed their own people secretly and strategically in the hotel lobby to identify who else was meeting with Exportkhleb. The spy games had begun.

Hilton Hotel, New York City   July 3, 1972

Misha and Gregor finished the breakfast they'd ordered from room service and awaited the arrival of their first guests. Misha scanned his notes, developed specifically for Michel Fribourg and the Continental Grain team, for the third time that morning. He wrestled with the jacket-on or jacket-off decision, trying to land on the right degree of formality. He settled with the more casual "jacket off, shirt sleeves long and necktie on" look. He had checked his watch five times in the last half hour. The hands moved agonizingly slowly, but he couldn't dwell on that. It didn't matter. He had all day to negotiate with Continental and either book some grain or send them back empty-handed. The tone and direction of the meeting would determine his reactions on the fly. He had to be nimble and he had to be flexible.

At 10:00 a.m. sharp a knock on the door signaled the arrival of the Continental contingent. Misha's stomach twisted again and his adrenaline rushed, as it had with Cargill. It was happening, right now, as he opened the suite door. This was the most important meeting of his life. Clarence Palmby stood at the front of the four-man entourage, and Misha recognized Continental Grain president Michel Fribourg at the rear.

"Good morning, gentlemen. It's very nice to see you again so soon, Clarence." Misha extended his hand to Palmby and in his firm, robust Russian manner shook everyone's hand as they entered the room. Fribourg was the last to enter. Misha was genuinely glad to see them and renew old friendships, but the pressure of the moment kept him on edge.

"Misha, my old friend, it's so good to see you." Fribourg was beaming as he made solid eye contact. "I hope you enjoyed your day in Washington yesterday with the Palmbys. Clarence really knows his way around." Fribourg's grin implied Clarence had more than geographical knowledge of the city.

Fribourg wasn't a tall man at five foot ten. He was slight of build and deeply tanned, just back from several weeks in the south of France. He had a distinct wave in his neatly trimmed brown hair and an engaging, genuine smile. He must buy his suits from the same tailor as Slaski, Misha thought; perfect fit, elegant material. One day. One day he would splurge on a custom-tailored suit.

"Clarence was an excellent, gracious host," Misha confirmed. "We are acquainted from his previous role in the US government, so it was nice to spend the day with him and his wife. Gregor and I really appreciate your invitation to Washington. I find American history quite fascinating."

Introductions were made all around: Fribourg, Palmby, Bernard Steinweg and Mike Laserson—the brain trust of their organization. The men settled into the configuration of comfortable chairs and tables. Misha decided to take control of the meeting by speaking first and laying out his intentions for a successful trade deal. The plan was to minimize Soviet needs and play up the problems of overproduction in the United States. When he was finished, he hoped to have them thinking he was doing them a huge favor.

Misha rose from his chair to address his audience. He remembered Frank Rowan from the CWB using this technique to gain a more dominant position in the room.

"Thank you all for meeting with us today. As I'm sure you already know, we are experiencing some winter wheat crop production problems, which threaten our plans for improved nutrition for our citizens as stipulated in our Five-Year Plan. We know there are large surplus stocks of wheat in the United States and another large crop already planted this year. We are here to secure a small portion of your surplus and open the door to ongoing trade relations between the Soviet Union and the United States. We value our trade relationship with Canada, but their ability to fulfill our orders from time to time is limited, as they serve many export nations. They have smaller production and try to service all of their traditional buyers every year. The long-term Soviet plan is based on diversifying our suppliers and reducing our risks.

"We are very pleased to start our buying mission with Continental Grain," Misha continued. "Michel, you have been a great ally of the Soviet Union in the past, and we look to you and your company to build on our relationship. I will confirm our interest, as outlined in the recent tender, in four million tonnes of hard red winter wheat. We released the information to allow you to prepare a competitive offer for today's meeting. We have numerous meetings scheduled, as you can imagine, so I ask you to provide your absolute best offer. We are prepared to deal today, in this room, but it is our preference to meet with a number of suppliers before finalizing any transactions."

He sat down. The last sentence was important, because it informed Fribourg that Misha had full trading authority. He didn't have to go back to his superiors at Exportkhleb to finalize any deals. But his intention remained to drag the discussions out, as per their plan.

Fribourg rose from his chair. Damn, Misha thought. He uses the same strategy. I probably shouldn't have yielded the floor. Lesson learned.

Fribourg was more formally dressed than Misha had expected. But this was likely normal attire for the European. He didn't do casual. He moved slowly and purposefully, with finesse. He actually made walking appear to be an art form in comparison to Misha's deliberate, heavy-footed maneuvers. He spoke with the softness, clarity and assurance of the well-educated professional he was.

"We are honored you are meeting with us first, Misha. You will recall, I'm sure, it was Continental Grain that provided a million tonnes of American wheat in 1964 when your country's production faltered. We are here again to supply the grain you need this year. Let me also say we can always count on you to get right to the point. Misha. You don't go on and on about the superior character and features of the communist society. We are also here to conduct business, and I think we might surprise you when you hear what we have in mind. I'm going to be fully transparent and put it right on the table for your consideration. We want to supply the Soviet Union with all of your wheat, all four million tonnes." Fribourg paused to add emphasis to this last statement. "If the government will agree to backstop the deal at the current subsidized export value, and you agree with our price, Continental Grain will commit to 100 percent of the supply. Right here, right now.

"But there's one stipulation we would like to include, Misha. We want exclusivity on any future business. If you need more grain you come to us—and only us. You can understand we don't want to be one of many who sell you grain and are left to compete with each other, running the market higher in the process. That's a position we don't want to try to manage." The other three Continental reps were smiling and nodding in agreement. "So, if we do commit to the full quantity of this tender today, you and Comrade Yeremenko can pack your bags and head back to Moscow tonight with your mission accomplished." Fribourg had spoken assertively and ended with a big smile.

The proposal caught Misha completely off guard. First, the quantity offered was larger than he expected. He thought he'd have to barter and cajole the sellers into offering higher quantities. But second, and most concerning, guaranteeing exclusivity would undermine his entire strategy. He had to retain the ability to book large blocks with multiple sellers. That stipulation just wouldn't work. On one hand, Continental's offer was too good to be true but, ironically, on the other, it could cause his entire plan to fall apart. He had to downplay his excitement and give Fribourg no reason to back away from the offer; however, he needed time to decide his next move. The offer was contrary to their tactical approach and not a possibility they had considered. Nimbleness was now required.

"Thank you, Michel. This is an offer I had not expected. As you can imagine, we are scheduled to meet with a number of other grain companies over the next few days and I would like to hear what they have to offer. But I must say your proposal is intriguing."

"Go ahead and meet with them, Misha. I'll go one better. If anyone gives you a better offer, I'll match it! As I said, we want to be your exclusive supplier, your source of grain from the USA. We are completely serious about this proposal to create a long-term, exclusive relationship."

Excellent, thought Misha. This could still work. With this substantial, flexible offer, he could continue with his scheduled meetings without alerting Fribourg to the possibility they might buy more than four million tonnes. If someone did come in cheaper or with better terms, he could go back to Continental for an adjustment. But even without any changes, the offer from them was more than he could have hoped for. This would most definitely change his negotiating strategy with the other companies. He could be more demanding for a break in price or terms. The exclusivity Fribourg was looking for was still a problem, but he decided he would deal with it later if he had to.

"If you are in agreement with this proposal, Misha, I only need one thing," Fribourg continued. "I need to call Carl Brunthaver at the Department of Agriculture and confirm they are willing to guarantee the export subsidy at today's level for the four million tonnes. I don't want to be on the hook for a subsidized price only to have the government change its mind."

A lot hung on the US government retaining the subsidy. Misha felt strongly they would. They had engaged in trade talks in Moscow just six weeks earlier, offered credit and appeared open to a larger, more sustained trading relationship with the Soviets. But if senior government officials said no or the Department of Agriculture got cold feet, he was sunk.

Fribourg asked Bernie Steinweg to make the call to Brunthaver, and Steinweg left the suite to do so. Apparently, Continental had booked a suite of their own at the Hilton so they could step out for private discussion if necessary. The two sides spent the next two hours sorting out details on price, quality, export ports, delivery schedule and payment terms. Fribourg wouldn't offer them credit. But if Pershin was successful in his negotiations with Agriculture Secretary Earl Butz and the US Department of Commerce, it wouldn't be a problem. During their discussions, Steinweg returned to the room and gave a single head nod to Fribourg, a pre-arranged signal that the US government would back them on the export subsidy.

"Excellent!" Fribourg exclaimed. "Bernie, please share with us what our good friend Carl had to say."

"Firstly, he was pleased to hear of the potential business. He indicated Secretary Butz and even President Nixon would be delighted with this news as well. They had no idea their meeting would result in tangible results so soon. I stressed to him it must remain confidential until the parties make an announcement. He's very trustworthy," Steinweg said. "The US government is eager to commence trade in grain and other commodities with the Soviet Union. Carl referred to President Nixon's visit in May as an example of new trade possibilities. This deal is incredibly good optics for the government in an election year, and closing the deal so quickly after their meetings is an example of their success. They couldn't be happier. Most importantly, he categorically assured me the government would guarantee the retention of the export subsidy program on registered sales through the remainder of this year."

"All right, Misha. Brunthaver's word is good enough for me. Is it good enough for you? Do we have an exclusive deal? Four million tonnes of wheat based on the base price of sixty US dollars per tonne loaded on a vessel at US eastern shipping ports during 1973."

"Michel, before we proceed to finalize our deal, I have a slight modification for your consideration. The Exportkhleb tender was for four million tonnes of wheat, but we also have interest in buying corn and other cereal grains for our expanding livestock industry. Would you be interested in discussing this today as well?" Misha took a risk and exposed this additional demand to Fribourg, recognizing it might expose their intent. But there was a reason for doing it. Misha hadn't planned on revealing this additional demand so soon but, as a seasoned trader, he felt the risk was worth it. And he had to manage Fribourg's request for exclusivity. This tactic might allow him to accomplish both.

"Like I said, Misha, I want Continental Grain to be Exportkhleb's exclusive supplier of grain. What are you looking for and how much?"

Misha felt a thrill at Fribourg's positive response. Outwardly he remained stoic as ever, but he knew his hunch was right—there was more on the table. "The actual quantity would be in the neighborhood of four million, five hundred thousand tonnes of corn and some small quantities of sorghum and barley," he replied calmly, as if he was accustomed to transacting deals of this magnitude on a regular basis. Internally he was vibrating.

"Does it all have to be US origin or can we supply corn from other countries?"

"We are flexible, as long as the landed price in the Soviet Union is the same regardless of the country of origin and, of course, the quality meets our minimum specifications."

"Very well. Can you give us some time to speak with our corn traders, Misha? I think we can settle this deal today, but we had been expecting to discuss wheat only."

"That sounds fine," Misha replied coolly. "Exportkhleb can guarantee exclusivity to Continental Grain on these cereal grains, Michel, but an exclusive on wheat is a big ask—not something we can commit to at this point. We have many international relationships that must be maintained. I hope you understand.

"We can finalize a deal on one further condition," Misha added, trying to draw as much benefit for the Soviet Union as possible. "It is critical this deal remains completely confidential. I don't want the other grain companies to learn we have filled our tender already. I want to be able to negotiate with them as if we are still uncommitted. And, as you proposed, we will accept your offer to match any lower prices or better terms. This too requires complete confidentiality."

"Misha, you can be damn certain we won't be announcing this deal to the public. We are bound to inform the government of this trade by the end of the month, but the actual amount and the details are not required to be disclosed. It is in our best interest to bury this deal and give our grain buyers time to cover the biggest trade in history," said Fribourg with a look of satisfaction.

Misha realized Fribourg's ego was getting a major boost from closing this deal. He wondered how cocky this French trader would be when Misha finished his buying spree.

"Certainly," Misha said. "Why don't we break for an hour and a half, have some lunch and reconvene here at one o'clock."

"Perfect. We will reconvene here in ninety minutes."

* * *

Misha and Gregor ordered room service for lunch so they could discuss their progress in private and review their next steps. Misha's actions had been bold, but he had read the thirst in Fribourg's eyes and the eagerness in his body language. Ego can be a powerful motivator. While Misha didn't let emotion drive his actions, he recognized it in others and was not averse to playing on it.

"Well done, Misha!" Gregor said. "This is an excellent start to our plan. I didn't expect you to make the corn request, but they jumped at the extra business, didn't they?"

"They most certainly did. I wasn't expecting such an aggressive approach from anyone. If the rest of our meetings are like this, we will be heading home sooner than we planned. We must stick to the strategy and focus on each company one by one. But this outcome is so fantastic for us. It puts us in a much stronger position as we work toward our targets. I'm extremely encouraged after our first meeting. If all the companies are this aggressive, we may have misjudged the circumstances, but we will still achieve our goals.

"We have more work to do with Conti this afternoon. If it takes all night to hammer this deal out, we must be prepared to finish. Tomorrow is America's Independence Day, so I didn't schedule any meetings. We will be able to see how their citizens celebrate their country. But let's stay focused on Conti right now. There are more details to confirm.

"It appears to me Michel and his team will come back with an offer for some or even all of the corn we requested. We will accept whatever they offer, but we should haggle on price a bit so as not to appear too eager.

"This could be one of the greatest days in Soviet agriculture history, Gregor," Misha said in a modest, confidential tone. "By the end of the day it is possible we might purchase as much as one third of our goal! But I am still concerned about the possibility of the US government removing the export subsidy, even after Michel assured us it wouldn't happen. If too many companies start calling the government to check on the subsidy status, they could react by ending the support. We are still at risk, but the more we buy, the more that risk transfers to them as sellers."

* * *

Promptly at one o'clock, Michel Fribourg and his three associates knocked on the suite door. The Russians had not scheduled meetings with any other companies on their first day in New York to be sure they could focus on Continental. It turned out to be an extremely good decision. Back in their original seats, the men resumed their negotiations. Once again Fribourg had the floor.

"Misha, Gregor, we want to start this afternoon by expressing our appreciation for your trust in our company and your open, forthright approach to negotiations. We discussed this over lunch at some length, and we are all agreed it is a pleasure to deal with you. In response to your request for four and one half million tonnes of corn and other parcels of cereal grains, we can say yes to your buying interest. I propose we agree on a base price for corn FOB NOLA—sorry, I should say on your boat in New Orleans, Louisiana— and we can negotiate the different grade spreads and origination points as spreads to the base point. Our teams can finalize the details. Importantly, we leave here committed to the full eight and a half million tonnes as a firm deal. That's 324 million bushels of grain, gentlemen. Easily the largest grain deal in history!"

Standing a little taller, Fribourg said, "I hope you are as proud of being a part of this as we are, my friends.

"We also want to reiterate our commitment to the confidentiality of this trade. It's in both our interests to keep this deal quiet for as long as possible. We are open to providing ocean freight for you if it would be helpful. Keeping those freight actions quiet is equally important. We track ocean freight bookings to monitor markets, and I'm sure other companies do as well. As to the exclusivity of the transaction, you proposed an exclusive on everything but wheat. We came here hoping to hammer out an exclusive deal on wheat only. So, in some part, this is a win for us, an exclusive on corn at least. We will table the exclusivity discussion on wheat for this tender, but we want to reiterate our desire to be Exportkhleb's single source of all imported grain and oilseeds from America. We believe it would be advantageous to us both. Lastly, we agree to complete confidentiality with respect to our dealings. No word of this deal will become public from our organization."

Fribourg's response both delighted and concerned Misha. The plan had been to slow-play the negotiations and ultimately buy as much as they could from everyone. Neither he nor Slaski had entertained a scenario where one company would offer double the tender quantity as an opening position. This was an aggressive tactic from Continental.

All considered, Conti's offer was exceptional. Misha wasn't likely to buy grain cheaper, and no other company, except for Cargill perhaps, was playing in the same league from a volume standpoint. Not only did this outcome remove the enormous stress and fear of failure he had been harboring, but it also put them in a stronger, leveraged negotiating position with the other grain companies. He could play hardball, as the Americans say. Misha was forced to decide on the spot: either stay with the original strategy to drag the dialogue out over the coming days, or seize this opportunity presented to him. He quickly decided the offer from Fribourg was too good to risk losing by playing games. While he hadn't expected this approach, it played into his hand perfectly, albeit in a different order.

"Michel, there was a reason we selected Continental Grain as our opening meeting in America. This decision has proved our relationship is strong. Exportkhleb has high confidence in the integrity of your company and your ability to perform. For those reasons and your innovative, aggressive proposition today, we accept your offer and look forward to finalizing the deal immediately.

"The offer to work with us on freight is also very good news, Michel. I will have our freight manager, Boris Gryzlov, contact you regarding our ocean freight situation.

"As a final point, I would like to request we baseline the price of corn included in this deal on the corn market close of last Wednesday, a dollar twenty-one per bushel on your Chicago September contract, I believe. The optics of this would be favorable for us personally, and I would consider it a favor."

Misha knew the Conti team would find a way to recoup the slightly higher price difference between Wednesday and the current day's close. It was less than five cents per bushel, but still a lot when you are talking about 177 million bushels. Nevertheless, he was correct; securing the much-needed grain at exceptionally low pricing improved the chances he would be viewed very positively for his negotiating acumen by his superiors.

Fribourg huddled with his team in response to his request. Misha knew they were doing the math on what amounted to a counterproposal reflecting a cost just shy of nine million dollars. He also doubted they would risk losing the deal for five cents per bushel. And he hadn't haggled on the wheat price, something he would surely do in future meetings with other exporters given that he had secured the wheat tonnage from Conti.

"That's a big 'give' on our part, Misha. It may mean we have to review the spreads on the various grades and shipping ports. And there's no export subsidy program on corn, so our asses are bare to the wind on that one." He grinned. "But if it reflects well on you with your bosses and if you can be a little flexible on relative prices for different grades of wheat, then we have a deal. This is a significant transaction, Misha. You and your team should be immensely proud of this accomplishment. I know I am proud of my team, but our hard work is just beginning while yours is coming to an end." He smiled.

Misha got up from his chair and approached Fribourg with his hand extended. Even as this unprecedented transaction neared completion with the pending handshake, he maintained his somber expression, a professional to the end. The time for celebrating would come soon enough. He knew Fribourg was right: this was the biggest grain deal in history, and he wasn't finished. But the satisfaction of executing a huge portion of this delicate phase of the plan was immensely satisfying on a personal level.

"We do indeed have a satisfactory deal from our perspective, Michel," Misha said as the two men shook hands. This gesture confirmed the deal. The paperwork would follow, but just like the open outcry of deals in the trading pit, the deals of physical grain are made on trust and verbal agreements. There's no reneging or changing minds. If your word is not trustworthy, your reputation is worthless.

"My agency will be extremely pleased to hear we have concluded a successful round of trade with Continental Grain. Once again you have shown yourself and your organization to be a friend of the Soviet Union, Michel. I am honored to invite you to come to Moscow later this summer, where we can conduct a formal signing of this agreement with our agriculture minister Matskevich and Exportkhleb president Pershin. We would be pleased to host your delegation and work toward building a stronger relationship with you."

"As you know, Misha, I travel to Moscow frequently, but this trip will be an exceptional pleasure. I look forward to coming to your homeland. Are you and Gregor free for dinner this evening? We would like to seal our negotiations over an exceptional New York steak if you would join us."

"Absolutely," Misha replied. Another free dinner, he thought—perfect! They agreed to meet in the hotel lobby at seven and spend the evening together.

Once the Conti group left, the two Russians hugged each other in exhilaration and then relaxed, finally able to let their guard down.

"What an exceptional day, Misha!" Gregor gushed almost as soon as the suite door closed. He was so animated as he youthfully jumped about the room, waving his arms in excitement. "I can't believe the deals you landed. President Pershin will be impressed. The Minister will be impressed."

"I think you are right, Gregor. This day exceeded all my expectations. I thought we would have to grind it out, but Michel really surprised me. I think we served our country well today."

"We are well on our way to pulling off one of the greatest deals in our country's history. You will be a national hero, my comrade!"

"Nah, there are many men above me who will manage to take any credit coming out of our efforts here, Gregor. Mark my word. But I am feeling better about our prospects in America. We are completing the task we set out to accomplish. If this first meeting is any indication of how the next couple of weeks will go for us, I am optimistic for the success of Operation Kuznechik." Misha's normally expressionless countenance finally relaxed into a broad grin as he began enjoying the moment a plan had come together.

"I'm going to lay down for a while, Gregor; rest my brain and let my nerves calm down."

"Okay. I'm going to go for a walk outside on this beautiful day and take in some American flavor."

"Okay, but don't even think about defecting!" Misha laughed, knowing Gregor to be a loyal countryman. Where did that thought come from, he wondered.

As he lay on his bed, he still had concerns about possible failure, even with this exceptional start. He feared the repercussions if they fell short of their final goal. His thoughts jumped back to 1964 and the ultimate fate of one of his heroes, Nikita Khrushchev, the former Premier and agricultural attaché. Like Misha, his career had begun in agriculture, and he had dedicated himself to his homeland, a fervent believer in communism. Yet, at the whim of a new power group in the Soviet Union, he was forced to resign and live out his last years in obscurity. Would dishonor be Misha's fate one day too? He was close to retirement, and he wondered more often these days what his future would be like. Lonely without Lily, no doubt.

Also in his thoughts were the comparably lavish experiences of international travel and his exposure to a way of life outside Russia. This taste of the more luxurious things in life was certainly in his mind and a source of conflict. It was a standard of extravagance he would never see in Moscow, or anywhere else in the Soviet Union. The special treatment he received from diplomats and grain traders reflected relationships he would not experience again once his working days came to an end.

It's no wonder he was in no hurry to retire, but if this assignment went badly, it would most certainly be his last. And yet, ironically, his success or failure in this task would most likely lead to the same outcome. One way or the other, he would be decommissioned and left to live out his days in either moderate comfort or, like Khrushchev, in obscurity.

* * *

On just the first day of meetings with grain exporters in the United States, Misha had managed to cover nearly one third of their country's projected shortfall and set the precedent for a locked-in US export subsidy as a further price incentive. Including the grain he had purchased in Canada, he was close to covering 50 percent of his target. The outcome of the first day's meetings had truly exceeded his expectations. They weren't out of the woods yet, he knew; they needed to remain vigilant.

Nevertheless, he was more optimistic than ever. Since he was now playing from a stronger hand, he decided to let the Cargill boys stew a little longer by canceling the meeting with them on Wednesday. A delay would really mess with them, he chuckled to himself. Slaski's sage advice had been right on point. Bringing him onto the team had been a wise move—no, more than that. It had been genius.

Before meeting Fribourg and Palmby for dinner, Misha and Gregor eagerly telephoned Viktor Pershin in Washington to update him on their glorious day.

"Fisenko! I hope your day went as well as mine!" Pershin bellowed exuberantly, not even waiting to hear what Misha had to say. "We negotiated a credit arrangement with the US government for 750 million dollars over three years. They backed me off from our one billion dollar request, but this is still a substantial total. We now have almost all of the financing we need to cover twenty-five million tonnes of grain at today's prices! The Soviet and US governments will make a joint, formal announcement on Saturday." He paused. "So, tell me, did you buy some grain from Continental today?"

Misha was very happy with Pershin's news about US government credit. "That is excellent news, President. Well done on your part. And, yes, we too have good news to share. Gregor and I were able to secure four million tonnes of winter wheat and four and one half million tonnes of corn from Continental Grain today. Prices are set at the current export subsidy level for wheat of a dollar sixty-three per bushel and a price on corn based on the close of the Chicago corn futures market last Wednesday of a dollar twenty-one per bushel."

"That is an outstanding effort, comrade! Now we are seeing progress, Misha. Excellent news!" Pershin was clearly pleased by this significant development. "I am breathing a big sigh of relief tonight, my friend."

"I agree," Misha said. "We were also assured by Michel Fribourg they will remain silent on this deal, allowing us both time to continue to buy. They think we are done, but we know otherwise. As an added benefit, if we find offers cheaper than the amount agreed with Conti, they will match the price. It's a 'no-lose' situation for us, Viktor."

"Ah, I look forward to advising Deputy Chairman Matskevich in the morning," Pershin said. "You are off to a fantastic start on our plan, Misha."

Now it's *our* plan, Misha thought. Pershin had been skeptical, but he was quick to get on board when the outcome appeared positive. This was as he'd expected. This was how it always worked in Russia. Even his good friend Pershin wasn't immune to the desire to look good in the eyes of his superiors.

"We have two more companies to meet this week." Misha didn't mention the couple of days off he had planned. "More meetings will follow next week; we will maintain a hectic pace. I think it would be wise to return to Winnipeg on Friday to exercise the option on the additional thirty million bushels from the Canadian Wheat Board before they learn of this business here. Their prices will most certainly rise once the full extent of our purchasing is revealed. There is no export subsidy program in Canada."

"I agree," said Pershin. "Go ahead and make your arrangements to return to Winnipeg and close the deal. I would join you, Misha, but I must return to Moscow to update the Politburo on these developments. You will then return to New York?"

"We understand, President. I wish you safe travels. And yes, if we have more deals to finalize, we will have to come back here before returning home. I will contact you later this week after we meet with both Bunge and Dreyfus."

14

Back to Plan A, The Dance - Round 3

Cargill Lake Office, Wayzata, Minnesota   July 3, 1972

Every commodity trader at the Lake Office received a summons Sunday afternoon from their department managers informing them of a must-attend meeting at seven o'clock Monday morning in the chateau's converted library, now the traders' boardroom. This wasn't just unusual; it was unprecedented. Something big was happening. Many traders had booked Monday off so they could enjoy a longer weekend around the Fourth of July holiday, but this call ended those plans. No one questioned the reasoning or even considered not attending.

Barney Saunders ran the meeting, which indicated the importance of the information he was about to share. All senior commodity managers and grain merchants were seated and ready to begin precisely at seven. Everyone knew this was not the time to wander in ten minutes late. The room was unusually silent; there was tension in the air, and the audience appeared anxious and curious.

Saunders scanned the room to make sure everyone was there. Men, women, young, old. Everyone was present. This mix of age and gender was part of Cargill's management development plan as an inclusive company relying on excellent training and mentoring to ensure a strong, diverse team and a successful future. The best of the best sat before him. Full attendance was essential to address some mighty challenges ahead of them.

Jim McCrea was one of those young merchants who had earned the opportunity to join this elite assemblage inside Cargill. This was his first emergency meeting. His emotions fluctuated between excitement and concern. He had no idea what was on the agenda.

"Ladies and gentlemen, on Saturday, Mel and I secretly met with the senior trader of Russia's Exportkhleb at the Madison Hotel in Washington."

His opening captured everyone's attention. Jim looked first at Middents and then around the table, noting the collective hum of excitement from the traders. The Russians were not regulars on Cargill's customer list.

"The Soviet Union has been an exporter of wheat for the past few years as they keep banging away at their aggressive goals to expand grain production. But, based on our market intelligence, we have suspected for some time that their winter wheat crop is short of their production goals. So short, in fact, they won't even have enough for their own needs, never mind exporting hard wheat.

"You all know Viktor sent out a tender for four million tonnes of wheat last week," Saunders continued. "For those of you new to the room, we use the nickname 'Viktor' when we're speaking about the Soviet Union. That name rings a bell with our global offices. I'm not even sure when we started using it... likely from meetings with Viktor Pershin, a great guy to deal with in the USSR.

"Anyway, back to the tender. This is the single largest request for a quotation we have ever received. It's in another league compared to the typical twenty-five thousand to forty thousand tonne cargo lots we normally trade. It sets a new standard. It may also be a harbinger of things to come. We need to take a long hard look at this, strategically and tactically. If the Russians establish trade financing, as they claim they will, and they start dealing with the United States this year, and possibly in the coming years, we could be entering a new era in agricultural commerce. This may be the biggest shift in commodity trade in everyone's career, young or old." He stressed the last phrase by pointing first at Jim and then back at himself.

"I'll give you a recap of our Saturday meeting. Their VP of agriculture, Misha Fisenko, shared with us, in confidence, that the US government is about to announce trade credit for as much as one billion dollars for Moscow to purchase US grain. At today's prices, it represents nearly one half billion bushels of grain. That's "billion" with a capital 'B,' folks, or fourteen million tonnes, likely spread out over the next three years. Like I said, this move by the Soviets could change the global grain trade. We can also share with you that Cargill Canada sold them 500 thousand tonnes of Canadian wheat last week, and the Soviets also bought a large parcel from the Canadian Wheat Board, probably several million tonnes based on Dick Dawson's best guess.

"On Saturday, Fisenko requested Cargill quote on two million tonnes each of wheat and corn," he continued. "We know they will be meeting a full roster of exporters while they are in New York this week. We intend to participate in this business, but we need to get on the right side of the market and we need to dig deep into whatever info we can find to make sure we assess the risk/reward of this business. We see this opportunity as the opening round of discussions toward a long-term relationship with Exportkhleb and a foundational affiliation we must establish. Honestly, on the financial side, if we break even on this deal during the coming year, we won't be too upset. We want to look at the long game. But make no mistake—I would prefer to make a lot of money on the deal this year if we can. If we are smart and quick, we should be able to get out in front of this one. We are already long wheat in anticipation of this buying interest, so that's a great start. Nice work, Mel!

"The follow-up to our meeting with Fisenko hasn't been set. We don't know when they will call us back, so we have to work fast. The first thing we need to do is get out of any short positions and move to the long side—wheat, corn, beans, everything! Covering our exposure is pretty obvious, and as other companies meet with the Russians they will come to the same conclusion. So review your positions and start buying—cash grain or futures, I don't care. Just get something bought! There are lots of companies who are bearish on markets. They may think prices are going down because we have so much on the supply side, but the numbers coming from Fisenko suggest we are about to witness a shift. Other grain companies don't have our network or intel, so let's play it to our advantage. I don't think we have much time to over analyze this guys.

"Mel, you and your team need to discover everything you can about winter and spring wheat crops in the Soviet Union countries. I'm not talking about US trade attaché garbage reports. Let's get the straight goods from our own sources. We have to be a party in this deal—but we don't want to lose a fortune in the process. And call Mike Slaski! I'm still pissed he left Tradax, but let's face it: he has the inside track over there and he's a great source of market info. You guys on the corn desk need to do the same thing. I want to know everything Fisenko knows. We will reconvene here at 3:00 p.m. to report on the status at the end of day. Got it? Any questions?... Okay, let's go!"

Saunders clapped his hands as if to start a race. Half the people were out of the room before the echo of the clapping had stopped. Jim quickly realized the proper speed now was full-on RUN. His mind went back to the meeting where Middents had predicted a call from Exportkhleb just two weeks ago. Would he ever reach that level of intuition? Impressive, Jim thought.

* * *

The assignment, researching data and searching for crop report information, was squarely in Jim's wheelhouse. He spent the rest of the day speaking with contacts, first with the wheat desk in Geneva and then with Dick Dawson in Winnipeg. Jim didn't know Mike Slaski, but Middents had said he would reach out to him. They were close friends. Jim also contacted the US government to gather whatever he could from them. He confirmed quantities of government-held stocks, reports of export activity and their latest assessment of crop quality and quantity across the Soviet plains. Finally, he made some strategic calls to Cargill's offices in wheat-growing regions. He didn't have time to call all of them, but he knew which ones were focal to his immediate needs.

This was the kind of exciting work Jim had signed up for when he'd interviewed with Cargill. He was on the leading edge of critical thinking and trailblazing action-oriented commerce in the commodity markets. He was thriving at this new, intense pace. By 3:00 p.m. he felt he had a strong summary and some interesting insights to share with the team. He ran it all by Middents, who gave him the green light to report his findings.

"We've got some important and surprising information to share," Middents said to get the meeting started. "Jim has unearthed key errors in USDA reports, and he also has the most recent crop information gathered from our global network. Jim, please share what you have learned with the group."

Could this get any better? Jim thought as all eyes in the room turned to him. Not only was he able to gather the necessary information, but Middents had the confidence in him to let him present.

"I'll start with crop conditions in the Soviet Union," Jim said. "Our guys in Geneva think things are a lot worse than anyone is letting on, mostly due to the adverse weather. Every day the temperatures are rising and there's little to no rain. The winterkill estimates are also high, based on extreme cold and a lack of adequate snow cover. Mel spoke with Mike Slaski and he confirmed crops aren't as lush as the Russians would like. He cautioned us to be careful and sell only what we know we can cover. The problems extend beyond the winter crops and are also affecting spring plantings. Germination has been poor and the hot dry weather has been a harsh, hostile environment for growth. The problems extend beyond the Russian border to almost all the Soviet bloc countries in the Asian region. In summary, we should expect the Soviets to fall far short of their 190 million tonne production target—possibly by as much as twenty million tonnes. It seems pretty certain they are going to need to buy more than four million tonnes of US grain or else get it from other countries.

"Here's something else I discovered during my investigation. The US Department of Agriculture quietly released a bulletin advising they have overstated inventories of winter wheat held under the Commodity Credit Corporation program. Sixty million bushels of wheat listed as winter wheat varieties is actually spring wheat. I know that's only one and a half million tonnes, a small amount in comparison to what the Soviets are likely to be seeking, but it will matter when a number of US exporters start trying to cover a spring wheat sale and discover supplies they were counting on don't exist."

"What?" Saunders blurted out. "Are you sure? That's a huge 'error.'"

"I'm sure," Jim replied. "I spoke with their chief statistician. Here's a copy of the bulletin advising the trade of the adjustment. This stuff generally gets overlooked as small-time edits. There's nothing small about this one."

"So, we should be pushing spring wheat on the Russians rather than winter wheat," Middents said. "Depending on how much winter wheat we and everyone else sells Russia, or any other buyers, it could result in a shortage."

"I agree, Mel," Saunders said. "Nice work, Jim. I knew we brought you here for a reason!" he said playfully.

The discussions proceeded as they covered other grains and critical services such as ocean freight, terminal capacity and scheduling. Spirits in the room were high. All these people got juice from these rare and exciting opportunities. The moment smacked of opportunity. Everyone knew they had the best team in the business and they exceled in moments and situations like this. But they did it through their own commitment to hard work and perseverance, not just because they were working for Cargill.

By 6:00 p.m. the plan was set. Over the course of the first day, commodity traders had managed to turn the ship on grain positions, buying 500 thousand bushels each of wheat and corn, 300 thousand bushels of sorghum and 200 thousand bushels of soybeans. They were now long all commodities in the market and planned to expand these positions judiciously in the coming days and weeks in preparation for Soviet buying. It would be "all buying—no selling" for the foreseeable future.

"These are big changes in our market positions," Middents said. "And they are big positions outright. Normally we don't take on this level of risk, preferring to work on handling margins. But these aren't normal times, people. Additional risk is necessary. So, we'll just call these trades 'anticipatory hedges,' shall we?" He smiled at the weak justification to take on such large outright long positions in the market, but the stakes had been raised by the Soviets, forcing a different and bold approach. These were definitely not times for the faint of heart. Saunders would have to report this activity to the Cargill family ownership group to make sure they were on board with the unprecedented risk to the family fortune.

It was decided that Jim would attend the next meeting with the Soviets in New York along with Saunders and Middents. He had earned the opportunity, and it looked like wheat would be the central focus of discussion—at least from Cargill's perspective. Saunders and Middents suggested that Misha might be trying to slow-play what was actually a dire situation. They also decided they would promote spring wheat to him as opposed to winter wheat. After all, there was a lot more of it in storage than most people realized. They were ready to trade. For now, they had to wait patiently until "Viktor" called.

Hilton Hotel, New York City   July 4, 1972

Misha was anxious to make another call after their meeting with Continental. He couldn't wait to update Slaski on his outstanding, unexpected success. He made the call early on Tuesday morning from the hotel suite.

"Hello, Mike. I have exceptionally good news to share. I think you will be shocked; I sure was. Our first meeting with Conti went flawlessly. I went off our tactical plan to delay buying, but you will understand why shortly. The results are so much better than we imagined.

You won't believe it, really. I'm having trouble accepting what we accomplished, and I was in the room when it happened!"

"You have my attention, my friend," Slaski said eagerly. "Let's hear the details. You're killing me here!"

Misha recapped the session with the Continental reps and defended his decision to accept Fribourg's offer. They spoke for nearly thirty minutes. It would be an expensive call from the hotel, but Misha didn't care. He'd needed to talk with Slaski.

"I'm stunned, Misha. I said you could pull it off, but I never dreamed you would come away with such an enormous deal so quickly, and from just one company. Nice work! I've never seen a grain company act so aggressively. I'll give them credit for being risk takers. Eight and a half million tonnes of grain…and financing from their government too? Jesus Christ! That's a helluva trade and a major coup for you, Misha. This has to be the largest single grain deal by anyone, ever. You'll be a legend!"

"Ha! A legend indeed." Misha blushed. "There will be a lot of people at Exportkhleb who must share in the glory of this deal if we succeed. I don't want to get too excited yet. We still have a lot to do."

"Of course, but it's smooth sailing from here. You can see how the situation has shifted in your favor. You are in complete control of the negotiations now. Who do you meet next?"

"It's Independence Day here in America today, as you know. We could have insisted on meeting, but I wanted to spread out the discussions, and I wasn't expecting we would close the deal with Fribourg in one day. Tomorrow is also open, and then on Thursday we meet with both Dreyfus and Bunge. My original plan was to meet with Cargill tomorrow, but now I favor waiting until next Monday before calling them. Hopefully, they will be more eager to deal and we will have a better idea of how much more we need to complete our mission. Saunders and Middents have the tender, but we haven't scheduled the next meeting yet. The delay will create some concern and uncertainty, which I hope will work in our favor."

"Good plan, Misha. The way this has evolved gives you some room to maneuver. If you lowball Dreyfus and Bunge on price, they can either deal at a discount or pass on this round. I think you will have a chance to book them later at the same price as Conti if they don't trade now. I love the way you're handling Cargill, like a fish on a line; pull them in close and then let them run off. Ha! That's probably my favorite part in this. Not to screw the guys at Cargill, just to make them work for it. They called me, by the way, to ask about crop conditions. My answer was pretty vague."

"Well, I'm glad this pleases you, Mike. It's certainly a stressor on me, but I'm less stressed tonight after a great day. We'll regroup with you after the next round of meetings to let you know how it goes, or doesn't go, as the plan unfolds."

As he hung up, a question regarding Slaski's motive, his loyalty and trustworthiness crossed Misha's mind. Was he being genuine with him or was he trying to help his old friends at Cargill avoid the trap they'd devised? As always, Slaski could be expected to have a plan within a plan, or even more layers. It reminded him of Ukrainian Medovik, a multi-layered honey cake. The image fit Slaski to a T. Misha didn't want to get caught in his own strategy by trusting the wrong person. Even though he had no reason not to trust Slaski, he was suspicious by nature, and that attribute had served him well over the years. He would pay close attention to their conversations and Cargill's behavior, watching for any signal that suggested he was becoming the rabbit in his own snare.

Misha made sure Gregor was out of the suite before making one additional call to Geneva. He had another piece of business to conduct, which had been dependent on his early North American meetings. The rapid progress of the day had forced him to decide on a separate, personal course of action—an irreversible, life-altering choice.

* * *

With no meetings scheduled for Tuesday or Wednesday, and an obvious cause for celebration, Misha suggested to Gregor they take in some of the sights and sounds of Manhattan. Gregor enthusiastically agreed. They wandered the streets of the Big Apple, taking in the zoo at Central Park, the Statue of Liberty and the Empire State building. The streets were loud and boisterous. People yelling across the streets to each other, music playing from many shops and an incessant blaring of horns coalesced into a fabric of sound and culture they had never experienced in their lives. It was chaos to Misha and Gregor, but apparently just a normal day for the locals who seemed to thrive in the pandemonium.

During the evening they ventured out to try hotdogs from a street vendor and take in Times Square and the sights and sounds of Broadway by night. That evening they were entertained by a glorious display of fireworks along the Hudson River and loud, spirited music. Where better to experience America's Independence Day festivities than in the heart of its largest city? The event was reminiscent of Russia's annual celebrations on October Revolution Day. It too paid tribute to sovereignty, but it was more about parades and the display of military might than explosions of color and boisterous dancing. Still shy of two hundred years old, America lacked the maturity of a long-standing nation like Russia. Its festivities made Misha think of a children's birthday party in comparison to a night at the opera—raucous and raw compared to civilized and sophisticated.

But both men had to admit they were having fun. New York was vibrant. There was a sense of joy and bravado in the Americans on the streets and in the restaurants and bars. Even the banter between customers and shop vendors had a tone of family squabble rather than anger. It was theater on the street for all to enjoy. Americans were riding a wave of success as a country; their economy was strong and their spirits were high. This effervescent mood stood in stark contrast to the seriousness and pathos of Russian citizens. Not that Russians weren't prideful, but they displayed it in a more sedate, solemn manner.

"These people in America can say and do whatever they want, can't they, Misha," Gregor said as they walked along Broadway. "There are police on the street, but they seem to be part of the whole experience rather than threatening enforcement."

"You're right, Gregor. This is capitalism at its primal level. Every one of these people can succeed or fail of their own accord. They come and go as they like, answering to no one. The whole thing seems chaotic and unorganized, doomed to fail. And yet, somehow, it works."

"You've traveled a lot more than me, Misha, to many cities and countries. Does living a life somewhere other than Russia appeal to you?"

Misha picked up on the subtle signal Gregor was sending. It was easy to fall prey to the bright lights and perpetual wall of sound of New York, he knew.

"This is too much for me, Gregor," Misha answered honestly. "I wouldn't last a month in a place like this. But I can definitely enjoy a night of their craziness, and their vodka is surprisingly good too!"

He didn't lie to Gregor, but he did dodge the specific question. New York was not a good fit for Misha—but he could think of a few places that were. It's no wonder the Russian government screened who was allowed to leave the country and monitored them while they were away. He didn't want to give Gregor the wrong idea or challenge his loyalty to the Soviet Union.

"Gregor, my comrade, let's have a couple more drinks before we end our day. We need to be sharp again tomorrow as we plan for the next day of meetings."

Hilton Hotel, New York City   July 6-7, 1972

The remainder of the week Misha danced with US grain traders and the export companies they represent. He downplayed deal sizes, speaking of 300 thousand to 750 tonne possibilities, which of course represented only portions of the four million tonne tender. This maintained the illusion of a total amount not exceeding four million tonnes. Misha and Gregor never spoke of their agreement with Continental Grain. The two Russians entertained negotiations with several major exporters, including Louis Dreyfus Corporation, Bunge Corporation, and Cook Industries. Each one left the suite at the Hilton Hotel frustrated. They had all failed to close a deal to capture part of this tempting, re-emerging Eastern European market. In every case, the point of resistance was price. The tonnage quantities of the pending deals and the shipping terms were all amenable, but Misha persisted on low-balling, citing the growing USA stockpile. His ideas on price were well below the current world values and outside the range of profitability for the exporters, even when they included the US government's export subsidy. The week ended with no additional deals and a bevy of frustrated, confused and exasperated exporters. But, as determined as Misha was to secure even lower prices, he was unable to crack the price floor of a dollar sixty-three a bushel. No one was prepared to take a risk and sell below current market values.

Western White House, San Clemente, California   July 8, 1972

On Saturday, as promised, the US Department of Commerce announced the largest trade credit deal with the Soviet Union in the history of the two superpowers. The United States was prepared to loan the Soviets 750 million dollars over three years for the purchase of American-produced cereal grains and oilseeds. The Soviets had agreed to utilize a minimum of 200 million dollars annually and pay interest on the loans. Agriculture Secretary Earl Butz confirmed these funds would stimulate the American farm economy by introducing a large new global customer. The ripple effect would be felt throughout the agricultural sector by creating income and jobs ranging from farm input dealers to equipment manufacturers and increased use of truck and rail transportation, grain handling and export terminal activity. The Nixon administration took full credit for the trade financing as a direct result of their persistent international negotiations.

The deal also hinted at the potential end for both production and export agriculture commodity subsidies and the return to a more market-driven economy. By eliminating the grain set-aside program, designed to take supply off the market and support domestic prices, the US government stood to save one and a half million dollars annually on grain storage costs and as much as forty million dollars annually in funding the program. No mention was made of eliminating the export subsidy, however, even in the face of the Soviet commitment and the US government's intelligence reporting of potential crop problems with Soviet winter crops.

In the government's view, this agreement was a huge win for both countries. The potential for higher commodity prices and increased exports was music to the ears of President Richard Nixon's campaign re-election team. This agreement would clinch voter support from rural America and virtually guarantee a win in November.

On Monday morning, the Chicago wheat market rallied one cent per bushel and ended the day lower than the close on Friday. The announcement of a trade deal with the Soviet Union for agricultural products didn't impress market traders. In fact, for the entire month of July 1972, the market was flat. Trade credit didn't mean actual deals, and market participants were skeptical that anything material would come out of the Republican party's touting of possible commerce.

15

Deals, Deals, Deals - Round 4

Hilton Hotel, New York City   July 10, 1972

During the following week, the Soviets changed their game plan. They shifted their tactics from being tire kickers to being dealmakers. On Monday morning, at 9:00 a.m. sharp Minneapolis time, Misha Fisenko called Cargill's Barney Saunders.

"Barney, can you and your grain team meet with us in our suite at the Hilton later today?"

"Yes, we can, Misha. We'll take our corporate jet." Getting right to the point, Saunders asked, "What grains are we talking about today?"

"Let's start with wheat," Misha replied. His wording implied other grains might be on the table for discussion.

"We will arrange a flight, and I'll let you know when we can get to your hotel."

"Excellent. See you later today."

Misha had deliberately waited until Monday morning to make the call to Cargill, purposely giving Saunders little time to prepare. It was all part of his strategy to keep the Cargill team off balance. He could have arranged the meeting anytime last week, but he wanted to make sure they felt left out. They already knew too much, Misha thought. He hoped this strategy would undermine their confidence.

Misha hung up the phone and walked straight into a meeting with Philip McCaull, the executive VP for Louis Dreyfus Corporation, another global grain-trading giant. Misha didn't feel the need to draw this out. It was time to make deals. In less than one hour, he had agreed to purchase 750 thousand tonnes of wheat from Dreyfus—nearly one fifth of the tender quantity. McCaull was ecstatic, clearly satisfied with the quantity and a price equivalent to world values with the US subsidy included.

Right after lunch, Misha closed another deal for 300 thousand tonnes of wheat with Ned Cook of Cook Industries, the smallest of the big six companies. Cook was an aggressive North American trader who wanted to expand his company's reach. Misha welcomed all sellers.

*   *   *

At 4:30 p.m. the Cargill team, including Jim McCrea, arrived to meet with Misha and Gregor. One more person didn't matter, as the jet was going anyway and there were open seats. If Jim was to play a role in assessing the potential risk/reward of this deal, it would be worthwhile exposing him to the Russian's presentation and deal making.

Saunders introduced Jim to Misha and Gregor.

"Your traders get younger every year, Barney," Misha joked as he eyed Jim over and shook his hand energetically.

"I wish this was true, Misha, but the painful reality is guys like you and me are just getting older."

"Ah, yes. It is true," he laughed. "But I don't need the reminder. It is nice to meet you, Jim. Thank you for joining us today."

Jim was impressed with Misha's English as well as his respectful manner. Fisenko obviously recognized his youth and obvious inexperience but was giving him respect as an equal in the meeting. A good first impression.

"Thank you, Vice President Fisenko." Jim responded formally, returning the respect. A good time to start building a relationship, Jim felt, harkening back to the words of Julius Hendel and his counsel on the importance of Cargill's customers.

All the men but Misha took seats.

"Based on our conversation last week, gentlemen, I would like to know what you can offer us in response to our tender. You have seen your commerce department's announcement confirming the 750 million dollar credit deal between our governments, so there is a good starting point for us to negotiate."

"Thank you for inviting us here today, Misha. We were beginning to wonder if you had filled your order and gone home," Saunders grinned. "We are pleased to be here now. So, let me turn things over to Mel to provide the details on our offer today."

"Thanks, Barney," Middents began. "Misha, Gregor, we put together offers on two million tonnes each of wheat and corn after speaking with you last weekend."

"Let's just deal with wheat today."

Misha's interruption brought confused looks to Saunders and Middents' face. He kept moving back and forth between wheat and corn, making it difficult to close a deal. Their team planning and preparation had made them ready for all possibilities, though.

"Okay, fine." Middents pressed on. "We can offer you one million tonnes of winter wheat FOB various US East Coast ports at a base price of sixty dollars five cents per tonne spread out from October 1972 through July 1973. We would also propose a small modification to your tender and ask you to consider our offer of an additional one million tonnes of spring wheat on those same terms."

Misha replied without hesitation. "My counter to your offer, gentlemen, is fifty-nine forty a tonne for the winter wheat. I'm not interested in spring wheat. The impurity from ergot fungus is a great concern to us. It is a deadly contaminant. We are reluctant to purchase this class of wheat based on your country's history."

"Misha, I can assure you, spring wheat grown in the United States is virtually ergot-free. Any product with disease problems does not enter the handling system. Full stop. You can expect top-quality grain from us, my friend."

"We are not prepared to purchase spring wheat on this mission, Mel," Misha said. "I will need further assurances before we even consider such a purchase."

"We thought you might feel that way, Misha. In order to address your concerns, we would be happy to host you on a tour of the spring wheat production area and show you firsthand how spring wheat is farmed and handled," Middents said. "We can introduce you to the plant breeders and farmers in the plains area of the United States and give you a full tour."

"I am not the best person to participate in a fact-finding mission regarding plant disease," Misha admitted. "But we could send a plant technician, maybe a cereals chemist and a breeder. I would join them for the tour on a future trip to the United States. Can we consider it for next month if we return to America?"

"Very well," Middents said. "Can we agree on one million tonnes of winter wheat at sixty dollars five cents per tonne?"

"We cannot," Misha replied. "I will show you a contract we signed earlier today with Cook Industries. Their price is fifty-nine point five two five per tonne. I am not inclined to pay more."

Middents looked at Saunders. Saunders nodded, and Middents agreed to the same price. "If we offer at your price, do we have a deal?"

"Yes, Exportkhleb would agree to those terms."

"Excellent! We have an agreement, then," said Middents.

"May I suggest we return tomorrow with a contract and we seal our agreement over dinner tomorrow evening?" Saunders asked.

* * *

Jim couldn't wait for the privacy of the hotel elevator to get a debriefing from Saunders and Middents on the meeting. What had just happened? They'd sold wheat, not corn, and got bullied on the price.

"We were buying corn, based on our first meeting with these guys. Now all they want to talk about is wheat, and we just locked in the largest single wheat sale in our company's history. We've got our work cut out for us, guys," Saunders blurted once the elevator doors had closed.

"No shit!" responded Middents. "We got out of our short wheat position last week, but this sale puts us back in the negative. But that's okay; we'll start covering in the Chicago market tomorrow. I just hope Cook and whoever else sold Viktor today doesn't hit the market with buying orders at the same time. We could all get killed."

"I agree with Dick. I think they'll buy more wheat if we offer it to them," Middents said. "If he bought a million from us and 300 thousand from Cook, you know he is dealing with Conti and several others. I'd bet he's already over four million tonnes. I'm not anxious to sell any more until we get this deal covered, but I still think we should push the spring wheat angle. Jim, can you arrange a tour in North Dakota? Let's try and resource experts through the university in Fargo and schedule a farm visit through our local elevator manager. Pick one of his best spring wheat growers and let's wow Fisenko with US crop production. Make tentative arrangements for some time in the middle of August, and we will finalize dates with him. I have another call scheduled with Mike Slaski Wednesday morning. Let's see if he has further insights on this situation."

"Wow, indeed! This is a memorable day for Cargill, boys. A million-tonne sale to Russia is a very encouraging outcome," Saunders said as they exited the Hilton to take a cab back to their hotel.

Hilton Hotel, New York City   July 11, 1972

Prior to signing Cargill's contracts the following day, Misha resumed his buying spree. He locked up 550 thousand tonnes of wheat from another of the Big Six grain companies, the Swiss firm Garnac.

Later in the morning, the three traders from Cargill arrived back at the suite with their contracts for one million tonnes of winter wheat to be signed. Before arriving at the hotel Cargill had reversed most of their long position in the corn market, replacing it with as many wheat futures as they could buy without triggering a run on the market. The day following the flurry of deals with the Russians, CBOT trading volume was higher than any day during the previous year. Farmers jumped at the chance to lock in slightly higher prices than they'd seen for more than a year.

The Cargill team persisted in their efforts to convince Misha the Soviets should consider buying spring wheat from the United States even though they were sensitive to his concerns about fungus. Saunders updated Misha on their crop tour offer.

"Misha, we have arranged for a visit to North Dakota to meet with plant geneticists and to tour a farm growing spring wheat. You and your scientists can get a firsthand look at the crop and speak with unbiased industry experts. We would be happy to host this tour."

"That is most generous of you, Barney. I think we would like to see it for ourselves. I will let you know when we might be able to arrange another trip to North America, sometime in the middle of August most likely. As I mentioned, I would like to bring some of our own plant geneticists and scientists. Is that acceptable to you?"

"Yes, let's get the right people talking to each other so we can lay the groundwork for spring wheat transactions. Are you and Gregor still free to join us for dinner this evening? We thought you might enjoy the food at the new Four Seasons Hotel, where we are staying."

"Most definitely." Misha was thankful for the invitation to another hosted dinner. "We will take a cab and meet you there for seven."

After making plans to continue their discussions over dinner, the Cargill contingent left, and Misha ordered room service for lunch.

* * *

After lunch, Michel Fribourg returned to the Hilton with copies of their Continental Grain contracts for signature. He was still open to deal more, as the market had not yet reflected any knowledge of the business they had conducted. He was certainly unaware of any additional trades Misha had finalized. During the afternoon session with Fribourg, Misha bought an additional one million tonnes, 850 thousand tonnes more of winter wheat and 150 thousand tonnes of soft white wheat.

The meeting with Conti went longer than expected, so when the phone rang at three o'clock, the time he had arranged to meet with Cook Industries, Misha was not prepared.

"Excuse me," he said to the Conti traders as he headed to the bedroom to take the call. "I'll just be a minute, and then we can conclude."

"Misha, Ned Cook here. Willard Sparkes and I are in the lobby. Let's trade some grain!" he said in his unique, engaging southern manner.

Cook and his team could wait, Misha thought. Conti was their primary supplier, and he had no intention of appearing to brush them off.

"I'm sorry, Mr. Cook. I will require a few more minutes. Can you call back in a half hour?"

"As long as you don't buy everything from someone else before we meet," Cook quipped.

"Well, we'll just have to see," Misha joked back.

Back in the main room, he re-engaged with the senior Conti traders. A stack of grain contracts for four million tonnes of wheat and four and one half million tonnes of corn sat on the table between them. The paperwork was symbolic of the largest grain transaction in history. Even given the enormity of the deal, it was irrevocable in the minds of these two seasoned traders because of their earlier verbal agreement. The contracts were necessary for legal purposes and evidence of export subsidy eligibility. Neither party hesitated to finalize the verbal agreements they had made.

"I will get another set of contracts for you for this additional million tonnes of wheat, Misha. I'll make sure they're delivered to the hotel. You can call me when they're signed and we'll pick them up at the front desk. Okay?"

"That sounds fine, Michel. Exportkhleb appreciates your efforts, and we value the strong relationship between us."

"As do I, Misha. As do I."

* * *

Michel Fribourg left the Soviet suite to return to his New York office. As he exited the elevator in the lobby, he encountered Ned Cook, who was obviously next on Fisenko's schedule of appointments.

"I'm guessing you're here for the same reason as me." Cook grinned as he rose to shake Fribourg's hand.

"Yes, Ned, I'm sure that's true."

"So, what can you tell me, Michel? Did you fill his order book already?"

"He's a difficult negotiator, Ned. We're trying our best, as usual, but Exportkhleb doesn't bend much on their terms. It's their way or not at all."

"I'll soften him up," Cook said confidently as he pulled out a bottle of his branded bourbon from a gift bag. "*Cook's Bourbon Blend*, fine southern whiskey. It's from our private stock."

"Misha's a vodka man. Bourbon is an acquired taste," Fribourg said. "But I'm sure he'll gladly accept your gift." He knew Misha's affinity for a good stiff drink.

The two traders measured each other, hoping to glean trade information, but neither revealed the deals they had already finalized with Fisenko. Secrecy was critical at this stage of dealings with the Soviets.

"Good luck, Ned," Fribourg said as he headed for the exit and Ned Cook and Willard Sparks headed to the elevator.

* * *

Cook and Sparks had never met Misha Fisenko before their meeting the previous day, although they both knew several of Exportkhleb's senior officials, Misha's bosses. When the door opened in response to their knock, they were welcomed by a large gregarious man with a huge smile on his face and a massive hand extended in greeting.

"Hello, Misha. It's great to see you again today," Cook gushed. "I brought contracts for you to sign for our three hundred thousand tonnes deal. And we are prepared to double the amount to six hundred thousand tonnes on the same terms right here and now!" Cook's bold and forthright style put it all out there for one to accept.

Misha found his Tennessee accent charming and even a little intoxicating. Cook had a genuinely pleasant persona and there was a likeability to him. His larger-than-life appearance was accented by a boney hawk-nose, and Misha had felt comfortable with him from the moment they'd met.

Willard Sparks was the polar opposite to Cook. He remained noticeably quiet during their meetings, but when he spoke or asked questions it was evident he had a deep and wide knowledge of the global agricultural scene. They were a formidable team.

"I think we can accommodate your additional offer, Ned," Misha replied. They had been on a first-name basis from their previous meeting at Ned's insistence. He was a very informal man, whereas Sparks maintained a professional decorum in both speech and dress. "I'm wondering if you might be interested in increasing the volume from an additional three hundred thousand tonnes to, say, five hundred thousand tonnes?"

"Well." Cook paused. "We hadn't considered a larger amount, Misha. What do you think, Willard?"

"I would like to re-assess the deal before adding more," Sparks said. "I'm comfortable with our new total of six hundred thousand tonnes, but I would like a little more time to consider more. We could be in a position to sell you soybeans if you're interested. Soybean meal is an excellent animal feed, Misha. It would be an option for you to consider as part of your expanding feed needs to meet your Five-Year Plan."

"That's an interesting proposal, Willard." Misha realized Sparks had done his homework and understood the new Soviet food plan. "Let us do a bit of research on the nutritional value and what we might be willing to pay."

"Listen," interjected Cook. "What are y'all's plans next week, Misha?"

"I am remaining here in New York for at least another week to finalize our program. Gregor is returning to Moscow on Friday."

"Well, that's perfect. Why don't you come to our home office as the guest of Cook Industries and we'll show you around the beautiful city of Memphis and the great state of Tennessee? You can tour some southern soybean operations and also enjoy our southern hospitality. Maybe you'll have some thoughts on buying beans and we can consider additional wheat tonnage."

Misha really had no idea what to expect from Cook and his company, but the potential to buy more grain was alluring, and the offer to travel to Tennessee was generous. He would have some free time next week. Why not, he thought.

"I will gladly accept your offer, Ned. I could leave New York late on the eighteenth as long as you can get me back here by Thursday. I have tentative plans to return to Moscow on Friday the twenty-first."

"Okay, we have a plan, then! I'll make our private jet available for you on those days. You and Willard can crunch the numbers and see if we can do some more dealing.

"Now I'd like to propose we seal the deal with a celebratory drink, Misha. I brought a bottle of Cook Industries custom-blend bourbon whiskey. We've been bottling this stuff for over thirty years. Started as a backwoods still, and now we are legal and sell it all over the world. I know you're a vodka man, but I think you might like the taste of our southern corn mash."

Misha glanced at Gregor. "I'd say our day is done. Can you get some ice from the machine in the hall, please, Gregor?"

Cook presented Misha with the bottle and went in search of some glasses. For the next hour the men sipped Cook's finest bourbon, toasted the grain deal, their new friendship and numerous other less important but otherwise toast-worthy items.

The past two days had gone well for Misha. He had secured another 3.9 million tonnes of grain. A good result by any measure. A small celebration was in order, although he had to drink in moderation, as he and Gregor had dinner plans with Cargill in a couple of hours.

"I'll get travel information to you tomorrow, Misha. I look forward to seeing you in Memphis next week."

"Maybe you could introduce me to your famous singer Elvis Presley when we are in Memphis?" Misha asked a bit sheepishly.

"Ha! Now, there are some miracles I can accomplish while others are just a little out of my reach," Ned said with a laugh. "Maybe, if you buy a million tonnes of soybeans from us, we'll see what we can do."

Everyone was in good spirits when Cook and Sparks left the Russians around five-thirty.

Four Seasons Hotel, New York City   July 11, 1972

Misha and Gregor met the three Cargill traders, Saunders, Middents and McCrea, for dinner later that evening at the elegant Four Seasons Hotel restaurant. During their earlier meeting, Misha had hoped to convince Cargill to increase the amount of their committed tonnage from one million tonnes to two or even three million. Cargill was either the largest or second largest privately owned grain company in the world, and they had the capacity to source more grain. Continental Grain was their adversary. Since both companies were private and exceptionally secretive, no one really knew which one was the largest. In Misha's mind it didn't matter, but it was curious how differently the two companies approached business with Exportkhleb. Both wanted to trade, but Conti's Michel Fribourg was much more aggressive and action oriented. If Conti was being so aggressive, why was Cargill being so conservative, he wondered.

Throughout dinner Saunders pressed the spring wheat variety but, until Misha got clearance from their crop scientists, he had to decline any of those offers. The plan was to stick with winter wheat. If their decision meant no more business with Cargill, then so be it. The other companies seemed willing to trade more.

For Jim McCrea, the evening provided his first opportunity to socialize and observe international buyers up close and personal. He wanted to understand their approach to business relationships, their motivation to trade and any subtle nuances the Russians might reveal about themselves, their tactics or their organization. He found them to be tremendously protective of their information, motivations and strategies. When it came to who was interrogating who, there was no question. Misha had many questions and very few answers. He was skilled at deflecting or evading questions and turning the discussion back to his own point of view.

Middents pursued their future trading needs. They knew from their last conversation with Misha that he planned to return to the United States later in August.

"Have you bought everything you came here to buy, Misha?" Middents asked. "Or do you plan to send out another tender to buy additional tonnage when you return next month?"

"This I honestly cannot tell you, Mel. I will return to Moscow and meet with the agricultural teams of our member countries to discuss their needs and allocate the grain we have purchased. It's no secret we want to use as much local production as possible, and you also know we have goals to improve overall food quality and quantity for our citizens. Future buying will depend on how far our government is prepared to take their pledge. My sense is we have secured enough," he lied.

"How much did you buy in total?"

"Ha! This I will not reveal, Mel," Misha said with a grin. "I would no more tell the other companies how much we bought from Cargill. This would betray a confidence and violate the covenant of a deal you and the other traders cherish so much. I will confirm we covered the amount we tendered here in the United States, and, as you well know, we bought our traditional quantity from the Canadian Wheat Board. I am hopeful this is all we will need this year." The truth was Misha had bought nearly triple the amount of their announced tender and he knew he wasn't done yet. But it was absolutely vital the industry viewed him as being done. More buying interest could spook the markets before they were finished securing their needs. This was the mistake Khrushchev had made and one he was determined not to repeat. He wanted to dispel any suspicions of additional demand, and the best way to give the impression of being done was to celebrate as if they were. And by "celebrating," he meant drinking!

Jim quickly discovered he was a lightweight when it came to drinking with the Russians. These guys partied hard and got louder and more boisterous as the evening wore on. He was relieved when Saunders announced they would have to leave to catch their plane home.

"As much as we would like to extend the celebration, Misha, we are scheduled to return to Minneapolis tonight. Jim will contact you regarding the trip to North Dakota. We hope you will gain confidence in our spring wheat. North Dakota isn't far from Canada, and you like their spring wheat, don't you?"

"We do, but the Canadian winters are long and cold. This controls a lot of plant disease and bug infestation. But we will be happy to learn more about US-grown spring wheat."

The Cargill team said goodbye to Misha and Gregor in the lobby of the Four Seasons as they headed to the Executive Airport. The Russians followed them out the door and headed down the streets of New York. They were primed and looking for some action, Jim thought. Heading back to Minnesota was a comforting thought to him as he considered what kind of trouble those two could find in one of the largest cities in the world.

* * *

The two Russians took a left turn, heading toward Broadway in Lower Manhattan in an apparent search for some American excitement. But they opted for fresh air on a short walk rather than another late night on the town. Misha wanted to return to the hotel and contact Slaski. A week had passed since they'd last spoken, and he felt the urge to update him on their progress. Back at the Hilton the men went to their separate rooms for the evening, and Misha made his call to Switzerland.

"Good morning, Mike. I'm sorry to call so early. I hope I didn't wake you."

"No, no. I'm an early riser, Misha. No problem. What time is it there?"

"Just after midnight. We had dinner tonight with your old friends from Cargill. We bought a million tonnes of wheat from them today."

"That's excellent news! Who did you meet with?"

"Saunders, Middents and a young new trader fresh out of the country system."

"Well, I hope you made them pay for dinner?"

"Porterhouse steaks all around, Mike. They paid. The food here is so fantastic! I think I'm gaining weight already." Misha chuckled.

"So, tell me what else has happened this week, Misha. Did you buy more than the million from Cargill?"

"Yes, we did. After shifting back to our plan and sending them all home without any business last week, we started to lock in tonnage, spreading our purchases between four companies: Dreyfus, Cook, Cargill and Garnac. And we secured another one million tonnes from Conti. So, all told, including the Canadian tonnage, we are just over fifteen million tonnes as of right now."

"Unbelievable, Misha! And the price? What are you having to pay?"

"There's the best part, Mike. The US government is holding firm on their export subsidy program, and we have locked in every single tonne at fifty-nine–fifty."

"I can't believe it! You are well on your way to pulling off one of the greatest grain heists in history, my friend. Even if you end up paying more for the remaining grain, you are so far ahead of what I imagined possible. I just can't believe it. What government idiot oversees those decisions?"

"You know I'm not the most political guy at Exportkhleb, Mike. I leave that stuff to Viktor. But he tells me the decisions are being made at the highest level. Nixon and Kissinger are calling the shots on their trade policy. They want to get re-elected in a few months, and we think they want to be seen as international trade heroes building bridges between our countries. They seem pretty determined to end the Cold War and go down in history with that legacy. As it happens, agriculture offers a way for them to achieve their goals. I sure didn't see this gift coming, but it has made the impossible possible.

"I'm wondering, Mike, could you come to Moscow and meet with the team when we return?" Misha asked. "I'm going back to Winnipeg this week to exercise our option on another million tonnes with the CWB, and we will finalize contracts and some freight discussions next week here in New York. I'd like you to join us for our team discussions the week of the twenty-fourth at the Exportkhleb office."

"I would love to join you and your team, Misha. I'll make arrangements to travel right away."

"Excellent. Maybe you and I can spend some time together before the team meeting. Can you arrive earlier on the twenty-third?"

"Definitely."

"Great. Let's plan on meeting around eleven at the Russian Historical Museum in Red Square."

"I know the distinguished building well, Misha, but I have never been inside. I look forward to it. I'll see you then."

"Dasvidaniya, my friend."

"Bye, Misha."

16

Cargill's Radar

Cargill Lake Office, Wayzata, Minnesota   July 12, 1972

Cargill's full complement of traders at the Lake Office convened in the boardroom at nine o'clock Wednesday morning for their weekly merchandising meeting, all anxious to hear the details on the dealings with the Russians. Internally, there were rumors of some huge trades with the Soviet buyer—"huge" as in the biggest deals in the company's history. News like this brought a heightened excitement to the marketplace in general and commodity traders individually. There was no chitchat among the traders as they anxiously awaited the update. The only sound in the room was the incessant clicking of a Reuters machine against a far wall. The traders were so accustomed to that noise they didn't even hear it.

"They're a shifty bunch," Middents began. "They tendered hard wheat, told us to come back with an offer on corn and then reversed again, buying the hard wheat and not even mentioning corn! I really can't figure out their tactics other than to say they are deliberately complicating the process to put us off. We have no idea if they're treating others the same way. I certainly hope so. We've dealt with the Russians before, but there's a lot of political angst between the Soviet and American leaders currently, and I think that's playing a part in their negotiating techniques. Based on the early meetings, I think it's safe to say we can't trust anything they say until we actually confirm a deal.

"To that point, we did manage to book one million tonnes of hard wheat with them," Middents said. This confirmed his reputation as a big dealmaker. The news brought a loud cheer from everyone in the room. Each of them recognized the significance of a trade of this magnitude—and the risk attached to it. "In case you didn't know, it is the single largest transaction in the company's history. And we think they're open to buy more. We have no idea how much they have acquired from others so far, but we know they met with all the major companies at least once already. Conti has been back and forth to the Hilton a few times. If the Russians stick to their tender amount of four million tonnes, then we locked in one quarter of their business.

"We didn't sell them any corn. In the end, they didn't even ask for an offer. We also couldn't convince them to consider buying spring wheat, although we did manage to get them to commit to a crop tour in North Dakota next month to learn more about it. The tour will cost us a few bucks, but it will be money well spent if we close a large deal like the hard wheat one. Let's go around the room and recap our grain positions."

One by one, the grain merchants summarized their positions in the market and the adjustments they had made based on feedback from dealings with the Russians.

Winter wheat – Short 650 thousand tonnes including this recent sale

Spring wheat – Long 240 thousand tonnes in anticipation of business

Corn – Close to even after learning the Russians weren't buyers

Soybeans – Long 150 thousand tonnes on spec

"All right," Middents said. "Let's get our hard wheat short position covered. That's our number one priority. I would prefer to buy cash grain now from farmers rather than cover the position with futures contracts. So, let's sweeten the cash price a bit more. We don't want to move the markets unnecessarily, and neither will the other grain companies. But I'm guessing most companies have sold something, so it's likely we're all short to the Russian now—a dangerous prospect.

"Any questions, folks? Okay, we'll meet again tomorrow morning. This will be a daily event for as long as the Russian is active. Meeting adjourned. Jim, come back here at ten and we'll reach out to Slaski. I scheduled another call with him for then."

* * *

At ten o'clock Jim met Middents back in the boardroom to get Slaski on the speaker phone.

"Good afternoon, Mike. Thanks for taking our call. I have our newest wheat merchant here in the room with me." Middents yelled at the speaker in the middle of the table as if he were trying to be heard across a vast distance. "Jim McCrea, meet Mike Slaski."

"Hi, Mel. You sound like you're inside a barrel with your fancy technology," Slaski laughed. "But I can hear you fine. Nice meeting you, Jim. How are you finding the Lake Office? I've spent a bit of time there in my days with Cargill."

"Hello, Mr. Slaski," Jim replied formally. "I would say intimidating and invigorating all at the same time."

"Mr. Slaski is my dad, Jim. Call me Mike."

"Will do, sir." Jim couldn't distance himself entirely from the formality and respect he held for senior traders.

"Mike, I'll get right to it," said Middents. "You know Exportkhleb is tendering for four million tonnes of US hard winter wheat. Fisenko is still in New York, and we think he's buying up a storm. We hope you have some additional intel on the Soviet wheat crops and maybe a little insight on what is happening over there."

"Yes, I knew of the tender. I'm also aware the Soviet winter wheat crop is under stress. That's obviously why Exportkhleb are buyers this year and not sellers. But how bad is it? I really don't know. They don't share crop info, as you well know, Mel.

"As I mentioned to you the last time we spoke, and just between us on this call, I think you need to tread carefully here. I can't say a lot, as I find myself in conflicting circumstances. I can't share numbers with you, but I can say the crop looks bleak. Like, really bleak. I know you want to be part of the deal. I know you already are—both in Canada and the US. But, guys, I wouldn't overextend on this one."

As Jim wondered how Slaski already knew about their dealings with Exportkhleb, Middents asked the question.

"Why would you think we've made deals already? How could you know this?"

"I know many things, Mel."

"I think you're playing me along now, Mike, trying to gather information."

"Would you like me to tell you how you ordered your steak at the Four Seasons Hotel last night, Mel?"

The Cargill men exchanged similar puzzled looks. It was clear the question had caught Middents completely off guard. He was speechless, in fact. They both realized there was only one way he could know—he was in direct, daily contact with Misha Fisenko.

This immediately changed the tone and direction of the call. And that was clearly Slaski's point: they'd better believe what he was telling them.

"That won't be necessary, Mike. But the offer certainly makes your point."

"Don't misunderstand, Mel. I made the point to let you know I'm being honest with you. I can't speak openly and I can't let our friendship interfere with my confidentiality to others. You would expect the same from me in different circumstances."

"Yes, of course I would," Middents agreed. "I'm just not sure how you can be very helpful to us today and still honor your client, which is obviously Exportkhleb."

"I think you're already getting the picture. Otherwise you would have sold more wheat to Fisenko. But look, as long as Kissinger and his cadre of ag guys keeps the export subsidy in place, you're protected from any big run in the markets. Right? I think they're idiots to leave the subsidy in place, but they aren't paying me for my opinion."

Who is paying you? Jim wanted to ask, but he remained silent.

After a brief pause, Slaski asked, "What do you think?"

"It's our biggest concern for sure, Mike. And you just never know what politicians will do, especially guys like Kissinger and Nixon. They look at things differently. They look at what will get them re-elected, not necessarily what is the right choice. God, I miss Harry Truman and politicians like him.

"But the US government clearly wants to trade with Russia, and even China, based on Nixon's recent trips to those countries," Middents said. "The trade credit puts their stamp of approval on these deals for us, along with assurances from Brunthaver and Butz. It feels like we're entering a new world of agricultural trade, and the stakes have been raised considerably."

"You see, Mel? You already know a lot more than me. I think you're more ahead than you might realize. Maybe resist the urge to do the biggest deal, but make the smartest one."

"Yup." Middents paused. "Good talking to you, Mike. Take care."

"See you, guys. Call me the next time you come this way." Slaski hung up.

Jim looked puzzled. "Who does he actually work for, Mel?"

"That's a good question, Jim. Not Cargill today, that's for sure. It sounds like he's working for Exportkhleb, but I think the only certain answer is Mike Slaski is working for Mike Slaski."

THE CHICAGO BOARD OF TRADE HEARTBEAT
July 3–12, 1972

Markets Are Calm, Quiet

After three weeks in Canada and the United States, hosting countless meetings and negotiation sessions, Misha Fisenko had managed to secure nearly sixteen million tonnes of grain for the Soviet Union from various sellers. His secret negotiations and purchases had not noticeably altered the acquisition price of

grain, and the futures prices on the CBOT had not yet reacted to the deals. The American wheat sellers remained quiet and careful, and the media hadn't been alerted to the business yet. Exportkhleb wasn't finished buying grain, and prospects looked good for continued commercial activity.

A look back at futures market prices for the previous year reveals a stable, low-priced market that was being artificially supported by the US government Wheat Export Subsidy and set-aside acreage programs. Price volatility was very low. The US farmer was an abundant producer of grain in quantities that far exceeded domestic and export demand. The result was a growing inventory of supply and a stagnant market trading in a narrow range fluctuating between a low of a dollar and forty cents per bushel to a high of a dollar and seventy-seven cents per bushel.

On July 3, 1972, the day the Soviets started buying grain from the United States, Chicago wheat futures closed at a dollar forty-nine and a half per bushel. By July 11, Fisenko had acquired over fifteen million tonnes of grain at roughly the same price of a dollar sixty-three per bushel in export position. The close of the market on July 12 was a dollar forty-nine and a half per bushel—no change. Their secret remained intact.

Hilton Hotel, New York City   July 12, 1972

Following three days of successful trade negotiations and contract signings with several American grain companies, Misha contacted Viktor Pershin to provide him with an update. He felt confident his superior would be more pleased with his progress this time.

"I have to say I am impressed, Misha," Pershin said after he'd summarized his purchases. "I was doubtful your low-key, one-man show would be successful, but there is no denying your results. I personally know the traders you have been meeting, and they are tough negotiators. Well done, comrade!"

"We have a lot of circumstances working in our favor, Viktor," Misha said. "Some things we knew, but other events have aligned in our favor. The large inventories of grain, another good crop on the way and the US government continuing their export subsidy program have all contributed to our results so far. Grain companies are falling over themselves to meet with us and make deals—well, most of them, at least.

"We are now just under sixteen million tonnes, more than two thirds of our goal." Misha repeated the numbers for context. "In the past week we met with the six major companies and struck deals with four of them. I am returning to Winnipeg tomorrow to exercise our option for the additional one million tonnes with the Wheat Board."

"That's an excellent idea, Misha. Once the CWB gets wind of these deals with American traders, they will most certainly increase their price or withdraw offers entirely."

John F Kennedy International Airport, New York City   July 13, 1972

Misha Fisenko and Gregor Yeremenko exited the taxi at the Departures level of JFK Airport just after 7:00 a.m. on Thursday. Both were exhausted from the past ten days of intense negotiation, long days and general disruption from their normal routines. In particular, the late evenings and concurrent food and alcohol consumption and cavorting in the "city that never sleeps" was taking a toll. They now had a better appreciation for that famous phrase.

Gregor was heading back home to Moscow, while Misha had a meeting the next day in Winnipeg. Gregor needed to start working with Boris Gryzlov on the huge logistical task of these pending grain imports, along with the in-country distribution to domestic processors.

Misha had some unfinished business with the Canadian Wheat Board: the matter of a contract option for an additional thirty million bushels of Canadian wheat.

At times Misha felt like a crazed shopper buying everything in sight. But he knew he still had more grain to buy to meet the estimated needs of his country. His task was not complete yet. The weather on the Russian plains wasn't improving. It remained hot and dry. Not that it mattered much anymore. There was less and less of a chance they would see any recovery in production and more and more of a likelihood the international trade would wake up to the impacts of drought across the Soviet Union. As tired as he was, he knew he had to keep working at this frenetic pace for as long as it took. He hoped another week would suffice, because stories of problems in the Soviet Union were starting to leak, mainly in Europe so far.

The flight to Winnipeg connected through Toronto and took up the entire day. He appreciated the break and enjoyed some quiet, private time to reflect on the past few weeks. He was proud of his results. His strategy and achievements would prevent his country from suffering great embarrassment, and the citizens of the Soviet Union, great hardship. Even though other people, higher in the Soviet chain of command, would most likely receive the accolades, he knew it was because of him and the insightful guidance of Mike Slaski. There was reason to celebrate.

Misha also appreciated that these results were achieved because he had a team behind him. From the office clerks to the Minister and everyone at Exportkhleb, they could all take credit for the unprecedented success. There were many pieces to this puzzle. Although his task wasn't quite complete, his confidence was soaring. If this turned out to be his last great accomplishment as a grain man at Exportkhleb, he would be satisfied and proud of this legacy.

Canadian Wheat Board, Winnipeg   July 14, 1972

Back at CWB headquarters, Misha and Frank Rowan sat in Rowan's office for a shortened second round of negotiations. Formalities were reduced and the number of participants was down to just the two of them. Misha liked the fact Rowan had full trading authority and could make a deal on the spot, often for exceptionally large quantities, as had been the case last month.

The agricultural agencies of both Canada and the Soviet Union valued their decades-old trading partner relationship. Since the 1930s, Canada had been a periodic supplier to the USSR when their production fell short of their Five-Year Plan targets; some years they traded a lot, other years minimal quantities. Nothing seemed unusual to Rowan in Exportkhleb's request to purchase several million tonnes in 1972. He told Misha he was confident Canadian farmers would have sufficient production to meet their needs.

After some friendly bantering and positioning, Misha was able to convince Rowan to exercise the one million tonne option at a favorable price. Rowan was satisfied to provide the additional optional tonnage they had agreed to just last month, although he did express surprise at how soon Misha had returned to Winnipeg to exercise this option; only eighteen days had passed. He had no idea Misha had changed the game entirely in the past two weeks. He would find out eventually, but that was the trading game—one day you're calling the shots and the next you're caught up in a tide of forces beyond your control.

"That's it for CWB selling for now, Misha. You have taken us out of the market. We'll wait to see what our production looks like before selling any more," Rowan said.

"Well, I'm glad I didn't take longer to get back to you, then. I might have missed this trade," Misha replied, again with a rare grin. The plan was nearing completion, he knew. One detail to lock down with the CWB remained, though.

"What can you tell me about our request for credit in the form of extended payment terms, Frank?"

"Ah, yes. I'm glad you asked. Our minister of agriculture spoke with the federal finance minister on your behalf. He was able to secure 150 million dollars Canadian toward the purchase of Canadian grains. Our current bank rate is 4.75 percent, but because you are dealing with the CWB, our government is willing to reduce it to 3 percent."

"Thank you, Frank. This is much appreciated and will be favorably communicated to our senior leadership."

"So what's next for you, Misha?" Rowan asked. "I mean over the weekend, not workwise."

"I return to New York on Sunday to finish some contracting arrangements with the grain companies there. And then I will return to Moscow one week from today."

"So you are free tomorrow?"

"I have no plans so far."

"I have an idea. Why don't we spend the day at one of our glorious Manitoba lakes? Dawson has a cabin at Grand Beach. I'll give him a call and make plans. How does a little quiet time sound?"

"I'd love to see how the wealthy people of Winnipeg relax," Misha said teasingly. "Honestly, after two weeks in New York, sitting beside a quiet lake listening to the call of the loons sounds glorious. If you would make those arrangements, I would be very grateful."

"Excellent. If Dick isn't around, we'll find someone else, but I know you two are good friends."

"Indeed we are, Frank. Indeed we are."

Misha felt fortunate to have built relationships with his Canadian friends over the years. They were good people, different from Americans. He didn't feel like he needed to keep his guard up quite so much. This little junket to Canada was turning out to be even better than he'd expected.

Sosland Publishing, Kansas City   July 17, 1972

"Who's calling, please?" Morton Sosland asked.

"I'm an editor with the Financial Times *in London," came the reply. The poor long-distance connection and the caller's European accent provided some unofficial authenticity to his claim. "It is our understanding that unprecedented volumes of grain are being traded between US exporters and Russia's Exportkhleb. We are looking for confirmation of these rumors. Can you comment on this from your end, Mr. Sosland?"*

Sosland hadn't caught the caller's name as he introduced himself, but he was inclined to believe the man had the role he said he did. But he couldn't quite believe what he was hearing. "Can you please repeat what you just asked? There's a crackle on the line and I'm not sure I heard you correctly."

"I said, Mr. Sosland, our paper is preparing to run a story today and we wanted third-party verification from you folks at Milling and Baking News. *We have learned, from a confidential source in the Soviet Union, that a Russian delegation has recently purchased five million tonnes each of wheat and corn from privately owned United States exporters. It appears they are interested in buying even more. We want to confirm the story before taking it to press. Does this match with your information?"*

Morton Sosland was the owner and senior editor of the Kansas City–based Milling and Baking News, *one of the most widely read grain publications in North America. The semi-weekly magazine had been in print for fifty years, reporting on cash grain prices, crop progress, transportation issues, weather reports and, most importantly, news on the market outlook. The focus of the periodical was wheat, in all its forms, from whole grain to flour and every possible derivative. There was always something to report in the world of wheat and flour. It was once stated that wheat is 13 percent protein and 87 percent politics. If the Soviets were indeed coming to North America to buy wheat, this statement wouldn't be more accurate.*

Sosland, the soft-spoken, bookish, bespectacled analyst, had heard rumors from the grain trade about possible Soviet buying. The rumor mill had been supported to some degree by higher trading volumes of wheat futures on the commodity exchanges as well as heavier than normal activity in ocean freight booking. But he knew the Americans were expecting another bumper crop to add to their ever-expanding grain inventory, so the impact of a trade to Russia, albeit newsworthy, didn't seem overly impactful to the market. Sosland was aware of the Soviet tender for four million tonnes, but he was unaware

of any confirmed trades. Not every tender resulted in business. And even four million tonnes wouldn't cause much of a ripple in wheat supply and demand. The likelihood grain prices would go higher on the announcement of a trade seemed remote due to those large grain stockpiles and the American government's export subsidy price cap. This widely shared view was based on the general industry consensus that the Soviet Union would purchase two to three million tonnes of wheat—not five million—along with similar quantities of corn. As well informed as the caller seemed to be, the numbers he was reporting sounded unlikely, unbelievable even, to Sosland.

"In my view, those numbers are overstated based on the information we have at hand," he said.

The caller persisted, assuring Sosland his source was reliable. He clearly had a good grasp of the global wheat market and the US situation in particular. "It would seem your President Nixon is prepared to deal with the Soviet Union on large quantities even though these sales might increase the price of food in the United States. At least your farmers will be happy if grain prices rise."

"The size of deals you are suggesting are unprecedented. We don't see market signals to suggest they are happening now."

"See what you can learn," the caller suggested. "I'll speak to you again soon."

Sosland called his editorial team together immediately, shared the conversation and instructed them to investigate. Calls to the major grain companies generated similar responses from each, namely disbelief, along with warnings not to print anything so incredible and potentially explosive to grain markets.

The London Times *wrote the article as reported, but it was largely ignored in North America and resulted in no real influence on market prices. Sosland chose to skip the story in his current edition and wait for more reliable sources to surface. He didn't want to cause a market price spike based on erroneous reporting. His concern for his publication's reputation and his own respect for the market would not allow him to behave irresponsibly.*

Cargill Lake Office, Wayzata, Minnesota   July 18, 1972

Five weeks had passed since Jim had first arrived at the Lake Office. Was it only five weeks ago? he thought. So much had happened in such a short period. His wheat desk trading role required a hectic pace and relentless focus. He had never felt so invigorated, so motivated to excel. His unprecedented access to information, and the exceptional trust senior management had sanctioned, boosted his confidence. He had never imagined this assignment and this level of responsibility when he joined the company, but he was thriving in his new position.

One week had passed since Cargill's record-breaking one million tonne wheat deal with Exportkhleb. They had no way of knowing their deal was minor in comparison to Continental's nine and a half million tonnes of wheat and corn. Cargill's country purchase strategy had been successful, and they secured over one million tonnes of grain from US farmers for delivery in the fall by raising their country bids. The question facing Jim and the wheat desk was whether they felt comfortable selling more.

He started his day by settling into his desk and turning on the monitor displaying market prices. Having access to live price feeds through a new electronic system was a luxury reserved for a few select traders in Cargill offices—yet another example of the technological sophistication of the organization. He noted futures prices were about five cents per bushel higher since they had sold wheat to Russia. Cash prices in the country were closer to ten cents higher as the basis, or discount to the futures, narrowed. Jim also checked the trading volume on the futures market and noted significant increases in daily trading volume in the past month. Thinking back to his training session with Julius Hendel, he remembered "increasing volume in a rising market indicated higher prices to come." If they were planning to sell more wheat to Russia in a future round of negotiations, Jim felt much more comfortable trading from a long position than a short one. *Felt.* He was already starting to feel the market as Doug Larson had described. Excellent!

Jim's plan for the day was to set the wheels in motion for the crop tour in the spring-wheat production area of North Dakota. He would reach out to Cargill's Fargo elevator manager, Bill Halvorson, and get a contact from him for the Cereal Science section at North Dakota State University. He wanted to find someone at NSDU with expertise in disease and pest management. He also sent a teletype message to Dick Dawson in Winnipeg to schedule a call later that day. It was risky to broaden the circle of people involved in these confidential deals, but Dawson already knew about it. Nevertheless, Jim was careful. He didn't want to be the guy who leaked information that could cost the company millions of dollars.

* * *

"Good morning, Bill. This is Jim McCrea calling from the wheat desk at the Lake Office."

"Well, a call from the castle!" Halvorson said with a chuckle. "What can I do for you, Jim?"

Jim explained the plan to host some dignitaries on a crop tour of the spring wheat belt and convince them their plant-disease concerns were unwarranted. He requested Halvorson's help in enlisting support from NDSU and asked him to arrange a field site visit to one of his successful wheat farmers as part of the trip. They would need ground transport for a dozen people and six to ten hotel rooms, depending on how many guests were coming. He couldn't give Halvorson a date yet but guessed it would be mid-August. He didn't mention that their guests were from

Russia. It wasn't necessary, and remaining silent on who the visitors were would preserve confidentiality.

"I'll take care of it, Jim. We'll show your guests how it's done here in North Dakota!"

Later, after the markets closed, Jim reached out to Dawson in Winnipeg.

"Hello, Jim," Dawson said in his now-familiar British accent. "How's the new job going?"

"Really great!" Jim sounded like an excited teenager. He was new to the job but not new to Dawson. Cargill merchants were handpicked by senior management and candidates were widely screened before selection. Dawson had been involved in the process of deciding who would occupy the Wayzata wheat desk seat.

"I want to speak with you about the Soviet delegation and Mikhail Fisenko, if you have some time."

"I certainly do, Jim, but I'll start by saying anything Misha told you about our bad behavior is a complete and utter falsehood. The man is a known liar and fabricator of ridiculous stories."

"He didn't tell me any stories about you, Dick."

"Oh. Well, then... never mind."

"Now you've got me curious, Dick."

"You don't want to be, I assure you."

The two men shared a laugh over Dawson's humorous response. It was a good icebreaker and testament to his ability to build relationships.

"Seriously, Jim, what can I help you with?"

"You know the background on the Soviet crop problems. I'm wondering what you were able to learn from Fisenko during his recent trips to Winnipeg. Do you think they are planning to buy only four million tonnes of wheat or are we looking at something larger?"

"I'll tell you about Misha Fisenko and Viktor Pershin, Jim," Dawson said. "You won't find two more upstanding men in the grain business anywhere in the world. But if they tell you something, it is, first and foremost, the Russian viewpoint. It may or may not be true depending on their needs at the time. Truth is not their main go-to response. What you must be concerned about is what they don't tell you. They are exceptionally good secret keepers. Even after many glasses of vodka I'm not much more enlightened than I was before the drinks started flowing. But I can say Misha was clear in communicating that I shouldn't leave myself short in the process of trading with them. He didn't come out and say it, but I still got the message."

"We got almost exactly the same message from Slaski when we spoke with him," Jim said.

"I haven't told you this yet, as it came up on short notice, but he was here in Winnipeg this weekend. I spent the day with him on Sunday along with the CWB wheat trader. It was pretty obvious he had purchased more wheat from them, but no one offered any details, even though they invaded my cabin for the day. Misha was pretty burned out, though, I could tell. He dozed on and off all day, sitting in the sun by the lake."

Jim marveled at the connection between these two savvy old grain traders. Friends from vastly different worlds bonded by dedicated careers in agriculture from politically diverse nations, they were able to rise above their jobs and sustain an obviously friendly relationship.

"You know we sold them one million tonnes last week, Dick, and we're considering selling them another lot if they come back for more. Mel thinks they might come back for a lot more. Given we have huge wheat inventories and another large crop nearing harvest, what are your thoughts on further commitments?"

"Here in Canada, the Wheat Board has folded their tents and closed off selling for a while," Dawson said. "They aren't offering any more wheat, so we're done for now. That only leaves the USA as a North American source. Do you have any idea how much wheat they've purchased so far?"

"No, not really," Jim admitted. "We're guessing they're already over the four million tonne mark. And the other thing is, we're hearing reports of terrible crop failures across Eastern Europe."

"Yes, I hear the same things as you, Jim. Honestly, it makes me feel nervous."

Another veteran trader describing his feelings for the market. Jim took note.

"Here's a thought, Jim. Do you care whether you sell one, two or even five million tonnes to Russia or to the guy who sold it to Russia?"

"I'm not sure I follow, Dick."

"I'm saying maybe it makes more sense to stand back, let the fireworks happen and then come back in as a seller, possibly at much higher levels. I wouldn't say no to another deal with the Russians, but make it small enough that you don't get hurt if the market takes off. You can re-enter as a seller and backfill the guys who do make the big international deals with Russia. You still make money, but your risks are greatly reduced. You also might get shut out entirely. It's a risk, but maybe the smaller risk of the two approaches."

"Okay, I see what you're suggesting. It makes sense, but don't we run the risk of being cut out of the deal entirely?"

"I don't think so, Jim. Your network of country elevators is key to buying directly from farmers. None of the other exporters have as great a reach. In the end, I think companies like Continental, Dreyfus, and Bunge will have to come to you. You may not get the glory and publicity of making big deals with the Russians, but you will likely make as much or even more money on your trades."

"Thanks for this, Dick. I'll share your views at our next meeting. I think you propose a brilliant strategic insight. One last question. Could you join me and some Russian visitors, including Fisenko, for a crop tour in Fargo next month? We're trying to convince them to buy spring wheat from a US origin. They love Canadian wheat but are afraid of the ergot problem in US spring wheat."

"I'm happy to spend time with you, but don't expect me to try and convince them your wheat is better than ours. That would be taking it too far," Dawson said teasingly.

"No, nothing of the kind. We just think your presence will build the relationship and maybe help us decide how far we push the deal. I'll send you some dates once we hear back from Fisenko. Thanks for your help, Dick."

17

Southern Hospitality

Cook Industries, Memphis, Tennessee   July 19, 1972

"Welcome to Memphis, Misha. Is this your first time here?" Ned Cook asked as he greeted Misha at a private hanger in the Memphis International Airport under a blazing Tennessee sun. Cook was far more casual today, wearing a golf shirt and slacks—clothes more suitable to the climate. The humidity in Memphis was intense. It was worse than New York due to the heat. Even at eleven in the morning it was already uncomfortably warm, and Misha was more than happy to get into Cook's air-conditioned Cadillac.

"I have never been to any of the US southern states, Ned. Thank you very much for sending your plane to bring me here."

"We're gonna be trading buddies, Misha; it's the least I can do." Cook gave Misha a spontaneous playful slap on his shoulder.

Misha was excited to see another part of the United States. The framework of the American colonies had always interested him, and Tennessee had so much folklore attached to it. Abraham Lincoln was born in the adjacent state, and the mighty Mississippi traced its route just to the west of the city of Memphis, separating Tennessee from Arkansas. Misha was also looking forward to hearing some of the famous Memphis blues in a local night club. He was here for only two days, and he hoped to take in as much as he could. But his primary task was to secure grain, and his mission remained uppermost in his mind.

If Cook wanted to sell him more wheat at the price he determined, this trip would be worthwhile.

As Cook drove through Memphis toward his corporate offices, Misha took in the scenery and obvious wealth of the people living there.

"I see a great many large homes here, Ned. At first I thought they were small hotels, but there are so many of them. Does everyone in Memphis live in a mansion?"

"Ha, ha! Well, no, not everyone, but I will say we spread out across the city a lot more than folks in the north. There is a lot of opulence in our history, and our homes reflect those grand days. We grew tons of cotton and tobacco in the past, but soybeans are the number one crop in Tennessee now. That's actually one of the things I want to talk to you about, Misha. I'm hoping we can make a deal on soybeans. Like I told you, beans make excellent feed for your cattle if you process them. The oil is really healthy, too. I really want you to take a look at importing our beans."

"We have imported soybeans before, Ned, but my focus on this trip is wheat. I'm not saying no; I'm just saying not yet. I'll speak with our nutritionists and get their views. Before I go, I'd like you to give me a price and the quantity you were thinking so I can do some comparisons."

"Well, we can talk about more wheat too, but I'll make you a hell of an offer on beans, my friend. I'm willing to start with one million tonnes. There's no sense buying a small amount if you're going to make changes to feed rations. A meaningful volume might help you make a decision."

"You just want to complicate my life, don't you, Ned?" Misha joked.

"No, no, not at all. I'm really serious. Balance out the wheat with some beans."

Cook wasn't aware Misha had already purchased a large quantity of corn from Continental along with barley and durum wheat from the CWB. His shopping cart was a lot more diverse than he knew.

But adding soybeans intrigued Misha, as long as the price was right. He would have to get his team back home investigating the market and the nutritional value and see if he could add a deal from Cook.

"Okay, make us an offer, and I will discuss it with our team when I return to Moscow."

"Excellent! I'd like you to be my guest at our house for the next two nights, Misha, if it's okay with you. But, before we get there, I wanted to stop and show you a little Memphis tradition."

Cook parked his car in the front driveway of the Peabody Hotel and led Misha through the front door into the elaborate, high-ceilinged lobby. They encountered a red carpet running from one of the main elevators to a fountain in the center of the lobby. Quite a few people stood near the carpet, and several children sat on the floor right at the edge, apparently waiting for something.

"What is this?" Misha asked.

"You just have to wait and see," Cook said.

After a few minutes, the elevator door opened and a man with a long red coat and a black cane exited. Right behind him waddled a half dozen full-grown ducks heading straight for the fountain. Startled, Misha expected someone to come out with a net to capture the intruders, but he soon realized they belonged to the hotel and were the center of this attraction. The children squealed with excitement as the ducks scurried past them to a small ramp leading to the watery refuge of the central fountain.

"What is happening?" Misha asked.

"They're mallards," Cook said. "This is the Peabody Hotel Duck March. One night, in 1933, the owner and some of his buddies left their hunting decoys in the fountain as a joke. There may have been some bourbon involved in that decision. But the guests loved it, and it wasn't long before the decoys became live ducks as an even bigger novelty. For nearly forty years now they have been coming down in the elevator every morning about this time and going back to their roost on the roof at five o'clock. Obviously these aren't the same ducks that started this tradition. Hell, we've got people training ducks to walk the big stage at the Peabody these days."

"Well, this moment is something I will most certainly remember," Misha chuckled. He wasn't at all certain if Ned was being truthful with him about training the ducks, but the whole event was unlike anything he had ever seen.

"I thought you might get a kick out of it, Misha. I promise we won't have duck for dinner tonight. It just wouldn't be right." Cook winked.

* * *

Misha welcomed another getaway from the pressure of negotiations and the stress of his responsibilities. His escape to a pristine Canadian lake followed by a brief immersion in the casual and quaint southern United States provided a wonderful week for unwinding and enjoying the company of old and new friends. Ned Cook was a fantastic host and knew how to pour a drink. He tried the bourbon Cook loved so much, but it just didn't compare to his beloved vodka, and Cook graciously served him all he could handle.

The next task before him would be returning to Moscow and the tedious preparation and delivery of many reports outlining his achievements and what was left to be completed. He would have to record all the contracts in their government system and get updates from Boris on the progress he was making with freight bookings and logistics and from Nadia on her progress in finalizing the financial arrangements.

If it was necessary for him to return to the United States for additional purchases, he knew it would have to be soon. There was no guarantee prices wouldn't increase and there was always the possibility sellers would withdraw further offers over supply concerns, changes in subsidy programs or escalating markets. Time was critical to the Soviets' task. While important steps had been taken, the Russians were still exposed to many areas of risk.

Inasmuch as Continental had pledged to supply all the grain Exportkhleb wanted to buy, Misha and Pershin had discussed the pros and cons of this proposed exclusivity during one of their calls. They decided it would be better to purchase grain from several suppliers rather than having everything locked in to a single company. They viewed this approach as less risky in terms of performance as well as confidentiality. It would be unwise to reveal all their business to just one company.

* * *

Misha returned to New York on the morning of July 21 in Ned Cook's private plane and boarded an overnight flight for Moscow. Normally he had no trouble sleeping for most of the eastbound trans-Atlantic flight, but on this occasion he was well rested and also had a great deal on his mind. He deliberated on the success of the past three weeks as he settled in for the ten-hour journey home. He knew he and his team had literally just executed the impossible. Even if they still needed to buy more grain in the next few weeks, it wouldn't change the business he had locked in at this point.

Through the course of the numerous meetings and conversations he'd conducted with North American traders, he had managed to enhance old relationships as well as build new bonds and trust. He knew these new connections would last well beyond the timelines of these deals. A monetary value couldn't be put on relationships, but in his mind the personal value of such outcomes was equally as important as the grain deals. This was the long game in grain trading. Trust meant so much, and it was one reason Misha exceled as a grain trader.

Hours into the flight, his thoughts turned to his future. Would he be recognized as a state hero for accomplishing a great commercial feat? Or was this just an example of him doing his job, an uncelebrated expectation? Some senior Soviet bureaucrats even felt the problem had been of Misha's making in that he had failed to develop the collective farming program properly in the first place. Since he had been at Exportkhleb for so long, he was an obvious target for the blame for the prolonged failure of the food production plan. He knew it was not his fault, but somewhere, someone would be looking for someone else to lay off culpability. Even his negotiating heroics in New York might not be enough to save him.

* * *

No welcoming party greeted him with cheers and banners on his arrival at the Moscow airport, no Fourth of July–type celebration. And of course no Liliya, who had always met him when he returned from international travel. His taxi home from the airport was a quiet and sterile return to his real life, his tiny apartment and lonely existence. Tomorrow he was scheduled to meet with Mike Slaski. The prospect brought a smile to his face.

THE CHICAGO BOARD OF TRADE HEARTBEAT
July 17–31, 1972

The Market Feels a Pulse of Action

Trading activity between US exporters and Exportkhleb during the preliminary round of negotiations had remained confidential. In the third week of July, the CBOT started to react but not to the extent it should have based on the magnitude of business conducted. But the market only reflects the combined influence of its users. By July 31, the wheat market closed at a dollar fifty-seven per bushel, showing a modest gain from the dollar forty-nine and a half low. One of the notable and telling measurements of trade on the CBOT is the volume of trade and the number of open contracts. The early part of July showed a trend toward increased activity. The market was growing in size and strength, representing new activity. These measurements are revealing to traders, but generally invisible to nearly everyone else. Something was happening, but with existing large US grain inventories and a promising crop just weeks away from harvest, it was hard to be bullish on wheat futures.

Few others except a small cadre of people inside Exportkhleb knew the extent of the volume of business conducted. However, the market was starting to react to rumor and speculation. But the problem of being short grain inventory was gradually being transferred from the Soviet agricultural agency to American grain companies. The risk of further price increases was also shifting to their ledgers.

Sosland Publishing, Kansas City   July 21, 1972

The mysterious caller contacted Morton Sosland again five days after his initial call.

"Do you believe me now, Mr. Sosland?" asked the European.

"I'm starting to," replied Morton. "I now know the Russians came to New York and met with some grain companies."

"Not some grain companies, my friend... all the grain companies. Deals were struck three weeks ago with Continental, Cargill, Cook, and Dreyfus. I believe Bunge may have finalized a transaction recently as well. The Russians have already purchased over ten million tonnes, and they are back again this week looking for more."

At this point, the reporter in Sosland came alive. These unprecedented volumes and the surreptitious activity surrounding the deals sounded unbelievable but tantalizing at the same time. Is it possible? he wondered.   He fired off questions in rapid succession, not even giving the caller time to respond.

"Where are you getting this information? How reliable is it? Who are you and what did you say your name was?"

"Very good. I seem to have your attention now, Mr. Sosland. As I said, my name is John Smith. I'm an editor for the London Financial Times *and my source is closely connected with Exportkhleb in Moscow.*

"I am sharing information that I have gathered from my confidential sources. The trades I reported to you were triggered by a serious crop failure in most of the Soviet Union countries. This isn't just a shortfall in Russia's winter wheat crop, Mr. Sosland. It appears the Soviet crop will be as much as thirty million tonnes below their target. And they have developed a plan to cover this shortfall with American grain."

"Wow!" Sosland exclaimed.

"Wow, indeed, Mr. Sosland."

"Call me Morton, please. I think we're going to be speaking often in the coming days and weeks. May I call you John?"

"Certainly."

* * *

Morton broke the news of this Soviet deal with the United States in the late July issue of Milling and Baking News. *Sosland's team of journalists reported that the Soviets had purchased five million tonnes of wheat from American exporters. The amount was lower than Smith was reporting, but it was an amount they had been able to confirm with their industry contacts. Based on the intel provided by Smith, Morton was reasonably confident his numbers were correct, but he needed to be certain.*

Before reporting larger amounts in future editions, he decided to phone the Financial Times *and speak with John Smith directly. The* Times *receptionist confirmed they did have an employee named Smith, but he worked as a literary editor, not a commodities reporter. Morton asked to speak with anyone involved in the story the* Times *had released on Russian grain buying and was connected to an editor.*

"The report we published came from a source we use periodically from East Germany. His name was Veovosky," said the editor.

Veovosky? Smith? Who is this guy and what is his game, Morton wondered. He was now officially a sketchy character in his opinion, but so far everything he had said had been accurate. What was his connection to Ex-

portkhleb and why would they be releasing confidential information on trading activity? It didn't add up, and it made Morton suspicious.

The revelation that Smith was lying about his connection with the London Financial Times clouded the story even more.

18

Looking Back - Looking Forward

Russian Historical Museum, Moscow   July 23, 1972

Misha's intense schedule continued into the fourth full week in July. Even on Sunday he felt driven to dedicate every waking moment to his work. He would have time to rest once this was all over, he thought... he hoped.

For his meeting in Moscow with Slaski, he had chosen one of his favorite places in the entire city: the State Historical Museum, located on the north end of Red Square, at the city's geographic epicenter. More than any other venue in Moscow, the museum held the history and symbolism of the country he loved. He and Liliya used to spend many hours walking the halls of the beautifully grand, red-brick wonder with its thousand ornate windows and castle-like towering minarets. It was here one could really appreciate the greatness of the Communist Party and the proud history of all those who had built the nation that was their home. This tribute to their ancestral heroes made him proud to be Russian.

Misha stood near the statue of a Russian soldier on horseback in front of the museum at 10:00 a.m. awaiting Slaski's arrival. He saw him coming part way along the parade route. He couldn't make out his face, but the walking stick and confident stride were unmistakable.

"This is an interesting place to meet, Misha," Slaski said as he extended his hand in greeting. "I can't wait to hear why you chose it."

"Good morning, Dr. Slaski," Misha offered in a jokingly formal manner, adding a bit of class to their meeting. "Welcome to the spectacular home of our national history. I used to spend a lot of time here, and it brings back fond memories for me. Have you toured the museum before?"

"No, I haven't, but I've always wanted to and just never had the time or opportunity. In my previous visits to Moscow my work always took priority over being a tourist. The building is so spectacular, such a prominent feature of Red Square, like many of the others here. Sadly, my previous trips have generally been limited to the Politburo or your offices at Exportkhleb. Are you planning to spend some time inside with me and give me your guided tour?"

This flattery brought a quick smile to Misha's face. He was no tour guide, but he was happy to show Slaski around.

"Before we start the tour," Slaski said, "I have a favor to ask of you. Could you please give this package to the ladies in your front office?"

"Certainly." Misha looked mystified. "Can I ask what it is?"

"Nylon stockings," Slaski said with a wink.

"Ahh, this is why the ladies like you so much, isn't it?"

"I don't know what you're talking about Misha," Slaski said with a grin. "But it never hurts to be in the good books of the people standing between me and anyone at Exportkhleb I need to speak with."

"Well, this answers an unresolved question I had about you, to be sure. I promise I will deliver the package. I might even tell them it's from you. Now let's get started, shall we?

"I will tell you why I asked you to meet me here in a moment, but first I would like you to take note of this grand statue. The man on the horse was a marshal of the Soviet Union during the Second World War. General Georgy Konstantinovich Zhukov is one of our most highly decorated war heroes. He led the Soviet army against the Germans and he, more than anyone, was the reason the Germans were defeated in the war. The world owes him a great debt of gratitude and yet, outside Russia, most people have never heard of him.

"Now, come inside, Mike. This is what I really want to show you."

The two men passed through the main doors of the museum into an enormous, five-story-high vestibule with a domed ceiling supported by five towering arched columns on either side. Every square inch of the walls and ceiling was painted with an elaborate vine and flower motif, and the ceiling portrayed a complex set of more than one hundred portraits. The vines formed a family tree effect connecting the oval images, each one containing the likeness of a distinguished man or woman dressed in the finest royal garb of their era.

At a distance of more than fifty feet from the floor, it was hard to make out the images on the ceiling clearly, but it was obvious to Slaski that these men and women had been historical Russian dignitaries of some kind.

"Here's a legend telling you about each of these people." Misha handed Slaski a leaflet. "As you might have guessed, this is the Tsar's family tree. They are the Russian monarchs dating back to Ivan the Terrible in 1530. The museum represents, to me, the greatness of Russia. We have much to be proud of as a nation and a people—such a rich, royal history."

"Are you trying to convince me or yourself, Misha?"

"What do you mean?"

"I'm saying, you speak of your country with pride and I hear that in your voice, and yet I hear doubts at the same time. I don't mean to be judgmental or argumentative, but you know I don't share your view that communism has been a success, Misha, and I think you are starting to harbor some of the same feelings and doubts. Is your country better off now than it was thirty or forty years ago? Are you more prosperous or satisfied than you were as a young employee of the government? How has your never-ending Five-Year Plan progressed?

"Don't misunderstand me, Misha. I too was born in a communist country, so my background is similar to yours. My own roots give me the right to have an opinion. And my opinion is, people in general are more motivated to work hard under a capitalist structure. They work hard because they want to, not because they have to. That's the simple but powerful difference in the two states.

"You just spent several weeks in New York, a city built on a capitalist concept and largely by immigrants from Europe looking for a better life in America. Did they seem happier to you than most people living here in Moscow?"

"It's different in America, Mike. There's no structure. Everywhere you go it feels like chaos. People coming and going, noise; there's a randomness I am not comfortable with at all."

"That's called freedom, Misha. People doing what they want whenever they want—within the laws of the land."

"But that's just it. There are so many people breaking the laws every day. It's chaos."

"I don't disagree. Freedom comes at a price, but a price most people are willing to pay. I personally escaped imprisonment as a young man by hiding in a tree during a communist invasion of my country. My personal views are deeply rooted in those moments." After a brief but uncomfortable silence, Slaski said, "That's enough political philosophy for the moment, Misha. Show me more of this magnificent museum."

They spent the next two hours touring some of Misha's favorite sections of the museum, including the historical-agriculture section and an ancient-artifacts area with remnants of exceptionally old civilizations in the country's history. They didn't talk any more business at the museum. It wasn't the right place. Instead, they took in the splendor of the halls and rooms in the museum, without question one of Moscow's most beautiful structures.

They enjoyed lunch in a small restaurant off Manege Square next to the museum and then decided to go to Slaski's suite at his invitation.

As they exited the taxi and headed toward the adjacent building, Misha recognized where they were.

"This is the same building where Cargill has a suite," he said.

"Well, yes. You're right, Misha. I gather you've been here before."

"I have, a couple of years ago. Don't they own it anymore?"

"Yes, they still own it. That's where we're headed." Slaski didn't offer any more information.

"How is it you are using the suite when you don't work for them anymore?" Misha was very confused.

"Well, you see… I still have a key." Slaski waved the door key and smiled broadly. "Let's see what Whitney has in the liquor cabinet, shall we?"

"Mike, Mike, Mike. You are a brazen bastard, aren't you?"

"That I am, Misha, that I am. Now let's get ourselves a drink and talk about your meetings in New York and what's next."

Once in Cargill's private suite, acting entirely like they belonged there, Slaski poured a couple of drinks and the men settled into comfortable, oversized chairs.

"I've given you the details on the discussions already, and you know we have purchased over sixteen million tonnes from Canada and the USA. But what I haven't told you, and what I find difficult to explain, is how easily all the pieces seemed to fall into place. Don't mention anything to my bosses, though. I think the strategy we developed played out well in our favor. I wasn't too anxious, and I made most of them wait before confirming deals. I also adopted a stubborn, unrelenting façade. But the truth is, they were all so eager to sell grain in large volumes and no one spoke at all of increasing the price during any of the meetings. It was not what I was expecting, but I'm pleased it worked out this way."

"I have to admit it's confusing to me too, Misha. They had to know you were buying more than you indicated, but you dealt with them individually and on a one-time basis, except for Continental. They didn't have the opportunity to communicate with each other and step the price higher on subsequent deals, did they?"

"True. But there is something else going on here. Something proving to be very favorable for the Soviet Union. I have a theory."

"Of course you do, Misha. Anyone in the business as long as you, develops a keen sixth sense about grain markets. You are particularly sensitive to events influencing supply and demand. Tell me your theory."

"Well, the first thing is, I believe the Americans have a better assessment of our crop conditions than we give them credit for. The big companies all have better crop surveillance and reporting systems than we do at Exportkhleb—even in our own countries in the Union! Call me suspicious, but I had a feeling in some meetings that they already knew we were coming.

"The second major factor is the huge inventory of grain in the United States and another large crop on the horizon. The practicality of it says the grain physically has to go somewhere. They can't just keep piling it up and either paying people not to grow more or subsidizing export trade. The costs will become unsupportable.

"But the biggest surprise to me was that during our entire buying spree, no one talked about raising prices—not one company. Every one of them called the US agriculture department and got the same reply from Brunthaver. He remained steadfast in supporting the sixty dollar per tonne guaranteed export price, even as our volumes grew and grew and futures market prices inched higher. Granted, he may not have known the full extent of our purchase activity. But they had to have a clue when so many companies started calling them to make sure the subsidy would remain in place. I also know the decision to keep selling to us was made at a higher level. It was President Nixon and his security advisor, Henry Kissinger, who called the shots. My theory is they wanted to make a big splash right before the American election later this year.

"They could have raised the price as we bought grain. And we would have had to pay more to get it. I'm sure the grain companies were advising the ag department to respond in that manner, but they just kept selling. I think I'm going back to New York early next month, and if they haven't moved the price higher, I expect we will buy more."

"I'm no political expert, Misha but the whole thing does sound like the motive is more about politicians getting re-elected than carving out the best deal for the US economy and its farmers. The market won't move higher until the government stops controlling prices or they move the stockpile of inventory."

"Exactly! That's the part I don't understand. Why have they been so accommodating to us at the expense of their own farmers and their own economy? Is there a longer game at play here I'm not seeing? To me, this behavior looks like a colossal blunder on the part of the US government."

"Okay, let's say it is so. Who really knows about it, Misha? How public are these deals? From what I see, it's in the best interests of the grain companies to stay quiet. It will take months for the shipments to start, and it will only be after inventories start declining that people will realize the possible magnitude of these deals. The impact to the consumer will be in small increments over a long time period. Honestly, most of them won't even notice bread is four cents a loaf higher or a cake mix is up a nickel. In the meantime, if your theory is right, Nixon will take credit for opening trade to the Soviets. From a business perspective, it's a stupid choice. But from a political standpoint, it's great leverage to retain power. If Nixon pulls off deals with China too, he will likely be unbeatable. I think your theory is on the money, Misha. I also have a theory, my friend. My theory is, we need another drink!"

"Who am I to argue with the architect of grain trading genius?" Misha nodded. "Tomorrow I must report my progress to Viktor and Deputy Chairman Matskevich. Do you have any advice, Mike?"

"I don't think you need much more help from me, Misha. You have accomplished the impossible. The Soviet Union owes you and your team a debt of gratitude. In my view, your trading activity this year will be a historic milestone in agricultural deals and international trading. They should throw rose petals in your path and give you a fancy Russian medal," he said teasingly.

"We both know rose petals won't be coming." Misha grinned at the thought, a little more relaxed as they filled their glasses for the third time. But yeah, a medal would be nice, he thought.

"I'll stay in Moscow for another day, Misha, and we can strategize more after you report and decide on your next steps. How's that?"

"That's a good plan, Mike. Better yet, why don't you to join us for our meeting with Viktor and Matskevich at the Politburo tomorrow morning? Your contribution in this success should be shared with my superiors, and I want you to hear the reaction for yourself."

"I look forward to it. Call me with the time and location and I will be there."

Russian Politburo, Department of Agriculture   July 24, 1972

At 9:00 a.m. MSK, Viktor Pershin was joined by Misha Fisenko and the entire Kuznechik team, including Mike Slaski, in the main Politburo boardroom of the Kremlin. They all stood proudly and confidently, awaiting the arrival of Deputy Chairman Matskevich. Misha, Pershin and Slaski had been in the impressive Grand Boardroom of the Politburo before, but for the rest of the members of Misha's team, this was a first. Their eyes swept the walls, taking in the lavish portraits and gilded frames of past rulers and political dignitaries. The elaborate décor and glimmering chandeliers seemed out of place in a boardroom and yet, in this setting, the furnishings seemed to belong while the people in modern clothes did not.

"Good morning, everyone," Matskevich said as he entered the room with his small entourage. He wore a stern, serious expression. "I am pleased to see you all this morning and am looking forward to an update on your grain-purchasing program. I have followed your weekly updates with great interest. Viktor, Misha, please proceed."

As the senior department head, Pershin spoke first.

"Good morning, Deputy Chairman. We are pleased to confirm our excellent success and provide you further information on our assignment this morning. I am sure you will be pleased and impressed with our progress."

"That's good; however, if you had done your jobs in the first place, we wouldn't be here at all now, would we?"

Ah, there it is, Misha thought. There's the reason for his apparent dour mood. Hopefully their report would bring a change.

"That's hard to say, sir." Pershin looked a little less happy at being the focus of Matskevich's glare.

"Let me start by acknowledging Dr. Michal Slaski, a former Cargill senior manager and now a private consultant working out of Geneva. I believe you are already acquainted. As you know, we enlisted Doctor Slaski to provide us with insight on grain companies in the United States and provide recommendations on strategy. His contribution has been instrumental in our success."

After the two men exchanged greetings, Pershin continued.

"Deputy Chairman, I am pleased to inform you that to date we have procured 75 percent of our targeted tonnage, secured 750 million dollars in government credit from the United States and 150 million dollars from Canada. We accomplished these deals without causing a ripple in the world price for wheat. I will let Vice President Misha Fisenko provide the details of his meetings and transactions."

"Thank you, President Pershin," Misha said. "Deputy Chairman, as President Pershin stated, we are most satisfied with our achievements to date. Over the past month our team traveled to Winnipeg and New York to meet with the major North American grain companies and the Canadian Wheat Board. Through a carefully planned strategy, designed with the assistance of Doctor Slaski, we executed a plan that has exceeded our expectations to this point."

Misha had to be careful not to be too self-aggrandizing, as it was up to senior officials to determine what was a success and who deserved praise. But he knew their results were irrevocably impressive, so he took a small liberty and promoted the team.

"To provide some high-level details, we contracted just over fifteen million tonnes of wheat and corn along with some miscellaneous feed grains. Our average price for the wheat is sixty dollars per tonne. The US and Canadian government credit is a bonus. President Pershin negotiated a deal where the Americans will loan us the money to buy grain from them, and at extremely attractive rates, I might add. Their department of agriculture continued to provide export subsidies to keep the export price at a fixed rate throughout the duration of our negotiations. Their domestic prices have increased, but our costs remain static.

"Nadia Makarov has secured financing from our Russian treasury for three billion dollars." Misha pointed in Nadia's direction. "This assures enough money to cover the program. And Comrade Gryzlov has taken on double duty, diligently re-engineering our grain-storage facilities to accommodate receiving rather than exporting grain and booking ocean freight to assure delivery of our purchases. The steps we have taken will guarantee that sufficient food supplies will reach our people in the coming year. The potential disaster has been avoided."

"Thank you, Comrade Fisenko," Matskevich said. "This certainly puts a dollar figure cost to the shortfall of grain production, doesn't it? I am relieved to know our people will not starve this winter but still disappointed with how we got into this predicament. It would appear you have the payment requirements secure, but I would like to hear more about your plans to modify our grain terminals and also an update on your progress in securing ocean freight. These seem to me to be critical components to your success."

"I agree with your assessment, Comrade Matskevich." Misha took a chance using a slightly less formal salutation. "These were the reasons we assigned one of our best people to lead the operations. I will let Boris present his report."

"Deputy Chairman," Boris began in a robust tone, "the tasks we have before us and the limited time to complete the work are challenging. I'll begin with a recap of our elevator terminal modifications. Some locations are easier to retrofit than others. Reversing the flow of grain from export to import requires some complex mechanics and, as you would expect, expensive modifications. Other locations have always been import terminals, so they are already able to start receiving grain. The good news is, we have staff at the elevators who can complete any modifications in time to receive grain by November. The work will be ongoing as we expand capacity and bring locations online in stages, but I am confident in our ability to meet the challenging schedule.

"Regarding the ocean freight, I fear we have a shortfall. Of course, we have our own vessels, but some US ports and labor unions still refuse to load Russian ships. This is a problem beyond my ability to resolve. My calculations indicate we have secured 60 percent of the required ocean freight for the coming year, but I'm not confident on the cost. Our increased demand is certain to escalate ocean freight rates."

"This does appear to be a weakness in an otherwise comprehensive program, Comrade Fisenko. Have you addressed Comrade Gryzlov's concern?" Matskevich asked.

"We have, sir, but aside from contacting more vessel owners and paying higher rates, we don't have a solution at this point."

Slaski raised his hand. "May I offer a suggestion?"

"Certainly," Matskevich said.

"This is the first I have heard of this potential problem, but I believe there may be a rather simple solution." He had everyone's attention.

"I assume you purchased the grain from most of the sellers on an FOB US port basis. That is the basis of the sixty dollars per tonne valuation, correct?"

"Yes, that's right," Misha said.

"Very well, then. Why don't you try to transfer the risk of ocean freight to your sellers along with the grain price risk?"

Everyone in the room looked puzzled except for Misha. He was already mentally running the idea across the spectrum of deals company by company.

"I'm not clear how one would accomplish this, Mike," Pershin said. "Can you explain?"

"It's not difficult for individual grain companies to take on the risk of delivering product and selling on a C and F basis rather than FOB. By C and F I mean cost and freight. They do it every day. They have huge freight departments trading ocean freight, rail and even truck freight. Transportation is a business in and of itself. I suggest you go back to the grain companies and see if they would be willing to convert your contracts to C and F, thereby eliminating the shipping risk for you. Any additional grain you buy should also be based on a delivered cost to avoid any further transportation risk for Exportkhleb."

"And this will be easy?" Matskevich asked.

"Not in all cases, but probably enough to cover your 40 percent shortfall."

"This is ingenious," Matskevich said. "I can see why you are on our team, Doctor Slaski. I am impressed."

Misha knew this was going to cost him a premium on Slaski's contract with Exportkhleb, but he had to admit it was another clever idea. The Canadian Wheat Board would be unwilling to change their contracts, but all the big trading companies should be open to a proposal.

"So, Misha, you will pursue this idea, I presume? And what are your remaining next steps? What is your department's estimate for additional grain purchases?"

"Yes, Comrade Matskevich. Mike's suggestion is an excellent one. I will include the plan in our next round of discussions with our suppliers. To answer your other questions, our team estimates that we will require an additional five million tonnes to reach a level of comfort in terms of the collective needs of the Soviet Union and our capacity to unload and store grain. I will return to New York in early August to address the freight and grain requirements. Cargill has invited us to travel to the American plains to inspect their spring wheat crops and meet academic agronomists. They have proposed we consider buying US production rather than relying solely on Canada and our own production of spring wheat. With your approval, I will arrange a team of agronomists to accompany me and comrade Yeremenko to North Dakota as guests of Cargill."

* * *

Outside the Kremlin thirty minutes later, at the base of six enormous white columns adorning the entrance, the Exportkhleb team gathered to debrief.

"You all conducted yourselves admirably," Pershin said. "A great deal has been accomplished in the past month thanks to your efforts. But we have much to do, as well. You know this. Mike, thank you for your guidance and trust. You are always welcome in Moscow."

"All right, let's get back to work!" Misha was half kidding and half serious. "Mike, can I drive you to the airport? We can talk on the way."

"That would be excellent, Misha. Thank you, Viktor, and the rest of you as well. Keep up the great work," Slaski said encouragingly.

* * *

"You're going to be a national hero, Misha!" Slaski exclaimed as they headed northeast out of the city center on the Leningradskoye Highway toward Sheremetyevo International Airport.

"What you have accomplished must have exceeded everyone's wildest expectations. I can already see the statue they will erect for you outside the Kremlin," he teased. "Right beside the World War II general!"

"Were that only true, Mike," Misha replied. "You heard Matskevich. We shouldn't have this problem in the first place. The Minister keeps going back to that as the real problem. He is probably right. I'm not out of the woods on this at all. So, never mind your national hero nonsense. But I really do appreciate everything you have done for us, my friend. One of the best things I did was to bring you on to our team.

"I hope to arrange for dignitaries from many of our suppliers to travel to Moscow and participate in official signing ceremonies and celebrations. It will be very formal and ceremonial. We really like those types of events so the political elites can prance about and take credit. If you would like to be part of that ceremony, I would be happy to invite you."

"I can assure you, Misha, those are the kinds of events I work strenuously to avoid, but I will make an exception out of respect to you." Slaski laughed and Misha joined in.

"So, how much do we owe you for your time and contribution?" Misha asked hesitantly.

"Well, you just keep driving and I'll start figuring it out, my friend."

"Ha! I was afraid you were going to say that." Misha grinned.

"On a more serious note, my friend." Misha was about to get to what he really wanted to discuss on the ride to the airport. "I have been thinking about what you said yesterday. About your comparison of capitalism and communism, about life inside and outside Russia. The past two months have forced me to think a lot more about my life, my future and what choices and options are open to me. I look at your life and those of my friends in North America, and comparing it all to the Soviet world makes me wonder about things."

"Good, Misha! You should be doing that. Wanting more from life doesn't make you a bad person or a bad citizen. It makes you human. You have pledged your life to making a better world for your fellow countrymen. I don't know anyone more dedicated to the Soviet way of life than you. I also know that questioning that way of life can be a dangerous thing, so this conversation is just between you and me."

"Thanks, Mike. I do trust you and I respect your opinion. I feel terribly torn between my loyalty to Russia and my growing realization that my country's blunt-force approach to problem solving and compulsory results aren't sustainable. I am going to accept Cargill's offer to tour their grain-production regions. I will see for myself how their industry compares to ours, how a capitalist production system works. Maybe I can learn some of their tricks and improve Soviet practices, or maybe I'm too small in the grand scheme of things to make any difference at all."

The two men traveled in silence for the remainder of the ride to the airport. Nothing more needed to be said.

Cargill Lake Office, Wayzata, Minnesota   July 28, 1972

Cargill's traders gathered for their daily merchandising meeting on the last Friday of the month. More than two weeks had passed since their transaction with Exportkhleb. The wheat market had been relatively flat during the period, suggesting either sellers were being remarkably disciplined or there was no additional buying from Russia. As far as Cargill management knew, the Exportkhleb traders were still in Russia.

At the same time, prospects were increasing for a bumper wheat crop in the United States—possibly a record production. The wheat market had actually dropped a few cents per bushel the previous day. Supply was exceeding demand in the eyes of most. It was starting to feel like the market was back into the doldrums of the period prior to the Soviet visit in early July—back to a time when government programs dictated a narrow price range determining a floor price due to the buy-back program and a ceiling due to the export subsidy program.

Mel Middents called the merchandising meeting to order.

"Jim, you have some news to share today?"

"Yes," Jim said. "I received a call from Misha Fisenko early this morning advising us they will be returning to New York next week. They're interested in buying more winter wheat from us and have accepted our invitation to travel to North Dakota to learn more about our spring wheat. I don't know if they have advised any other companies about their intention to return for more wheat, but let's assume they have. They called us to confirm the crop tour, so it's possible we have an early advantage on their travel and trade plans."

"All right people, what does this mean?" Middents asked rhetorically. "It means they went back to Moscow, tallied their purchases, took another look at their crop and then decided they need to buy more wheat. How much more, we have no idea!

"Based on the glut of wheat we have in the United States, we should be shorting the hell out of the market," he continued. "But the downside is limited by government programs—so is the upside, for that matter. The US government intervention has caused one helluva mess! And they could pull the rug out from under us at any moment by discontinuing their support. What are your thoughts, people?"

Jim had been to enough morning meetings to know to stay quiet while Middents went on one of his anti-government rants. But he felt the time was right to recap Dawson's recommendations.

After giving Dawson full credit for his advice, Jim recapped the idea to stand back in this round and watch to see where the chips fall. This was an unusual strategy for Cargill, a company known to be a market leader and innovator, especially when it came to opening new markets for American production. But in those cases, Cargill was always the biggest player in the room. This one was different. This time they were dealing with an entity much larger and more powerful even than themselves.

"An interesting approach, Jim. I respect Dick's judgment, and he is certainly closer to the Russians than anyone else from Cargill in North America. Slaski is also sending us big red-flag signals. Maybe we should ride this one out a bit."

"What is our current wheat position?" asked Barney Saunders.

"We are long 1.3 million tonnes," Middents said.

"So we could sell a million tonnes, make a profit and still carry a smaller, manageable position forward, right? I would be happy to lighten our load and cash in. What is the government going to do with subsidies?"

"Everything we hear from Brunthaver says they are maintaining them," Middents said. "My view is that Kissinger and Nixon are determined to make political gains out of new trade deals by maintaining the program right through the November election. As politicians often do, they are buying votes with taxpayer money. The only thing potentially forcing their hand is a rapid rise in wheat prices. The cost of subsidies would increase at the same rate to maintain the lower export price. It would be madness to keep paying higher and higher rates. At some point, somebody is going to make it a public issue."

"So, another risk for us as an exporter is getting caught short and losing the subsidy. Dick's suggestion to step aside is sounding better all the time," said Saunders.

"When does Fisenko want to meet with us, Jim?" Middents asked.

"It sounds like they want us to come to New York and wine and dine them next weekend and then fly to North Dakota on Monday the seventh. We can arrange the tour and meeting at NDSU on Monday.

Dawson has agreed to fly in from Winnipeg and join us for the trip. I think it would make sense for him to come to Wayzata the day before so we can brief him and get aligned on a strategy."

"Yeah, right! Screw the Russians' weekend plans, Jim," Middens said. "Tell them you will pick them up on Sunday afternoon and fly into Minneapolis. We can bring them here to the chateau on Monday to negotiate a second deal and buy them dinner here on Monday night. We'll use the jet to fly everyone directly to Fargo early Tuesday morning. You can be the tour guide; it will be your show from there."

"Okay," Jim replied. "I can do that."

19

Grain Deals - Round 5

Hilton Hotel, New York City   August 1, 1972

In the second month of the summer of 1972, Misha returned to New York City, emboldened for another round of buying. This could be trickier, he anticipated. The grain companies knew he had purchased all of, and likely more than, the four million tonnes they had initially indicated. Showing his hand to buy even more this time would be a strong signal the Soviets had a problem and prices should move higher. The big question was, would this new demand exceed the anticipated surplus of American wheat?

Interestingly, since his first trip to New York, the Chicago futures market had not shown any inclination to move higher. Maybe there was still a window of opportunity. Maybe, thanks to bountiful North American crops and generous government subsidy programs, the market wouldn't react to Soviet purchases at all. The futures market should move higher, he felt, but US government intervention in the open market created a false economy. In truth, he didn't care about the effect of the actions of American politicians as it related to the American market. He just needed to be able to find ways to capitalize on their actions for the benefit of the Soviet Union.

Pershin had accompanied Misha on this trip to America. He was keen to reconnect with old acquaintances and meet some of the new trading partners who would be integral to meeting their new and urgent needs as a grain importer. He hoped it wouldn't be the case for future years, but being prepared for differing outcomes was what created advantage. This mission had taken a decidedly favorable tone and become considerably more interesting and exciting than he had imagined at the outset.

"Do you really think we will be able to buy another five million tonnes during this trip, Misha?" Pershin asked. "We are agreed it is our current estimated shortfall after considering our own production and the purchases we've made to date."

"Yes, I believe we can, but the real unknown remains—at what price? We've lost the strategic advantage of surprise we enjoyed last month. I feel like we are an open book, but it's probably just my paranoia affecting my perspective. No one on this side of the Atlantic Ocean really knows our plans.

"We also have some other considerations this time," he continued. "Ned Cook made a good argument for us to consider buying soybeans for animal feed. And Cargill thinks we should be open to buying spring wheat from somewhere else besides Canada. I'll see if they can convince us when we travel to one of their elevators in the Midwest states."

"When is the crop tour trip scheduled, Misha, and who is coming here to join you?"

"Crop production manager Gregor Yeremenko has selected two of our crop scientists to join him, and they will meet us in Minneapolis next Monday. Cargill has offered to fly us to the spring-wheat production area in their state of North Dakota. I know your plans don't include the crop tour, Viktor, but I'm glad you are here to meet with our suppliers. I think it is important for you to be part of the Minneapolis session with Cargill. I know you want to see their fancy French mansion in Wayzata just as much as I do."

"I've had enough of your dusty crop tours this year, Misha," Pershin said with a smile and a nod, recalling the horrendous trip to the Volga plains. "But I definitely want to sit at the table with my old friends at Cargill."

"And we're flying in their jet, so it won't cost us anything," Misha added.

"I feel like we should be able to buy more wheat from Cargill than we have to date, Misha. How do you suggest we negotiate another wheat deal with them?"

"I agree. They have been hesitant to offer us more, especially in comparison to Conti, who have been surprisingly aggressive. But, as we discussed, we have purchased all we should from Continental. They're in for more than ten million tonnes, and we don't want to rely on a single supplier in case they fail to perform. The stakes are too high. But Cargill has only committed one million tonnes so far, and they are capable of selling us a lot more. I believe our best approach is to try to get them to commit on a higher volume of winter wheat. We can agree to lock in prices for both winter and spring varieties subject to us agreeing to try their spring wheat. Then we can investigate whether ergot infestation is an issue and determine if we want to buy the spring wheat or not."

"Okay, your plan sounds good, Misha. Let's see how much we can buy from some of the other companies this week in advance and then try and finalize our needs with Cargill."

"One other point we need to address is the conversion of some of our contracts from FOB US ports to delivered Russian ports," Misha said. "This is a time-sensitive issue and is closely linked to the amount of grain we buy. Since the bulk of our purchases are with Conti, they are the obvious ones to approach."

"Yes, right, Misha," Pershin said. "You have the detail on ports, quantities and delivery periods. Let's make that a priority to satisfy the Minister's concern."

"Conti has already offered to work with us on securing ocean freight. Let's see if we can drop that on them for a large portion of the grain we bought last month. I'll call them and try to arrange another dinner with their team tonight."

Misha made a call to Continental Grain's New York office and asked to speak with Michel Fribourg. Bernie Steinweg took the call when

Misha identified himself, and the two agreed to arrange a dinner meeting that evening as a follow-up discussion related to their deal. Misha emphasized they were not interested in buying more grain at this point, but he did want to introduce his boss to senior Continental executives and wished to discuss matters related to ocean freight. They agreed to meet in the Hilton Hotel dining room at seven.

* * *

"We're pleased you called today, Misha. It's nice to meet you, Viktor," Steinweg said in greeting as Misha handled introductions. "Dinner was an excellent idea. It gives us an opportunity for you to meet more of our New York team. You mentioned you wanted to discuss freight, so I brought along our senior commodity trader and vice president, Mike Laserson, and our ocean freight department manager, Gerry McClintock. Unfortunately, Michel is back in Europe and not able to meet with you gentlemen."

As dinner proceeded and small talk ran out of steam, Misha opened the dialogue for the matter at hand.

"Bernie, we would like to accept Michel's offer to work with us on securing ocean freight. As you know, our hands are somewhat tied due to your American longshoremen's unwillingness to loading Soviet vessels. We would like to discuss converting many of our contracts to a delivered basis and leave it in your expert hands to book freight."

"We suspected his request might come up, Misha. I think we can help you with this problem. Mike, Gerry, do you agree?"

Both men nodded.

"Not only can we use our freight division, Stellar Charting and Brokerage, to secure all the foreign-flag cargo ships you will need," McClintock said, "we can do it anonymously on your behalf. That will prevent the freight market from getting too overcooked and expensive, at least for a few weeks while we try to secure enough cargo space for you."

"Excellent!" Misha was obviously relieved. "We would like to include Gregor Yeremenko, who would take the lead from our side on further discussions with your team."

"That's fine with us, however you want to handle it," Laserson responded. "We can and should move quickly to make sure we have shipments booked so we can keep our delivery schedule. This is going to be a significant task to get all this grain moved."

Misha nodded in agreement. And he doesn't even know about all the other commitments we have on the books, he thought. We'll just keep that secret to ourselves, and I'll stress secrecy with Gregor during his meetings. So many details. So many things that could go wrong.

Hilton Hotel, New York City   August 2, 1972

The next day Misha started another round of purchasing. In their first meetings they purchased grain from five of the big six global grain companies: Continental, Cargill, Louis Dreyfus, Garnac, and Cook.

In this round of negotiations he decided to meet with Bunge first, expecting them to be the most eager to make a deal. Misha greeted the traders first thing in the morning and did all the talking while Pershin played the observer in the negotiations. His distinguished but silent presence in the room was unsettling to the traders.

Bunge was a South American–based grain exporting and processing company originally founded in Amsterdam in the early 1800s. They were global traders, albeit smaller players in the United States. They made it clear they were eager to get some kind of a deal done with the Russians. With the export subsidy still in place, the Bunge traders were happy to price wheat at the same price, fifty-nine forty a tonne, as the other sellers because the export markets still reflected the unchanged value. The futures markets had increased by ten cents per bushel and domestic prices were rising, but the export subsidy had increased by an equal amount to maintain the dollar sixty-three per bushel export target price set by the government. They soon agreed on 600 thousand tonnes of winter wheat.

"They were very eager to deal, almost falling over themselves to make the sale, weren't they?" Pershin said after the meeting. "But that's just 10 percent of our objective for this round."

"It's true, Viktor. This is how it went last month. I expected to be negotiating long, hard hours to hammer out deals in our favor, but these companies have been bolstered by their government allowing them to be aggressive. No one as much as Continental, mind you, but all of them eager to trade. There are no political philosophies standing between us. It's just about making a deal. This is a good start, and we have more meetings scheduled. Don't worry, be patient; we will get the job done."

Hilton Hotel, New York City   August 3, 1972

The following day Misha began reconnecting with the major grain companies that already had deals with him. A loud knock on the door signaled the unmistakable arrival of Ned Cook.

"Misha!" Cook bellowed before the suite door was even opened and with no concern for other hotel guests. This time he was meeting with them on his own. It was quite different dealing with the man who owns the company rather than traders for the larger grain conglomerates. It was evident that Cook called the shots.

"Hello, Ned. It's nice to see you again. I'd like to introduce the president of Exportkhleb, Viktor Pershin."

"Welcome to the United States, Vic!" Cook said in his casual southern style. "It's great to meet more people from Russia. I'm coming over there later this year to meet your whole team and see your beautiful country!"

"We will be delighted to host you, Mr. Cook."

"Ah, shit! Call me Ned, please."

"Very well, Ned. And thank you for the wheat we have purchased from your company already and for hosting Misha in Memphis."

"No problem. We had a great time. I'd call it just ducky, wouldn't you, Misha?" He looked at Misha and winked. "And now we have more business to conduct, I hope. I'm here to finalize a deal on the soybeans we discussed last time. Did you think about our proposal, Misha?"

"Yes, we did, Ned. We would like you to give us an offer on the one million tonne quantity you discussed. It comes with an introduction to Elvis Presley, I believe." Misha had offered a rare moment of levity during negotiations. Pershin seemed unimpressed with the comment, but Cook roared.

"Well, how does three eighty-five per bushel for the beans sound? The conversion to metric tonnes is the same as wheat, so it's one hundred forty-one dollars and 50 cents per tonne. And let me see what I can do about Elvis." He grinned, carrying on the joke.

"One hundred forty-one dollars and forty-six cents per tonne is my calculation," Misha said. The four-cent difference represented forty thousand dollars, which was significant, but moving Ned off his price was equally important for a trader.

"Well, I guess your calculator has more decimal places than mine." Cook laughed. "All right, is it a trade, then?"

"It is, if you can add another 300 thousand tonnes of wheat at the same price as the other deals."

"Ugh, Misha, you're killing me! All right, but I need an exclusive on the soybeans. I don't want a bunch of other traders mucking about in the market while I cover this deal. There's no export subsidy on soybeans, so I'm taking some serious risk on this one."

"We understand your position, Ned, and your terms are acceptable to us. We have two new deals with Cook Grain. And the soybeans will be an exclusive arrangement—for this crop year only, though."

"Excellent! It's a little early in the day to celebrate with a shot of Tennessee bourbon, but why don't we have dinner tonight, gentlemen?"

Misha enjoyed Cook's company and his charming personality very much, but he needed to check with his superior. A quick glance in his direction earned a nod from Pershin.

"Dinner would be very nice, Ned. Why don't we meet in the lobby around seven?"

"Done! See you then."

Cook rose and shook both men's hands in his vigorous, unique style. This gesture locked in the deal for both parties. The lawyers and accountants all needed signed paperwork, but this was all these merchants of grain needed. Paperwork was simply a necessary evil.

* * *

Later that day, Dreyfus's Philip McCaull met with the Russians in their twenty-sixth floor suite at the Hilton. He came prepared to deal.

"Gentlemen, we at Louis Dreyfus have been long-standing traders with Exportkhleb, and we hope our relationship is as important to you as it is to us. We appreciate the opportunity to trade additional tonnage with you. At this time, we are prepared to offer an additional one point five million tonnes at the same price as our previous transaction."

"Thank you, Philip," Misha said. "We would prefer buying additional tonnage from you on a delivered basis and converting our original purchase to delivered Soviet Union ports as well. Can you give us a few moments to meet privately and consider your offer?"

"Certainly. I don't see a problem in allowing us to handle the ocean freight. Why don't I step out and return in thirty minutes? Would that be adequate?"

"It would be perfect. We'll see you at two thirty."

Misha quietly and solemnly escorted McCaull to the door. Once the door closed, Pershin jumped up from his seat.

"What are you doing, Misha? Why didn't you close the deal?" He was obviously perplexed.

"Can you believe these guys?" Misha said. "I can't believe how eager they are. For most of them, the size of these deals is bigger than anything they have ever closed before. And yet they keep coming back to sell us more. He just offered us double what we bought from them last month! Honestly, Viktor, I just didn't want to appear too eager. We will lock him in most definitely. But I wanted to plant at least some seeds of doubt. It's just a little diversion, but it keeps us in control of the pace and the tone of dealing."

"All right. What you are doing is working, so I'm not going to second-guess you, but maybe give me a little warning next time you go crazy, Misha!"

* * *

Precisely at two thirty, Philip McCaull returned to the Soviets' suite and closed the biggest deal in the history of Louis Dreyfus Corporation: one and a half million tonnes of wheat worth ninety million dollars. His handshake was not nearly as assertive as the one earlier in the day, but it was every bit a confirmation of the deal.

"That's nearly three million tonnes, Misha." Viktor said afterward, flashing his notebook to show the entries. "A solid deal with Cargill will finish up the task at hand."

"Yes, you're correct. But it's important to spread the risk of shipping between multiple companies, Viktor. Boris has advised us of pending problems with loading and unloading these huge quantities of grain, so we still need to spread our business around."

* * *

Dinner with Ned Cook would prove to be an evening to remember. Ironically, the next morning, both Misha and Pershin found the one thing neither of them could do very well was just that—remember.

The evening had started innocently enough with a few vodkas of differing brands followed by a plethora of bourbons recommended by Cook. Misha recalled him entertaining them with stories of the cotton industry, the source of the Cook family's wealth. Misha remembered none of the details. He did remember suggesting they go for dinner on numerous occasions, to which Cook had replied, "Sure. Let's have one more drink and then we'll go." They may have eaten... he wasn't sure.

Misha was glad Jim McCrea had called earlier in the day and arranged to pick them up in New York on Sunday rather than Friday, as he had originally requested. It would take them a day or more to recover from their overindulgence with Cook.

Misha was a bigger drinker than Pershin, but neither held a candle to the man from Tennessee. From a night club to a comedy bar to a blues bar, Cook could have gone on all night and, to the best of Misha's recollection, that's what they did. They had rolled Pershin into a cab around 2:00 a.m. and sent him back to the hotel. Misha and Cook had continued. The evening again validated the saying Misha had heard earlier: New York was the city that never sleeps.

Misha woke on Friday at around noon.

"I'm blind! I can't see!" he said with panic. Instinctively his hands flew to his eyes and started rubbing them aggressively. His head pounded in response to the rubbing, but gradually light started to penetrate the eyelids that were more or less glued together. His other senses weren't faring much better. His mouth was dry, his ears ringing and his nose wasn't exactly right either. Slowly he gathered his thoughts, reviewed the previous day and, as the memories of some of the night's events intermittently came back to him, hoped Ned Cook felt as bad as he did.

After a much-needed room service lunch and more than three cups of black coffee, Misha felt well enough to call Slaski to give him the latest update. He especially wanted to inform him of their progress in securing freight coverage from Continental and Dreyfus.

"That is exceptional, Misha. Well done. Converting those contracts to delivered will make your lives abundantly easier. Conti will have more success in loading Soviet vessels on your behalf than if you tried to do it on your own. And you bought almost three million tonnes more and you still have to meet with Cargill? I'm utterly amazed at what you have accomplished, my friend. In my wildest dreams I would not have predicted this outcome. You are essentially done your part. Now it's on the elevator operations and transportation teams to execute these deals, isn't it?"

"Yes, true. From here we are heading to Cargill's Lake Office on Sunday to conclude our dealings and take the crop tour."

"Well, get ready to be shocked at the modern farms and country operations, Misha. They are much more sophisticated than on Soviet farms. You can learn from them."

"Our production manager, Gregor, is joining us for the tour for just this reason, Mike. We want to see how they manage large production and handling in North America. The spring wheat thing is mostly an excuse for us to spy on them."

"Good luck, then. We will speak again when you return home."

"We will, Mike. And thanks again for your counsel. You made a difference in the outcome."

Sosland Publishing, Kansas City   August 7, 1972

Two weeks passed before John Smith called Morton Sosland for the third time. This call was to confirm the Russians had most definitely purchased over ten million tonnes of wheat and corn in early July. He also offered Sosland a tip: the Russians were back in New York with the intention of buying more. Their appetite for wheat remained strong, even after these record purchase quantities. Reuters was also reporting unusual Soviet buying based on a "reliable source." John Smith was not exclusive to M&B News, *Sosland suspected.*

How did Smith, or Veovosky, or whoever he was, have such good intel on the Soviets, Sosland kept wondering. His information was so specific and accurate. He had to be on the inside of the Soviet Politburo or know someone who was. This was shaping up to be the biggest story in international grain trading history, and somehow Smith had the inside track on everything. If his latest tip was correct, the Soviets had already locked in more than twelve million tonnes of grain purchases. This was a staggering quantity, which was sure to impact the US food economy and could easily send grain prices soaring. And, he wondered, what did this mean for the US export subsidy program? Aren't we just giving the Russians free money? He made a note to contact Carl Brunthaver at the US ag department and get a response from him.

Even though Smith had misrepresented his position with the London Financial Times, Sosland was reluctant to challenge his identity yet for fear he might lose the source. He also wondered about Smith's motive. Was he simply a market investor trying to send commodity prices higher? Or was his strategy more politically motivated and devious? Could it actually be the Russians planting information after they locked in their supplies in order to drive world prices higher for nations not aligned with the Soviet Union—such as China? That seemed elaborate but not impossible.

In the August 2 edition of Milling and Baking News, *Morton Sosland reported a conservative estimate of Soviet purchases tallying seven million tonnes of wheat to Russia. He knew it was low—really low, in fact—but this was still all he could confirm from exporters.*

* * *

Not knowing who John Smith was or what his motives might be finally pushed Sosland to confront him on his next call.

"I know you aren't who you say you are, John. You don't work for the Financial Times."

"They are publishing the articles and transactions I am reporting to you, aren't they, Morton?"

"Yes, but based on tips from an East German named Veovosky," Sosland said. "That's you too, isn't it?"

"Ever the newsman, confirming his sources aren't you, Morton?"

"You bet I am, and when a source turns out to be someone other than who he represents himself to be, I get very concerned."

"Here's what I can tell you, Morton. Everything I've told you is true and accurate. I work for a secret information service in London. The motives of myself and my employer shall remain confidential, but I will not steer you wrong or embarrass you in any way."

"So, you're James Bond? Is this what you're telling me, 007?"

"Hardly." Smith laughed. "I'm just a purveyor of facts, an instrument of the truth."

"Well, that's a load of crap. But as long as you're honest with me, I will try and work with you. I can live with some opacity, but I'm reporting only what I can verify elsewhere."

"It's certainly your choice, Morton. I'm glad we could get past your concerns. I can give you another interesting update today. The Russians aren't in New York anymore."

"They're not? Did they go back to Moscow? Where are they?"

"Wayzata"

"The Cargill chateau?"

"Exactly."

20

The Crop Tour

Cargill Lake Office, Wayzata, Minnesota   August 7, 1972

North Dakota holds bragging rights as the state with the largest production of spring wheat in the USA. Harvest generally occurs between the middle and end of August every year, weather permitting. The timing of the Russian crop tour, hosted by Cargill, aligned perfectly with the development of the wheat crop and the presence, if any, of plant disease—ergot specifically. The distinct and potentially lethal black fungus is identical in size and shape to wheat kernels. Cargill had a lot riding on their ability to convince the Russians of the control measures in place in the Fargo area and the high quality of their spring wheat. Americans consumed this wheat, which should be adequate evidence of its safety.

Misha and Pershin arrived in Minnesota, after their five-day stop in New York, on the evening of August 6. They were accompanied by three additional Russians: Gregor Yeremenko and two of the top Russian plant agronomists from Exportkhleb, all eager to see a part of American industry few Soviets had the opportunity to study.

Jim McCrea met the group and took everyone to the Marriott Hotel near the Minneapolis–Saint Paul International Airport. After dinner, Jim arranged to meet Pershin and Fisenko at 8:00 a.m. Monday and drive them to the Lake Office.

The limousine Jim rented for the occasion added a little flair and prestige to the morning drive. By 8:20 a.m. they'd arrived at the great circular driveway leading up to the front door of the Cargill chateau on Lake Minnetonka. The front entrance to Cargill headquarters was rarely used. On this day, however, it was considered most appropriate. Their guests represented the largest trading entity in the world. "If we don't use the front door today for these guests, when will we ever use it?" Barney Saunders had asked Jim.

"Good morning, Viktor, Misha," Saunders said as he opened the massive wooden door for him and Mel Middents to welcome the vehicle's occupants as they exited. "It's nice to see you again so soon, Misha, and nice to reconnect with you, Viktor. It's been over a year since we met in Geneva. I trust your flight from New York and the local accommodations are suitable?"

"Thank you, Barney. Hello to you, Mel." Pershin responded as the senior official. "Everything is excellent. The hotel is fine, and we appreciate Jim driving us this morning in grand style. As for this mansion"—he turned to scan the building in front of him—"I applaud your attention to detail in what you call an office. I'm a student of European architecture, and this is truly a testament to French design. I would love to see more if you would indulge me."

"Absolutely. We can tour the castle during a break in our meeting this morning," Saunders said. "But first, let's move inside to the boardroom where we can discuss the wheat market and our plans for the next two days."

Saunders led the entourage into the same room the merchants used for their weekly sessions, the Reuters machine against the wall perpetually clicking out fresh news. The senior management boardroom was on the upper floor of the chateau, but the trading boardroom was more suitable for their purposes. Dick Dawson had flown in from Winnipeg and joined the group enroute to the meeting room, exchanging hearty greetings with both of his good Russian friends along the way.

"Let me start by thanking you for joining us here in Wayzata, gentlemen. It's our honor to host you," Middents said. "For our travels tomorrow, we have arranged a meeting with independent plant agronomists from North Dakota State University, a tour of our grain elevator in Fargo and a trip to a local farmer's operation just west of town. The crop in North Dakota this year is excellent and nearing harvest. We are confident you will be impressed by the quality and purity of America spring wheat. So confident, in fact, we are prepared to offer you one million tonnes of the spring wheat at the same price as the winter wheat we sold you last month."

Misha took that opportunity to step into his role as the trader for the Soviet group.

"Thank you, Mel. We would like to secure additional wheat, but we would like to conclude our purchases of winter wheat, and your one million tonne offer would accomplish our goal. Can we agree on additional winter wheat and then discuss spring wheat after we finish the tour?"

"For several reasons, Misha, I'm afraid we are not able to make you an offer on additional winter wheat, and I'll tell you why."

Misha was caught off guard by the first refusal of a deal by anyone in the five weeks he had been negotiating for American grain. He knew it would come eventually, but Cargill's commitment to them was comparatively small. He was more than a little curious to hear Middents' reasoning.

"You have purchased a lot more winter wheat than the original four million tonnes you tendered. By our best estimate, you have secured at least double that amount, maybe more. This will affect our available supply. Also, we can share with you that the US government figures on winter wheat inventory are overstated, so we are reluctant to sell more of a product that may not be readily available. Lastly, our concern is that the government may change the rules on the export subsidy program as they learn more of these facts. The price of wheat on the Chicago Exchange is up over twenty cents per bushel this week alone—coincidently, since you returned to buy more grain. That means government subsidy rates have increased as well. Brunthaver says the government will continue to finance the subsidy, but they can always change their mind and leave us stuck with low price sales. These added costs to the government come out of general revenues and, much to the chagrin of politicians, there is a limit to available funds. Wheat trading has suddenly become a lot more political. It's a big risk, we feel."

Middents had managed to craft a message to express logical reasons why they were reluctant to sell more winter wheat. He was careful not to reveal their strategy to step aside on this initial round of trade and let others incur the preliminary risk. Selling some spring wheat carried less risk in Cargill's view, but another one million tonnes was still a huge amount, and it was the most they wanted to sell at this time.

"So, in response to your request, Misha, we will have to decline. We can offer you spring wheat, but no more winter wheat."

"What about you, Dick?" Misha looked conspiratorially over at Dawson. "Can you offer us a million tonnes of Canadian wheat?"

Misha was cleverly trying to introduce competition within the different branches of Cargill's network, but to no avail.

"Not a hope, Misha," Dawson said. "You tapped us out and you took the CWB out of the market too. Your last trip to Winnipeg was their final deal. They have been following the activity between the Soviet Union and the USA and know when to fold their tent and shut it down. They may revisit things after harvest, but if the price keeps climbing, they will likely wait even longer."

"Perhaps this is a good time to take a break, Barney. Give Viktor and me some time to confer and, most importantly, enjoy a tour of your beautiful lodgings."

"Splendid idea, Misha. Let's go," Saunders said without hesitation.

* * *

"Tell me what you've gathered from our meeting here so far, Jim," Middents said as Saunders took the Russian guests on a short tour of the global Cargill headquarters.

"They seem very relaxed to me, Mel. Their body language and reactions suggest they aren't anxious or stressed. My feeling is if we don't make this deal with them, they are confident in their ability to cover it elsewhere. I'm fairly sure they are spreading the business around."

"That's what I think too," Middents said. "I'm not eager to sell more than the one million tonnes we decided on, though. Dick, do you see it otherwise?"

"No, I don't. You are spot on in assessing them as relaxed, Jim. Misha is hard to read, but I know him well, and if he felt any pressure, I could tell. He's cool as an English cucumber today."

"Okay, we stay the course and try and lock in the spring wheat," Middents said. "But that isn't likely to happen, if at all, until they see the quality of the crop for themselves. You're sure we have them meeting the right people in Fargo, Jim?"

Jim nodded.

"Good. We can make some money on a deal when the real stock situation becomes common knowledge in the marketplace. Let's grab another coffee and meet them back here. Jim, can you catch them and let them know we will give them the room for a while before we reconvene?"

"Sure."

Jim caught up with the Russians in the lower-level cafeteria getting coffee and a pastry.

"Misha, you and Viktor can use the meeting room for some privacy, and we will join you again in a half hour. Is that enough time? Do you need a phone line to speak with anyone?"

"No, this is fine, thanks, Jim. Would it be okay if Viktor and I went outside and took in the beauty of the small lake I saw as we drove in?"

"By all means. Take a stroll and come back to the meeting room when you're ready. Can you find your way back okay?"

"I think so," Misha said.

* * *

The two men strolled along the edge of the pond and enjoyed the manicured landscaping of the gardens.

"Do you think the boardroom is bugged, Misha?" Pershin asked.

"I don't know, but I don't want to risk it. If it were reversed, we would be listening in on them, wouldn't we?"

"Most definitely," Pershin replied with a grin.

Misha shifted to the business at hand. "I think we should agree to purchase the spring wheat. That's assuming the quality is on par with Canadian wheat, of course. We are starting to reach the end of offers from other companies, I feel, and we are close to achieving our goal for this trip. Others may start turning us down like Mel just did."

"Yes, I agree, Misha. Let's be realistic. We are only a few hundred miles away from Canada. How much different will the spring wheat be? As long as we get some guarantees on quality from them as sellers, we can always reject the shipments if they don't meet our standards."

"Exactly. And we can learn something from their scientists and farmers as part of this exercise. Okay, then. I'll accept the offer conditional on the tour and we can close our book on buying for now—and hopefully forever."

* * *

Subject to Misha's conditions, an agreement on terms for one million tonnes of spring wheat was reached shortly after the group reconvened. The deal finalized their plan to secure additional tonnage on this trip and ran their tally on total purchases from Canada and the USA to twenty-four million tonnes. The final average price was much lower than they'd projected. Performance risk had been mitigated by purchasing from seven different sellers, including the Canadian Wheat Board, and much of the freight risk had also been offloaded to the sellers. They had secured credit for nearly one quarter of the purchases and positioned themselves with sufficient gold reserves to pay for the remainder.

Misha felt the burden lift off his shoulders as they locked in the symbolic final purchase with Cargill. From the Soviets' initial planning, the goals of the Kuznechik team had been identified and fulfilled as of today. Misha was confident they could claim victory in their challenge.

"All right, gentlemen, we have a deal," Middents said. "Let's go have some lunch and relax a bit."

"Before we eat, let's confirm plans for tomorrow," Saunders said. "How many of your team will be flying with us tomorrow, Misha?"

"There will be four of us," he said. "Viktor has meetings in Washington."

"Yes," Pershin said. "I have plans to meet with Carl Brunthaver and Earl Butz to thank them for their support in preserving the export subsidy and honoring President Nixon's commitment to develop trade between our nations. We are pleased to contribute in a great step toward a warming of the Cold War and achieving détente. I also hope to extend those credit terms based on recent, expanded business with the United States."

"Well, good luck with your meeting, Viktor. We mean that seriously. Federal government credit goes a long way to building our confidence in the deals. Dick, you're coming with us to Fargo, right?"

"Yes, I am, Barney."

"Okay, six in total, adding you in, Jim. I'll leave it to you to get everyone to the airport, Jim. I'll make sure the plane is ready to go by eight."

* * *

Once the Russians left in the limousine, the Cargill wheat team reconvened for a follow-up session in the traders' boardroom.

"Did you hear Viktor's comment about expanded business in the United States?" Saunders asked.

"I sure did," Middents replied. "What do you make of his choice of words?"

"We could still be grossly underestimating the size of this deal."

"He also mentioned Russia is trying to secure more credit. There's another signal more deals have been struck or they are planning more purchases from America in the coming years. Either way, this is further evidence of a brand-new ball game in international trade."

"Jim, you and Dick need to try and draw out more info from these guys over the next couple of days. Barney, let's make sure the liquor cabinet on the plane is well stocked. Lots of vodka. We need to find out as much as we can. Get the booze flowing and loosen their tongues."

"That's going to take a lot of booze," Dawson said.

Cargill Corporate Jet, Forty-one Thousand Feet over Minnesota
  August 8, 1972

Flying northwest out of Minneapolis on the one-hour trip to Fargo, North Dakota, Cargill's jet passed over the feeder-lakes-system tributary to the Great Lakes. The land base around Fargo was the north-eastern-most section of the US Great Plains, ten states ranging from the Canadian border to the Gulf of Mexico. It was also the section of the growing area in the United States most similar to Russia's Volga Plain latitude and growing conditions. The view of the landscape from eight miles high was an impressive grid of square-mile plots of wheat, corn and soybeans that resembled a multi-shaded green quilt. About one quarter of the land mass was brown earth, summer fallow, allowing the soil to rest and recover for sustainability, critical to the farming sector.

Six men boarded Cargill's corporate jet at 8:00 a.m. Joining Jim Mc-Crea, Dick Dawson and Misha Fisenko were Gregor and the two crop scientists flown in from Exportkhleb in Moscow to assess the veracity of the spring wheat crop with a special focus on ergot contamination. The Soviet grain agency had developed a level of trust and confidence in Canadian spring wheat, but rumors persisted about an ongoing problem in the United States wheat-production area. Ergot fungus was a geographic and climate-specific parasite largely uncontrollable without a comprehensive, dedicated effort to eradicate it from the land. Their goal today was to learn as much as they could about US wheat production and their success in controlling a concerning and potentially deadly contaminant.

From the fuselage of the sleek private jet, the Russians gazed out the windows, high above the earth's surface. They were simultaneously in awe of the productivity and jealous of the efficiency and comprehensive use of the land. The flight offered a unique view of rural United States and the intensive farming practices that resulted in better yields than in any other country in the world.

The occupants had paired off in seats for the flight; the two Soviet scientists sat together. Their English was minimal, so they were more comfortable in their own company. Dawson encouraged Gregor to sit with him, giving Jim an opportunity to get to know Misha and try to extract whatever information he could from the wily Russian trader.

Jim invited Misha to join him in a row with optimal views of the ground below. Sitting in one of the luxurious leather seats closest to the window, Misha found himself captivated by the beauty and symmetry of the agricultural land below as the jet rose to altitude and left the urbanization of Minneapolis behind. The images below validated the order and abundance of American grain production.

"Your family farms this land, Jim?" Misha asked, continuing to stare out the window as he spoke.

"No, our family farm is in Illinois, nearly one thousand miles south and east of here. This is wheat country. We grow corn and soybeans mostly. But the business of farming is the same, and I certainly feel a kinship with all American farmers."

"Are you not in competition with every farmer to get the best deal?"

"Not really. We make our own decisions on what to grow, when to sell and who we deal with. There's a lot of independence in the way we run our farm businesses."

"All this land is owned by individual farmers, correct? The government doesn't own land or run farming business; is this the truth?"

"The government buys grain from time to time to support prices, but they don't own land or conduct farming activities. We would definitely consider land ownership as direct government competition."

"How much land does each farmer own? Is it the same amount for everyone?" Misha turned back from the window to make eye contact with Jim. He was looking for some aspect in common with Soviet agriculture.

"Each of the squares on the grid you see is one square mile, or a section of land. Farmers generally own anywhere from two to forty sections of land, and they manage all of the operations, from seeding, fertilization, harvest, marketing and equipment maintenance. Farming is big business in America," Jim said.

The farm sizes didn't surprise Misha. Russian collective farms were just as large. But the fact they were owned by individuals rather than the government was the difference. How could this be fair distribution of resources, he wondered. One person could have so much while another might have far less.

"This seems so unfair to me, Jim," Misha said. "Are smaller farmers jealous and angered by the larger farmers? Do they feel cheated?"

"I wouldn't describe it that way. Everyone works and lives within their means, striving to maintain their business or expand it if getting bigger is their ambition. But farming in America is more than just a business. It's a lifestyle. Farmers are the most independent people in the country. They are their own bosses. Living their lives in rural America is more important to them than making money. They live off the land and feed the country. It's a moral imperative. What about you, Misha? Do you have a farming background?"

"No, I've never been a farmer, Jim. My family were not farmers, either. I'm a bureaucrat. My role in Soviet agriculture has always been on the business side. I currently oversee the collective farm operations and manage production for our country. I'm having to change my role from an exporter to an importer this year, but Exportkhleb's primary role is to export surplus production. We have the land base and labor necessary to be the primary wheat supplier to all of Europe."

"How successful are your farms in Russia, Misha? How do your farmers feel about their lives?"

"I admit we could do better, and we will. But our farmers work for the good of the country, for all people, not for their individual benefit. That is the Soviet way. Farmers haven't owned their land in Russia since 1917."

"I've researched the history of Soviet agriculture as part of my university studies, Misha. I'm no expert, but I learned farmers who opposed the move to collective farms were killed or imprisoned, and the production of the state farms is far below their potential. Is this a factor in your need to buy so much grain this year?"

"No one was killed or imprisoned, Jim. Your classes do an injustice to Russian history. It's true, we are suffering a drought in parts of the country and yes, that's the reason we are buying American grain. We have been self-sufficient during many years of agricultural collectivization, and we will be exporters of grain in the near future. This year is an anomaly."

"Well, the timing of our surplus and your deficit is a good fit," Jim said.

"It is kismet."

Misha turned his head to gaze out the window again, signaling the conversation had taken a turn he did not care to pursue. He was adamant in protecting the reputation of his homeland and insulted by Jim's mention of killing Russian citizens being sanctioned by the government. He knew it to be true but would never admit it, especially to an American.

* * *

With Misha checking out of the conversation and the flight about half over, Jim thought it was a good time to switch seats with Dick and get to know Gregor and understand his role with the delegation better. Jim was more likely to build a relationship with Gregor, the younger of the two Soviet delegates, than with Misha. Misha was Dawson's contemporary and his career with Exportkhleb was closer to its end. More importantly, he knew Dawson stood a better chance of learning any of Misha's secrets. Without being too obvious, they had to continue their mission to extract information from the vault of Fisenko's mind.

Jim made his way to Dawson and Gregor's seats and tapped Dawson lightly on the shoulder, signaling it was time to switch. Without uttering a word, Dawson raised his eyebrows, inquiring about Jim's success, to which Jim replied with his own, silent response: a single shake of his head indicating no progress. Dawson rose, excused himself from Gregor's company and headed to Misha. Jim slid into the seat beside Gregor and took on the hosting role with him.

"Misha, my friend," Dawson said as he took the aisle seat beside him. "This is quite a spectacular view from up here, isn't it? Tell me, are you still buying grain on this mission of yours?"

"You don't waste any time 'schmoozing,' as you call it, do you, Dick?"

"Nope, don't need to with you, Misha. You know me too well."

"If the quality is good, I think the one million tonnes of wheat we have agreed to buy from Cargill after this trip will be the last of it," Misha said. In fact, he spoke the truth, but Dawson had no way of knowing that or how much they had already purchased in total. What he really needed to know was how much they had purchased since his trip to Winnipeg just five short weeks ago. That would provide the full story the Cargill team was seeking. How deep was Soviet purchasing, and what might that mean for wheat markets?

"It sounds like you bought more than the four million tonnes you had tendered to the US grain companies. Maybe double that amount?"

"Maybe yes… maybe no," Misha said mischievously. "One day I'll tell you the story, Dick. And it's a good one. But probably not today."

"Ah, Misha. You're such a hard-ass to deal with." Dawson grinned back and gave his shoulder a playful push. Both men laughed at the moment, knowing each was just doing their job. They sat in silence as the plane began its descent to the Fargo airport, just under an hour after departing Minneapolis.

Misha stared out the plane portal pensively. He knew his mission was coming to an end. His grain-volume targets had been reached and secured at prices better than his government's most optimistic expectations. His thoughts turned to his own future. What was next? Would he be recognized as a hero in his country? Would a statue like the one for World War II hero General Zhukov be erected? The odds were slim, he knew. Would he be expected to go back to his desk and small office in Moscow and his ordinary tasks? That sounded most likely. The adrenalin rush he had experienced through much of the grain-buying campaign was subsiding. The stress was gone, but so was the elation of their successes day after day. Had it only been a little more than a month? It felt like they arrived in New York a long time ago. He knew he had aged more than a mere thirty days, that was certain!

Hector International Airport, Fargo, North Dakota   August 8, 1972

Fargo's Hector International Airport was a small terminal in comparison to the larger centers of Minneapolis, New York and Moscow. It didn't offer a separate building for private jets, but it wasn't difficult to navigate the Arrivals level. The local Cargill elevator agent was easily recognized with his bright green jacket and cap and his exuberant wave to the deplaning contingent of Russians and Americans. Jim McCrea approached Bill Halvorson and introduced himself and the others traveling with him.

"Welcome to all of you," Halvorson said, his accent drawing out the vowels with a cadence that revealed his Scandinavian/German roots in the area. "It's a pleasure to show you the great state of North Dakota." He was beaming. "I've got a van outside we can all fit in. We'll start the day at the North Dakota State University's Cereal Science department, because it's close to the airport here, and then take a tour of our local elevator. We can have lunch and then wrap up the day with a visit to one of our finest local farming operations. How does that sound?"

"Sounds perfect, Bill," Jim replied. "Let's go!"

Halvorson escorted his six guests to the large passenger van he had arranged for the tour. It wasn't unusual for Cargill senior management to visit Fargo, but four Russians was a rare event indeed. He had scheduled a busy day for them in keeping with McCrea's specific requests. The scientists were waiting, his plant had been cleaned and tuned for presentation, and one of his best wheat growers was teed up for their arrival. The preparations were top-notch.

* * *

Professor Charlie Johnson was the head of the Cereal Science department at NDSU. He was the youngest and, by all measures, the most enthusiastic professor at the college, maybe in the entire state. Johnson had been raised on a cotton farm near Lubbock, Texas, and attended Texas A&M, where he graduated in 1968. He moved to Fargo and took on the professorship just two years after graduating. That aside, going by his keenness, you would think he was born and bred in North Dakota—except for the accent. His Texan drawl added a delightful if confusing note to the Scandinavian undertones of most residents. They did share a common trait of taking a long, slow approach to speaking.

"It's really nice to meet y'all!" Johnson said. "It's a real honor and pleasure to meet some fellow agronomists from Russia and share knowledge.

"Did Bill give you a tour of Fargo yet? It's a great town with a whole lot of history. Did y'all know this is the place where the music died? It's true. Back in 1959, the plane carrying Buddy Holly crashed right here in Fargo. Terrible tragedy. Don McLean wrote a song about it. "American Pie." Holly came from my hometown of Lubbock, Texas." Johnson didn't give anyone a chance to respond or get a word in edgewise. He just motormouthed his way along.

"But let me tell you what North Dakota is best known for. It's our wheat!" He took a rare pause. "We're best known for the hardiest, highest-protein wheat in the country. We do it better than anywhere else in the world. With all due respect," he added, nodding and smiling at his Soviet guests.

Finally, Jim thought. He's finally getting to the point of the meeting. You can't rush a Texan, though; he knew that.

"Thanks for a little bit of local history, Professor Johnson," Jim said. "I'm not sure our guests know much about American musicians, but we appreciate your sharing. And yes, we're here to talk about spring wheat, so your comments and insight are welcome. In particular, our Russian friends would like to know more about the ergot problem in North

American wheat crops. How bad is it and what are we doing to manage this plant disease?"

"That's a great question, Jim, and you've come to the right place for an answer," Johnson answered, obviously happy to be talking again. Everyone could see his eyes twinkle at the prospect of delving deep into plant anatomy.

"As I'm sure y'all know, ergot is a plant disease caused by the fungus Claviceps purpurea," he began as Misha interpreted for the two Russian scientists. "It infects the developing seeds of cereals and grasses. Ergot bodies called sclerotia form in place of the kernels. You probably also know that ergot poisoning from eating contaminated rye flour led to deaths in the Middle Ages. Human symptoms can include impaired blood circulation followed by gangrene of extremities, referred to as Saint Anthony's Fire. That sounds like a tough way to go, doesn't it? Nervous convulsions may also occur, leading to eventual death. It's a real bad one." Johnson spoke as if lecturing a class.

"Grazing animals that consume grains and grasses contaminated with ergot suffer disorientation and muscle spasms due to the presence of lysergic acid derivatives in ergot. It's called 'paspalum staggers' in cattle. Human experimentation with this drug has been popular in the past decade. You've heard of it right? LSD? It's a powerful hallucinogenic."

Jim noted the Russian scientists exchanged knowing glances as Johnson spoke. The direction of Charlie's presentation, while educational, wasn't furthering their case when it came to convincing the decision-makers at Exportkhleb that it was safe to buy American spring wheat. He knew he needed to manage the message in a hurry.

"I think the Soviet team knows a lot about the downside of ergot, Charlie," Jim said. "What they want to hear from you is what we are doing here in America to mitigate the problem and how widespread the presence of ergot in wheat crops is today."

"Sure thing, Jim. Actually, knowing as much as we do about the problem has allowed us to develop tools and techniques to control it in US spring wheat."

That's what Jim wanted to hear from the professor—solutions, not problems.

"The most effective tool in managing ergot is crop rotation year over year. Planting wheat on the same field in consecutive years encourages plant disease to gain a stronger foothold. Switching from grass crops to broadleaf plants really helps manage all kinds of disease problems. Resting the land by summer fallowing every third or fourth year is also a great strategy. Another effective technique is the development of ergot-resistant varieties. Eradication generally takes a few years, but we are having excellent success there as well."

"So, how bad is the ergot problem today in your spring wheat crop?" Misha asked, getting right to the point.

"This year I can say it is virtually nonexistent," Johnson answered confidently. Jim breathed a quiet sigh of relief.

"Really?" Misha raised his shaggy eyebrows.

"Yes," replied the professor. "I can't say we have eliminated the problem, because spores have a way of surviving and returning. And when we do encounter the rare year of extreme moisture in the Central Plains, we should expect a potential outbreak in some areas. But, for the most part, ergot is a bit like tuberculosis: controlled but never eliminated."

* * *

The session at the university was a good start, Jim felt. It showed Cargill's willingness to be transparent and speak to the scientific concerns and solutions. The Soviet scientists had a few questions, and Misha managed to relay them to the university team. Their responses generally initiated nods and expressions of agreement from the Soviets, giving Jim confidence in their progress. After two hours of meetings, grain-sample inspections and questions, Misha's team was satisfied and ready to move on.

The next stop, the Cargill elevator in Fargo, was more for Misha and Gregor's benefit than the scientists'. The Fargo elevator team generally kept a clean plant, but they had gone the extra mile to prepare for visitors. The amount of grain storage and the load-out capabilities impressed Misha.

"Your plant is remarkable," he said to Halvorson. "This is one of Cargill's larger country facilities, I gather?"

"No," Halvorson said. "This is pretty typical of the elevators we have across the United States. There are a couple of hundred just like this one."

Misha responded with a rare look of surprise. Generally, his reactions were contained but this revelation was genuinely unexpected. The handling and storage capacity was superior to most of the plants in the Soviet Union, certainly the inland receiving facilities. The guided tour through the impressive elevator gave him some insight as to how the Americans were able to maintain high shipments and large inventories.

"Can you show me your railcar loading system?" Misha asked.

"You bet," said Halvorson. "We can load a hundred railcars in an eight-hour shift. Each one holds just over three thousand bushels, or eighty-five tonnes in your measure."

"Eighty-five hundred tonnes in eight hours?"

"Yup, as long as we have the grain in-store or scheduled to arrive to meet the shipment. It runs like clockwork."

Misha and Gregor headed for the rear of the elevator to inspect the railcar loading system while Halvorson hung back with Jim.

"Why are we sharing information with the Russians, Jim? I've always thought they were an enemy of America. I don't understand what's happening here."

"I think the best answer, Bill, is… times are changing," Jim said. "What's happening here and now may be the first step toward finding peace or reduced tension between our countries. I don't have any kids yet, but when I do, I want their world to be a more peaceful and safer place to live. Don't you?"

"I hadn't thought about it, really. I never saw myself having any influence in the relations between America and our enemies, so I just kind of go with the flow."

"I guess I thought that way too, at least until I started spending time with these guys and understanding the power that food might have in building bridges between nations. Meeting Misha and Gregor and getting to know them has been an opportunity for me to put a face to Russia. They are regular people, just like us, kind of going with the flow of their government too. Maybe more so than us, I'm discovering. But you can't get to a more basic requirement of life than food, you know. We've got it, they need it, and our government is falling all over themselves to make a deal possible."

"Maybe I've watched too many movies showing Russia as the bad guy," Halvorson said. "Stuff on communism, world domination and crap like that. Remember the movie *Dr. Strangelove*? Man, I laughed my ass off watching that one! This still feels weird to me, but I'll trust you on it, Jim. You seem to have given it some thought already. You wouldn't be here with them if you and the bosses at the Lake Office didn't think it was the right thing to do."

"You're right, Bill. The farm tour this afternoon will be the most important part of this whole trip, I think. I'm looking forward to turning them loose on a solid American farm. But first we'd better get some food in all of us. I'm hungry."

"Me too! I've set up a great spot for lunch."

* * *

At Jim's request, Halvorson had arranged a lunch at one of Fargo's finest roadside diners. What better taste of true rural America than Kroll's Diner? They specialized in a blend of German and American food with one of the flashiest neon signs in the area. The group turned full plates of food into full stomachs in short order and then boarded the van for their next scheduled stop, one of Halvorson's best customers and most successful farmers. But Misha Fisenko had another plan in mind.

Making sure everyone was safe on board the van, Halvorson climbed in behind the wheel. Misha occupied the front passenger seat for the best view of the countryside. The Russians were all given window seats so they could take in the vast North Dakota vista while enjoying the cool air-conditioned cabin, a necessity on a typical hot, dry August day in Fargo.

Halvorson headed west from Fargo on Interstate 94 and north at the hamlet of Mapleton. The view of the robust North Dakota crops along the highway gave the visiting Soviets a perspective that was different from the bird's-eye view from the plane. The golden wheat gently swayed to the rhythm of the summer breeze, revealing tall stands of even crop maturity approaching harvest readiness. There were no indications of plant disease or insect damage from ground level. The fields were free of weeds and volunteer grains left from previous crops. Misha was duly impressed with the progress of the crop and eager to walk among the narrowly spaced rows of plants to inspect the seeds for himself.

"The farm we are going to is about four miles north of here," Halvorson said, pointing in their direction of travel.

"This is a field of wheat we are passing, isn't it?" Misha asked.

"Well, yes it is." Halvorson seemed a bit confused by Misha's question.

"Stop here, then," Misha said. "I wish to speak with the farmer who lives here."

"But we haven't spoken with him. They aren't expecting us," Halvorson said.

"Precisely why I want to stop here. They are not expecting us and have not prepared for a meeting. Is there a reason we shouldn't make a random stop?"

"Well… no." Halvorson looked over his shoulder at Jim for some direction.

"Let's stop here," Jim said. He didn't want it to look like they were hiding anything or the farm they had chosen was a set-up. He realized they were rolling the dice, not knowing who or what lay ahead of them with an unannounced visit from businesspeople—especially when half of them were Russian. For all he knew, the farmer might greet them with a shotgun and even pull the trigger if he heard Russian accents.

This could be a complete disaster, Jim thought. He looked over at Dawson and saw the same concern in his expression.

Halvorson backtracked on the country road to find the driveway to the farmhouse adjacent to the field of wheat. He found the home nestled in a grove of trees and followed the slightly curved road, past a half dozen grain bins, to the main house and utility barn. He parked the van.

"Maybe just wait here while I see if the owner is at home and is willing to speak with us," Halvorson said. "Jim, you want to come with me?"

Not even a little bit, Jim thought, but he joined Halvorson out of necessity, considering the situation.

Halvorson tentatively knocked on the back door, a bit uncertain about how this was going to go. This was going to be a confusing call for the farmer who'd come to the door.

"Good afternoon. I'm Bill Halvorson, the manager at the Cargill elevator in Fargo, and this is Jim McCrea, one of our wheat traders from Minneapolis. We are wondering if you might have time to answer a few questions for some international dignitaries we have visiting us today."

The farmer peered over Halvorson's shoulder at the van and then back at the two men before him, clearly perplexed by their arrival.

"Well, I guess so, Bill. Name's Ernie. Nice to meet you," he said as he extended his hand. "Who are they?"

"One of them is a senior Cargill executive from Winnipeg, and the rest are a delegation of Russian scientists interested in buying our spring wheat. They asked to see a typical North Dakota wheat farm and speak with the farmer who works the land. They randomly picked your farm while we were driving down the road. We were heading to Brewin's place up the road, but they asked to stop here at your farm. I'm sorry if it's an imposition, but we won't stay long. They just want to learn about how we grow wheat in North Dakota."

"Russians? In North Dakota?" Ernie looked even more bewildered.

"I'm surprised too, Ernie," Jim said. "But the Russians have already bought a lot of our winter wheat this year, and now they are considering buying more—spring wheat, this time."

"It's a good thing, I think," added Halvorson. "We have a lot of wheat backing up in the country, right? These guys could be big buyers. Really big! Their buying will help move grain, which would help grain prices move higher."

The last comment caught Ernie's attention. "You don't have to tell me," he said. "My grain bins are full of wheat, and I have a really good crop close to harvest. I could use some new markets, especially at a higher price. Bring 'em over to the Quonset and we can have a chat."

For the next hour and a half Misha and his scientists asked questions and listened intently to Ernie. Misha and Gregor translated back and forth for their team and privately exchanged many thoughts in their own language. The dialogue was congenial, the mood positive. They walked in wheat fields, inspected samples of grain and marveled at the quantity and quality of machinery this one farmer had at his disposal.

"You own all of these tractors, combines and sprayers?" Misha asked.

"Well, me and my friends at the bank," Ernie said. "I carry some operating debt, but it's part of the business of farming these days."

"How many acres do you farm?" Misha asked. "How many bushels per acre do you harvest? What chemicals do you use to control disease and pests?"

The questions covered the full breadth and depth of farming in North America, and Ernie had all the answers. It was clear to Jim: Ernie was a proud and successful farmer and was turning out to be a real gem for their messaging objective.

Satisfied with the experience, although a little disappointed he hadn't been able to find any flaws in the US spring wheat crop, Misha and his team were becoming convinced of its quality and consistency.

"If there aren't any more questions, I think we should let Ernie get back to his work," Jim said. "We all have planes to catch in a few hours."

Thanking Ernie for his time and expertise, they shook hands and climbed back into the van for the trip back to Fargo. Ernie stood in his driveway, waving as the van of grain men pulled away.

"So, what do you think after our meetings today, Misha?" Jim asked. "Do you have enough confidence now to include spring wheat on your shopping list?"

"I think so." Misha looked at his team for their nods of approval or head shakes indicating concern. "We had a lot of questions answered, and nothing gives us a reason to hesitate. I have to admit I hoped to catch you off guard and uncover a hidden truth, but you either got lucky with this farmer or the crop is as good as you say it is. I am willing to proceed."

"Excellent!" Jim said, not sure what he should do next.

But Misha had the answer.

"Go back to Barney and Mel and tell them you managed to talk me into buying one million tonnes of your spring wheat. Tell them I was reluctant, but you finally convinced me to close the deal. I'm sure Mr. Dawson here will support this version of events, right, Dick?" Misha nodded his head encouragingly.

"We have already agreed to a price and shipping period, as you know. The purpose of this trip was to address our concerns, and you have done your job here today."

As the traders talked, Halvorson navigated back to the Interstate, heading east toward Hector International Airport. The day had been a success for everyone, and the light moods and smiling faces revealed a calm completion of their individual missions. Each person's agenda was different, but today felt like one of those win-win days, a rare thing in the zero-sum world of commodity trading.

* * *

As the entourage of Russian, Canadian and American grain specialists waited to board their respective planes and head in different directions, Dawson and Misha embraced in a robust, manly hug, as two old friends often do. Misha would return to Minneapolis with his team on the Cargill private jet and then go home to Moscow. Dawson had a short flight north, back to Winnipeg.

As they shared goodbyes, Misha moved closer to Dawson for a confidential conversation.

"You asked me how many tonnes of grain we bought, Dick. I told you I would tell you the story, but 'not today.' Well, I've changed my mind and I will tell you now. Just between us, our country had an extremely poor production year, and we purchased just shy of twenty-five million tonnes from Canada and the United States."

Dawson pulled back, startled, looking Misha straight in the eye to assess the sincerity of his statement. As Misha nodded as if to confirm what he'd said, Dawson understood immediately that he was being completely honest and forthcoming.

"Wow! You have secured all of this already? Without the market exploding?"

"Yes. The US export subsidy kept the lid on prices while we completed our purchasing. And all grain companies, including Cargill, are keeping the information confidential. I won't tell you who is involved or how much we bought from any company, but you're smart. You guys can figure it out."

"The US government can't know the total amount," Dawson said. "They would have removed the support sooner if they knew."

"They know. Nixon wants to get re-elected. He will use American taxpayer dollars to make himself look better. Capitalism at its finest!" Misha said mockingly.

Dawson was dumbfounded by the magnitude of the deal. Counting the one million tonnes Misha just agreed to purchase, Cargill had two million tonnes of US-origin grain and 500 thousand tonnes of Canadian grain on the books with the Soviets, only one-tenth of the total Misha claimed. How was the purchase of twenty-five million tonnes even possible?

Even though he had shared this information with Dawson confidentially, Misha knew he would report back to the Cargill brass in Minneapolis. In fact, he was counting on it. His own personal plan was dependent on the news leaking out and grain markets reacting to this unprecedented volume of business. If markets started moving higher in response to this information becoming public, it wouldn't be harmful to the Soviets. They had their exposure covered.

Before they boarded their flights, Dawson quickly pulled Jim aside. While he appeared to be wishing Jim a safe trip home, he quietly said he had an urgent need to speak with everyone on the wheat desk.

"Misha just dropped an information bomb in my lap, Jim. There's a lot more going on here than we estimated. A lot more! We need to get everyone together and talk about it first thing in the morning. Can you arrange a call?"

"For sure. What's going on?"

"It's too much to discuss now. Tomorrow morning... eight o'clock. Okay?"

"I'll look after it. Have a safe trip, Dick."

21

The Picture Comes into Focus

THE CHICAGO BOARD OF TRADE HEARTBEAT
August 1–8, 1972

The Market Wakes Up

After the second round of grain purchases by Exportkhleb, the futures market started to respond to a new world grain order. Misha Fisenko's "Kuznechik" team had purchased twenty-four million tonnes of wheat, corn and soybeans from the most sophisticated and experienced traders on the planet. He did it without raising the price of grain a single cent per bushel, and his team had even managed to use the US government money to help pay for the grain.

Now, as grain companies scrambled to cover their sales to the Soviets with both physical grain purchases and futures contracts on the Board of Trade, the realities of a tightening supply and demand balance started to become evident. In ten short days, the Chicago December wheat contract rose from a dollar fifty-nine per bushel to a new high of a dollar eighty-seven and

a half per bushel. That represented an increase of 18 percent in value, more than the change in price during the entire previous year. Daily trading volumes continued to increase and the open interest, the number of contracts created through trade, was growing steadily. The market was sending a bullish signal to its participants and the world at large: demand for grain had increased—significantly. The exchange was serving its function in communicating this shift in the market.

Cargill Lake Office, Wayzata, Minnesota   August 9, 1972

"Tell us what you know, Dick. We're all on the edge of our seats," Middents said. He was in the boardroom in the company of Barney Saunders and other Cargill senior management, along with a half dozen wheat and corn traders including Jim McCrea.

"Good morning, everyone," Dawson said. "You all know we spent some time with Misha Fisenko and his team of agronomists in North Dakota yesterday. Just before leaving Fargo, Misha confided to me that the Soviets have purchased nearly twenty-five million tonnes of grain in the past month. You heard me right, in spite of my accent: twenty-five… million… tonnes. That's triple what we had speculated internally, isn't it, Mel?"

"Twenty-five million? Are you sure?" Middents said. "Who would supply such a quantity? Who would take on the risk?"

"Conti is my guess. It helps explain the market rally in the past week, doesn't it. Some speculators are reacting to emerging news stories, while others may be trying to cover their sales."

"Well, yes, but I just can't accept the US government allowing this kind of volume and still guaranteeing the export subsidy. That's just plain stupid!"

"Misha assured me the US government is aware of the amount of business and is backstopping the risk through the subsidy program. You've checked into it too and received the same assurance, right?"

"We have, but we thought the government was securing ten million, not two and a half times that amount. They can't know the amount is twenty-five million. It would be exceptionally bad judgment on their part," Middents said in disbelief.

"You might think so, but I've given it some thought since yesterday. Misha told me the assurances come from Brunthaver, Kissinger and even Nixon himself," Dawson said. "It's the politics of international commerce. Nixon has been looking for ways to leverage his trips to Russia and China and demonstrate real trade for the USA. It also gets the government out of the cost of storage payments on grain they own. And it stimulates commercial activity in the agricultural sector. That buys votes!"

"Here's my burning question, Dick. Why would he tell you?" Saunders asked.

"I've been asking myself the same question, Barney. I think the answer is simple—he's done. Higher prices don't hurt the Soviets now. If the market moves higher, it makes Misha look good at Exportkhleb and within the Politburo. And then of course, the more political answer is, higher markets make food more costly for their enemies, namely China. And if it turns out costing the Americans a bit more for food, it really isn't his problem. He will never have to answer for it. The US government will."

"So, what do we do to protect our position and make some money on this intel, guys? Where are we at risk?" Mel Middents—ever the trader.

"There's a very real possibility the US, and even the Canadian, government will wake up. They could impose an export embargo on additional business to the Soviet Union and maybe expand it further to all export destinations," Saunders said.

"I think we need to speak with all our contacts in the US ag department and take the temperature for this deal and possible interventions, without revealing the magnitude Fisenko is reporting," Middents said. "Barney, can you reach out to Brunthaver and Butz or even Kissinger on this?"

"Definitely, Mel. Let's find out as much as we can and regroup here at one o'clock. Jim, can you touch base with the guys on the trading floor and get their read on action in the wheat market? Who's buying, how much, how far out—you know what I mean."

"Sure, Barney. I'll do it, and I'll reach out to some of the analysts I've been talking to in Washington. They always seem to like to talk about what's going on in their world."

"Good idea," Saunders said. "Dick, see what you can squeeze out of Rowan and his team at the Wheat Board. And Mel, can you reconnect with Slaski again?"

"I'll call him, Barney. He was pretty vague during our last call but, at the same time, possibly sending warning signals to us. He might be good for some private Soviet intel if we tell him we know how much has actually traded."

"Okay, team," Saunders said. "Let's get to work!"

* * *

At one o'clock sharp, the same group of people, assignments completed, reconvened for an information-share and strategy session.

"Okay, I'll start, Saunders said. "I spoke with both Butz and Brunthaver this morning. They reiterated their continued support of subsidies for wheat trade to the Soviet Union. They are firmly behind the newly developing business and assured me Kissinger and Nixon are keeping close watch on the action. It's pretty clear the highest levels of government power are indeed pulling the strings on this deal—not the ag department.

"I asked them how many tonnes had been reported for subsidy payments, and their answer was less than seven million. They have no idea the final number could be three to four times larger. Nor do they have a grasp of the impact this volume of business could have on grain markets and the handling and transportation systems. When it comes to commerce, these political clowns bring a knife to a gun fight every time.

"Does anyone have a theory on why there is such a large gap between the USDA numbers and Fisenko's admission?"

"I might have, Barney," Jim said. "There's another play on this whole deal we haven't discussed."

"What's that?" Middents asked.

"The way the export subsidy program works, the exporter reports the trade when it happens and the government guarantees the seller the difference between the current world value and the baseline of a dollar sixty-three per bushel. So, if you don't report the trade right away and world values move higher, the subsidy gets bigger. When you do report the sale, you get the higher subsidy. It's risky, but the larger the potential volume of trade, the lower the risk of markets dropping. If the market goes up one cent per bushel and you delay reporting on a million tonnes, you can bank a cool three hundred and sixty-seven thousand dollars. With these volumes we're discussing, the opportunities are huge. But you can't take advantage of it if you aren't in the game."

"That's a great insight, Jim. We've never considered essentially being long or short subsidy payments," Middents said.

"Just look at what has happened on the subsidy since the Soviets started buying." Jim passed a paper around to the traders. "It's gone from five cents per bushel to thirty-one cents as of yesterday, just in thirty-five days. That's a lot of cash flowing from the US Treasury to the Soviet Union or our competitors."

"You've got that right!" Middents said as everyone looked over Jim's paper. "The important discovery here, Barney, is the US government really doesn't have a clue. When they catch up to the facts, their decision to continue subsidies could change. In fact, if they have any brains at all, it will change. Let's keep a close eye on the subsidy rates and be sure we're covered against any risk of it being terminated. I don't want to get caught exposed, given what we know now."

"Jim, did you learn anything from your Washington guys?"

"More or less the same," Jim said. "They described a similar range of reported trades. Remember, they are tracking only wheat for export payment purposes. If the Soviets are buying corn or even soybeans, they won't even register in the totals."

"Shit!" This was unusual language for Middents. "That's right! Fisenko did play with us a bit on corn offers, didn't he? I wonder if he bought some from another exporter. That could explain why he didn't follow through with us."

"What's happening in Canada, Dick?" Saunders was moving on to another dimension of this unprecedented puzzle.

"Frank Rowan was more than a little vague about their dealings with Exportkhleb. But he was clear the CWB was not a seller today. They are happy to wait until the grain harvest is completed before committing additional tonnage," Dawson said. "There are no plans to embargo anyone, but they don't have to since they are the single-desk seller. They can accomplish the same thing by withdrawing from the market. We are free to sell to the Soviets, but we have to buy it from the CWB, so it's not a risk worth taking. There would have to be a strong political reason to embargo the Soviet Union. Including our business, there's at least five million tonnes on the books from Canada, and that's where it is likely to stay unless somebody takes a flyer and shorts the Board."

"Thanks, Dick," Middents said. "I managed to find Slaski in Geneva. He didn't offer anything more than he had already but did give another warning that we should be cautious. I asked him outright if the Soviets were in the market for twenty-five million tonnes. He hesitated a bit and then turned it back on me and asked about our intel on their crop production and what it told us. He's a clever bugger and a bit irritating at times, but we have to remember he's working for Exportkhleb now and that tells us something right there. Why do they need him? What is he strategizing for them?"

The merchandising meeting carried on for more than two hours as the team threw ideas out for discussion and strategized their own plan to mitigate their risk and capitalize on the events. Saunders summarized the point from his notes.

"We need an action plan to come out of this session, gentlemen. We're convinced Fisenko was honest with us, and we also feel the full impact of their buying hasn't hit the market yet. I think it goes without saying that we make sure we are on the long side of the market indefinitely—anticipatory hedging. Right, Mel? But Cargill is in the grain-handling business. We have grain-collection facilities to operate and rail cars and grain terminals to utilize. How do we maximize those investments if we aren't involved in this business at more than current levels?"

"If Fisenko is being forthright with us, then we know we can't sell any more grain to Exportkhleb," Middents said. "But, as we had planned earlier, we can sell it to the grain companies short to him now. Wheat futures are higher by fifteen cents a bushel in the past week. That's almost equal to the total trading range for all of last year, just in the past week! I think we're in for a bumpy ride on price volatility and trading grain.

"I also think we could see a sharp reaction from the government if and when they finally get wind of what is really happening here. I think we have an opportunity, or, maybe better stated, a need, to draft some internal contracts between our global offices so we have transactions in place just in case the politicians decide to flex their muscles and shut the door to further trade."

"What are you suggesting, Mel?" Saunders asked.

"Let's put some trades on the books between our North American Cargill offices and our Tradax team in Europe. We can report them just like other export deals. If we do get an embargo, we have some wiggle room to keep trading. If nothing happens, we cancel the trades—no harm, no foul. I think we need to do this right away. Like today, I'm saying."

"That sounds like a good idea, Mel, but it's late in the day and our offices here are mostly closed," Saunders said. "Do you really think this is something we have to do before tomorrow?"

"I do, actually. We may have triggered an internal government investigation just by making those calls today; you never know. Why risk waiting? We have west coast offices still open and capable of issuing contracts. It might be better to have them issued from trading locations rather than head office anyway. We can instruct our Portland regional office from here and, Dick, you can use the Vancouver export office in Canada. We might as well spread it around."

"Who have we got in these offices to entrust with this?" Saunders asked.

"We have a good team in Portland who can take this on," Middents said.

"Yes, in Canada the Vancouver guys are still at work and can make it happen today," Dawson added.

"All right," Middents said. "How many tonnes should we put on the books? We need to be reasonable but aggressive at the same time."

"We don't have to report anything in Canada," Dawson said. "But I feel like two million tonnes over a twelve-month period would be prudent. I don't mind carrying some deals on the books just in case."

"Good. Let's say five million from the US side," Middents said. "Jim, you'll need to wake the trading manager in Geneva, bring him up to speed and get his team going on this. Don't worry; he's used to being wakened in the middle of the night to do a deal."

Sosland Publishing, Kansas City   August 24, 1972

"Do you believe me now, Morton?" asked John Smith. "I told you the Soviets had a massive buying program, and that is exactly what has occurred. It's taken a while for the futures markets to react to the events of the past two months, but prices are now higher by about 30 percent since we first spoke. And I don't think the market has fully absorbed the impact of what has happened. Do you?"

"I really don't know, John," Sosland said. "This is new territory for me and for North American wheat markets."

"*They are now over twenty million tonnes of purchases from US exporters, my friend. It's the largest grain trade package in history. Can you envision the significance of what has transpired and how it affects global trade and prices going forward? It's a pivotal point in commodity markets, Morton.*"

"*I'm still struggling to understand how the Soviets managed to pull this off. They purchased our entire carry-over of wheat, used American credit to pay for it and profited from the government export subsidies on one hundred percent of the tonnage. It's almost incomprehensible. I feel like we're the victims of a hold-up.*"

"*Your government failed to react, Morton. They got entangled in the euphoria of the deal but don't have the capacity to comprehend the impact on markets or your domestic economy. The long-term effects will be felt for months and even years, I suspect.*

"*This is likely the last time we will speak, Morton. The deal has been done and the news is out there. I'll leave it to you to finish the story for your readers and interpret the impact. It's been my pleasure to work with you to uncover this fantastic story.*"

"*Don't say never, John. If you learn of more news, I want you to keep us in the loop,*" *Sosland said.* "*You certainly had the inside track on this one. Thanks for sharing with us, and keep in touch. Can you leave me a number where I can reach you?*"

"*I think not. I'll call you if necessary.*"

"*A mystery to the end, John Smith. It's been a pleasure. Goodbye.*"

"*Dasvidaniya, my friend.*"

22

The Game Changes

Cargill Lake Office, Wayzata, Minnesota   August 23, 1972

Armed with his knowledge of the largest international grain trade in history, Jim McCrea was in the enviable position of being able to capture a windfall profit from the commodity market. His first step was to cover the exposure created by Cargill's sale of spring wheat to Exportkhleb. His second step was to just keep buying. Buying contracts on the CBOT was a good start, but the real gain for Cargill would be in owning and handling physical grain. The demand in the market wasn't speculative; it was for real, physical commodities. He knew he needed to sweeten the price in their country elevators and start locking in tonnage.

Farmers were selling wheat for fall delivery. They liked the higher prices available at the country elevator this fall and were eager to cash in on rising prices at harvest as opposed to the typical seasonal price drop during this period of sustained deliveries. It made it easier for all the grain companies to cover their sales to the Soviets. For Cargill, it gave them the opportunity to build their long position for a future sale to either the Russians or their export competitors.

THE CHICAGO BOARD OF TRADE HEARTBEAT
August 11 to September 11, 1972

The Market Takes the News in Stride

Trading activity on the CBOT surged from mid-August to mid-September with trading volumes as much as ten times greater than earlier in the year. But the market absorbed this sustained new buying, limiting upward price movement to twelve cents a bushel. The reports from publications like *Milling and Baking News* did little to signal the major shift taking place in the global grain markets.

Perhaps traders felt the twelve-cents-per-bushel market increase reflected the impact of what was assumed to be ten to twelve million tonnes of business rather than the original tender of four million tonnes. As long as the government export program remained in place, the market wasn't likely to go much higher. The domestic consumer of wheat was paying a little more for processed goods, but international buyers were not. They remained protected by the export subsidy.

* * *

"We've been invited to Russia," Barney Saunders said as he approached Jim McCrea and Mel Middents in the trading room. He waved a sheet of paper and tossed it on Middents' desk. "They would like us to join them in a formal ceremony in Moscow to sign the contracts and celebrate our business. I gather all the grain companies will be there at the same time. It's a bit unusual, but they do love the pomp and circumstance of these events. I think it's a positive sign for ongoing trade."

"But we already have signed contracts with them," Jim said.

"Yes, you're right, Jim," Saunders said. "This is entirely ceremonial. Where we prefer to keep our dealings confidential, the Russians like to wave the flag and demonstrate their might. I suggest we attend, though. Declining their invitation would be viewed as an insult."

"Well, you and Jim can go," Middents said. "Somebody will have to stay here and watch the business."

"Fine suggestion, Mel. It would be a good experience for you, Jim. The date of the ceremony is September 19, so let's plan to fly over on the eighteenth. We can stay in our Moscow suite, and I suggest we plan on a day in the Tradax office in Geneva while we're in the neighborhood," Saunders said.

This just gets better and better, Jim thought. A trip to Moscow, hanging out in Cargill's suite and then some time in Geneva. And not Geneva, Illinois—Geneva frickin' Switzerland! He ran through a mental checklist: he'd need to update his passport, buy some new clothes and try to stay calm, cool and collected while his brain was exploding with excitement. Life was good for the young trader.

THE CHICAGO BOARD OF TRADE HEARTBEAT
September 11–19, 1972

Export Subsidy Program Ends

For much of the summer of 1972, the markets digested the news of a large new buyer and the changing dynamics this could represent. Daily trading volumes were robust, traders were happy, farmers were happy and the Soviets were extremely happy. Then, in mid-September the rules of the game changed.

On September 11, the US Department of Agriculture notified the grain trade they would have two weeks to report all outstanding export trades eligible for export subsidy. On September 25, 1972, the US government posted a zero-dollar amount for export subsidies of hard red spring wheat. At its peak, the current

subsidy had been as high as thirty-eight cents per bushel. This meant sales of wheat to the Soviet Union would be at world value. The market was now free to reflect this true demand in price, something it had not done for many years. Free of the influence of government price tampering, the market could operate on the influence of basic supply and demand fundamentals.

In the week that followed, the market rose just under forty cents per bushel, an increase of 20 percent. Futures trading volumes hit record levels for the contracts and new highs were achieved daily as the market rose to the permissible limit of ten cents per bushel for three consecutive days.

Russian Kremlin, Moscow   September 19, 1972

"Thank you all for joining us," agriculture minister Matskevich said. "Our department celebrates the success of our traders and the new and renewed relationships with many international trading firms who are here today. Our agriculture department, led by Exportkhleb president Viktor Pershin, has accomplished magnificent results in the face of a potentially disastrous crop failure. With the help of the American and Canadian governments and the many companies represented here today, we are able to supply food to our citizens and maintain our nutritional goals. We look forward to the official signing of contracts between ourselves and the representatives of our trading partners. But before we do that, I have some awards to bestow."

The elaborate ballroom in the Kremlin was filled with dignitaries from North American and Eastern European countries. Frank Rowan was there to represent the Canadian Wheat Board along with Dick Dawson and his boss, Roger Murray from Cargill Canada. Michel Fribourg led a contingent from Continental Grain. Jim McCrea and Barney Saunders were there from Cargill USA along with other US-based traders, including the affable Ned Cook. Representatives from various countries of the Soviet Union, including Joe the Blinker, were also in attendance for the ceremony. A gathering such as this was more than unusual for grain companies. Buyers and sellers of grain never associate in such an open, transparent manner, but this is how the Soviets wanted to recognize the dealing, so everyone accommodated their request.

"For outstanding leadership, I am proud to recognize President Viktor Pershin as a Hero of Socialist Labor, and for his service to his country in this difficult time I award him the Order of Lenin," Matskevich said.

Pershin, dressed in one of his finest Italian suits, beamed with pride as the Minister placed the broad, yellow-trimmed red ribbon with its elaborate medallions around his neck.

"I am also proud to recognize Vice President Mikhail Fisenko as recipient of the Order of Lenin for his bold and successful campaign to replenish our shortfall in grain production." Even now, thought Misha, he can't let go of our crop failure. An award and a slap in the same sentence.

But Misha stood proudly and seemed a little bit taller as the Minister placed the award around his neck. This recognition meant a great deal to Misha. It was confirmation of his dedication to his country and a measure of his success. It was one of the proudest moments in his life. He was sorry his parents and Liliya could not be there to share this great honor with him.

"So, this is the pomp and ceremony you mentioned?" Jim asked Saunders.

"Sure is. Can you imagine any other buyers inviting us to an event and then awarding their buyers for shoving it down our throats?" Saunders' disgust was clear. "It's not enough to get one over on us, which they most definitely did, but they have to rub it in our faces. Yeah, I don't like this part of the business much. Well, I better get over to the table and smile and sign off on this deal."

As the signing ceremony proceeded, the other guests congregated casually in an open area of the ballroom. Jim approached Misha to congratulate him, even though he was engaged in a conversation already. He didn't know who Misha was taking to but he had an idea, and he really wanted to meet this person.

"Jim. Hello," Misha said. "I'm so glad to see you here. Come, let me introduce you to Mike Slaski, an ex-Cargill employee. You may have heard of him. Mike, this is the young Cargill trader I told you about. He took us on a glorious tour of North Dakota wheat fields last month."

"I've spoken with Mr. Slaski but we haven't met," Jim said. "It's nice to meet you, Mike. I didn't expect to see you here."

"Misha was kind enough to invite me," Slaski replied. "It's a pleasure to meet you, Jim. I've heard a lot about you."

Misha hadn't missed Jim's comment that he had spoken with Mike and wondered how that might have happened. Had Slaski been tipping off his old associates? Oh, well; no matter. The deals were done and Russia had come out on top. That's all that should matter now, he thought.

"I don't see Mel here with you, Jim. Didn't he make the trip?"

"No, he sent me while he stayed home to watch the shop."

"Good thing too, I suspect," Slaski said. "The wheat market has been limit up for the past three days. I'll bet he's a little busy."

"I would agree," said Jim. "I think the combination of the end of the export subsidy program and the poorly kept secret that we're all celebrating in Moscow today have triggered a buying frenzy. It's not your typical harvest price dip this year, that's for sure."

Jim turned to Misha. "Congratulations on your award, Misha," he said as he admired the distinguished-looking medal resting high on Misha's chest. "I think this is a well-deserved honor."

"I agree with you, Jim," Slaski said. "Misha was the mastermind behind this whole deal. His country owes him a huge debt of gratitude. A medal is hardly enough, but I know it is high praise for you, isn't it, my friend?"

"Thank you both. I'm just doing my job, but it's definitely nice to be noticed."

"I'll warn you, Misha: we won't be caught off guard again. This was your one-time shot at it," Jim said with a grin. Although he'd said it playfully, he was quite serious. The Russians had pulled off a significant strategic maneuver around the grain companies in general and the US government specifically, but the next time they came shopping, sellers would be much more cautious and suspicious.

"Yes, you'll need to pull another rabbit out of a hat," Slaski said.

Misha wondered what a rabbit and a hat had to do with the point they were making, but he smiled and nodded anyway. He knew there wasn't going to be a "next time" for him, so it didn't really matter.

Jim spotted Saunders speaking with another guest and excused himself to join them. Saunders introduced him to Continental's Michel Fribourg as the two continued their conversation.

"As I was saying, Barney, we're extremely disappointed in the irresponsible actions of the US government and the USDA. There was no reason for them to ignore our counsel to terminate the export subsidy program sooner. We are all in a vulnerable position with sales on the books to the Soviets at extremely low prices. It was irresponsible of Kissinger and Nixon to support this program for their own political gains."

"I agree, Michel, but I suspect some of us are more exposed than others." Saunders was trying to elicit a rise out of his competitor. Michel didn't bite. "These politicians have succeeded in reducing America's overstocked grain supplies and opened a door for trade to the Soviets, though, and that's the business we are in. The long-term value would appear to outweigh the short-term costs we might have to absorb."

"Don't try to defend their actions, Barney. You know as well as I do what their motivation has been. I have no patience for this self-serving behavior."

Looking for a way to extricate themselves from Fribourg's rant, Saunders suggested he and Jim congratulate Viktor Pershin. They excused themselves to move on.

"Yikes!" Jim said. "He's a little upset, isn't he."

"I think you would be, too, if you had his book of sales to manage. He makes a point, though, Jim, and I don't disagree with him on it. The involvement of government in freely functioning markets takes its toll. Their interference often does more harm than good."

After a brief conversation with Pershin, Saunders was ready to separate himself from the ceremony and his competitors. "I think we're done here, Jim. Let's go take in some of the sights of Moscow, shall we?"

"Absolutely," Jim said. And the two traders headed for the door.

Cargill's Tradax Office, Geneva, Switzerland   September 20, 1972

The following day, Jim McCrea and Barney Saunders took the same Aeroflot flight from Moscow to Geneva that Misha had taken three months earlier. They too arrived at 11:15 a.m. and were met by Tradax's wheat trader, Eberhard Nietzer.

"Welcome to Geneva, Barney," said Nietzer. "Jim, nice to finally meet you. We have spoken many times, and now we have faces to go with the voices. Ha! How are our good friends in Russia? Full of celebration, I suspect."

"You've got that right, Eber," Saunders said. "They are in their glory, handing out awards and prancing about the palace."

"Well, they did pull one over on the Americans, didn't they? It appears Conti has the biggest share, though, and not us. I don't think I would want their book of trades right now."

"We have a plan for that, Eber," said Saunders. Let's go to the office and get our heads together to figure out how to play this out next year and beyond. We're starting to feel like this is the start of a new global trading dynamic."

* * *

Tradax's office in Geneva was in the core of the downtown financial district. The office and furnishings were of modern design with an emphasis on efficiency. The single purpose of the traders was to manage trading activities in and out of Europe. The city was also a tax haven for the Cargill empire.

The meeting room was a far cry from the expansive boardrooms at the Lake Office, but it served the purpose and had been the genesis of many successful trades in recent years. All of the merchants in the office joined Eberhard and manager Huub Spierings in the meeting. These were elite traders from around the world brought together to manage corporate risk and initiate bold trading strategies. Jim was honored to be in the same room as many company legends.

"Global grain markets are shifting to a new state of normalcy, gentlemen," Saunders said. "The world population continues to expand, and many developing countries now have disposable cash as their people demand more and better food than ever before. The Soviets managed to hide a potentially catastrophic shortfall in production from us this year but, as Jim warned Fisenko, we won't be caught again."

"Good for you, Jim!" Eber said.

"As you are all aware, Exportkhleb tendered for four million tonnes of grain and bought over twenty million, plus another five million from Canada. That wasn't a clerical error. It was a clever, tactical strategy, no doubt formulated by our old friend and associate, Mike Slaski."

The mention of Slaski's name triggered a rumble of discontent. A few audible "boos" were mostly meant in good fun, but some traders had hard feelings about his departure and subsequent career choice as an independent global consultant. Perhaps a small amount of jealousy was thrown in as well.

"From our perspective in the United States, we feel this round of buying is done. This has been confirmed by both Fisenko and Pershin. Take that for what it's worth, because they lied to us from the outset. But we feel like we're right on this much, at least.

"The remaining opportunity for us lies in the demand for physical grain to fill the orders. That list of buyers is now made up of the Big Six grain companies. With our strong country network, we see a great opportunity to supply those unfulfilled commitments. Jim McCrea will be taking the lead in this assignment for Cargill North America. So, tell me, guys—what does this Soviet caper look like from your perspective here in Europe?"

"Our views agree with yours," Spierings said. "We knew the crops were in tough shape and suspected for a long time that Russia would be a buyer, not a seller. But not to the extent they have shown. They really caught us all by surprise. We've been long for a while now and have a nice little gain in our trading accounts. But we're in no hurry to take it to the bank just yet.

"As far as a longer-term view," he continued, "I feel we have seen the lows in the market and it may continue to set new highs. After all, we know there is less than ten cents worth of wheat in a loaf of bread and less than a nickel's worth of barley in a pint of beer. When grain prices double, the consumer doesn't see a big impact. There is room for markets to go higher for sure."

"That's a valid point, Huub, but let's not forget it takes two to three pounds of grain to make one pound of chicken meat and ten pounds to make one pound of beef. The increasing demand for meat means a lot more grain production will be going into animal feed. That comes at a cost, and it will be inflationary for food prices on the whole; there's no escaping it. Now that the US wheat export subsidies are gone, we will have to see if the global consumer will pay higher prices to maintain and improve their food choices or if this price rally is a one-time event supported by a crop failure in the Soviet wheat belt."

"My money is on the consumer," Spierings stated.

"You mean Cargill's money, don't you?" Saunders said.

"But of course." Spierings grinned.

"Jim, what's your plan to use all those elevators and railcars in the US to make some money for the company?" Eber asked.

"It's all about buying physical grain in the right drawing area in close proximity to our export ports," Jim said. "We can do that by bidding up for grain in areas that work for us. Companies like Continental will have to come to the plate at some point to buy real grain to load in real vessels. That's where we can prosper, we believe. As long as wheat markets stay at this level or higher, I don't think we'll have trouble buying it from farmers—especially if futures markets continue to rise and pay them more. Without government intervening in market pricing, for the first time in a long time markets have the opportunity to find their own levels and farmers can make an excellent profit. They will be buying new equipment like crazy in the coming years with this influx of cash. You can bet on that too, Huub!"

"It's a new game, guys," Saunders summarized. "New players, new rules and a new score card currently standing at 1-0 for the Soviets. But now it's our turn up to bat."

THE CHICAGO BOARD OF TRADE HEARTBEAT
September 20 to December 31, 1972

The Market Continues to Set New Highs

The Chicago wheat market continued its steady upward trend through the remainder of 1972, reaching a new peak of two dollars and seventy-three cents per bushel as demand continued to outpace supply. The price of wheat had nearly doubled since June—an unprecedented rally. Gradually, the market became aware of the magnitude of the Soviet purchasing and started to digest the possibility and the impact of a pending clearance of all surplus inventories of grain. For the final quarter of 1972, there were more buyers than sellers.

Trading volumes were brisk day after day as physical commodities changed hands, futures contracts traded and traditional deals to normal markets continued. The wheat market reached new all-time highs spurred on by persistent buying support.

Where was the top? When would the demand diminish? No one knew the answer as wheat prices reached uncharted territory. Was this a one-year phenomenon or a shift in market value? The exchange would continue to discover prices, but it offered no insight into where the market was going. The warning "past performance was no indication of future direction" was never truer as 1972 drew to a close.

Cargill Lake Office, Wayzata, Minnesota   October 20, 1972

"How was harvest on your family's farm, Jim?" Mel Middents asked.

"It was really fun!" Jim replied. "This is the first time since college I've been able to take vacation this time of year to get back to the farm. When I worked in the elevator in Tuscola, it was all hands on deck, twelve hours a day. There was no chance to take time off and help my dad. I really appreciated being able to go home for a couple of weeks. I discovered I have developed a very different view of what we're doing and how our farm fits into the food-supply system. It didn't feel like work at all, and I felt more significance in what we were doing than ever before. I shared in my father's pride in being a farmer more than ever before."

"You're lucky to have those farming roots, Jim. Don't ever lose touch with them."

"I won't. My dad won't let me. He thinks I'm some sort of marketing genius now and wants me to help him market his grain. Boy, is that ever a change from a few years ago!"

"Well, he's not wrong, is he? You do have more information and insight than just about everyone else on the planet, Jim. I don't see anything wrong in you helping your family make the best marketing choices."

Like Jim's dad, Cargill made money in the fall of 1972 by playing the market from the long side and handling more wheat in their country elevator system than any quarter in their company's history. Jim led the corporate strategy to optimize port terminals and their feeder networks by concentrating grain purchasing in hard-wheat production areas close to export terminals best suited to Soviet destinations.

"This isn't the easiest money we will ever make, Jim, but it could be close," Middents said. "It's a rare opportunity when we know our competitors' positions with a high degree of certainty. It won't last forever, but let's make the most of it while we can."

"Understood, Mel. The pace of business has increased along with the volatility in the markets, but we seem to have landed in a post-harvest price range that works for everyone. Looking forward, my concern is with what happens if the Soviets come back next year. We'll be ready for them, that's for sure. But next year we won't have the large grain inventories to fill new demand. We will only have production from the new crop."

"The thing to watch, Jim, is how fast we fill the twenty million tonnes Fisenko bought," Middents said. "It's supposed to be a three-year deal. At least that is the length of their credit terms with the US government. If they stay on course and take seven to eight million tonnes this year, then we should see the markets remain calm, all other things being equal. But if they behave like they did when they bought the wheat, it's another story."

"How's that, Mel?"

"Well, they said they wanted four million tonnes and they bought nearly twenty. Call it a lie or misdirection; it amounts to the same. Then they said they wanted it over three years, but if they take it all in one year it's very likely they'll be back for another big order next year."

"I'll make a point of monitoring the pace of export movement over the next few months," Jim said. "Those are stats they can't hide from us."

"That's a good idea," Middents said. "My only warning at this stage is let's not get caught short in this market, Jim. It's on you to manage the program without slipping up. More market risk is being created by the increased fluctuation in price and the higher prices. There are a lot of moving parts in our organization, so we need a clear and communicated plan. We buy and sell wheat all across North America. Let's make sure we're buying more than we're selling or we might get caught.

"I want you to keep talking to Fisenko, Canada and Tradax. That's how we'll be successful. And don't be shy in calling Oscar to get his feel on futures activity. He often sees things on the floor we miss from the outside. You're in charge of the wheat desk now, Jim. There'll be a lot going on in the days and weeks to come. Cargill stands to make a lot of money, but we could also lose our shirts. No pressure—but don't mess it up."

23

The Fireworks of 1973

Misha's strategy had worked to perfection. Exportkhleb had avoided a potential disaster and the cost was far less than the Soviets had feared. The US government had survived the experience unscathed politically and financially, now free from export and acreage set-aside payment subsidies. The US farmers' outlook had improved substantially with the higher prices and, more importantly, shipment of their grain, which had been stockpiling for the past two years.

But the book wasn't closed on this record-breaking season of trade. One hundred percent of the risk of higher prices had been transferred from the Soviets to the export traders. All six major grain companies now carried the risk in varying amounts. They still needed to execute the contracts they had entered into with Exportkhleb. They needed to secure grain from farmers, which became more challenging as the Soviets exercised their options by calling for more and more grain on the front end of their three-year agreements. The export subsidy payments covered off some of the price risk, but grain markets had increased in value well beyond the value of the subsidies.

Cargill Lake Office, Wayzata, Minnesota   April 16, 1973

Jim monitored the exports of US wheat to the Soviet Union countries through the winter of 1972. The Soviets had already shipped their projected annual quantity of eight million tonnes by Christmas. If they

288

maintained this pace, they would take the full three-year quantity in the first year. A quick call to Dick Dawson in Winnipeg confirmed the same pace of shipments out of Canadian ports. All things pointed to the Soviets shipping everything they'd purchased in a single year.

In spite of this public data, the market didn't react. It didn't send out the alarms one might expect from the escalation in shipments. The reaction was quite the opposite, in fact. Wheat futures prices drifted lower as seeding approached in the spring of 1973. Trade and shipping were steady and robust, and all parts of the system were working in harmony. But for Jim, it didn't add up. Prices should be moving higher, he felt.

At the weekly merchandising meeting Jim shared his observations with the other traders and senior management.

"Six months ago, Mel, you suggested we keep a close eye on Soviet exports," Jim began. "I'm sure you remember." Middents nodded. "Your intuition was spot on… again."

"The Soviets are taking more than one third in the first year, I take it?" Middents asked.

"They took more than one third in the first three months. They are well into Year 2 quantities as we reach the end of the second quarter of the crop year. I fully expect them to take all twenty million tonnes, and the five million tonnes from Canada, in this single calendar year," Jim said. "They have a huge and urgent need for wheat. Based on these shipments, I feel we should expand our long position significantly."

"Aside from the companies who are actually short to Exportkhleb," Jim continued, "we are very likely the only ones who really know how large this deal is, other than Slaski, of course. And those companies probably still have grain to buy to satisfy their sales."

"I need more convincing, Jim," Middents said. "Since the price rally last fall, the markets have been very calm. Our long position hasn't generated any of the profit we expected. I'm losing faith in our plan. What other factors should we be considering? Let's talk about the political situation right now. Barney, do you foresee a repeat of the US government's interference in the markets this year?"

"Not from an ag policy perspective," replied Saunders. "With his reelection in November, Nixon doesn't need to cater to the rural voter for a while. That's a 'mission accomplished' file for him. He's got his hands full with this whole Watergate scandal, so I think ag policy and international trade are a lot lower on his list of priorities right now. As I see it, with all subsidy programs inactivated, the markets will have free rein to find their own levels. I will say there's no ceiling on market price to consider. But we haven't seen any real market reaction from the Nixon administration's devaluation of the dollar in February yet, either."

"What are you expecting from that, Barney?" Jim inquired. This wasn't something Julius Hendel had covered during his training session.

"Nixon devalued the US dollar by 10 percent in an effort to make our exports even more competitive internationally. That's made everything cheaper for buyers. It also dropped the cost on goods that haven't been shipped and paid for yet. I'm referring to the wheat the Soviets bought. Their costs just dropped by 10 percent, or roughly sixteen cents per bushel. Another gift to the Soviets from the US government and American taxpayers!"

"Geez, this deal just keeps getting better and better for them, doesn't it?" Jim said. "America got spanked on this deal, didn't we?"

"Some exporters did," Middents said. "Not Cargill, though. But the biggest cost goes to the taxpayers, as Barney said. As a country I think we'll be wearing a badge of shame for quite a long time on this one. Most American consumers won't even be aware of the cost to them, but since they are the only real source of tax dollars the cost is inevitable.

"Let's get back to our wheat-position strategy. What price is the farmer looking for net in his jean pockets, people? And how does that translate into a futures price forecast?"

"Right now, I think we'll start seeing farmers contract for fall delivery at the two dollars fifty per bushel mark," Jim said. "That's another twenty to thirty cents higher than today's country bid for October delivery."

"So, we shouldn't expect to see any heavy farmer selling before that number?" Middents asked. "Does anyone see it differently?" He paused for responses. "No? Okay, Jim; this is your call here. How do you recommend we proceed?"

Jim hadn't thought this through to the point where he would be put on the spot for a marketing strategy already. But he felt on pretty safe ground continuing to play the market from the long side. The question was, how large of a long position should he propose—fifty million bushels? A hundred? Five hundred? These were still uncharted waters for him, but he knew he had to make a call.

"Let me crunch some numbers and I'll put something together for next week's meeting," he said.

THE CHICAGO BOARD OF TRADE HEARTBEAT
January to May 1973

The Market Finds a Trading Range

The market settled into a new trading range for the first five months of 1973. A doubling of commodity prices in the previous year had been a windfall for North American farmers and a new paradigm for the agricultural economy. Everyone was making money. The market slowed down to catch its breath.

The abundant harvest of the 1972/'73 wheat crop appeared to be satisfying domestic and export demand at these new, higher levels. The market reflected that in terms of steady daily trading volumes and a market price hovering between two dollars and ten cents and two dollars and eighty cents per bushel. The outlook for an even larger crop in 1973 provided another buffer against a further rise in prices in the coming year.

* * *

For the next month Jim masterminded the accumulation of a larger long position in the US wheat market. He collaborated with traders in Canada, Europe and South America. He had two mechanisms in play to amass the position: grain purchases from farmers in the cash market and futures contracts on the various global exchanges. Farmer selling was light, as expected, so he was forced to accumulate his position in the futures market. By the end of April, his wheat book was long fifty million bushels, and by mid-May that number had doubled to one hundred million. His persistent buying, along with forced coverage by other companies who were short in the market, provided underlying support in the futures markets.

In mid-May the market adjustment, based on the dollar devaluation Saunders had predicted, began. Global currency traders started selling US dollars, which caused a collapse in the currency market mirrored by a simultaneous rise in commodity markets. Wheat futures rose by fifty cents per bushel in two weeks, peaking at the magical and unprecedented three-dollars-per-bushel mark. Jim McCrea's wheat position generated a profit of forty million dollars.

In the midst of these new high-water marks in futures prices, farmer selling backed off. They became cautious and curious. How high could this market go? Also, during this period, the Soviets remained quiet. Was this their new strategy, or were they hoping to become exporters again in the space of one short year?

"What can you tell us about the wheat markets today, Jim?" \Middents said during the weekly merchandising meeting.

"We're just over one hundred million long. We averaged forty cents per bushel in gains, and the market is making new all-time highs. It's a scary ride, I have to admit. But market signals continue to remain bullish."

"I knew it was going to be good, Jim, but this is unprecedented. Well done!"

* * *

Often the hardest part of trading grain is being patient and waiting for your plan to unfold. Watching the Chicago wheat market in June of 1973 was like watching crops grow. Every day was the same; not much happened. Three small rallies were followed by three small retracements. It's tempting to lose faith in your analysis and there is always pressure to deploy the money tied up in the position elsewhere. It's all about return on investment, and right now Jim's wheat position wasn't generating a return.

One undeniable fact was that the huge stockpile of wheat in the United States was disappearing to offshore destinations at record pace. The safety net of supply keeping American food prices low, in particular for flour and baked goods, was vanishing. For the first time in a decade, the risk of higher prices due to lower crop supplies was a distinct possibility. American consumers were exposed to the potential of an adverse consequence caused by the Soviet grain grab that had begun just a year ago.

THE CHICAGO BOARD OF TRADE HEARTBEAT
July 18 to August 22, 1973

A Limit Up Frenzy

In early July, the weather forecasts turned to an extended period of heat with no perceptible precipitation. Great for playing on the beach, but not for growing lush crops. The first indicators of a problem led to a thirty-cent rally on the market in the first half of the month. Then a long-term forecast on July 18 triggered uncontested buying. The following day, the market closed limit up: ten cents per bushel in a single trading session. With many more buyers than sellers, the futures market started running scared.

Over the next month, the market price for wheat nearly doubled to a high of five dollars and forty-three cents per bushel. It traded limit up an unprecedented seventeen of twenty-one trading days in July. The dry-weather forecast created the perfect storm of light farmer selling, short traders trying to cover positions and market longs running the market up with no sellers in sight.

Cargill Lake Office, Wayzata, Minnesota   August 15, 1973

The Lake Office traders gathered in their meeting room after the market closed on what had been a wild and crazy day that topped off an even more wild and crazy month. The range in price for the day had spanned a high–low of thirty-seven cents per bushel. That used to be a typical trading range for an entire year. After a spectacular heart-pounding thirty-day price rally, the markets took a breath. No one knew where the top was, and trading volumes disappeared as prices kept climbing.

Spirits were high and the traders were almost giddy. After a month of near-vertical ascent, the market had finally taken a breather. For those traders who followed chart patterns, today's trade signaled a "key reversal"—a term that describes a trading range above and below the previous day's close with a settlement opposite to the recent trend. Whether they trade according to chart patterns or fundamental supply and demand influences, it always makes sense for traders to follow what is happening in both schools of thought.

Mel Middents sat on the edge of his chair, his hands parallel and palms down on the table in front of him. "Give us the latest scoop, Jim. Where are we at in the wheat market?"

"It appears the legacy of the Soviet shopping spree has a long tail." Jim was referring to the long tail of a bull versus the short tail of a bear, implying higher, or bullish, markets. "We lightened the load on our wheat position by about half on the way up. That was at three-eighty per bushel, or about a dollar ago. Today was a rare down day in the market. A lot has happened in the past month, but as you all know it really started a year ago when the Soviets came to New York. All hell has broken loose since then. We have no idea where the top is, and there hasn't even been much trade for the past two weeks. The bell rings on the floor, traders scream their heads off for two minutes until they peg the market at limit up and that's it for the day. It's unbelievable. I don't feel like the lower market today is the beginning of a collapse, but I think it's time to take some profit."

"I would agree with you, Jim," said Middents. There are bulls and bears in the market, and then there are pigs—the ones who get greedy. Let's not be one of those."

The comment brought a round of laughter from the merchants. They'd heard the phrase before but couldn't contain their collective joy and comradery in the moment.

"I think it's safe to say we have navigated the tricky waters of one of the most complicated and impactful experiences in Cargill's history. I can't say if it was just lucky we didn't connect with Exportkhleb on more tonnage than we did, but I don't think it was all chance. Our conservative approach and solid research helped guide us through the process. This drought rally we have just experienced was exacerbated by the reduction in stocks, no question. Being long in the market for that was mostly luck, but I'll take it!"

24

The Aftermath

In America...

The impact of Soviet grain purchases in 1972 was a historic turning point in global commodity prices. Exchange futures prices for wheat, corn and soybeans never returned to the low levels of the early 1970s—ever. The seventies offered a bountiful windfall for farmers around the world. Commodity prices soared, land values increased and farming became big business almost overnight.

US government price-support programs were terminated. They were no longer needed, as market values reflected a new reality. This was good news for American taxpayers who had been footing the bill for set-aside acres and export subsidies as well as paying higher prices for commodity-based goods than international buyers. While it did mean an end to those hidden costs, what replaced them was a much larger grocery bill every month due to higher ingredient prices. Food prices moved sharply higher, accounting for an increase of 30 percent for North American consumers.

Most grain companies didn't fare as well as Cargill. Some struggled mightily to cover short positions. One company in particular, Cook Grain, wasn't able to survive the economic blow, although it took another three years for them to disappear from the list of the Big Six grain companies.

Some companies found other ingenious ways to profit from the structure of government subsidies and reporting. For example, exporters registered wheat sales for subsidies well after consummating deals. In a report to the US government, the US comptroller general identified five deals that were registered several weeks after the deals were made (in August 1972). The subsidy paid was $604,493. If the deals had been registered at the time of sale, the subsidy would have been $286,188. This amounts to a profit to the exporter of $318,305 in excess subsidies. Looking at the entire export program, the total difference could be as high as 1.7 million of taxpayer dollars siphoned out of the subsidy programs.

In the Soviet Union...

The good fortune of the Russian government agricultural agency persisted beyond the basement-price acquisition of the largest ever quantity of grain supported by US government credit to pay for it. In February 1973, the US government devalued its currency by 10 percent. This meant the Russian government could sell 10 percent less gold to secure the US funds they needed to pay for their grain. President Nixon's intent was to make American goods more competitive in world markets. In reality, it dropped the price the Soviets had to pay by a further sixteen cents per bushel.

But that wasn't the end of it. In yet another unforeseen benefit of this trade, the price of gold began an unprecedented upward trend. When the Russians first estimated how much gold they would have to draw from their treasury, it was trading at thirty-five US dollars an ounce. But by the end of 1972, gold was worth sixty-two dollars an ounce and rose to over one hundred by May 1973. Rather than drawing down nearly eighty-six million ounces of their gold reserves, they needed to liquidate only thirty-five to forty million ounces. That extra fifty million ounces resulted in a saving of five billion dollars for the Soviet Union.

These additional windfalls were not of Misha Fisenko's making, but they most certainly add to the legend of one of the most amazing stories in commodity trading history. The event has been described as "The Great Grain Robbery." In retrospect, the grain trade of July 1972 was a turning point in global agricultural prices. Markets for grain and oilseed commodities never ever reached the low point preceding the Russian purchases. For a decade, the agricultural economy soared, enriching the farm community and associated industries.

Our Heroes

Where do you promote the guy who just made more money for Cargill in a single year than anyone else in the company's history? In keeping with Cargill's corporate strategy to round out their traders and expose them to many elements of the organization's operations, Jim McCrea was offered a transfer to Geneva, Switzerland. He went on to manage global trading activities in the company of elite traders like himself.

Misha Fisenko never received the honors truly due to him. He was awarded the Order of Lenin, which pleased him greatly, but it didn't change his life in Moscow. But he had a plan for that as well...

25

Epilogue

Lausanne, Switzerland   October 1973

Strong, persistent winds blew across the widest part of Lake Geneva between the Chablais and Bernese Alps ranges. Fed by the Rhone River, the broad middle section of the lake was a popular sailing destination. Visible from the shores of Lausanne, dozens of sailboats crisscrossed the lake in all directions, defying the singular direction of the wind. The boats brought life to the view thanks to their bright and bold spinnaker sails of many colors and patterns that represented countries, corporations or bold graphic designs. Autumn in Switzerland was magical.

The blended sounds of the scene were familiar to a lakeside wharf. Seagulls cackled their incessant demand for food scraps. The Eurasian coots, or *foulque macroule*, as they were known locally, were returning to the area as winter approached. They disappeared from the water's surface frequently, diving for the lush vegetation at the bottom of the lakeshore. The familiar tinkling of the metal sail pulleys clanging against aluminum masts in the brisk wind provided a symphony of background noise for the marina orchestra.

Two men strolled casually along the lakefront path, the stockier of the two gesturing and smiling, clearly in a jovial mood. The second man waved a cane, rather than relying on it for support, as he listened and shared in the jocularity. They soaked in the early morning sights and sounds of one of the most beautiful places on earth. This route had been traveled by Roman soldiers in the second century and Celtic settlers before them. Now it was an avenue for tourists, joggers and locals to enjoy.

"You aren't wearing your medal today, Misha," Mike Slaski said teasingly.

"No, not today, not here. It's in my drawer now, a memory of another time and another place."

"Let's go back to that place, Misha. I still have some questions about the whole deal now that a year has passed. As I watched the markets and the world economy unfold, I got a strong hunch there was more to it than you buying a record quantity of grain at the bottom of the market. What haven't you shared with me?"

"I don't follow you, Mike. What are you asking me?"

"I'm talking about the gold market and the devaluation of the US dollar. What did those two events mean to the Soviets? You must have saved big time on your deal with the Americans."

"Oh, that part." Misha grinned. "Well, you're right. President Nixon's decision to devalue the US dollar was helpful to us. My best guess is we saved about ninety million US dollars thanks to that.

"But that's small in comparison to the impact of the gold market. We were able to save about five billion dollars thanks to higher prices when we needed to sell. I admit it was simply good luck for us, but what part of this deal hasn't been good luck, I ask you?

"So, there you have it. The whole deal went our way. We couldn't have planned for a better outcome. What do you think?"

"I think I need to charge you a higher fee for my services, Misha," Slaski said. "You guys made out like bandits. But I continue to believe you are the person who made it all happen. Your knowledge of world grain markets and your strategic thinking were critical.

"Not only did I underestimate your knowledge of US farm policy, but I certainly did not see this surprise coming." Slaski waved his arm across the expanse of Swiss mountains. "I understand why you didn't share your secret plan with me during the negotiations with the Americans, but I'm dying to know how you pulled off your own heist at the same time you pulled one over on the most sophisticated and experienced grain traders in the world."

"Well, maybe not all of them, Mike. That smart young kid from Cargill had it figured out. But I bettered enough of them to do my duty to my country and craft a retirement strategy for myself at the same time. I have to say, the motivation to locate here and live the rest of my life in a place like this helped make my future a whole lot better than I could have predicted in the Soviet Union." He laughed as he pointed to the ground of his new home.

"So, please, Misha; tell me how you did it."

"I'd been contemplating this for a long time, Mike, long before the crop failure. I knew I had privileged information due to my position at Exportkhleb, but I had to wait for the right time to turn it to my advantage. I knew I would have only one shot at it. Do you remember when I first came to visit you in Geneva in June last year?"

"Yes, I do. You and your grasshopper plan," Slaski grinned.

"Right. Well, before I returned to Moscow, I went to the Julius Baer Bank and opened an account. My diplomatic status gives me some leeway on government oversight, and my loyalty to Russia was unquestioned, so I was able to move larger sums of money out of Russia. Between my trip to your house and two others, I was able to transfer the equivalent of ten thousand US dollars. I chose the Baer Bank because they offered banking as well as securities and commodity trading for their clients. I never communicated with them from Russia, only when I was out of the country."

"Cautious. That was wise."

"I know how things work in government circles and with the Soviet police. I had to be extremely careful. Fortunately, there wasn't a need for frequent communications. Once I closed the deal with Continental for nearly ten million tonnes, I knew it was the time to choose. It was now or, possibly, never. I called the Baer Bank from New York and invested all my money in Chicago December wheat futures. I remember buying seventy thousand bushels at an average price of a dollar forty-two per bushel thanks to the leveraging power of margin trading. From there I was able to expand my position from profits as markets went higher. My final long position was close to two million bushels.

"Jesus Christ, Misha! Two million bushels?"

"Yup."

"I will admit, Misha, I made a few trades for my own account during this little adventure. I may have influenced the market a bit myself, although no one will ever know I did. It was just too good an opportunity, wasn't it? The table was set. We just had to sit down and eat."

"Some of us might have had a little more than our share." Misha patted his round belly as a joke.

"Okay, I have to ask … and you don't have to tell me, but I really want you to tell me so I can enjoy the moment with you. How much did you personally make on your trading?"

"Just between you and me, Mike?"

"Of course. You know you can trust me."

"I averaged a profit of three dollars per bushel overall and made just a little more than six million US dollars," he whispered.

"Jesus Christ! Fantastic! Well done, my friend."

"It was nerve wracking, especially as markets drifted lower from time to time, but I hung in there. My two favorite words when I checked the market ticker in the evenings became 'limit up.' I sold out the position this past summer once I no longer had the opportunity to influence the market. Besides, there is some question about trading with inside knowledge, so I don't want to take risk anymore."

"You don't need to, do you?"

"No, I don't. I'm happily established here in Lausanne in a nice small home. Nothing as fancy as your mountain retreat, Mike, but, compared to my suite in Moscow, it is a palace. Everything is so close to Geneva; the great cities of Paris, Monaco, Venice, Florence and Frankfurt are within easy reach. I love to visit the old museums, and there are hundreds of them within a two-hour train ride from here."

As the men enjoyed the serenity of Lake Geneva, a tour boat heading out for a half-day voyage navigated into the cluster of sails, honking its horn loudly even though the sailboats had the right of way. The sun glistened off the rippling lake as the wind stirred up rough waters. In spite of the activity and noise, Misha felt settled in his new home, at peace in the mountain retreat. He had anguished at first over the decision to leave Mother Russia, but now he was content with his choice to become a capitalist. It was a pretty nice way to live, he thought, especially with the means to enjoy some of the luxuries life had to offer.

"I couldn't have done this without your help and inspiration, Mike. I can never express my thanks to you enough. But we are neighbors now, so I hope we can spend time growing old together."

"Nothing would please me more, Misha. What do you say, for starters, we go over to the men's clothing store and get you a new suit? And then head into the city and have lunch with "that smart young kid from Cargill"?"

Author's Comments

The story depicted in *Limit Up* is fictional although based on actual events around what has been cleverly called The Great Grain Robbery of 1972. Some of the characters in the story are real people known by the author such as Dick Dawson, Mike Laserson and Jim McCrea. Many people referenced in the book are real public figures and were indeed participants in this story. Some people referred to are real but their names have been changed. Lastly, some characters are fictional and have been added in order to tell a more complete tale. Some literary licence has been taken to fill in gaps or develop the characters, but the real, true story is likely even more entertaining than this fictional version if it could ever be told accurately.

The underlying theme of political philosophies of central planning versus free market can be debated endlessly, although the ultimate failure of collective farming in favor of market pricing suggests a victory for the western world, at least in agriculture. No system is perfect, and it can certainly be said that the grass is always greener on the other side. What is in question is the need to build walls and use military might to force people to stay in a country as virtual prisoners or build walls to keep foreigners out.

The US political aspect of the story is factual. President Nixon, Henry Kissinger and Carl Brunthaver did indeed extend the Wheat Export Subsidy Program longer than necessary. The Soviets could have and would have paid more for America's surplus stocks. Americans very well might have received more in proceeds from wheat sales in 1972. It is also likely that the sales created a positive image for Richard Nixon and resulted in his re-election the same year. And he accomplished this result using taxpayer money—not the first or last politician to utilize a similar advantage.

One version of this story suggests the Americans actually initiated this round of trade back in 1971 in an attempt to negotiate a peaceful settlement for the war in Vietnam in exchange for favorable terms on a massive wheat deal. Their actions have been described as deliberate, driven by a broader goal than just the commercial deal. Nixon and Kissinger may have been the architects of this event all along but did they leave something on the table?

Looking back, we can see the broader, long-term impact of the 1972 deal. Massive stockpiles of grain, incurring huge storage and interest costs, were reduced. Grain production continued to expand and, importantly, farm revenues increased during the remainder of the decade. Grain and oilseed prices never reached the low levels of the early 1970s ever again—ever. The American economy benefited in many ways from these sales, including increased employment revenues for jobs in transportation and handling. The government viewed large grain inventory as a liability rather than an asset. The costs of maintaining ever-expanding inventories were reduced and the financial incentives supporting the export subsidy program were terminated that year. As bad as the senior government choices appeared to trading companies at the time, they can't deny that history shows long-term benefit in their actions.

I had the good fortune to find traders alive today who were part of this historic tale. Their minds are still sharp and their recollections most spectacular. I owe a great debt of gratitude to three industry veterans in particular, who shared their memories and their own opinions on the events of 1972. They make the story richer in the telling. My sincere thanks to my mentors, and actual participants in the events detailed here, Richard Dawson, Cargill VP and senior trader and Myron "Mike" Laserson, senior VP of Continental Grain. I would also like to thank Eugene Bannikov, senior advisor to the president of Exportkhleb who provided excellent Soviet insight but does not appear in the story.

www.ingramcontent.com/pod-product-compliance
Lightning Source LLC
Chambersburg PA
CBHW030802210726
48290CB00002B/385